Scenes
from
American Life

Books by Joyce Carol Oates

Wonderland

The Wheel of Love

Them

Expensive People

A Garden of Earthly Delights

Upon the Sweeping Flood

With Shuddering Fall

By the North Gate

Anonymous Sins (poems)

Love and Its Derangements (poems)

Scenes from American Life

Contemporary Short Fiction

Edited by Joyce Carol Oates

University of Windsor, Canada

Random House, New York

Copyright © 1973 by Joyce Carol Oates.

All rights reserved under International and Pan-American Copyright Conventions.
Published in the United States by Random House, Inc., and simultaneously in
Canada by Random House of Canada Limited, Toronto.
Library of Congress Cataloging in Publication Data

Oates, Joyce Carol, 1938–   comp.
Scenes from American life: contemporary short fiction.

CONTENTS: The bitter bread, by J. H. Ford.—Flight, by J. Updike.—The
boat, by A. MacLeod. [etc.]
1. Short stories, American. I. Title.
PZ1.O115Co [PS648.S5] 813'.01 72–4721
ISBN 0-394-31683-5

Manufactured in the United States of America by The Kingsport Press,
Kingsport, Tenn.

Typography by Karin Gurski Batten

First Edition 987654321

ACKNOWLEDGMENTS

JOHN BARTH. "Autobiography" from *Lost in the Funhouse*, by John Barth. Copyright © 1968 by John Barth. Reprinted by permission of Doubleday & Company, Inc.

ROBERT COOVER. "The Hat Act" from *Pricksongs & Descants*, by Robert Coover. Copyright © 1969 by Robert Coover. Published by E. P. Dutton & Co., Inc., and used with their permission.

HARRIS DOWNEY. "The Hunters" from *Epoch* (1950). Reprinted by permission of the author and publisher.

JESSE HILL FORD. "The Bitter Bread" from *Fishes, Birds and Sons of Man*, by Jesse Hill Ford. Copyright © 1966, 1967 by Jesse Hill Ford; and Sara Davis Ford and Katherine Kieffer Musgrove, Trustees. Reprinted by permission of Atlantic-Little, Brown and Co.

GAIL GODWIN. "A Sorrowful Woman." Copyright © 1971 by Esquire, Inc. Reprinted by permission of Paul R. Reynolds, Inc., 599 Fifth Avenue, New York, N.Y. 10017.

ALISTAIR MACLEOD. "A Boat" from *The Massachusetts Review*, 9 (Spring 1968). © 1968 The Massachusetts Review, Inc. Reprinted by permission of the publisher.

DAVID MADDEN. "The Singer" from *The Poetic Image in Six Genres*, by David Madden. Copyright © 1969 by Southern Illinois University Press. Reprinted by permission of Southern Illinois University Press.

Acknowledgments

BERNARD MALAMUD. "My Son the Murderer" from *Esquire* (November 1968). Copyright © 1968 by Bernard Malamud. Reprinted by permission of Russell & Volkening, Inc.

WILLARD MARSH. "Mending Wall" from *Southern Review* (Autumn 1969). © 1972 by George Rae Marsh. Reprinted by permission of George Rae Marsh and Virginia Kidd, agent of the author's widow.

JAMES ALAN MCPHERSON. "Of Cabbages and Kings" from *Hue and Cry*, by James Alan McPherson. Copyright © 1969 by James Alan McPherson. Reprinted by permission of Atlantic-Little, Brown and Co.

W. S. MERWIN. "The Dachau Shoe," "Make This Simple Test," and "Postcards from the Maginot Line," from *The Miner's Pale Children*, by. W. S. Merwin. Copyright © 1969, 1970 by W. S. Merwin. "Postcards from the Maginot Line" originally appeared in *The New Yorker*. Reprinted by permission of Atheneum Publishers, Inc.

CHARLES NEWMAN. "A Dolphin in the Forest, A Wild Boar on the Waves" from *Chicago Review*, Vol. 17, nos. 2 and 3, 7 and 16. Reprinted by permission of the author.

JOYCE CAROL OATES. "Plot" from *Paris Review*, 52 (Summer 1971). Copyright © 1971 by Joyce Carol Oates. Reprinted by permission of the author and Blanche C. Gregory, Inc.

FLANNERY O'CONNOR. "Revelation" from *Everything That Rises Must Converge*, by Flannery O'Connor. Copyright © 1964, 1965 by the Estate of Mary Flannery O'Connor. Reprinted by permission of Farrar, Straus & Giroux, Inc.

JEAN STAFFORD. "In the Zoo" from *The Collected Stories*, by Jean Stafford. Copyright © 1953, 1969 by Jean Stafford. Reprinted by permission of Farrar, Straus & Giroux, Inc.

HOLLIS SUMMERS. "The Third Ocean" from *The Hudson Review*, XXII (Summer 1969). Copyright © 1969 by The Hudson Review, Inc. Reprinted by permission of the publisher.

PETER TAYLOR. "The Fancy Woman" from *The Collected Stories*, by Peter Taylor. Copyright 1941 by Peter Taylor, copyright renewed 1968 by Peter Taylor. Reprinted by permission of Farrar, Straus & Giroux, Inc.

JOHN UPDIKE. "Flight" from *Pigeon Feathers and Other Stories*, by John Updike. Copyright © 1962 by John Updike. "Flight" originally appeared in *The New Yorker* in another version. Reprinted by permission of Alfred A. Knopf, Inc.

EUDORA WELTY. "The Demonstrators" from *The New Yorker*. Copyright © 1966 by Eudora Welty. Reprinted from *The New Yorker* by permission of Random House, Inc.

SOL YURICK. "The Siege" from *Someone Just Like You*, by Sol Yurick. Copyright © 1963 by Sol Yurick. Reprinted by permission of Harper & Row, Publishers, Inc.

A number of paragraphs in the story "A Sorrowful Woman," by
Gail Godwin, were accidentally transposed in the collection
Scenes from American Life (pages 249-254), edited by Joyce
Carol Oates. The following is the complete story in its
proper order.

A SORROWFUL WOMAN

GAIL GODWIN

Once upon a time there was a wife and mother one too many times

One winter evening she looked at them: the husband durable, receptive, gentle; the child a tender golden three. The sight of them made
her so sad and sick she did not want to see them ever again.

She told the husband these thoughts. He was attuned to her; he
understood such things. He said he understood. What would she
like him to do? "If you could put the boy to bed and read him the
story about the monkey who ate too many bananas, I would be grateful." "Of course," he said. "Why, that's a pleasure." And he sent
her off to bed.

The next night it happened again. Putting the warm dishes away
in the cupboard, she turned and saw the child's grey eyes approving
her movements. In the next room was the man, his chin sunk in the

---

GAIL GODWIN received a Ph.D. in English from the University of Iowa. She
is currently a post-doctoral fellow at the Center for Advanced Study in
Urbana, Illinois. She has published two novels, *The Perfectionists* and
The Glass People.

1

without that treasure of a girl. "Why don't you stay here with me in bed," the woman said.

Next morning she fired the girl who cried and said, "I loved the little boy, what will become of him now?" But the mother turned away her face and the girl took down the watercolors from the walls, sheathed the records she had danced to and went away.

"I don't know what we'll do. It's all my fault, I know. I'm such a burden, I know that."

"Let me think. I'll think of something." (Still understanding these things.)

"I know you will. You always do," she said.

With great care he rearranged his life. He got up hours early, did the shopping, cooked the breakfast, took the boy to nursery school. "We will manage," he said, "until you're better, however long that is." He did his work, collected the boy from the school, came home and made the supper, washed the dishes, got the child to bed. He managed everything. One evening, just as she was on the verge of swallowing her draught, there was a timid knock on her door. The little boy came in wearing his pajamas. "Daddy has fallen asleep on my bed and I can't get in. There's not room."

Very sedately she left her bed and went to the child's room. Things were much changed. Books were rearranged, toys. He'd done some new drawings. She came as a visitor to her son's room, wakened the father and helped him to bed. "Ah, he shouldn't have bothered you," said the man, leaning on his wife. "I've told him not to." He dropped into his own bed and fell asleep with a moan. Meticulously she undressed him. She folded and hung his clothes. She covered his body with the bedclothes. She flicked off the light that shone in his face.

The next day she moved her things into the girl's white room. She put her hairbrush on the dresser; she put a note pad and pen beside the bed. She stocked the little room with cigarettes, books, bread and cheese. She didn't need much.

At first the husband was dismayed. But he was receptive to her needs. He understood these things. "Perhaps the best thing is for you to follow it through," he said. "I want to be big enough to contain whatever you must do."

All day long she stayed in the white room. She was a young queen, a virgin in a tower; she was the previous inhabitant, the girl with all the energies. She tried these personalities on like costumes, then discarded them. The room had a new view of streets she'd never seen that way before. The sun hit the room in late afternoon and she took to brushing her hair in the sun. One day she decided to write a poem. "Perhaps a sonnet." She took up her pen and pad and began working from words that had lately lain in her mind. She had

4

FICTION
DREAMS
REVELATIONS

All art is autobiographical. It is the record of an artist's psychic experience, his attempt to explain something to himself: and in the process of explaining it to himself, he explains it to others. When a work of art pleases us it is often because it recounts for us an experience close to our own, something we can recognize. And so we "like" the artist, because he is so human.

But there are works of art that explain nothing, that dispel order and sanity; works of art that contradict our experience and are therefore deeply offensive to us; works of art that refuse to make sense, that are perhaps dangerous because they are unforgettable. Picasso tells us that "Art is a lie that leads to the truth," and we understand by this paradox that a lie can make us see the truth, a lie can illuminate the truth for us, a lie—especially an extravagant, gorgeous lie—can make us sympathize with a part of the truth we had always successfully avoided. Instinctively, we want either lies that we can know as lies, or truth that we can know as truth. A newspaper in the mid-South declares bluntly: "We Print Only the Truth—No Fiction." But the two are hopelessly mixed together, mysteriously confused. Nothing human is simple.

Every person dreams, and every dreamer is a kind of artist. The formal artist is one who arranges his dreams into a shape that can be experienced by other people. There is no guarantee that art will be understood, not even by the artist; it is not meant to be understood but to be experienced. Emotions flow from one personality to another, altering someone's conception of the world: this is the moment of art, the magical experience of art. It is a revelation. This impact of another personality upon us—our terrible, reluctant, unavoidable acknowledgment of another person, other people, all the consciousness outside ourselves that we cannot control and cannot possess, despite our deepest wishes—all that is humanly sacred is present in this exchange, which is art.

This collection of contemporary American short fiction has been put together for use in college classrooms, but hopefully its interest will be more general. In its range of subject and style it is representative of much of the vitality of current writing; but a collection of stories that did justice to the richness of our contemporary literature would be several thousand pages long. This anthology begins with stories that appear—like our most innocuous dreams—to be "realistic," "normal." It concludes with strange stories that call attention to themselves as artificial constructions, daring us to believe in them. The gradual movement from one to the other, from lies that seem quite plausible to lies that exhibit themselves proudly as lies, is not meant to suggest any development, any progress from simple to complex—and certainly it is not meant to suggest any degeneration, any fashionable decadence! Behind the steady, straightforward narrative of Jesse Hill Ford's "The Bitter Bread," and behind the perplexing reflection of a narrative yet to be written of John Barth's "Autobiography" there are the same kinds of human emotions, someone's vivid psychic experience. As formal fantasy breaks down—plot, characters, setting, "theme,"—the artist himself emerges, creating his art and himself while we stare in bewilderment: is this new character more or less fictional than the old-fashioned characters of fiction?

Most of the stories in this collection are moving, in their separate ways. A few are irritating, puzzling, unpleasant. Like certain people, they are not "likeable"—yet, like certain people, they are irresistible and it would be a shame to have missed them. Why should we like only those people who please us, especially those who contrive to please us? Why should we want to be pleased at all? It is only through disruption and confusion that we grow, jarred out of ourselves by the collision of someone else's private world with our own.

Joyce Carol Oates

CONTENTS

Contents

Scenes
from
American Life

THE BITTER BREAD

JESSE HILL FORD

It was after Christmas, towards the end of December. There had come a sudden thaw. The roads got soft—the Devil was baking his bread, as the saying is, getting ready to pass out the hard luck for the New Year.

"Yes, yes," said the midwife, coming behind Robert in the narrow lane, toting her black suitcase. "It happen this way every year."

Maybe, thought Robert, maybe not. The damp cold tugged at his hands. Tonight the roads would freeze again. He looked back. "Can't you walk no faster?" he said.

"The first chile always slow," she replied.

"She alone by herself though," Robert said. "Lemme tote that bag—"

JESSE HILL FORD lives in Humboldt, Tennessee. In addition to his story collection, *Fishes, Birds and Sons of Men*, he is the author of the novels *The Liberation of Lord Byron Jones* and *Mountains of Gilead*, and the play *The Conversion of Buster Drumwright*.

"Don't nobody tote this bag but me."

He waited up until she came alongside him and then, reluctantly, he matched his pace with her own. A hawk went hunting rabbits above the dun-colored fields to the left, patiently tracing back and forth, hovering along the shaggy fence rows. Woods already dark with the cold shadows of winter lay to the right of the lane.

He smelled woodsmoke. His dog, a little brown fice, yapped three times, nervously, like a fox, and ran under the house.

"He won't bite," Robert said leading the way across the porch and entering the little room ahead of the midwife. On the bed beside the fireplace, Jeannie had not raised up.

"It's just me," said the midwife. Jeannie stirred. "How old is she?"

"She seventeen," Robert said. He squatted down and set two hickory logs into the fire. The logs hissed. Flame flickered from the red and yellow embers. It fluttered above the logs in the smoke. "How you feeling, Jeannie?" He asked without looking at the bed.

"No, no, *no*," said the midwife. Robert stood up. He looked around. The midwife had opened her suitcase. "We must take her to the hospital. Wrap her up warm. See how drowsy she is? Feel her?"

"Yes'm."

"Fever," said the midwife. "You ain't got a truck?"

"No."

"Wagon?"

"No."

"Then we have to tote her. Down to the main road we can flag somebody." The midwife leaned over the bed. "We got to get you to town, understand me? Can you hear me? You too drowsy—hear?"

"Yes," Jeannie said. She did not open her eyes.

"How you feel?" Robert said.

"I hurt some," Jeannie said in a sleepy voice.

Robert got her shoes from the hearth.

"Don't bother with that. We'll wrap her up like a baby, see here? Now, lift her," said the midwife. "That's the time."

"She feel hot," Robert said.

The midwife was ahead of him, out the door and across the bare yard. "Makase," she said, going ahead of him almost at a trot now. Carrying Jeannie held close against his chest, his powerful arms under her knees and her shoulders, Robert followed the midwife down the lane. The mud was already beginning to freeze crisp. Sunset made a dark red glow in the sky beyond soft fields of dead grass. Ahead and above him he saw the stars of evening.

Dark had come swiftly down by the time they reached the embankment to the highway. The midwife took off her scarf and waved at the first approaching headlights. A pickup truck stopped. The midwife opened the door. "This girl need to go to the hospital. . . ."

"Get in," said the white man.

Robert climbed into the warm cab, holding Jeannie on his lap like a child. The midwife closed the door and waved good-bye. The truck moved down the highway.

"Has she got anything catching?" said the white man.

"She having a baby."

"Oh." The white man turned the heater up and stepped harder on the gas pedal. Robert's feet began to tingle and get warm. The lights of Somerton appeared. At the Negro entrance to the hospital, down a narrow drive at the rear of the flat wooden building, the white man stopped the truck. He climbed out and came around to Robert's side. He opened the door.

"How much I owe you?" Robert said, climbing down with Jeannie in his arms.

"Nothing," the man said. "I was coming in town anyhow." He walked ahead and opened the door to the hospital.

"I'm much obliged to you," Robert said.

"You're welcome," said the man. "Good luck." And he was gone.

In one corner of the waiting room there was a statue of Lord Jesus, standing on a pedestal. Beside the Coca-Cola machine in the hall stood another statue, Mary, dressed in blue robes. "Yes, can I help you?" The white nurse came from behind a counter.

"We need the white doctor," Robert said.

"What's her trouble?"

"Baby," said Robert.

The nurse turned and walked up the corridor. She came back rolling a narrow hospital cart.

Now it's going to be all right, Robert thought. He put Jeannie on the cart.

"Straight down that hall to the front office. You'll see a window. The sign says 'Hospital Admissions.'"

"What about the doctor, please ma'am?"

"After she's admitted to the hospital we'll call the doctor. Meanwhile she can lie here in the hall. She seems to be resting."

"Yes'm," Robert said.

He went down the strange corridor. The woman behind the admissions window was a Sister in black robes. Robert answered her questions one after the other while she filled in a white form.

"Fifty dollars," the Sister said.

"Yes'm. Put it on the book. I'll pay it."

"Cash, now," she said.

He reached into the pocket of his denim jacket and brought out the bills and the change, six dollars and forty-seven cents. He laid it out for her. "I can put this here down."

"Didn't you hear me just explain to you a while ago? We have rules. Your wife can't be admitted until you've paid fifty dollars cash in advance."

"Fifty dollars," Robert said.

"Fifty dollars," the Sister said. "I didn't make the rule."

"She need the white doctor," Robert said.

"I'm sure she does, and we'll call the doctor as soon as we can get her into a hospital bed. The doctor can't deliver babies out in the hall. I'll hold these papers while you go for the money."

"Yes'm. I don't have it."

"Then you'll have to borrow it, won't you?"

"Yes'm."

She turned away in the bright, silent room beyond the glass, bent about other business. Robert went out the front door and walked quickly down the road. For the first time he knew he had been sweating in the warm corridor because the cold came through his clothes. The sweat combined with it to chill him. He pushed his hands into the pockets of his coat and set off walking. Fear caught at him then. He began suddenly to run down the side of the road. He turned and waved at the lights of a car. It passed him slowly by, its exhaust making a steamy white plume in the air that was freezing him. He began running again. He ran down towards the intersection, past a row of neat white houses. Dogs rushed down the lawns and leaped the ditch, barking. He walked then. The dogs backed nervously away, whining at the strange smell of him.

At the corner he stopped. There was a filling station on his right, well lit, and painted blue and red. Inside the station two white men warmed themselves beside a kerosene heater. He crossed the street. A sidewalk took up on the other side and he began running again. He had a glimpse of white faces peering at him from the passing cars. He ran doggedly on, sweating again, breathing through his mouth, and tasting the bite of the cold air. By now, he thought, the land would be frozen—nearly hard as this sidewalk, by now.

He passed the last houses in the white section of town. He saw the cotton gin and the railroad crossing. He stopped running and walked long enough for his heart to stop pounding so, long enough for the ache inside to ease a bit. Beyond the rail crossing and up a side street he saw Joe-Thell's barbecue stand and the beer hall.

Robert had passed some time in the place on Saturday evenings at strawberry harvest and during cotton season. He ran up the street and pushed through the flimsy door. Joe-Thell looked up, frightened. "What's wrong?" he said. "Say, Robert?" There were no customers in the place.

"I need to borrow fifty dollars," Robert said.

"That quick," said Joe-Thell. He was an old man, wise in the ways of the world and never at a loss for words. He listened as Robert explained, nodding to let Robert know he had heard the same story six dozen times before. Joe-Thell nodded, sadly amused. He struck a kitchen match and lit his cigarette. He wiped his hands on his apron.

"*This* time of year though," said Joe-Thell, "peoples ain't got any work. Peoples ain't got any money, and you got nothing to hock."

"If it was another time of year I wouldn't need to borrow," Robert said. "I can pay back."

"If I had it you could have it," said Joe-Thell. "But I don't have it. Here it is already after dark."

"Then who does have it?" Robert said. "Jeannie up there laying in the hall."

"You got to have a lender, Robert. Mama Lavorn about the only one I know that might go that high with you this time of the year."

"Mama Lavorn?"

"Sure," Joe-Thell said. "Over to the Cafe and Tourist. Don't you know the Cafe and Tourist?" Joe-Thell was smiling a weary smile. "Look here, Robert. Go back to the crossing and then follow the dirt street by the tracks, that's south on a dirt street that angles and slants off. Mama Lavorn got a red light that winks on and off above her front entrance. It's up that road on the right-hand side."

"Mama Lavorn," Robert said.

"Tell her I sent you. Say to her Joe-Thell said she might go that high."

Robert was already backing away to the door. He turned suddenly out into the cold again, running back the way he had come, crossing the railroad and running; running then up the dark dirt side street. He suddenly sprawled. He fell, crashing through thin ice into a puddle of freezing water. He leaped up, the front of him wet through. He was stung by the cold water. Almost without knowing it he was running again, but carefully now, watching for the pale gleam of the frozen puddles. His thin clothes began to stiffen in front where the puddle had wet them. His hands burned.

He crossed the porch beneath the blinking red light bulb and opened the front door. He saw Mama Lavorn smiling at him. She sat in a high chair behind the cash register. She was a fat, dark woman in a purple dress. She wore earbobs that glittered like ice when she moved her head.

"Lord, look here!" said Mama Lavorn. "I mean *somebody's* in a hurry!"

Her smile disappeared as he began talking. "So you need fifty dollars," she said. "You know anyplace else you can get it?" She didn't wait for him to say no, but went on: "Because if you do I'm going to give you good advice. Go there and get it. I'm a lender. If you get it here it's going to cost you money— *if* you get it."

"Please . . ." he said.

"The interest on a dollar for one week is two bits—twenty-five cents," she said. "In a week this fifty dollars gonna come to sixty-two fifty. Put it another way, you can bring me twelve and a half dollars every Saturday to take care of the interest and keep the fifty dollars until strawberry season if you have to."

Robert nodded. "Sign here, on this line." She pushed him a check on the Farmers and Merchants Bank. She handed him her fountain pen. He signed the check. "If you come up and don't pay, or if you miss a payment, all I have to do is take this check to court and they'll come after you. It means jail then, don't you know?"

"Yes'm."

She counted the money out of the cash drawer and into his big hand. "How come you so wet?"

"I fell," he said. Clutching the money, he made himself walk out the door. Then he ran.

Now, he was thinking, it *will* be all right. Running was easier now. The way back seemed shorter. The sidewalk started again. Almost before he knew it he saw the blue-and-red filling station, then the two white men, standing inside as before, beside the heater. Again the dogs rushed down at him but he hardly minded them. They drew back as though astonished and let him pass. Lightly he bounded over the dead short grass on the hospital lawn and took his time then, opening the front door and approaching the admissions window. He laid the five bills on the black marble shelf.

Silently the Sister took the money, counted it, and pushed him a receipt. "Take this to the nurse."

"The doctor?"

"The doctor will be called."

He went down to the Negro waiting room. The nurse took the receipt. "Do you have a regular doctor?"

"No," he said. "No, ma'am."

The nurse picked up the phone. Robert walked around the corner and into the hall to the cart. The hallway was dim. It didn't seem proper to touch his wife, not here.

"What took me so long," he said softly, "I had to go after the money."

Jeannie made no answer. Resting, he thought.

He walked back to the waiting room. It was deserted. Only Christ and Mary looked at him from pale, hard eyes. The red eye in the cold-drink machine said "Nickels Only." The doctor came briskly up the hall, nodded in Robert's direction, and muttered something to the nurse.

The two of them went into the dim hallway. Presently they came back.

"Should have called me at once!" the doctor said. "How long ago did you bring her in?"

"I think. . . ."

"You *think?*" The doctor came slowly from behind the counter. "Robert?" The doctor's white face had a smooth powdered look. His eyes were soft and blue.

"Sir?"

"Your wife's dead. She's been dead maybe half an hour. Sister will refund your fifty dollars. There'll be no fee for my services. There's the body to be taken care of—I usually call the L. B. Jones Funeral Parlor for Colored."

"And they bury her?"

"Well, they fix her and arrange a burial for her, yes. You have a burial policy?"

"I don't have one," Robert said.

"Doctor?" It was the nurse. The doctor went to the counter. He took out his fountain pen. In a moment he returned, holding a slip of paper. He handed the paper to Robert.

"That's the death certificate. However you decide about handling the burial will be all right. Whoever does it will need this."

"Thank you, sir," Robert said. He sat down on the yellow patterned sofa. The doctor went away.

Presently a priest appeared. "I'm sorry about your wife, my son. She's in the arms of God now. She's with God. Are you a Catholic?"

"No, sir."

"We always ask. Not many Negroes are Catholics. We've a few converts among the Negro personnel who work here at the hospital."

"Yes, sir."

"Can I help you in any way? With arrangements?"

The nurse handed something to the priest, who then handed it to Robert—the fifty dollars. Robert put the bills in the damp, cold pocket of his cloth jacket. He carefully folded the death certificate then. The embarrassment of grief had begun to blind him a little—

to make him dizzy. He stood up and pushed the slip of white paper into the watch pocket of his overalls.

A big man, taller than the white people, he felt better standing up.

"We can't keep the body here," the nurse was saying.

Robert walked down the hall to the cart. He pulled the white sheet away. Then he wrapped Jeannie carefully in her quilt. He lifted her in his arms.

"If I can help in any way," the priest was saying. "If there's anyone I can call. . . ."

"Just open the door, please sir," Robert said.

The priest looked at the nurse. "Oh, this happens, it happens," the nurse said. "Wait till you've been here long as I have."

The priest opened the door. "God love you," he said.

Robert stepped into the cold. He walked slowly at first, until he reached the road, then he shifted his burden to his shoulder. It rested lightly. He walked at a quick pace and was soon out of town, beyond the last yellow street lamp. He chose the longer way, by the old road, a hard, narrow winding road that soon played out to gravel wending between the frozen fields.

At last he crossed the highway, climbed down the embankment, and entered the lane. His shoulder was numb. His side had begun to ache. As he had known it would be, the earth in the lane was frozen hard. The ground everywhere would be hard this night. Like a taste of sudden sickness, grief welled up inside him again, bone-hard and hard as the frozen ground, yet after the first few strokes of the pick the crust finally would give way. He knew the spade would bite and bite again, deeper and deeper still.

FLIGHT

JOHN UPDIKE

At the age of seventeen I was poorly dressed and funny-looking, and went around thinking about myself in the third person. "Allen Dow strode down the street and home." "Allen Dow smiled a thin sardonic smile." Consciousness of a special destiny made me both arrogant and shy. Years before, when I was eleven or twelve, just on the brink of ceasing to be a little boy, my mother and I, one Sunday afternoon—my father was busy, or asleep—hiked up to the top of Shale Hill, a child's mountain that formed one side of the valley that held our town. There the town lay under us, Olinger, perhaps a thousand homes, the best and biggest of them climbing Shale Hill toward us, and beyond

---

JOHN UPDIKE, winner of the National Book Award for his novel *The Centaur*, is the author of a number of books, including the novels *Rabbit Redux; Rabbit, Run; Couples;* and the short story collections *Olinger Stories, The Music School,* and *Bech: A Book.* He lives in Ipswich, Massachusetts.

them the blocks of brick houses, one- and two-family, the homes of my friends, sloping down to the pale thread of the Alton Pike, which strung together the high school, the tennis courts, the movie theatre, the town's few stores and gasoline stations, the elementary school, the Lutheran church. On the other side lay more homes, including our own, a tiny white patch placed just where the land began to rise toward the opposite mountain, Cedar Top. There were rims and rims of hills beyond Cedar Top, and looking south we could see the pike dissolving in other towns and turning out of sight amid the patches of green and brown farmland, and it seemed the entire county was lying exposed under a thin veil of haze. I was old enough to feel embarrassment at standing there alone with my mother, beside a wind-stunted spruce tree, on a long spine of shale. Suddenly she dug her fingers into the hair on my head and announced, "There we all are, and there we'll all be forever." She hesitated before the word "forever," and hesitated again before adding, "Except you, Allen. You're going to fly." A few birds were hung far out over the valley, at the level of our eyes, and in her impulsive way she had just plucked the image from them, but it felt like the clue I had been waiting all my childhood for. My most secret self had been made to respond, and I was intensely embarrassed, and irritably ducked my head out from under her melodramatic hand.

She was impulsive and romantic and inconsistent. I was never able to develop this spurt of reassurance into a steady theme between us. That she continued to treat me like an ordinary child seemed a betrayal of the vision she had made me share. I was captive to a hope she had tossed off and forgotten. My shy attempts to justify irregularities in my conduct—reading late at night or not coming back from school on time—by appealing to the image of flight were received with a startled blank look, as if I were talking nonsense. It seemed outrageously unjust. Yes, but, I wanted to say, yes, but it's *your* nonsense. And of course it was just this that made my appeal ineffective: her knowing that I had not made it mine, that I cynically intended to exploit both the privileges of being extraordinary and the pleasures of being ordinary. She feared my wish to be ordinary; once she did respond to my protest that I was learning to fly, by crying with red-faced ferocity, "You'll never learn, you'll stick and die in the dirt just like I'm doing. Why should you be better than your mother?"

She had been born ten miles to the south, on a farm she and her mother had loved. Her mother, a small fierce woman who looked more like an Arab than a German, worked in the fields with the men, and drove the wagon to market ten miles away every Friday. When still a tiny girl, my mother rode with her, and my impression of those rides is of fear—the little girl's fear of the gross and beery men who grabbed and hugged her, her fear of the wagon breaking, of the produce not selling, fear of her mother's possible humiliation and of her father's condition when at nightfall they returned. Friday was his holiday, and he drank. His drinking is impossible for me to picture; for I never knew him except as an enduring, didactic, almost Biblical old man, whose one passion was reading the newspapers and whose one hatred was of the Republican Party. There was something public about him; now that he is dead I keep seeing bits of him attached to famous politicians—his watch chain and his plump square stomach in old films of Theodore Roosevelt, his high-top shoes and the tilt of his head in a photograph of Alfalfa Bill Murray. Alfalfa Bill is turning his head to talk, and holds his hat by the crown, pinching it between two fingers and a thumb, a gentle and courtly grip that reminded me so keenly of my grandfather that I tore the picture out of *Life* and put it in a drawer.

Laboring in the soil had never been congenial to my grandfather, though with his wife's help he prospered by it. Then, in an era when success was hard to avoid, he began to invest in stocks. In 1922 he bought our large white home in the town—its fashionable section had not yet shifted to the Shale Hill side of the valley—and settled in to reap his dividends. He believed to his death that women were foolish, and the broken hearts of his two must have seemed specially so. The dignity of finance for the indignity of farming must have struck him as an eminently advantageous exchange. It strikes me that way, too, and how to reconcile my idea of those fear-ridden wagon rides with the grief that my mother insists she and her mother felt at being taken from the farm? Perhaps prolonged fear is a ground of love. Or perhaps, and likelier, the equation is long and complex, and the few factors I know—the middle-aged woman's mannish pride of land, the adolescent girl's pleasure in riding horses across the fields, their common feeling of rejection in Olinger—are enclosed in brackets and heightened by coefficients that I cannot see. Or perhaps it is not love of land but its absence that needs explaining, in my grandfather's fastidiousness and pride. He believed that as a boy he had been abused, and bore his father a grudge that my mother could never understand. Her grandfather to her was a saintly slender giant, over six feet tall when this was a prodigy, who knew the names of everything, like Adam in Eden. In his old age he was blind. When he came out of the house, the dogs rushed forward to lick his hands. When he lay dying, he requested a Gravenstein apple from the tree on the far edge of the meadow, and his son brought him a Krauser from the orchard near the house. The old man refused it, and my grandfather made a second trip, but in my mother's eyes the outrage had been committed, a savage insult insanely without provocation. What had his father done to him? The only specific complaint I ever heard my grandfather make was that when he was a boy and had to fetch water for the men in the fields, his father would tell him sarcastically, "Pick up your feet; they'll come down themselves." How incongruous! As if each generation of parents commits atrocities against their children which by God's decree remain invisible to the rest of the world.

I remember my grandmother as a little dark-eyed woman who talked seldom and who tried to feed me too much, and then as a hook-nosed profile pink against the lemon cushions of the casket. She died when I was seven. All the rest I know about her is that she was the baby of thirteen children, that while she was alive she made our yard one of the most beautiful in town, and that I am supposed to resemble her brother Pete.

My mother was precocious; she was fourteen when they moved, and for three years had been attending the county normal school. She graduated from Lake College, near Philadelphia, when she was only twenty, a tall handsome girl with a deprecatory smile, to judge from one of the curling photographs kept in a shoebox that I was always opening as a child, as if it might contain the clue to the quarrels in my house. My mother stands at the end of our brick walk, beside the elaborately trimmed end of our privet hedge—in shape a thick square column mounted by a rough ball of leaf. The ragged arc of a lilac bush in flower cuts into the right edge of the photograph, and behind my mother I can see a vacant lot where there has been a house ever since I can remember. She poses with a kind of country grace in a long fur-trimmed coat, unbuttoned to expose her beads and a short yet somehow demure flapper dress. Her hands are in her coat pockets, a beret sits on one side of her bangs, and there is a swank about her that seemed incongruous to me, examining this picture on the stained carpet of an ill-lit old house in the evening years of the thirties and in the dark of the warring forties. The costume and the girl in it look so up-to-date, so formidable. It was my grandfather's pleasure, in his prosperity, to give her a generous clothes allowance. My father, the penniless younger son of a Presbyterian minister in Passaic, had worked his way through Lake College by waiting on tables, and still speaks with mild resentment of the beautiful clothes that Lillian Baer wore. This aspect of my mother caused me some pain in high school; she was a fabric snob, and insisted on buying my slacks and sports shirts at the best store in Alton, and since we had little money, she bought me few, when of course what I needed was what my classmates had—a wide variety of cheap clothes.

At the time the photograph was taken, my mother wanted to go to

New York. What she would have done there, or exactly what she wanted to do, I don't know; but her father forbade her. "Forbid" is a husk of a word today, but at that time, in that quaint province, in the mouth of an "indulgent father," it apparently was still viable, for the great moist weight of that forbidding continued to be felt in the house for years, and when I was a child, as one of my mother's endless harangues to my grandfather screamed toward its weeping peak, I could feel it around and above me, like a huge root encountered by an earthworm.

Perhaps in a reaction of anger my mother married my father, Victor Dow, who at least took her as far away as Wilmington, where he had made a beginning with an engineering firm. But the depression hit, my father was laid off, and the couple came to the white house in Olinger, where my grandfather sat reading the newspapers that traced his stocks' cautious decline into worthlessness. I was born. My grandmother went around as a cleaning lady, and grew things in our quarter-acre yard to sell. We kept chickens, and there was a large plot of asparagus. After she had died, in a frightened way I used to seek her in the asparagus patch. By midsummer it would be a forest of dainty green trees, some as tall as I was, and in their frothy touch a spirit seemed to speak, and in the soft thick net of their intermingling branches a promise seemed to be caught, as well as a menace. The asparagus trees were frightening; in the center of the patch, far from the house and the alley, I would fall under a spell, and become tiny, and wander among the great smooth green trunks expecting to find a little house with a smoking chimney, and in it my grandmother. She herself had believed in ghosts, which made her own ghost potent. Even now, sitting alone in my own house, a board creaks in the kitchen and I look up fearing she will come through the doorway. And at night, just before I fall asleep, her voice calls my name in a penetrating whisper, or calls, "*Pete.*"

My mother went to work in an Alton department store, selling inferior fabric for $14 a week. During the daytime of my first year of life it was my father who took care of me. He has said since, flattering me as he always does, that it was having me on his hands that kept him from going insane. It may have been this that has made my affection for him so inarticulate, as if I were still a wordless infant looking up into the mothering blur of his man's face. And that same shared year helps account, perhaps, for his gentleness with me, for his willingness to praise, as if everything I do has something sad and crippled in it. He feels sorry for me; my birth coincided with the birth of a great misery, a national misery—only recently has he stopped calling me by the nickname "Young America." Around my first birthday he acquired a position teaching arithmetic and algebra in the Olinger high school, and though he was so kind and humorous he couldn't enter a classroom without creating uproarious problems of discipline, he endured it day by day and year by year, and eventually came to occupy a place in this alien town, so that I believe there are now one or two dozen ex-students, men and women nearing middle age, who carry around with them some piece of encouragement my father gave them, or remember some sentence of his that helped shape them. Certainly there are many who remember the antics with which he burlesqued his discomfort in the classroom. He kept a confiscated cap pistol in his desk, and upon getting an especially stupid answer, he would take it out and, wearing a preoccupied, regretful expression, shoot himself in the head.

My grandfather was the last to go to work, and the most degraded by it. He was hired by the borough crew, men who went around the streets shoveling stones and spreading tar. Bulky and ominous in their overalls, wreathed in steam, and associated with dramatic and portentous equipment, these men had grandeur in the eyes of a child, and it puzzled me, as I walked to and from elementary school, that my grandfather refused to wave to me or confess his presence in any way. Curiously strong for a fastidious man, he kept at it well into his seventies, when his sight failed. It was my task then to read his beloved newspapers to him as he sat in his chair by the bay window, twiddling his high-top shoes in the sunshine. I teased him, reading too fast, then maddeningly slow, skipping from column to column to create one long chaotic story; I read him the sports page, which did not interest him, and mumbled the editorials. Only the speed of his feet's twiddling betrayed vexation. When I'd stop, he would plead mildly in his rather beautiful, old-fashioned, elocutionary voice, "Now just the obituaries, Allen. Just the names to see if anyone I know is there." I imagined, as I viciously barked at him the list of names that might contain the name of a friend, that I was avenging my mother; I believed that she hated him, and for her sake I tried to hate him also. From her incessant resurrection of mysterious grievances buried far back in the confused sunless earth of the time before I was born, I had been able to deduce only that he was an evil man, who had ruined her life, that fair creature in the beret. I did not understand. She fought with him not because she wanted to fight but because *she could not bear to leave him alone.*

Sometimes, glancing up from the sheet of print where our armies swarmed in retreat like harried insects, I would catch the old man's head in the act of lifting slightly to receive the warm sunshine on his face, a dry frail face ennobled by its thick crown of combed corn-silk hair. It would dawn on me then that his sins as a father were likely no worse than any father's. But my mother's genius was to give the people closest to her mythic immensity. I was the phoenix. My father and grandmother were legendary invader-saints, she springing out of some narrow vein of Arab blood in the German race and he crossing over from the Protestant wastes of New Jersey, both of them serving and enslaving their mates with their prodigious powers of endurance and labor. For my mother felt that she and her father alike had been destroyed by marriage, been made captive by people better yet less than they. It was true, my father had loved Mom Baer, and her death made him seem more of an alien than ever. He, and her ghost, stood to one side, in the shadows but separate from the house's dark core, the inheritance of frustration and folly that had descended from my grandfather to my mother to me, and that I, with a few beats of my grown wings, was destined to reverse and redeem.

At the age of seventeen, in the fall of my senior year, I went with three girls to debate at a high school over a hundred miles away. They were, all three, bright girls, A students; they were disfigured by A's as if by acne. Yet even so it excited me to be mounting a train with them early on a Friday morning, at an hour when our schoolmates miles away were slumping into the seats of their first class. Sunshine spread broad bars of dust down the length of the half-empty car, and through the windows Pennsylvania unravelled in a long brown scroll scribbled with industry. Black pipes raced beside the tracks for miles. At rhythmic intervals one of them looped upward, like the Greek letter Ω. "Why does it do that?" I asked. "Is it sick?"

"Condensation?" Judith Potteiger suggested in her shy, transparent voice. She loved science.

"No," I said. "It's in pain. It's writhing! It's going to grab the train! Look out!" I ducked, honestly a little scared. All the girls laughed.

Judith and Catharine Miller were in my class, and expected me to be amusing; the third girl, a plump small junior named Molly Bingaman, had not known what to expect. It was her fresh audience I was playing to. She was the best dressed of us four, and the most poised; this made me suspect that she was the least bright. She had been substituted at the last moment for a sick member of the debating team; I knew her just by seeing her in the halls and in assembly. From a distance she seemed dumpy and prematurely adult. But up close she was gently fragrant, and against the weary purple cloth of the train seats her skin seemed luminous. She had beautiful skin, heartbreaking skin a pencil dot would have marred, and large blue eyes equally clear. Except for a double chin, and a mouth too large and thick, she would have been perfectly pretty, in a little woman's compact and cocky way. She and I sat side by side, facing the two senior girls, who more and more took on the wan slyness of matchmakers. It was they who had forced the seating arrangements.

We debated in the afternoon, and won. Yes, the German Federal Republic *should* be freed of all Allied control. The school, a posh castle on the edge of a miserable coal city, was the site of a statewide cycle of debates that was to continue into Saturday. There was a dance Friday night in the gym. I danced with Molly mostly, though to my annoyance she got in with a set of Harrisburg boys while I conscientiously pushed Judith and Catharine around the floor. We were stiff dancers, the three of us; only Molly made me seem good, floating backward from my feet fearlessly as her cheek rumpled my moist shirt. The gym was hung with orange and black crepe paper in honor of Hallowe'en, and the pennants of all the competing schools were fastened to the walls, and a twelve-piece band pumped away blissfully on the year's sad tunes—"Heartaches," "Near You," "That's My Desire." A great cloud of balloons gathered in the steel girders was released. There was pink punch, and a local girl sang.

Judith and Catharine decided to leave before the dance was over, and I made Molly come too, though she was in a literal sweat of pleasure; her perfect skin in the oval above her neckline was flushed and glazed. I realized, with a little shock of possessiveness and pity, that she was unused to attention back home, in competition with the gorgeous Olinger ignorant.

We walked together to the house where the four of us had been boarded, a large white frame owned by an old couple and standing with lonely decency in a semi-slum. Judith and Catharine turned up the walk, but Molly and I, with a diffident decision that I believe came from her initiative, continued, "to walk around the block." We walked miles, stopping off after midnight at a trolley-car-shaped diner. I got a hamburger, and she impressed me by ordering coffee. We walked back to the house and let ourselves in with the key we had been given; but instead of going upstairs to our rooms we sat downstairs in the dark living room and talked softly for more hours.

What did we say? I talked about myself. It is hard to hear, much less remember, what we ourselves say, just as it might be hard for a movie projector, given life, to see the shadows its eye of light is casting. A transcript, could I produce it, of my monologue through the wide turning point of that night, with all its word-by-word conceit, would distort the picture: this living room miles from home, the street light piercing the chinks in the curtains and erecting on the wallpaper rods of light the size of yardsticks, our hosts and companions asleep upstairs, the incessant sigh of my voice, coffee-primed Molly on the floor beside my chair, her stockinged legs stretched out on the rug; and this odd sense in the room, a tasteless and odorless aura unfamiliar to me, as of a pool of water widening.

I remember one exchange. I must have been describing the steep waves of fearing death that had come over me ever since early childhood, about one every three years, and I ended by supposing that it would take great courage to be an atheist. "But I bet you'll become one," Molly said. "Just to show yourself that you're brave enough." I felt she overestimated me, and was flattered. Within a few years, while I still remembered many of her words, I realized how touchingly gauche our assumption was that an atheist is a lonely rebel; for mobs of men are united in atheism, and oblivion—the dense lead-like sea that would occasionally sweep over me—is to them a weight as negligible as the faint pressure of their wallets in their hip pockets. This grotesque and tender misestimate of the world flares in my memory of our conversation like one of the innumerable matches we struck.

The room filled with smoke. Too weary to sit, I lay down on the floor beside her, and stroked her silver arm in silence, yet still was too timid to act on the wide and negative aura that I did not understand was of compliance. On the upstairs landing, as I went to turn into my room, Molly came forward with a prim look and kissed me. With clumsy force I entered the negative space that had been waiting. Her lipstick smeared in little unflattering flecks into the skin around her mouth; it was as if I had been given a face to eat, and the presence of bone—skull under skin, teeth behind lips—impeded me. We stood for a long time under the burning hall light, until my neck began to ache from bowing. My legs were trembling when we finally parted and sneaked into our rooms. In bed I thought, "Allen Dow tossed restlessly," and realized it was the first time that day I had thought of myself in the third person.

On Saturday morning, we lost our debate. I was sleepy and verbose and haughty, and some of the students in the audience began to boo whenever I opened my mouth. The principal came up on the stage and made a scolding speech, which finished me and my cause, untrammeled Germany. On the train back, Catharine and Judith arranged the seating so that they sat behind Molly and me, and spied on only the tops of our heads. For the first time, on that ride home, I felt what it was to bury a humiliation in the body of a woman. Nothing but the friction of my face against hers drowned out the echo of those boos. When we kissed, a red shadow would well under my lids and eclipse the hostile hooting faces of the debate audience, and when our lips parted, the bright inner sea would ebb, and there the faces would be again, more intense than ever. With a shudder of shame I'd hide my face on her shoulder and in the warm darkness there, while a frill of her prissy collar gently scratched my nose, I felt united with Hitler and all the villains, traitors, madmen, and failures who had managed to keep, up to the moment of capture or death, a woman with them. This had puzzled me. In high school, females were proud and remote; in the newspapers they were fantastic monsters of submission. And now Molly administered reassurance to me with small motions and bodily adjustments that had about them a strange flavor of the practical.

Our parents met us at the station. I was startled at how tired my mother looked. There were deep blue dents on either side of her nose, and her hair seemed somehow dissociated from her head, as if it were a ragged, half-gray wig she had put on carelessly. She was a heavy woman, and her weight, which she usually carried upright, like a kind of wealth, had slumped away from her ownership and seemed, in the sullen light of the railway platform, to weigh on the world. I asked, "How's Grandpa?" He had taken to bed several months before with pains in his chest.

"He still sings," she said rather sharply. For entertainment in his increasing blindness my grandfather had long ago begun to sing, and his shapely old voice would pour forth hymns, forgotten comic ballads, and camp-meeting songs at any hour. His memory seemed to improve the longer he lived.

My mother's irritability was more manifest in the private cavity of the car; her heavy silence oppressed me. "You look so tired, Mother," I said, trying to take the offensive.

"That's nothing to how you look," she answered. "What happened up there? You stoop like an old married man."

"Nothing happened," I lied. My cheeks were parched, as if her high steady anger had the power of giving sunburn.

"I remember that Bingaman girl's mother when we first moved to town. She was the smuggest little snip south of the pike. They're real old Olinger stock, you know. They have no use for hillbillies."

My father tried to change the subject. "Well, you won one debate, Allen, and that's more than I would have done. I don't see how you do it."

"Why, he gets it from you, Victor. I've never won a debate with you."

"He gets it from Pop Baer. If that man had gone into politics, Lillian, all the misery of his life would have been avoided."

"Dad was never a debater. He was a bully. Don't go with little women, Allen. It puts you too close to the ground."

"I'm not *going* with *any*body, Mother. Really, you're so fanciful."

"Why, when she stepped off the train from the way her chins bounced I thought she had eaten a canary. And then making my poor son, all skin and bones, carry her bag. When she walked by me I honestly was afraid she'd spit in my eye."

"I had to carry somebody's bag. I'm sure she doesn't know who you are." Though it was true I had talked a good deal about my family the night before.

My mother turned away from me. "You see, Victor—he defends her. When I was his age that girl's mother gave me a cut I'm still bleeding from, and my own son attacks me on behalf of her fat little daughter. I wonder if her mother put her up to catching him."

"Molly's a nice girl," my father interceded. "She never gave me any trouble in class like some of those smug bastards." But he was curiously listless, for so Christian a man, in pronouncing this endorsement.

I discovered that nobody wanted me to go with Molly Bingaman. My friends—for on the strength of being funny I did have some friends, classmates whose love affairs went on over my head but whom I could accompany, as clown, on communal outings—never talked with me about Molly, and when I brought her to their parties gave the impression of ignoring her, so that I stopped taking her. Teachers at school would smile an odd tight smile when they saw us leaning by her locker or hanging around in the stairways. The eleventh-grade English instructor—one of my "boosters" on the faculty, a man who was always trying to "challenge" me, to "exploit" my "potential"—took me aside and told me how stupid she was. She just couldn't grasp the principles of syntax. He confided her parsing mistakes to me as if they betrayed—as indeed in a way they did—an obtuseness her social manner cleverly concealed. Even the Fabers, an ultra-Republican couple who ran a luncheonette near the high school, showed malicious delight whenever Molly and I broke up, and persistently treated my attachment as being a witty piece of play, like my pretense with Mr. Faber of being a Communist. The entire town seemed ensnarled in my mother's myth, that escape was my proper fate. It was as if I were a sport that the ghostly elders of Olinger had segregated from the rest of the livestock and agreed to donate in time to the air; this fitted with the ambiguous sensation I had always had in the town, of being simultaneously flattered and rejected.

Molly's parents disapproved because in their eyes my family was virtually white trash. It was so persistently hammered into me that I was too good for Molly that I scarcely considered the proposition that, by another scale, she was too good for me. Further, Molly herself shielded me. Only once, exasperated by some tedious, condescending confession of mine, did she state that her mother didn't like me. "Why not?" I asked, genuinely surprised. I admired Mrs. Bingaman—she was beautifully preserved—and I always felt gay in her house, with its white woodwork and matching furniture and vases of iris posing before polished mirrors.

"Oh, I don't know. She thinks you're flippant."

"But that's not true. Nobody takes himself more seriously than I do."

While Molly protected me from the Bingaman side of the ugliness, I conveyed the Dow side more or less directly to her. It infuriated me that nobody allowed me to be proud of her. I kept, in effect, asking her, Why was she stupid in English? Why didn't she get along with my friends? Why did she look so dumpy and smug?—this last despite the fact that she often, especially in intimate moments, looked beautiful to me. I was especially angry with her because this affair had brought out an ignoble, hysterical, brutal aspect of my mother that I might never have had to see otherwise. I had hoped to keep things secret from her, but even if her intuition had not been relentless, my father, at school, knew everything. Sometimes, indeed, my mother said that she didn't care if I went with Molly; it was my father who was upset. Like a frantic dog tied by one leg, she snapped in any direction, mouthing ridiculous fancies—such as that Mrs. Bingaman had sicked Molly on me just to keep me from going to college and giving the Dows something to be proud of—that would make us both suddenly start laughing. Laughter in that house that winter had a guilty sound. My grandfather was dying, and lay upstairs singing and coughing and weeping as the mood came to him, and we were too poor to hire a nurse, and too kind and cowardly to send him to a "home." It was still his house, after all. Any noise he made seemed to slash my mother's heart, and she was unable to sleep upstairs near him, and waited the nights out on the sofa downstairs. In her desperate state she would say unforgivable things to me even while the tears streamed down her face. I've never seen so many tears as I saw that winter.

Every time I saw my mother cry, it seemed I had to make Molly cry. I developed a skill at it; it came naturally to an only child who had been surrounded all his life by adults ransacking each other for the truth. Even in the heart of intimacy, half-naked each of us, I would say something to humiliate her. We never made love in the final, coital sense. My reason was a mixture of idealism and superstition; I felt that if I took her virginity she would be mine forever. I depended overmuch on a technicality; she gave herself to me anyway, and I had her anyway, and have her still, for the longer I travel in a direction I could not have taken with her, the more clearly she seems the one person who loved me without advantage. I was a homely, comically ambitious hillbilly, and I even refused to tell her I loved her, to pronounce the word "love"—an icy piece of pedantry that shocks me now that I have almost forgotten the context of confusion in which it seemed wise.

In addition to my grandfather's illness, and my mother's grief, and my waiting to hear if I had won a scholarship to the one college that seemed good enough for me, I was burdened with managing too many petty affairs of my graduating class. I was in charge of yearbook writeups, art editor of the school paper, chairman of the Class Gift Committee, director of the Senior Assembly, and teachers' workhorse. Frightened by my father's tales of nervous breakdowns he had seen, I kept listening for the sounds of my brain snapping, and the image of that gray, infinitely interconnected mass seemed to extend outward, to become my whole world, one dense organic dungeon, and I felt I had to get out; if I could just get out of this, into June, it would be blue sky, and I would be all right for life.

One Friday night in spring, after trying for over an hour to write thirty-five affectionate words for the yearbook about a dull girl in the Secretarial Course I had never spoken a word to, I heard my grandfather begin coughing upstairs with a sound like dry membrane tearing, and I panicked. I called up the stairs, "Mother! I must go out."

"It's nine-thirty."

"I know, but I have to. I'm going insane."

Without waiting to hear her answer or to find a coat, I left the house and got our old car out of the garage. The weekend before, I had broken up with Molly again. All week I hadn't spoken to her, though I had seen her once in Faber's, with a boy in her class, averting her face while I, hanging by the side of the pinball machine, made wisecracks in her direction. I didn't dare go up to her door and knock so late at night; I just parked across the street and watched the lit windows of her house. Through their living-room window I could see one of Mrs. Bingaman's vases of hothouse iris standing on a white mantel, and my open car window admitted the spring air, which delicately smelled of wet ashes. Molly was probably out on a date with that moron in her class. But then the Bingamans' door opened, and her figure appeared in the rectangle of light. Her back was toward me, a coat was on her arm, and her mother seemed to be screaming. Molly closed the door and ran down off the porch and across the street and quickly got into the car, her eyes downcast in their sockets of shadow. *She came.* When I have finally forgotten everything else, her powdery fragrance, her lucid cool skin, the way her lower lip was like a curved pillow of two cloths, the dusty red outer and wet pink inner, I'll still be grieved by this about Molly, that she came to me.

* * *

After I returned her to her house—she told me not to worry, her mother enjoyed shouting—I went to the all-night diner just beyond the Olinger town line and ate three hamburgers, ordering them one at a time, and drank two glasses of milk. It was close to two o'clock when I got home, but my mother was still awake. She lay on the sofa in the dark, with the radio sitting on the floor murmuring Dixieland piped up from New Orleans by way of Philadelphia. Radio music was a steady feature of her insomniac life; not only did it help drown out the noise of her father upstairs but she seemed to enjoy it in itself. She would resist my father's pleas to come to bed by saying that the New Orleans program was not over yet. The radio was an old Philco we had always had; I had once drawn a fish on the orange disc of its celluloid dial, which looked to my child's eyes like a fishbowl.

Her loneliness caught at me; I went into the living room and sat on a chair with my back to the window. For a long time she looked at me tensely out of the darkness. "Well," she said at last, "how was little hot-pants?" The vulgarity this affair had brought out in her language appalled me.

"I made her cry," I told her.

"Why do you torment the girl?"

"To please you."

"It doesn't please me."

"Well, then, stop nagging me."

"I'll stop nagging you if you'll solemnly tell me you're willing to marry her."

I said nothing to this, and after waiting she went on in a different voice, "Isn't it funny, that you should show this weakness?"

"Weakness is a funny way to put it when it's the only thing that gives me strength."

"Does it really, Allen? Well. It may be. I forget, you were born here."

Upstairs, close to our heads, my grandfather, in a voice frail but still melodious, began to sing, "There is a happy land, far, far away, where saints in glory stand, bright, bright as day." We listened; and his voice broke into coughing, a terrible rending cough growing in fury, struggling to escape, and loud with fear he called my mother's name. She didn't stir. His voice grew enormous, a bully's voice, as he repeated, "Lillian! Lillian!" and I saw my mother's shape quiver with the force coming down the stairs into her; she was like a dam; and then the power, as my grandfather fell momentarily silent, flowed toward me in the darkness, and I felt intensely angry, and hated that black mass of suffering, even while I realized, with a rapid light calculation, that I was too weak to withstand it.

In a dry tone of certainty and dislike—how hard my heart had become!—I told her, "All right. You'll win this one, Mother; but it'll be the last one you'll win."

My pang of fright following this unprecedentedly cold insolence seemed to blot my senses; the chair ceased to be felt under me, and the walls and furniture of the room fell away—there was only the dim orange glow of the radio dial down below. In a husky voice that seemed to come across a great distance my mother said, with typical melodrama, "Goodbye, Allen."

THE BOAT

ALISTAIR MACLEOD

There are times even now, when I awake at four o'clock in the morning with the terrible fear that I have overslept; when I imagine that my father is waiting for me in the room below the darkened stairs or that the shorebound men are tossing pebbles against my window while blowing their hands and stomping their feet impatiently on the frozen steadfast earth. There are times when I am half out of bed and fumbling for socks and mumbling for words before I realize that I am foolishly alone, that no one waits at the base of the stairs and no boat rides restlessly in the waters by the pier.

At such times only the gray corpses on the overflowing ashtray beside my bed bear witness to the extinction of the latest spark and silently await the crushing out of the most recent of their fellows.

ALISTAIR MACLEOD was born in North Battleford, Saskatchewan. Currently he teaches English and Creative Writing at the University of Windsor and is fiction editor of the *University of Windsor Review*.

And then because I am afraid to be alone with death, I dress rapidly, make a great to-do about clearing my throat, turn on both faucets in the sink and proceed to make loud splashing ineffectual noises. Later I go out and walk the mile to the all-night restaurant.

In the winter it is a very cold walk and there are often tears in my eyes when I arrive. The waitress usually gives a sympathetic little shiver and says, "Boy, it must be really cold out there; you got tears in your eyes."

"Yes," I said, "it sure is; it really is."

And then the three or four of us who are always in such places at such times make uninteresting little protective chitchat until the dawn reluctantly arrives. Then I swallow the coffee which is always bitter and leave with a great busy rush because by that time I have to worry about being late and whether I have a clean shirt and whether my car will start and about all the other countless things one must worry about when he teaches at a great Midwestern university. And I know then that that day will go by as have all the days of the past ten years, for the call and the voices and the shapes and the boat were not really there in the early morning's darkness and I have all kinds of comforting reality to prove it. They are only shadows and echoes, the animals a child's hands make on the wall by lamplight, and the voices from the rain barrel; the cuttings from an old movie made in the black and white of long ago.

I first became conscious of the boat in the same way and at almost the same time that I became aware of the people it supported. My earliest recollection of my father is a view from the floor of gigantic rubber boots and then of being suddenly elevated and having my face pressed against the stubble of his cheek, and of how it tasted of salt and of how he smelled of salt from his red-soled rubber boots to the shaggy whiteness of his hair.

When I was very small, he took me for my first ride in the boat. I rode the half mile from our house to the wharf on his shoulders and I remember the sound of his rubber boots galumphing along the gravel beach, the tune of the indecent little song he used to sing and the odor of the salt.

The floor of the boat was permeated with the same odor and in its constancy I was not aware of change. In the harbor we made our little circle and returned. He tied the boat by its painter, fastened the stern to its permanent anchor and lifted me high over his head to the solidity of the wharf. Then he climbed up the little iron ladder that led to the wharf's cap, placed me once more upon his shoulder and galumphed off again.

When we returned to the house everyone made a great fuss over my precocious excursion and asked, "How did you like the boat?"

"Were you afraid in the boat?" "Did you cry in the boat?" They repeated "the boat" at the end of all their questions and I knew it must be very important to everyone.

My earliest recollection of my mother is of being alone with her in the mornings while my father was away in the boat. She seemed to be always repairing clothes that were "torn in the boat," preparing food "to be eaten in the boat" or looking for "the boat" through our kitchen window which faced upon the sea. When my father returned about noon, she would ask, "Well how did things go in the boat today?" It was the first question I remember asking, "Well how did things go in the boat today?" "Well how did things go in the boat today?"

The boat in our lives was registered at Port Hawkesbury. She was what Nova Scotians called a Cape Island boat and was designed for the small inshore fishermen who sought the lobsters of the spring and the mackerel of summer and later the cod and haddock and hake. She was thirty-two feet long and nine wide, and was powered by an engine from a Chevrolet truck. She had a marine clutch and a high speed reverse gear and was painted light green with the name *Jenny Lynn* stenciled in black letters on her bow and painted on an oblong plate across her stern. Jenny Lynn had been my mother's maiden name and the boat was called after her as another link in the chain of tradition. Most of the boats that berthed at the wharf bore the names of some female member of their owner's household.

I say this now as if I knew it all then. All at once, all about boat dimensions and engines, and as if on the day of my first childish voyage I noticed the difference between a stenciled name and a painted name. But of course it was not that way at all, for I learned it all very slowly and there was not time enough.

I learned first about our house which was one of about fifty which marched around the horseshoes of our harbor and the wharf which was its heart. Some of them were so close to the water that during a storm the sea spray splashed against their windows while others were built farther along the beach as was the case with ours. The houses and their people, like those of the neighboring towns and villages, were the result of Ireland's discontent and Scotland's Highland Clearances and America's War of Independence. Impulsive emotional Catholic Celts who could not bear to live with England and shrewd determined Protestant Puritans who, in the years after 1776, could not bear to live without.

The most important room in our house was one of those oblong old-fashioned kitchens heated by a wood and coal burning stove. Behind the stove was a box of kindlings and beside it a coal scuttle. A heavy wooden table with leaves that expanded or reduced its dimensions stood in the middle of the floor. There were five wooden home-made chairs which had been chipped and hacked by a variety of knives. Against the east wall, opposite the stove, there was a couch which sagged in the middle and had a cushion for a pillow, and above it a shelf which contained matches, tobacco, pencils, odd fish hooks, bits of twine, and a tin can filled with bills and receipts. The south wall was dominated by a window which faced the sea and on the north there was a five-foot board which bore a variety of clothes hooks and the burdens of each. Beneath the board there was a jumble of odd footwear, mostly of rubber. There was also, on this wall, a barometer, a map of the marine area and a shelf which held a tiny radio. The kitchen was shared by all of us and was a buffer zone between the immaculate order of ten other rooms and the disruptive chaos of the single room that was my father's.

My mother ran her house as her brothers ran their boats. Every-thing was clean and spotless and in order. She was tall and dark and powerfully energetic. In later years she reminded me of the women of Thomas Hardy, particularly Eustacia Vye, in a physical way. She fed and clothed a family of seven children, making all of the meals and most of the clothes. She grew miraculous gardens and magnifi-cent flowers and raised broods of hens and ducks. She would walk miles on berry-picking expeditions and hoist her skirts to dig for clams when the tide was low. She was fourteen years younger than my father whom she had married when she was twenty-six, and had been a local beauty for a period of ten years. My mother was of the sea as were all of her people, and her horizons were the very literal one she scanned with her dark and fearless eyes.

Between the kitchen clothes rack and barometer a door opened into my father's bedroom. It was a room of disorder and disarray. It was as if the wind which so often clamored about the house succeeded in entering this single room and after whipping it into turmoil stole quietly away to renew its knowing laughter from without.

My father's bed was against the south wall. It always looked rum-pled and unmade because he lay on top of it more than he slept within any folds it might have had. Beside it, there was a little brown table. An archaic goose-necked reading light, a battered table radio, a mound of wooden matches, one or two packages of tobacco, a deck of ciga-rette papers and an overflowing ashtray cluttered its surface. The brown larvae of tobacco shreds and the gray flecks of ash covered both the table and the floor beneath it. The once-varnished surface of the table was disfigured by numerous black scars and gashes inflicted by the neglected burning cigarettes of many years. They had tumbled from the ashtray unnoticed and branded their statements permanently and quietly into the wood until the odor of their burning caused the snuffing out of their lives. At the bed's foot there was a single window which looked upon the sea.

Against the adjacent wall there was a battered bureau and beside it there was a closet which held his single ill-fitting serge suit, the two or three white shirts that strangled him and the square black shoes that pinched. When he took off his more friendly clothes, the heavy woolen sweaters, mitts and socks which my mother knitted for him and the woolen and doeskin shirts, he dumped them unceremoniously on a single chair. If a visitor entered the room while he was lying on the bed, he would be told to throw the clothes on the floor and take their place upon the chair.

Magazines and books covered the bureau and competed with the clothes for domination of the chair. They further overburdened the heroic little table and lay on top of the radio. They filled a baffling and unknowable cave beneath the bed, and in the corner by the bureau they spilled from the walls and grew up from the floor.

The magazines were the most conventional: *Time, Newsweek, Life, MacLeans, The Family Herald, The Reader's Digest.* They were the result of various cut-rate subscriptions or of the gift subscriptions associated with Christmas, "the two whole years for only $3.50."

The books were more varied. There were a few hard-cover magnificents and bygone Book of the Month wonders and some were Christmas or birthday gifts. The majority of them, however, were used paperbacks which came from those second-hand bookstores which advertise in the backs of magazines: "Miscellaneous Used Paperbacks 10¢ Each." At first he sent for them himself, although my mother resented the expense, but in later years they came more and more often from my sisters who had moved to the cities. Especially at first they were very weird and varied. Mickey Spillane and Ernest Haycox vied with Dostoyevsky and Faulkner, and the Penguin Poets' edition of Gerard Manley Hopkins arrived in the same box as a little book on sex technique called *Getting the Most Out of Love.* The former had been assiduously annotated by a very fine hand using a very blue-inked fountain pen while the latter had been studied by someone with very large thumbs, the prints of which were still visible in the margins. At the slightest provocation it would open almost automatically to particularly graphic and well-smudged pages.

When he was not in the boat, my father spent most of his time lying on the bed in his socks, the top two buttons of his trousers undone, his discarded shirt on the ever ready chair and the sleeves of the woolen Stanfield underwear, which he wore both summer and winter, drawn halfway up to his elbows. The pillows propped up the whiteness of his head and the goose-necked lamp illuminated the pages in his hands. The cigarettes smoked and smouldered on the ashtray and on the table and the radio played constantly, sometimes low and sometimes loud. At midnight and at one, two, three and four, one could sometimes hear the radio, his occasional cough, the rustling thud of a completed book being tossed to the corner heap, or the movement necessitated by his sitting on the edge of the bed to roll the thousandth cigarette. He seemed never to sleep, only to doze and the light shone constantly from his window to the sea.

My mother despised the room and all it stood for and she had stopped sleeping in it after I was born. She despised disorder in rooms and in houses and in hours and in lives, and she had not read a book since high school. There she had read *Ivanhoe* and considered it a colossal waste of time. Still the room remained, like a solid rock of opposition in the sparkling waters of a clear deep harbor, opening off the kitchen where we really lived our lives, with its door always open and its contents visible to all.

The daughters of the room and of the house were very beautiful. They were tall and willowy like my mother and had her fine facial features set off by the reddish copper-colored hair that had apparently once been my father's before it turned to white. All of them were very clever in school and helped my mother a great deal about the house. When they were young they sang and were very happy and very nice to me because I was the youngest and the family's only boy.

My father never approved of their playing about the wharf like the other children, and they went there only when my mother sent them on an errand. At such times they almost always overstayed, playing screaming games of tag or hide-and-seek in and about the fishing shanties, the piled traps and tubs of trawl, shouting down to the perch that swam languidly about the wharf's algae-covered piles, or jumping in and out of the boats that tugged gently at their lines. My mother was never uneasy about them at such times, and when her husband criticized her she would say, "Nothing will happen to them there," or "They could be doing worse things in worse places."

By about the ninth or tenth grade my sisters one by one discovered my father's bedroom and then the change would begin. Each would go into the room one morning when he was out. She would go with the ideal hope of imposing order or with the more practical objective of emptying the ashtray, and later she would be found spellbound by the volume in her hand. My mother's reaction was always abrupt, bordering on the angry. "Take your nose out of that trash and come and do your work," she would say, and once I saw her slap my youngest sister so hard that the print of her hand was scarletly emblazoned upon her.daughter's cheek while the broken-spined paperback fluttered uselessly to the floor.

Thereafter my mother would launch a campaign against what she had discovered but could not understand. At times although she was not overly religious she would bring in God to bolster her arguments saying, "In the next world God will see to those who waste their lives reading useless books when they should be about their work." Or without theological aid, "I would like to know how books help anyone to live a life." If my father were in, she would repeat the remarks louder than necessary, and her voice would carry into his room where he lay upon his bed. His usual reaction was to turn up the volume of the radio, although that action in itself betrayed the success of the initial thrust.

Shortly after my sisters began to read the books, they grew restless and lost interest in darning socks and baking bread, and all of them eventually went to work as summer waitresses in the Sea Food Restaurant. The restaurant was run by a big American concern from Boston and catered to the tourists that flooded the area during July and August. My mother despised the whole operation. She said the restaurant was not run by "our people," and "our people" did not eat there, and that it was run by outsiders for outsiders.

"Who are these people anyway?" she would ask, tossing back her dark hair, "and what do they, though they go about with their cameras for a hundred years, know about the way it is here, and what do they care about me and mine, and why should I care about them?"

She was angry that my sisters should even conceive of working in such a place and more angry when my father made no move to prevent it, and she was worried about herself and about her family and about her life. Sometimes she would say softly to her sisters, "I don't know what's the matter with my girls. It seems none of them are interested in any of the right things." And sometimes there would be bitter savage arguments. One afternoon I was coming in with three mackerel I'd been given at the wharf when I heard her say, "Well I hope you'll be satisfied when they come home knocked up and you'll have had your way."

It was the most savage thing I'd ever heard my mother say. Not just the words but the way she said them, and I stood there in the porch afraid to breathe for what seemed like the years from ten to fifteen, feeling the damp moist mackerel with their silver glassy eyes growing clammy against my leg.

Through the angle in the screen door I saw my father who had been walking into his room wheel around on one of his rubber-booted heels and look at her with his blue eyes flashing like clearest ice beneath the snow that was his hair. His usually ruddy face was drawn and gray, reflecting the exhaustion of a man of sixty-five who had been working in those rubber boots for eleven hours on an August day, and for a fleeting moment I wondered what I would do if he killed my mother while I stood there in the porch with those three foolish mackerel in my hand. Then he turned and went into his room and the radio blared forth the next day's weather forecast and I retreated under the noise and returned again, stamping my feet and slamming the door too loudly to signal my approach. My mother was busy at the stove when I came in, and did not raise her head when I threw the mackerel in a pan. As I looked into my father's room, I said, "Well how did things go in the boat today?" and he replied, "Oh not too badly, all things considered." He was lying on his back and lighting the first cigarette and the radio was talking about the Virginia coast.

All of my sisters made good money on tips. They bought my father an electric razor which he tried to use for a while and they took out even more magazine subscriptions. They bought my mother a great many clothes of the type she was very fond of, the wide-brimmed hats and the brocaded dresses, but she locked them all in trunks and refused to wear any of them.

On one August day my sisters prevailed upon my father to take some of their restaurant customers for an afternoon ride in the boat. The tourists with their expensive clothes and cameras and sun glasses awkwardly backed down the iron ladder at the wharf's side to where my father waited below, holding the rocking *Jenny Lynn* in snug against the wharf with one hand on the iron ladder and steadying his descending passengers with the other. They tried to look both prim and windblown like the girls in the Pepsi-Cola ads and did the best they could, sitting on the thwarts where the newspapers were spread to cover the splattered blood and fish entrails, crowding to one side so that they were in danger of capsizing the boat, taking the inevitable pictures or merely trailing their fingers through the water of their dreams.

All of them liked my father very much and, after he'd brought them back from their circles in the harbor, they invited him to their rented cabins which were located high on a hill overlooking the village to which they were so alien. He proceeded to get very drunk up there with the beautiful view and the strange company and the abundant liquor, and late in the afternoon he began to sing.

I was just approaching the wharf to deliver my mother's summons when he began, and the familiar yet unfamiliar voice that rolled down from the cabins made me feel as I had never felt before in my young life or perhaps as I had always felt without knowing it, and I was ashamed yet proud, young yet old and saved yet forever lost, and there was nothing I could do to control my legs which trembled nor my eyes which wept for what they could not tell.

The tourists were equipped with tape recorders and my father sang for more than three hours. His voice boomed down the hill and bounced off the surface of the harbor, which was an unearthly blue on that hot August day, and was then reflected to the wharf and the fishing shanties where it was absorbed amidst the men who were baiting their lines for the next day's haul.

He sang all the old sea chanties which had come across from the Old World and by which men like him had pulled ropes for generations, and he sang the East Coast sea songs which celebrated the sealing vessels of Northumberland Strait and the long liners of the Grand Banks, and of Anticosti, Sable Island, Grand Manan, Boston Harbor, Nantucket and Block Island. Gradually he shifted to the seemingly unending Gaelic drinking songs with their twenty or more verses and inevitable refrains, and the men in the shanties smiled at the coarseness of some of the verses and at the thought that the singer's immediate audience did not know what they were applauding nor recording to take back to staid old Boston. Later as the sun was setting he switched to the laments and the wild and haunting Gaelic war songs of those spattered Highland ancestors he had never seen, and when his voice ceased, the savage melancholy of three hundred years seemed to hang over the peaceful harbor and the quiet boats and the men leaning in the doorways of their shanties with their cigarettes glowing in the dusk and the women looking to the sea from their open windows with their children in their arms.

When he came home he threw the money he had earned on the kitchen table as he did with all his earnings but my mother refused to touch it and the next day he went with the rest of the men to bait his trawl in the shanties. The tourists came to the door that evening and my mother met them there and told them that her husband was not in although he was lying on the bed only a few feet away with the radio playing and the cigarette upon his lips. She stood in the doorway until they reluctantly went away.

In the winter they sent him a picture which had been taken on the day of the singing. On the back it said, "To Our Ernest Hemingway" and the "Our" was underlined. There was also an accompanying letter telling how much they had enjoyed themselves, how popular the tape was proving and explaining who Ernest Hemingway was. In a way it almost did look like one of those unshaven, taken-in-Cuba pictures of Hemingway. He looked both massive and incongruous in the setting. His bulky fisherman's clothes were too big for the green and white lawn chair in which he sat, and his rubber boots seemed to take up all of the well-clipped grass square. The beach umbrella jarred with his sunburned face and because he had already been singing for some time, his lips which chapped in the winds of spring and burned in the water glare of summer had already cracked in several places producing tiny flecks of blood at their corners and on the whiteness of his teeth. The bracelets of brass chain which he wore to protect his wrists from chafing seemed abnormally large and his broad leather belt had been slackened and his heavy shirt and underwear were open at the throat revealing an uncultivated wilderness of white chest hair bordering on the semi-controlled stubble of his neck and chin. His blue eyes had looked directly into the camera and his hair was whiter than the two tiny clouds which hung over his left shoulder. The sea was behind him and its immense blue flatness stretched out to touch the arching blueness of the sky. It seemed very far away from him or else he was so much in the foreground that he seemed too big for it.

Each year another of my sisters would read the books and work in the restaurant. Sometimes they would stay out quite late on the hot summer nights and when they came up the stairs my mother would ask them many long and involved questions which they resented and tried to avoid. Before ascending the stairs they would go into my father's room and those of us who waited above could hear them throwing his clothes off the chair before sitting on it or the squeak of the bed as they sat on its edge. Sometimes they would talk to him a long time, the murmur of their voices blending with the music of the radio into a mysterious vaporlike sound which floated softly up the stairs.

I say this again as if it all happened at once and as if all of my sisters were of identical ages and like so many lemmings going into another sea and, again, it was of course not that way at all. Yet go they did, to Boston, to Montreal, to New York with the young men they met during the summers and later married in those faraway cities. The young men were very articulate and handsome and wore fine clothes and drove expensive cars and my sisters, as I said, were very tall and beautiful with their copper-colored hair and were tired of darning socks and baking bread.

One by one they went. My mother had each of her daughters for fifteen years, then lost them for two and finally forever. None married a fisherman. My mother never accepted any of the young men, for in her eyes they seemed always a combination of the lazy, the effeminate, the dishonest and the unknown. They never seemed to do any physical work and she could not comprehend their luxurious vacations and she did not know from whence they came nor who they were. And in the end she did not really care, for they were not of her people and they were not of her sea.

I say this now with a sense of wonder at my own stupidity in thinking I was somehow free and would go on doing well in school and playing and helping in the boat and passing into my early teens while streaks of gray began to appear in my mother's dark hair and my father's rubber boots dragged sometimes on the pebbles of the beach as he trudged home from the wharf. And there were but three of us in the house that had at one time been so loud.

Then during the winter that I was fifteen he seemed to grow old and ill at once. Most of January he lay upon the bed, smoking and reading and listening to the radio while the wind howled about the house and the needlelike snow blistered off the ice-covered harbor and the doors flew out of people's hands if they did not cling to them like death.

In February when the men began overhauling their lobster traps he still did not move, and my mother and I began to knit lobster trap headings in the evenings. The twine was as always very sharp and harsh, and blisters formed upon our thumbs and little paths of blood snaked quietly down between our fingers while the seals that had drifted down from distant Labrador wept and moaned like human children on the ice floes of the Gulf.

In the daytime my mother's brother who had been my father's partner as long as I could remember also came to work upon the gear. He was a year older than my mother and was tall and dark and the father of twelve children.

By March we were very far behind and although I began to work very hard in the evenings I knew it was not hard enough and that there were but eight weeks left before the opening of the season on May first. And I knew that my mother worried and my uncle was uneasy and that all of our very lives depended on the boat being ready with her gear and two men, by the date of May the first. And I knew then that *David Copperfield* and *The Tempest* and all of those friends I had dearly come to love must really go forever. So I bade them all good-bye.

The night after my first full day at home and after my mother had gone upstairs he called me into his room where I sat upon the chair beside his bed. "You will go back tomorrow," he said simply.

I refused then, saying I had made my decision and was satisfied.

"That is no way to make a decision," he said, "and if you are satisfied I am not. It is best that you go back." I was almost angry then and told him as all children do that I wished he would leave me alone and stop telling me what to do.

He looked at me a long time then, lying there on the same bed on which he had fathered me those sixteen years before, fathered me his only son, out of who knew what emotions when he was already fifty-six and his hair had turned to snow. Then he swung his legs over the edge of the squeaking bed and sat facing me and looked into my own dark eyes with his of crystal blue and placed his hand upon my knee. "I am not telling you to do anything," he said softly, "only asking you."

The next morning I returned to school. As I left, my mother followed me to the porch and said, "I never thought a son of mine would choose useless books over the parents that gave him life."

In the weeks that followed he got up rather miraculously and the gear was ready and the *Jenny Lynn* was freshly painted by the last two weeks of April when the ice began to break up and the lonely screaming gulls returned to haunt the silver herring as they flashed within the sea.

On the first day of May the boats raced out as they had always done, laden down almost to the gunwales with their heavy cargoes of traps. They were almost like living things as they plunged through the waters of the spring and maneuvered between the still floating icebergs of crystal white and emerald green on their way to the traditional grounds that they sought out every May. And those of us who sat that day in the high school on the hill, discussing the water imagery of Tennyson, watched them as they passed back and forth beneath us until by afternoon the piles of traps which had been stacked upon the wharf were no longer visible but were spread about the bottoms of the sea. And the *Jenny Lynn* went too, all day, with my uncle tall and dark, like a latter-day Tashtego standing at the tiller with his legs wide apart and guiding her deftly between the floating pans of ice and my father in the stern standing in the same way with his hands upon the ropes that lashed the cargo to the deck. And at night my mother asked, "Well, how did things go in the boat today?"

And the spring wore on and the summer came and school ended in the third week of June and the lobster season on July first and I wished that the two things I loved so dearly did not exclude each other in a manner that was so blunt and too clear.

At the conclusion of the lobster season my uncle said he had been offered a berth on a deep-sea dragger and had decided to accept. We all knew that he was leaving the *Jenny Lynn* forever and that before the next lobster season he would buy a boat of his own. He was expecting another child and would be supporting fifteen people by the next spring and could not chance my father against the family that he loved.

I joined my father then for the trawling season, and he made no protest and my mother was quite happy. Through the summer we baited the tubs of trawl in the afternoon and set them at sunset and revisited them in the darkness of the early morning. The men would come tramping by our house at 4:00 A.M. and we would join them and walk with them to the wharf and be on our way before the sun rose out of the ocean where it seemed to spend the night. If I was not up they would toss pebbles to my window and I would be very embarrassed and tumble downstairs to where my father lay fully clothed atop his bed, reading his book and listening to his radio and smoking his cigarette. When I appeared he would swing off his bed and put on his boots and be instantly ready and then we would take the lunches my mother had prepared the night before and walk off toward the sea. He would make no attempt to wake me himself.

It was in many ways a good summer. There were few storms and we were out almost every day and we lost a minimum of gear and seemed to land a maximum of fish and I tanned dark and brown after the manner of my uncles.

My father did not tan—he never tanned—because of his reddish complexion, and the salt water irritated his skin as it had for sixty years. He burned and reburned over and over again and his lips still cracked so that they bled when he smiled, and his arms, especially the left, still broke out into the oozing saltwater boils as they had ever since as a child I had first watched him soaking and bathing them in a variety of ineffectual solutions. The chafe-preventing bracelets of brass linked chain that all the men wore about their wrists in early spring, were his the full season and he shaved but painfully and only once a week.

And I saw then, that summer, many things that I had seen all my life as if for the first time and I thought that perhaps my father had never been intended for a fisherman either physically or mentally. At least not in the manner of my uncles; he had never really loved it. And I remembered that, one evening in his room when we were talking about *David Copperfield*, he had said that he had always wanted to go to the university and I had dismissed it then in the way one dismisses his father's saying he would like to be a tightrope walker, and we had gone on to talk about the Peggotys and how they loved the sea.

And I thought then to myself that there were many things wrong with all of us and all our lives and I wondered why my father, who was himself an only son, had not married before he was forty and then I wondered why he had. I even thought that perhaps he had had to marry my mother and checked the dates on the flyleaf of the Bible where I learned that my oldest sister had been born a prosaic eleven months after the marriage, and I felt myself then very dirty and debased for my lack of faith and for what I had thought and done.

And then there came into my heart a very great love for my father and I thought it was very much braver to spend a life doing what you really do not want rather than selfishly following forever your own dreams and inclinations. And I knew then that I could never leave him alone to suffer the iron-tipped harpoons which my mother would forever hurl into his soul because he was a failure as a husband and a father who had retained none of his own. And I felt that I had been very small in a little secret place within me and that even the completion of high school was for me a silly shallow selfish dream.

So I told him one night very resolutely and very powerfully that I would remain with him as long as he lived and we would fish the sea together. And he made no protest but only smiled through the cigarette smoke that wreathed his bed and replied, "I hope you will remember what you've said."

The room was now so filled with books as to be almost Dickensian, but he would not allow my mother to move or change them and continued to read them, sometimes two or three a night. They came with great regularity now, and there were more hard covers, sent by my sisters who had gone so long ago and now seemed so distant and so prosperous, and sent also pictures of small red-haired grandchildren with baseball bats and dolls which he placed upon his bureau and which my mother gazed at wistfully when she thought no one would see. Red-haired grandchildren with baseball bats and dolls who would never know the sea in hatred or in love.

And so we fished through the heat of August and into the cooler days of September when the water was so clear we could almost see the bottom and the white mists rose like delicate ghosts in the early morning dawn. And one day my mother said to me, "You have given added years to his life."

And we fished on into October when it began to roughen and we could no longer risk night sets but took our gear out each morning and returned at the first sign of the squalls; and on into November when we lost three tubs of trawl and the clear blue water turned to a sullen gray and the trochoidal waves rolled rough and high and washed across our bows and decks as we ran within their troughs. We wore heavy sweaters now and the awkward rubber slickers and the heavy woolen mitts which soaked and froze into masses of ice that hung from our wrists like the limbs of gigantic monsters until we thawed them against the exhaust pipe's heat. And almost every day we would leave for home before noon, driven by the blasts of the northwest wind, coating our eyebrows with ice and freezing our eyelids closed as we leaned into a visibility that was hardly there, charting our course from the compass and the sea, running with the waves and between them but never confronting their towering might.

And I stood at the tiller now, on these homeward lunges, stood in the place and in the manner of my uncle, turning to look at my father and to shout over the roar of the engine and the slap of the sea to where he stood in the stern, drenched and dripping with the snow and the salt and the spray and his bushy eyebrows caked in ice.

But on November twenty-first, when it seemed we might be making the final run of the season, I turned and he was not there and I knew even in that instant that he would never be again.

On November twenty-first the waves of the gray Atlantic are very very high and the waters are very cold and there are no signposts on the surface of the sea. You cannot tell where you have been five minutes before and in the squalls of snow you cannot see. And it takes longer than you would believe to check a boat that has been running before a gale and turn her ever so carefully in a wide and stupid circle, with timbers creaking and straining, back into the face of storm. And you know that it is useless and that your voice does not carry the length of the boat and that even if you knew the original spot, the relentless waves would carry such a burden perhaps a mile or so by the time you could return. And you know also, the final irony, that your father like your uncles and all the men that form your past, cannot swim a stroke.

The lobster beds off the Cape Breton coast are still very rich and now, from May to July, their offerings are packed in crates of ice, and thundered by the gigantic transport trucks, day and night, through New Glasgow, Amherst, St. John and Bangor and Portland and into Boston where they are tossed still living into boiling pots of water, their final home.

And though the prices are higher and the competition tighter, the grounds to which the *Jenny Lynn* once went remain untouched and unfished as they have for the last ten years. For if there are no signposts on the sea in storm there are certain ones in calm and the lobster bottoms were distributed in calm before any of us can remember and the grounds my father fished were those his father fished before him and there were others before and before and before. Twice the big boats have come from forty and fifty miles, lured by the promise of the grounds, and strewn the bottom with their traps and twice they have returned to find their buoys cut adrift and their gear lost and destroyed. Twice the Fisheries Officer and the Mounted Police have come and asked many long and involved questions and twice they have received no answers from the men leaning in the doors of their shanties and the women standing at their windows with their children in their arms. Twice they have gone away saying: "There are no legal boundaries in the Marine area"; "No one can own the sea"; "Those grounds don't wait for anyone."

But the men and the women, with my mother dark among them, do not care for what they say, for to them the grounds are sacred and they think they wait for me.

It is not an easy thing to know that your mother lives alone on an inadequate insurance policy and that she is too proud to accept any other aid. And that she looks through her lonely window onto the ice of winter and the hot flat calm of summer and the rolling waves of fall. And that she lies awake in the early morning's darkness when the rubber boots of the men scrunch upon the gravel as they pass beside her house on their way down to the wharf. And she knows that the footsteps never stop, because no man goes from her house, and she alone of all the Lynns has neither son nor son-in-law that walks toward the boat that will take him to the sea. And it is not an easy thing to know that your mother looks upon the sea with love and on you with bitterness because the one has been so constant and the other so untrue.

But neither is it easy to know that your father was found on November twenty-eighth, ten miles to the north and wedged between two boulders at the base of the rock-strewn cliffs where he had been hurled and slammed so many many times. His hands were shredded ribbons as were his feet which had lost their boots to the suction of the sea, and his shoulders came apart in our hands when we tried to move him from the rocks. And the fish had eaten his testicles and the gulls had pecked out his eyes and the white-green stubble of his whiskers had continued to grow in death, like the grass on graves, upon the purple, bloated mass that was his face. There was not much left of my father, physically, as he lay there with the brass chains on his wrists and the seaweed in his hair.

THE FANCY WOMAN

PETER TAYLOR

He wanted no more of her drunken palaver. Well, sure enough. Sure
enough. And he had sent her from the table like she were one of his
half-grown brats. *He,* who couldn't have walked straight around to
her place if she *hadn't* been lady enough to leave, sent *her* from the
table like either of the half-grown kids he was so mortally fond of. At
least she hadn't turned over three glasses of perfectly good stuff during
one meal. Talk about vulgar. She fell across the counterpane and
slept.

She awoke in the dark room with his big hands busying with her
clothes, and she flung her arms about his neck. And she said, "You
marvelous, fattish thing."

PETER TAYLOR, of the English Department of the University of Virginia, has
won a number of distinguished awards for his short fiction. His most recent book is *The Collected Stories of Peter Taylor.* He is currently at
work on a new novel.

His hoarse voice was in her ear. He chuckled deep in his throat. And she whispered: "You're an old thingamajig, George."

Her eyes opened in the midday sunlight, and she felt the back of her neck soaking in her own sweat on the counterpane. She saw the unfamiliar cracks in the ceiling and said, "Whose room's this?" She looked at the walnut dresser and the wardrobe and said, "Oh, the kids' room"; and as she laughed, saliva bubbled up and fell back on her upper lip. She shoved herself up with her elbows and was sitting in the middle of the bed. Damn him! Her blue silk dress was twisted about her body; a thin army blanket covered her lower half. "He didn't put that over me, I know damn well. One of those tight-mouth niggers sneaking around!" She sprang from the bed, slipped her bare feet into her white pumps, and stepped toward the door. Oh, God! She beheld herself in the dresser mirror.

She marched to the dresser with her eyes closed and felt about for a brush. There was nothing but a tray of collar buttons there. She seized a handful of them and screamed as she threw them to bounce off the mirror, "This ain't my room!" She ran her fingers through her hair and went out into the hall and into her room next door. She rushed to her little dressing table. There was the bottle half full. She poured out a jigger and drank it. Clearing her throat as she sat down, she said, "Oh, what's the matter with me?" She combed her hair back quite carefully, then pulled the yellow strands out of the amber comb; and when she had greased and wiped her face and had rouged her lips and the upper portions of her cheeks, she smiled at herself in the mirror. She looked flirtatiously at the bottle but shook her head and stood up and looked about her. It was a long, narrow room with two windows at the end. A cubbyhole beside the kids' room! But it *was* a canopied bed with yellow ruffles that matched the ruffles on the dressing table and on the window curtains, as he had promised. She went over and turned back the covers and mussed the pillow. It might not have been the niggers! She poured another drink and went down to get some nice, hot lunch.

The breakfast room was one step lower than the rest of the house; and though it was mostly windows the venetian blinds were lowered all round. She sat at a big circular table. "I can't make out about this room," she said to the Negress who was refilling her coffee cup. She lit a cigarette and questioned the servant, "What's the crazy table made out of, Amelia?"

"It makes a good table, 'spite all."

"It sure enough does make a strong table, Amelia." She kicked the toe of her shoe against the brick column which supported the table top. "But what *was* it, old dearie?" She smiled invitingly at the servant and pushed her plate away and pulled her coffee in front of her. She stared at the straight scar on Amelia's wrist as Amelia reached for the plate. What big black buck had put it there? A lot these niggers had to complain of in her when every one of them was all dosed up.

Amelia said that the base of the table was the old cistern. "He brung that top out f'om Memphis when he done the po'ch up this way for breakfas' and lunch."

The woman looked about the room, thinking, "I'll get some confab out of this one yet." And she exclaimed, "Oh, and that's the old bucket to it over there, then, with the vines on it, Amelia!"

"No'm," Amelia said. Then after a few seconds she added, "They brung that out f'om Memphis and put it there like it was it."

"Yeah . . . yeah . . . go on, Amelia. I'm odd about old-fashioned things. I've got a lot of interest in any antiques."

"That's all."

The little Negro woman started away with the coffee pot and the plate, dragging the soft soles of her carpet slippers over the brick floor. At the door she lingered, and, too cunning to leave room for a charge of impudence, she added to the hateful "That's all" a mutter, "Miss Josephine."

And when the door closed, Miss Josephine said under her breath, "If that black bitch hadn't stuck that on, there wouldn't be another chance for her to sneak around with any army blankets."

George, mounted on a big sorrel and leading a small dapple-gray horse, rode onto the lawn outside the breakfast room. Josephine saw him through the chinks of the blinds looking up toward her bedroom window. "Not for me," she said to herself. "He'll not get *me* on one of those animals." She swallowed the last of her coffee on her feet and then turned and stomped across the bricks to the step-up into the hallway. There she heard him calling:

"Josie! Josie! Get out-a that bed!"

Josephine ran through the long hall cursing the rugs that slipped under her feet. She ran the length of the hall looking back now and again as though the voice were a beast at her heels. In the front parlor she pulled up the glass and took a book from the bookcase nearest the door. It was a red book, and she hurled herself into George's chair and opened to page sixty-five:

nity, with anxiety, and with pity. Hamilcar was rubbing himself against my legs, wild with delight.

She closed the book on her thumb and listened to George's bellowing: "I'm coming after you!"

She could hear the sound of the hoofs as George led the horses around the side of the house. George's figure moved outside the front windows. Through the heavy lace curtains she could see him tying the horses to the branch of a tree. She heard him on the veranda and then in the hall. Damn him! God damn him, he couldn't make her ride! She opened to page sixty-five again as George passed the doorway. But he saw her, and he stopped. He stared at her for a moment, and she looked at him over the book. She rested her head on the back of the chair and put a pouty look on her face. Her eyes were fixed on his hairy arms, on the little bulk in his rolled sleeves, then on the white shirt over his chest, on the brown jodhpurs, and finally on the blackened leather of his shoes set well apart on the polished hall floor. Her eyelids were heavy, and she longed for a drink of the three-dollar whiskey that was on her dressing table.

He crossed the carpet with a smile, showing, she guessed, his delight at finding her. She smiled. He snatched the book from her hands and read the title on the red cover. His head went back, and as he laughed she watched through the open collar the tendons of his throat tighten and take on a purplish hue.

At Josephine's feet was a needlepoint footstool on which was worked a rust-colored American eagle against a background of green. George tossed the red book onto the stool and pulled Josephine from her chair. He was still laughing, and she wishing for a drink.

"Come along, come along," he said. "We've only four days left, and you'll want to tell your friend-girls you learned to ride."

She jerked one hand loose from his hold and slapped his hard cheek. She screamed, "Friend-girl? You never heard me say friend-girl. What black nigger do you think you're talking down to?" She was looking at him now through a mist of tears and presently she broke out into furious weeping.

His laughter went on as he pushed her across the room and into the hall, but he was saying: "Boochie, Boochie. Wotsa matter? Now, old girl, old girl. Listen: You'll want to tell your girl friends, your *girl friends*, that you learned to ride."

That was how George was! He would never try to persuade her. He would never pay any attention to what she said. He wouldn't argue with her. He wouldn't mince words! The few times she had seen him before this week there had been no chance to talk much. When they were driving down from Memphis, Saturday, she had gone through the story about how she was tricked by Jackie Briton and married Lon and how he had left her right away and the pathetic part about the baby she never even saw in the hospital. And at the end of it, she realized that George had been smiling at her as he probably would at one of his half-grown kids. When she stopped the story quickly, he had reached over and patted her hand (but still smiling) and right away had started talking about the sickly-looking tomato crops along the highway. After lunch on Saturday when she'd tried to talk to him again and he had deliberately commenced to play the victrola, she said, "Why won't you take me seriously?" But he had, of course, just laughed at her and kissed her; and they had already begun drinking then. She couldn't resist him (more than other men, he could just drive her wild), and he would hardly look at her, never had. He either laughed at her or cursed her or, of course, at night would pet her. He hadn't hit her.

He was shoving her along the hall, and she had to make herself stop crying.

"Please, George."

"Come on, now! That-a girl!"

"Honest to God, George. I tell you to let up, stop it."

"Come on. *Up* the steps. *Up! Up!*"

She let herself become limp in his arms but held with one hand to the banister. Then he grabbed her. He swung her up into his arms and carried her up the stairs which curved around the back end of the hall, over the doorway to the breakfast room. Once in his arms, she didn't move a muscle, for she thought, "I'm no featherweight, and we'll both go tumbling down these steps and break our skulls." At the top he fairly slammed her to her feet and, panting for breath, he said without a trace of softness: "Now, put on those pants, Josie, and I'll wait for you in the yard." He turned to the stair, and she heard what he said to himself: "I'll sober her. I'll sober her up."

As he pushed Josephine onto the white, jumpy beast he must have caught a whiff of her breath. She knew that he must have! He was holding the reins close to the bit while she tried to arrange herself in the flat saddle. Then he grasped her ankle and asked her, "Did you take a drink upstairs?" She laughed, leaned forward in her saddle, and whispered: "Two. Two jiggers."

She wasn't afraid of the horse now, but she was dizzy. "George, let me down," she said faintly. She felt the horse's flesh quiver under her leg and looked over her shoulder when it stomped one rear hoof.

George said, "Confound it, I'll sober you." He handed her the reins, stepped back, and slapped the horse on the flank. "Hold on!" he called, and her horse cantered across the lawn.

Josie was clutching the leather straps tightly, and her face was almost in the horse's mane. "I could kill him for this," she said, slicing out the words with a sharp breath. God damn it! The horse was galloping along a dirt road. She saw nothing but the yellow dirt. The hoofs rumbled over a three-plank wooden bridge, and she heard

George's horse on the other side of her. She turned her face that way and saw George through the hair that hung over her eyes. He was smiling. "You dirty bastard," she said.

He said, "You're doin' all right. Sit up, and I'll give you some pointers." She turned her face to the other side. Now she wished to God she hadn't taken those two jiggers. George's horse quickened his speed and hers followed. George's slowed and hers did likewise. She could feel George's grin in the back of her neck. She had no control over her horse.

They were galloping in the hot sunlight, and Josie stole glances at the flat fields of strawberries. "If you weren't drunk, you'd fall off," George shouted. Now they were passing a cotton field. ("The back of my neck'll be blistered," she thought. "Where was it I picked strawberries once? At Dyersburg when I was ten, visiting some God-forsaken relations.") The horses turned off the road into wooded bottom land. The way now was shaded by giant trees, but here and there the sun shone between foliage. Once after riding thirty feet in shadow, watching dumbly the cool blue-green underbrush, Josie felt the sun suddenly on her neck. Her stomach churned, and the eggs and coffee from breakfast burned her throat as it all gushed forth, splattering her pants leg and the brown saddle and the horse's side. She looked over the horse at George.

But there was no remorse, no compassion, and no humor in George's face. He gazed straight ahead and urged on his horse.

All at once the horses turned to the right. Josie howled. She saw her right foot flying through the air, and after the thud of the fall and the flashes of light and darkness she lay on her back in the dirt and watched George as he approached on foot, leading the two horses.

"Old girl . . ." he said.

"You get the hell away from me!"

"Are you hurt?" He kneeled beside her, so close to her that she could smell his sweaty shirt.

Josie jumped to her feet and walked in the direction from which they had ridden. In a moment George galloped past her, leading the gray horse and laughing like the son-of-a-bitch he was.

"Last night he sent me upstairs! But this is more! I'm not gonna have it." She walked through the woods, her lips moving as she talked to herself. "He wants no more of my drunken palaver!" Well, he was going to get no more of her drunken anything now. She had had her fill of him and everybody else and was going to look out for her own little sweet self from now on.

That was her trouble, she knew. She'd never made a good thing of people. "That's why things are like they are now," she said. "I've never made a good thing out of anybody." But it was real lucky that she realized it now, just exactly when she had, for it was certain that there had never been one whom more could be made out of than George. "God damn him," she said, thinking still of his riding by her like that. "Whatever it was I liked about him is gone now."

She gazed up into the foliage and branches of the trees, and the great size of the trees made her feel real small, and real young. If Jackie or Lon had been different she might have learned things when she was young. "But they were both of 'em easygoin' and just slipped out on me." They *were* sweet. She'd never forget how sweet Jackie always was. "Just plain sweet." She made a quick gesture with her right hand: "If only they didn't all get such a hold on me!"

But she was through with George. This time *she* got through first. He was no different from a floorwalker. He had more sense. "He's educated, and the money he must have!" George had more sense than a floorwalker, but he didn't have any manners. He treated her just like the floorwalker at Jobe's had that last week she was there. But George was worth getting around. She would find out what it was. She wouldn't take another drink. She'd find out what was wrong inside him, for there's something wrong inside everybody, and somehow she'd get a hold of him. Little Josephine would make a place for herself at last. She just wouldn't think about him as a man.

At the edge of the wood she turned onto the road, and across the fields she could see his house. That house was just simply as old and big as they come, and wasn't a cheap house. "I wonder if he looked after getting it fixed over and remodeled." Not likely. She kept looking at the whitewashed brick and shaking her head. "No, by Jesus," she exclaimed. "*She* did it!" George's wife. All of her questions seemed to have been answered. The wife had left him for his meanness, and he was lonesome. There was, then, a place to be filled. She began to run along the road. "God, I feel like somebody might step in before I get there." She laughed, but then the heat seemed to strike her all at once. Her stomach drew in. She vomited in the ditch, and, by God, it was as dry as cornflakes!

She sat still in the grass under a little maple tree beside the road, resting her forehead on her drawn-up knees. All between Josie and her new life seemed to be the walk through the sun in these smelly, dirty clothes. Across the fields and in the house was a canopied bed and a glorious new life, but she daren't go into the sun. She would pass out cold. "People kick off in weather like this!"

Presently Josie heard the voices of niggers up the road. She wouldn't look up, she decided. She'd let them pass, without looking up. They drew near to her and she made out the voices of a man and a child. The man said, "Hursh!" and the voices ceased. There was only the sound of their feet padding along the dusty road.

The noise of the padding grew fainter. Josie looked up and saw that the two had cut across the fields toward George's house. Already she could hear the niggers mouthing it about the kitchen. That little yellow Henry would look at her over his shoulder as he went through the swinging door at dinner tonight. If she heard them grumbling once more, as she did Monday, calling her "she," Josie decided that she was going to come right out and ask Amelia about the scar. Right before George. But the niggers were the least of her worries now.

All afternoon she lay on the bed, waking now and then to look at the bottle of whiskey on the dressing table and to wonder where George had gone. She didn't know whether it had been George or the field nigger who sent Henry after her in the truck. Once she dreamed that she saw George at the head of the stairs telling Amelia how he had sobered Miss Josephine up. When she awoke that time she said, "I ought to get up and get myself good and plastered before George comes back from wherever he is." But she slept again and dreamed this time that she was working at the hat sale at Jobe's and that she had to wait on Amelia who picked up a white turban and asked Josie to model it for her. And the dream ended with Amelia telling Josie how pretty she was and how much she liked her.

Josie had taken another hot bath (to ward off soreness from the horseback ride) and was in the sitting room, which everybody called the back parlor, playing the electric victrola and feeling just prime when George came in. She let him go through the hall and upstairs to dress up for dinner without calling to him. She chuckled to herself and rocked to the time of the music.

George came with a real mint julep in each hand. His hair was wet and slicked down over his head; the part, low on the left side, was straight and white. His cheeks were shaven and were pink with new sunburn. He said, "I had myself the time of my life this afternoon."

Josie smiled and said that she was glad he had enjoyed himself. George raised his eyebrows and cocked his head to one side. She kept on smiling at him, and made no movement toward taking the drink that he held out to her.

George set the glass on the little candle stand near her chair and switched off the victrola.

"George, I was listening . . ."

"Ah, now," he said, "I want to tell you about the cockfight."

"Let me finish listening to that piece, George."

George dropped down into an armchair and put his feet on a stool.

His pants and shirt were white, and he wore a blue polka dot tie.

"You're nice and clean," she said, as though she had forgotten the victrola.

"Immaculate!" There was a mischievous grin on his face, and he leaned over one arm of the chair and pulled the victrola plug from the floor socket. Josie reached out and took the glass from the candle stand, stirred it slightly with a shoot of mint, and began to sip it. She thought, "I *have* to take it when he acts this way."

At the dinner table George said, "You're in better shape tonight. You look better. Why don't you go easy on the bottle tonight?"

She looked at him between the two candles burning in the center of the round table. "I didn't ask you for that mint julep, I don't think."

"And you ain't gettin' any more," he said, winking at her as he lifted his fork to his lips with his left hand. This, she felt, was a gesture to show his contempt for her. Perhaps he thought she didn't know the difference, which, of course, was even more contemptuous.

"Nice manners," she said. He made no answer, but at least he could be sure that she had recognized the insult. She took a drink of water, her little finger extended slightly from the glass, and over the glass she said, "You didn't finish about the niggers having a fight after the chickens did."

"Oh, yes." He arranged his knife and fork neatly on his plate. "The two nigs commenced to watch each other before their chickens had done scrapping. And when the big rooster gave his last hop and keeled over, Ira Blakemoor jumped over the two birds onto Jimmy's shoulders. Jimmy just whirled round and round till he threw Ira the way the little mare did you this morning." George looked directly into Josie's eyes between the candles, defiantly unashamed to mention that event, and he smiled with defiance and yet with weariness. "Ira got up and the two walked around looking at each other like two black games before a fight." Josie kept her eyes on George while the story, she felt, went on and on and on.

That yellow nigger Henry was paused at the swinging door, looking over his shoulder toward her. She turned her head and glared at him. He was not even hiding this action from George, who was going on and on about the niggers' fighting. This Henry was the worst hypocrite of all. He who had slashed Amelia's wrist (it was surely Henry who had done it), and probably had raped his own children, the way niggers do, was denouncing her right out like this. Her heart pounded when he kept looking, and then George's story stopped.

A bright light flashed across Henry's face and about the room which was lit by only the two candles. Josie swung her head around, and through the front window she saw the lights of automobiles that were moving through the yard. She looked at George, and his face said absolutely nothing for itself. He moistened his lips with his tongue.

"Guests," he said, raising his eyebrows. And Josie felt that in that moment she had seen the strongest floorwalker weaken. George had scorned and laughed at everybody and every situation. But now he was ashamed. He was ashamed of her. On her behavior would depend his comfort. She was cold sober and would be *up* to whatever showed itself. It was her real opportunity.

From the back of the house a horn sounded, and above other voices a woman's voice rose, calling "Whoohoo!" George stood up and bowed to her beautifully, like something she had never seen, and said, "You'll excuse me?" Then he went out through the kitchen without saying "scat" about what she should do.

She drummed on the table with her fingers and listened to George's greetings to his friends. She heard him say, "Welcome, Billy, and welcome, Mrs. Billy!" They were the only names she recognized. It was likely the Billy Colton she'd met with George one night.

Then these *were* Memphis society people. Here for the night, at least! She looked down at her yellow linen dress and straightened the lapels at the neck. She thought of the women with their lovely profiles and soft skin and natural-colored hair. What if she had waited on one of them once at Jobe's or, worse still, in the old days at Burnstein's? But they had probably never been to one of those cheap stores. What if they stayed but refused to talk to her, or even to meet her? They could be mean bitches, all of them, for all their soft hands and shaved legs. Her hand trembled as she rang the little glass bell for coffee.

She rang it, and no one answered. She rang it again, hard, but now she could hear Henry coming through the breakfast room to the hall, bumping the guests' baggage against the doorway. Neither Amelia nor Mammy, who cooked the evening meal, would leave the kitchen during dinner, Josie knew. "I'd honestly like to go out in the kitchen and ask 'em for a cup of coffee and tell 'em just how scared I am." But too well she could imagine their contemptuous, accusing gaze. "If only I could get something on them! Even catch 'em toting food just once! That Mammy's likely killed enough niggers in her time to fill Jobe's basement."

Josie was even afraid to light a cigarette. She went over to the side window and looked out into the yard; she could see the lights from the automobiles shining on the green leaves and on the white fence around the house lot.

And she was standing thus when she heard the voices and the footsteps in the long hall. She had only just turned around when George stood in the wide doorway with the men and women from Memphis. He was pronouncing her name first: "Miss Carlson, this is Mr. Roberts, Mrs. Roberts, Mr. Jackson, Mrs. Jackson, and Mr. and Mrs. Colton."

Josie stared at the group, not trying to catch the names. She could think only, "They're old. The women are old and plump. George's wife is old!" She stared at them, and when the name Colton struck her ear, she said automatically and without placing his face, "I know Billy."

George said in the same tone in which he had said, "You'll excuse me?" "Josie, will you take the ladies upstairs to freshen up while the men and I get some drinks started? We'll settle the rooming question later." George was the great floorwalker whose wife was old and who had now shown his pride to Josie Carlson. He had shown his shame. Finally he had decided on a course and was following it, but he had given 'way his sore spots. Only God knew what he had told his friends. Josie said to herself, "It's plain he don't want 'em to know who I am."

As Josie ascended the stair, followed by those she had already privately termed the "three matrons," she watched George and the three other men go down the hall to the breakfast room. The sight of their white linen suits and brown and white shoes in the bright hall seemed to make the climb a soaring. At the top of the stairs she stopped and let the three women pass ahead of her. She eyed the costume of each as they passed. One wore a tailored seersucker dress. Another wore a navy-blue linen dress with white collar and cuffs, and the third wore a striped linen skirt and silk blouse. On the wrist of this last was a bracelet from which hung a tiny silver dog, a lock, a gold heart.

Josie observed their grooming: their fingernails, their lipstick, their hair in tight curls. There was gray in the hair of one, but not one, Josie decided now, was much past forty. Their figures were neatly corseted, and Josie felt that the little saggings under their chins and under the eyes of the one in the navy blue made them more charming; were, indeed, almost a part of their smartness. She wanted to think of herself as like them. They were, she realized, at least ten years older than she, but in ten years, beginning tonight, she might become one of them.

"Just go in my room there," she said. She pointed to the open door and started down the steps, thinking that this was the beginning of the new life and thinking of the men downstairs fixing the drinks. And then she thought of the bottle of whiskey on her dressing table in the room where the matrons had gone!

"Oh, hell," she cursed under her breath. She had turned to go up the two steps again when she heard the men's voices below. She heard her own name being pronounced carefully: "Josie Carlson." She went down five or six steps on tiptoe and stood still to listen to the voices that came from the breakfast room.

"You said to come any time, George, and never mentioned having this thing down here."

George laughed. "Afraid of what the girls will say when you get home? I can hear them. 'In Beatrice's own lovely house,'" he mocked.

"Well, fellow, you've a shock coming, too," one of them said. "Beatrice has sent your boys down to Memphis for a month with you. They say she has a beau."

"And in the morning," one said, "your sister Kate's sending them down here. She asked us to bring them, and then decided to keep them one night herself."

"You'd better get *her* out, George."

George laughed. Josie could hear them dropping ice into glasses.

"We'll take her back at dawn if you say."

"What would the girls say to that?" He laughed at them as he laughed at Josie.

"The girls are gonna be decent to her. They agreed in the yard."

"Female curiosity?" George said.

"Your boys'll have curiosity, too. Jock's seventeen."

Even the clank of the ice stopped. "You'll every one of you please to remember," George said slowly, "that Josie's a friend of yours and that she met the girls here by appointment."

Josie tiptoed down the stairs, descending, she felt, once more into her old world. "He'll slick me some way if he has to for his kids, I think." She turned into the dining room at the foot of the stairs. The candles were burning low, and she went and stood by the open window and listened to the counterpoint of the crickets and the frogs while Henry, who had looked over his shoulder at the car lights, rattled the silver and china and went about clearing the table.

Presently, George had come and put his hand on her shoulder. When she turned around she saw him smiling and holding two drinks in his left hand. He leaned his face close to hers and said, "I'm looking for the tears."

Josie said, "There aren't any to find, fellow"; and she thought it odd, really odd, that he had expected her to cry. But he was probably poking fun at her again.

She took one of the drinks and clinked glasses with George. To herself she said, "I bet they don't act any better than I do after they've got a few under their belts." At least she showed her true colors! "I'll keep my eyes open for their true ones."

*   *   *

If only they'd play the victrola instead of the radio. She liked the victrola so much better. She could play "Louisville Lady" over and over. But, *no*. They all wanted to switch the radio about. To get Cincinnati and Los Angeles and Bennie this and Johnny that. If they liked a piece, why did they care who played it? For God's sake! They wouldn't dance at first, either, and when she first got George to dance with her, they sat smiling at each other, grinning. They had played cards, too, but poker didn't go so well after George slugged them all with that third round of his three-dollar-whiskey drinks. Right then she had begun to watch out to see who slapped whose knee.

She asked George to dance because she so liked to dance with him, and she wasn't going to care about what the others did any more, she decided. But finally when two of them had started dancing off in the corner of the room, she looked about the sitting room for the other four and saw that Billy Colton had disappeared not with his own wife but with that guy Jackson's. And Josie threw herself down into the armchair and laughed aloud, so hard and loud that everybody begged her to tell what was funny. But she stopped suddenly and gave them as mean a look as she could manage and said, "Nothin'. Let's dance some more, George."

But George said that he must tell Henry to fix more drinks, and he went out and left her by the radio with Roberts and Mrs. Colton. She looked at Mrs. Colton and thought, "Honey, you don't seem to be grieving about Billy."

Then Roberts said to Josie, "George says you're from Vicksburg."

"I was raised there," she said, wondering why George hadn't told her whatever he'd told them.

"He says you live there now."

Mrs. Colton, who wore the navy blue and was the fattest of the three matrons, stood up and said to Roberts, "Let's dance in the hall where there are fewer rugs." And she gave a kindly smile to Josie, and Josie spit out a "Thanks." The couple skipped into the hall, laughing, and Josie sat alone by the radio wishing she could play the victrola and wishing that George would come and kiss her on the back of her neck. "And I'd slap him if he did," she said. Now and again she would cut her eye around to watch Jackson and Mrs. Roberts dancing. They were at the far end of the room and were dancing slowly. They kept rubbing against the heavy blue drapery at the window and they were talking into each other's ears.

But the next piece that came over the radio was a hot one, and Jackson led Mrs. Roberts to the center of the room and whirled her round and round, and the trinkets at her wrist tinkled like little bells. Josie lit a cigarette and watched them dance. She realized then that Jackson was showing off for her sake.

When George came with a tray of drinks he said, "Josie, move the victrola," but Josie sat still and glared at him as if to say, "What on earth are you talking about? Are you nuts?" He set the tray across her lap and turned and picked up the little victrola and set it on the floor.

"Oh, good God!" cried Josie in surprise and delight. "It's a portable."

George, taking the tray from her, said, "It's not for you to port off, old girl."

The couple in the center of the room had stopped their whirling and had followed George. "We like to dance, but there are better things," Jackson was saying.

Mrs. Roberts flopped down on the broad arm of Josie's chair and took a drink from George. Josie could only watch the trinkets on the bracelet, one of which she saw was a little gold book. George was telling Jackson about the cockfight again, and Mrs. Roberts leaned over and talked to Josie. She tried to tell her how the room seemed to be whirling around. They both giggled, and Josie thought, "Maybe we'll get to be good friends, and she'll stop pretending to be so swell." But she couldn't think of anything to say to her, partly because she just never did have anything to say to women and partly because Jackson, who was not at all a bad-looking little man, was sending glances her way.

It didn't seem like more than twenty minutes or half an hour more before George had got to that point where he ordered her around and couldn't keep on his own feet. He finally lay down on the couch in the front parlor, and as she and Mrs. Roberts went up the stairs with their arms about each other's waists, he called out something that made Mrs. Roberts giggle. But Josie knew that little Josephine was at the point where she could say nothing straight, so she didn't even ask to get the portable victrola. She just cursed under her breath.

The daylight was beginning to appear at the windows of Josie's narrow little room when waking suddenly she sat up in bed and then flopped down again and jerked the sheet about her. "That little sucker come up here," she grumbled, "and cleared out, but where was the little sucker's wife?" Who was with George, by damn, all night? After a while she said, "They're none of 'em any better than the niggers. I knew they couldn't be. Nobody is. By God, nobody's better than I am. Nobody can say anything to me." Everyone would like to live as free as she did! There was no such thing as . . . There was no such thing as what the niggers and the whites liked to pretend they were. She was going to let up, and do things in secret. Try to look like an angel. It wouldn't be as hard since there was no such thing.

It was all like a scene from a color movie, like one of the musicals. It was the prettiest scene ever. And they were like two of those lovely wax models in the boys' department at Jobe's. Like two of those models, with the tan skin and blond hair, come to life! And to see them in their white shorts spring about the green grass under the blue, blue sky, hitting the little feather thing over the high net, made Josie go weak all over. She went down on her knees and rested her elbows on the window sill and watched them springing about before the people from Memphis; these were grouped under a tree, sitting in deck chairs and on the grass. George stood at the net like a floorwalker charmed by his wax manikins which had come to life.

It had been George's cries of "Outside, outside!" and the jeers and applause of the six spectators that awakened Josie. She ran to the window in her pajamas, and when she saw the white markings on the grass and the net that had sprung up there overnight, she thought that this might be a dream. But the voices of George and Mrs. Roberts and Phil Jackson were completely real, and the movements of the boys' bodies were too marvelous to be doubted.

She sank to her knees, conscious of the soreness which her horse-back ride had left. She thought of her clumsy self in the dusty road as she gazed down at the graceful boys on the lawn and said, "Why, they're actually pretty. Too pretty." She was certain of one thing: she didn't want any of their snobbishness. She wouldn't have it from his two kids.

One boy's racket missed the feather thing. George shouted, "Game!" The group under the tree applauded, and the men pushed themselves up from their seats to come out into the sunlight and pat the naked backs of the boys.

When the boys came close together, Josie saw that one was six inches taller than the other. "Why, that one's grown!" she thought. The two of them walked toward the house, the taller one walking with the shorter's neck in the crook of his elbow. George called to them, "You boys get dressed for lunch." He ordered them about just as he did her, but they went off smiling.

Josie walked in her bare feet into the little closet-like bathroom which adjoined her room. She looked at herself in the mirror there and said, "I've never dreaded anything so much in all my life before. You can't depend on what kids'll say." But were they kids? For all their prettiness, they were too big to be called kids. And nobody's as damn smutty as a smart-alecky shaver.

Josephine bathed in the little, square, maroon bathtub. There were maroon and white checkered tile steps built up around the tub, so that it gave the effect of being sunken. After her bath, she stood on the steps and powdered her whole soft body. Every garment which she put on was absolutely fresh. She went to her closet and took out her new white silk dress and slipped it over her head. She put on white shoes first, but, deciding she looked too much like a trained nurse, she changed to her tan pumps. Josie knew what young shavers thought about nurses.

She combed her yellow hair till it lay close to her head, and put on rouge and lipstick. Someone knocked at the bedroom door. "Yeah," she called. No answer came, so she went to the door and opened it. In the hall stood one of the boys. It was the little one.

He didn't look at her; he looked past her. And his eyes *were* as shiny and cold as those on a wax dummy!

"Miss Carlson, my dad says to tell you that lunch is ready. And I'm Buddy."

"Thanks." She didn't know what the hell else she should say. "Tell him, all right," she said. She stepped back into her room and shut the door.

Josie paced the room for several minutes. "He didn't so much as look at me." She was getting hot, and she went and put her face to the window. The people from Memphis had come indoors, and the sun shone on the brownish green grass and on the still trees. "It's a scorcher," she said. She walked the length of the room again and opened the door. Buddy was still there. Standing there in white, his shirt open at the collar, and his white pants, long pants. He was leaning against the banister.

"Ready?" he said, smiling.

As they went down the steps together, he said, "It's nice that you're here. We didn't know it till just a few minutes ago." He was a Yankee kid, lived with his mother somewhere, and rolled his *r*'s, and spoke as though there was a lot of meaning behind what he said. She gave him a quick glance to see what he meant by that last remark. He smiled, and this time looked right into her eyes.

After lunch, which Josie felt had been awful embarrassing, they traipsed into the back parlor, and George showed off the kids again. She had had a good look at the older one during lunch and could tell by the way the corners of his mouth drooped down that he was a surly one, unless maybe he was only trying to keep from looking so pretty. And all he said to the questions which George asked him about girls and his high school was "Yeah" or "Aw, naw." When Henry brought in the first round of drinks, and he took one, his daddy looked at him hard and said, "Jock?" And the boy looked his daddy square in the eye.

Buddy only shook his head and smiled when Henry offered him a drink, but he was the one that had started all the embarrassment for her at lunch. When they came into the dining room he pulled her chair out, and she looked back at him—knowing how kids like to jerk chairs. Everybody laughed, but she kept on looking at him. And then she knew that she blushed, for she thought how big her behind must look to him with her bent over like she was.

The other thing that was awful was the question that Mrs. Jackson, the smallest matron and the one with the gray streak in her hair, asked her, "And how do *you* feel this morning, Miss Carlson?" It was the fact that it was Jackson's wife which got her most. But then the fool woman said, "Like the rest of us?" And Josie supposed that she meant no meanness by her remark, but she had already blushed; and Jackson, across the table, looked into his plate. Had this old woman and George been messing around? she wondered. Probably Mrs. Jackson hadn't meant anything.

As they all lounged about the sitting room after lunch, she even felt that she was beginning to catch on to these people and that she was going to start a little pretense of her own and make a good thing out of old Georgie. It was funny the way her interest in him, any real painful interest, was sort of fading. "I've never had so much happen to me at one time," she said to herself. She sat on the floor beside George's chair and put her hand on the toe of his brown and white shoe.

Then George said, "Buddy, you've got to give us just one recitation." And Buddy's face turned as red as a traffic light. He was sitting on a footstool and looking down at his hands.

Jock reached over and touched him on the shoulder and said, "Come on, Buddy, the one about 'If love were like a rose.'" Buddy shook his head and kept his eyes on his hands.

Josie said to herself, "The kid's honestly kind-a shy." It gave her the shivers to see anybody so shy and ignorant of things. But then he began to say the poetry without looking up. It was something about a rose and a rose leaf, but nobody could hear him very good.

George said, "Louder! Louder!" The boy looked at him and said a verse about "sweet rain at noon." Next he stood up and moved his hands about as he spoke, and the blushing was all gone. He said the next one to Mrs. Roberts, and it began:

If you were life, my darling,
And I, your love, were death . . .

That verse ended with something silly about "fruitful breath." He went then to Billy Colton's wife, and the verse he said to her was sad. The boy *did* have a way with him! His eyes were big and he could look sad and happy at the same time. "And I were page to joy," he said. He actually looked like one of the pages they have in stores at Christmas.

But now the kid was perfectly sure of himself, and he had acted timid at first. It was probably all a show. She could just hear him saying dirty limericks. She realized that he was bound to say a verse to her if he knew that many, and she listened carefully to the one he said to Mrs. Jackson:

If you were April's lady,
And I were lord in May,
We'd throw with leaves for hours
And draw for days with flowers,
Till day like night were shady
And night were bright like day;
If you were April's lady,
And I were lord in May.

He turned on Josie in his grandest manner:

If you were queen of pleasure,
And I were king of pain,
We'd hunt down love together,
Pluck out his flying-feather
And teach his feet a measure,
And find his mouth a rein;
If you were queen of pleasure,
And I were king of pain.

And Josie sat up straight and gave the brat the hardest look she knew how. It was too plain. "Queen of pleasure" sounded just as bad as whore! Especially coming right after the verse about "April's lady." The boy blushed again when she glared at him. No one made a noise for a minute. Josie looked at George, and he smiled and began clapping his hands, and everybody clapped. Buddy bowed and ran from the room.

"He's good, George. He's good," Jackson said, squinting his beady little eyes. Jackson was really a puny-looking little guy in the light of day! And he hadn't thought the boy was any better than anybody else did. It was just that he wanted to be the first to say something.

"He's really very good," Mrs. Jackson said.

George laughed. "He's a regular little actor," he said. "Get's it from Beatrice, I guess." Everybody laughed.

George's wife was an actress, then! She'd probably been the worst of the whole lot. There was no telling what this child was really like.

"How old is he, Jock?" Jackson asked. How that man liked to hear his own voice!

"Fourteen and a half," Jock said. "Have you seen him draw?" He talked about his kid brother like he was his own child. Josie watched him. He was talking about Buddy's drawings, about the likenesses. She watched him, and then he saw her watching. He dropped his eyes to his hands as Buddy had done. But in a minute he looked up; and as the talking and drinking went on he kept his eyes on Josephine.

It wasn't any of George's business. It wasn't any of his or anybody's how much she drank, and she knew very well that *he* didn't really give a damn! But it *was* smarter'n hell of him to take her upstairs, because the boys had stared at her all afternoon and all through supper. That was really why she had kept on taking the drinks when she had made up her mind to let up. She had said, "You're jealous. You're jealous, George." And he had put his hand over her mouth, saying, "Careful, Josie." But she was sort of celebrating so much's happening to her, and she felt good, and she was plain infuriated when George kissed her and went back downstairs. "He was like his real self comin' up the steps," she said. He had told her that she didn't have the gumption God gave a crab apple.

Josie went off to sleep with her lips moving and awoke in the middle of the night with them moving again. She was feeling just prime and yet rotten at the same time. She had a headache and yet she had a happy feeling. She woke up saying, "Thank your stars you're white!" It was something they used to say around home when she was a kid. She had been dreaming about Jock. He was all right. She had dreamed that together she and Jock had watched a giant bear devouring a bull, and Jock had laughed and for some reason she had said, "Thank your stars you're white!" He was all right. She was practically sure. His eyes were like George's, and he was as stubborn.

It would have been perfectly plain to everybody if supper hadn't been such an all-round mess. What with Jackson's smutty jokes and his showing off (trying to get her to look at him), and Mrs. Colton's flirting with her husband (holding his hand on the table), nobody but George paid any attention to Jock. And she was glad that she had smacked Jackson when he tried to carry her up the stairs, for it made Jock smile his crooked smile.

"They all must be in bed," she thought. The house was so quiet that she could hear a screech owl, or something, down in the woods.

She thought she heard a noise in her bathroom. She lay still, and she was pretty sure she had heard it again. She supposed it was a mouse, but it might be something else; she had never before thought about where that door beside the bathtub might lead. There was only one place it could go. She got up and went in her stocking feet to the bathroom. She switched on the light and watched the knob. She glanced at herself in the mirror. Her new white silk dress was twisted and wrinkled. "Damn him," she whispered to herself. "He *could* have made me take off this dress." Then she thought she had seen the knob move, move as though someone had released it. She stood still, but there wasn't another sound that night.

In the morning when she turned off the bathroom light, she was still wondering. She looked out of the window; the high net was down. No one was in sight.

What they all did was to slip out on her before she woke up! And in the breakfast room that morning Amelia wanted to talk, but Josephine wasn't going to give the nigger the chance. There was no telling what they had let the niggers hear at breakfast. Amelia kept coming to the breakfast room door and asking if everything was all right, if Miss Josephine wanted this or wanted that, but Miss Josephine would only shake her head and say not a word after Amelia had once answered, "They've went back to Memphis." For all she knew, George and the kids had gone too. It would have been like him to leave her and send after her, just because he had promised her she could stay a week. (He talked like it was such a great treat for her. She hadn't given a copper about the place at first. It had been *him*.) But he'd damned well better not have left her. She'd got a taste of this sort of thing for its own sake now, and she'd stay for good!

Buddy opened the outside door of the breakfast room.

"Good morning, Miss Carlson," he said.

"Hello," Josie said. She did wonder what Jock had told Buddy, what he had guessed to tell him. Buddy wasn't at dinner last night, or she couldn't remember him there.

He was wearing khaki riding pants and a short-sleeved shirt. He sat down across the table from her. "I guess we're all that's left," he said. He picked up the sugar bowl and smiled as he examined it. The corners of his mouth turned up like a picture kids draw on a blackboard.

"Did Jock and George go to Memphis? Did they?"

"Jock did."

"He did?"

"Yes, he did. And Henry told me he didn't much want to go. I was off riding when they all got up this morning. Daddy wanted me to go too, but I wasn't here." He smiled again, and Josie supposed he meant that he'd been hiding from them.

* * *

"Where's your dad?"

"He? Oh, he went to the village to see about some hams. What are you going to do now?"

Josie shrugged her shoulders and began to drink her coffee. Jack was gone. He might have just been scorning her with those looks all the time. She should have got that door open somehow and found out what was what. "Why didn't Jock want to go?" she asked Buddy.

"Our pleasant company, I suppose," he said. "Or yours."

She looked at him, and he laughed. She wondered could this brat be poking fun at her? "Queen of pleasure!" she said out loud, not meaning to at all.

"Did you like that poem?" he asked. It was certain that he wasn't timid when he was alone with somebody, not at least when alone with her.

"I don't know," she said. Then she looked at him. "I don't like the one you picked for me."

"That's not one of the best, is it?"

Neither of them spoke while Josie finished her coffee. She put in another spoonful of sugar before taking the last few swallows, and Buddy reddened when she motioned for him to give up the sugar bowl. Amelia came and removed the breakfast plate and the butter plate. She returned for Josie's coffee cup, and, finding it not quite ready, she stood behind Buddy's chair and put her hands on his shoulders. The scar was right beside his cheek. Buddy smiled and beat the back of his head against her ribs playfully. Finally Josie put her cup down and said, "That's all."

She went upstairs to her room. Jock had tried to get in through her bathroom last night, or he had been so on her mind that her ears and eyes had made up the signs of it. Maybe Buddy had caught Jock trying to open the door and had told George. At any rate George had sent Jock away. If he sent him away, then Jock had definitely had notions. Josie smiled over that one. She was sitting on the side of her little canopied bed, smoking a red-tipped cigarette. There was the noise of an automobile motor in the yard. George was back! Josie went to her dressing table and drank the last of her whiskey.

She sat on the stool before her dressing table, with her eyes on the hall door. She listened to George's footsteps on the stairs, and sat with her legs crossed, twitching the left foot, which dangled. George came in and closed the door behind him.

"I've bought you a ticket on the night train, Josie. You're goin' back tonight."

So he wasn't such a stickler for his word, after all! Not in this case. He was sending her home. Well, what did he expect her to say? Did he think she would beg to stay on? She would clear out, and she wasn't the one beaten. George was beaten. One of his kids that he was so mortally fond of, one for sure had had notions. "Almost for sure." George opened the door and left Josie staring after him. In a few minutes she heard his horse gallop past the house and out onto the dirt road.

She folded her white dress carefully and laid it on the bottom of her traveling bag. She heard Buddy somewhere in the house, singing. She wrapped her white shoes in toilet paper and stuck them at the ends of the bag. Buddy seemed to be wandering through the house, singing. His voice was high like a woman's, never breaking as she sometimes thought it did in conversation. It came from one part of the house and then another. Josie stopped her packing. "There's no such thing," she said.

She went down the steps like a child, stopping both feet on each step, then stepping to the next. One hand was on her hip, the other she ran along the banister. She walked through the front parlor with its bookcases and fancy chairs with the eagles worked in needlepoint, and through the back parlor with the rocking chairs and the silly candle stand and the victrola. She stepped down into the breakfast room where the sunlight came through the blinds and put stripes on the brick wall. She went into the kitchen for the first time. Mammy, with a white dust cap on the back of her head, had already started supper. She stood by the big range, and Amelia sat in the corner chopping onions. Josie wasn't interested in the face of either. She went through the dark pantry and into the dining room. She looked through the windows there, but no one was in the yard. She went into the hall.

Buddy was near the top of the stairway which curved around the far end of the long hall, looking down at her. "Why don't you come up here?" He pronounced every word sharply and rolled his *r*'s. But his voice was flat, and his words seemed to remain in the hall for several minutes. His question seemed to float down from the ceiling, down through the air like a feather.

"How did he get up there without me hearing him?" Josie mumbled. She took the first two steps slowly, and Buddy hopped up to the top of the stair.

The door to the kids' room was open and Josie went in. Buddy shut the white paneled door and said, "Don't you think it's time you did something nice for me?"

Josie laughed, and she watched Buddy laugh. Queen of pleasure indeed!

"I want to draw you," he said.

"Clothes and all, Bud . . . ?"

"No. That's not what I mean!"

Josie forced a smile. She suddenly felt afraid and thought she was going to be sick again but she couldn't take her eyes off him.

"That's not what I mean," she heard the kid say again, without blinking an eye, without blushing. "I didn't know you were that sort of nasty thing here. I didn't believe you were a fancy woman. Go on out of here. Go away!" he ordered her.

As Josie went down the steps she kept puckering her lips and nodding her head. She was trying to talk to herself about how many times she had been up and down the steps, but she could still see the smooth brown color of his face and his yellow hair, and she could also see her hand trembling on the banister. It seemed like five years since she had come up the steps with the matrons from Memphis.

In the breakfast room she tore open the frail door to George's little liquor cabinet and took a quart of Bourbon from the shelf. Then she stepped up into the hall and went into the sitting room and took the portable victrola and that record. As she stomped back into the hall, Buddy came running down the steps. He opened the front door and ran out across the veranda and across the lawn. His yellow hair was like a ball of gold in the sunlight as he went through the white gate. But Josie went upstairs.

She locked her door and threw the big key across the room. She knocked the bottle of toilet water and the amber brush off her dressing table as she made room for the victrola. When she had started "Louisville Lady" playing, she sat on the stool and began to wonder. "The kid's head was like a ball of gold, but I'm not gonna think about him ever once I get back to Memphis," she told herself. "No, by damn, but I wonder just what George'll do to me." She broke the blue seal of the whiskey with her fingernail, and it didn't seem like more than twenty minutes or half an hour before George was beating and kicking on the door, and she was sitting on the stool and listening and just waiting for him to break the door, and wondering what he'd do to her.

OF
CABBAGES
AND
KINGS

JAMES
ALAN
McPHERSON

Claude Sheats had been in the Brotherhood all his life, and then he had tried to get out. Some of his people and most of his friends were still in the Brotherhood and were still very good members, but Claude was no longer a good member because he had tried to get out after over twenty years. To get away from the Brotherhood and all his friends who were still active in it, he moved to Washington Square and took to reading about being militant. But, living there, he developed a craving for whiteness the way a nicely broke-in virgin craves sex. In spite of this, he maintained a steady black girl, whom he saw at least twice a month to keep up appearances, and once he took both of us

JAMES ALAN MC PHERSON, graduated in 1968 from Harvard Law School, is a contributing editor of *Atlantic Monthly*, and a Fellow of College V, University of California at Santa Cruz. His first collection of stories is *Hue and Cry*.

with him when he visited his uncle in Harlem who was still in the Brotherhood.

"She's a nice girl, Claude," his uncle's wife had told him that night, because the girl, besides being attractive, had some very positive ideas about the Brotherhood. Her name was Marie, she worked as a secretary in my office, and it was on her suggestion that I had moved in with Claude Sheats.

"I'm glad to see you don't waste your time on hippies," the uncle had said. "All our young men are selling out these days."

The uncle was the kind of fellow who had played his cards right. He was much older than his wife, and I had the impression that night that he must have given her time to experience enough and to become bored enough before he overwhelmed her with his success. He wore glasses and combed his hair back and had that oily composure that made me think of a waiter waiting to be tipped. He was very proud of his English, I observed, and how he always ended his words with just the right sound. He must have felt superior to people who didn't. He must have felt superior to Claude because he was still with the Brotherhood and Claude had tried to get out.

Claude did not like him and always seemed to feel guilty whenever we visited his uncle's house. "Don't mention any of my girls to him," he told me after our first visit.

"Why would I do that?" I said.

"He'll try to psych you into telling him."

"Why should he suspect you? He never comes over to the apartment."

"He just likes to know what I'm doing. I don't want him to know about my girls."

"I won't say anything," I promised.

He was almost twenty-three and had no steady girls except Marie. He was well built so that he had no trouble in the Village area. It was like going to the market for him. During my first days in the apartment the process had seemed like a game. And once, when he was going out, I said: "Bring back two."

Half an hour later he came back with two girls. He got their drinks, and then he called me into his room to meet them.

"This is Doris," he said, pointing to the smaller one, "and I forgot your name," he said to the big blonde.

"Jane," she said.

"This is Howard," he told her.

"Hi," I said. Neither one of them smiled. The big blonde in white pants sat on the big bed, and the little one sat on a chair near the window. He had given them his worst bourbon.

"Excuse me a minute," Claude said to the girls. "I want to talk to Howard for a minute." He put on a record before we went outside into the hall between our rooms. He was always extremely polite and gentle, and he was very soft-spoken in spite of his size.

"Listen," he said to me outside, "you can have the blonde."

"What can I do with that amazon?"

"I don't care. Just get her out of the room."

"She's dirty," I said.

"So you can give her a bath."

"It wouldn't help much."

"Well, just take her out and talk to her," he told me. "Remember, you asked for her."

We went in. "Where you from?" I said to the amazon.

"Brighton."

"What school?"

"No. I just got here."

"From where?"

"*Brighton!*"

"Where's that?" I said.

"*England*," she said. Claude Sheats looked at me.

"How did you find Washington Square so fast?"

"I got friends."

She was very superior about it all and showed the same slight irritation of a professional theater critic for a late performance to begin. The little one sat on the chair, her legs crossed, staring at the ceiling. Her white pants were dirty too. Both girls looked as though they would have been relieved if we had taken off our clothes and danced for them around the room and across the bed, and made hungry sounds in our throats with our mouths slightly opened.

I said that I had to go out to the drugstore and would be back very soon; but once outside, I walked a whole hour in one direction, and then I walked back. I passed them a block away from our apartment. The were walking fast and did not slow down or speak when I passed them.

Claude Sheats was drinking heavily when I came into the apartment.

"What the hell are you trying to pull?" he said.

"I couldn't find a drugstore open."

He got up from the living room table and walked toward me. "You should have asked me," he said. "I got more than enough."

"I wanted some mouthwash too," I said.

He fumed a while longer, and then told me how I had ruined his evening because the amazon would not leave the room to wait for me and the little one would not do anything with the amazon around. He suddenly thought of going down and bringing them back, and he went out for a while. But he came back without them, saying that they had been picked up again.

"When a man looks out for you, you got to look out for him," he warned me.

"I'm sorry."

"A hell of a lot of good *that* does. And that's the last time I look out for *you*, baby," he said. "From now on it's *me* all the way."

"Thanks," I said.

"If she was too much for you I could of taken the amazon."

"It didn't matter that much," I said.

"You could of had Doris if you couldn't handle the amazon."

"They were both too much," I told him.

But Claude Sheats did not answer. He just looked at me.

After two months of living with him I concluded that Claude hated whites as much as he loved them. And he hated himself with the very same passion. He hated the country and his place in it, and he loved the country and his place in it. He loved the Brotherhood and all that being in it had taught him, and he still believed in what he had been taught, even after he had left it and did not have to believe in anything.

"This Man is going *down*, Howard," he would announce with conviction.

"Why?" I would ask.

"Because it's the Black Man's time to rule again. They had five thousand years, now we get five thousand years."

"What if I don't *want* to rule?" I asked. "What happens if I don't want to take over?"

He looked at me with pity in his face. "You go down with the rest of the country."

"I guess I wouldn't mind much anyway," I said. "It would be a hell of a place with nobody to hate."

But I could never get him to smile about it the way I tried to smile about it. He was always serious. And once, when I questioned the mysticism in the teachings of the Brotherhood, Claude almost attacked me. "Another man might kill you for saying that," he had said. "Another man might not let you get away with saying something like that." He was quite deadly, and he stood over me with an air of patient superiority. And because he could afford to be generous and forgiving, being one of the saved, he sat down at the table with me under the single light bulb and began to teach me. He told me the stories about how it was in the beginning before the whites took over, and about all the little secret significances of black, and about the subtle infiltration of white superiority into everyday objects.

"You've never seen me eat white bread or white sugar, have you?"

"No," I said. He used brown bread and brown sugar.

"Or use bleached flour or white rice?"

"No."

"You know why, don't you?" He waited expectantly.

"No," I finally said. "I don't know why."

He was visibly shocked, so much so that he dropped that line of instruction and began to draw on a pad before him on the living room table. He moved his big shoulders over the yellow pad to conceal his drawings and looked across the table at me. "Now I'm going to tell you something that white men have paid thousands of dollars to learn," he said. "Men have been killed for telling this, but I'm telling you for nothing. I'm warning you not to repeat it because if the whites find out, you know, you could be killed too."

"You know me," I said. "I wouldn't repeat any secrets."

He gave me a long, thoughtful look.

I gave him back a long, eager, honest look.

Then he leaned across the table, and whispered: "Kennedy isn't buried in this country. He was the only President who never had his coffin opened during the funeral. The body was in state all that time, and they never opened the coffin once. You know why?"

"No."

"Because he's not *in it!* They buried an empty coffin. Kennedy was a Thirty-third Degree Mason. His body is in Jerusalem right now."

"How do you know?" I asked.

"If I told you, it would put your life in danger."

"Did his family know about it?"

"No. His lodge kept it secret."

"No one knew?"

"I'm telling you, *no!*"

"Then how did you find out?"

He sighed, more from tolerance than from boredom with my inability to comprehend the mysticism of pure reality in its most unadulterated form. Of course I could not believe him, and we argued about it, back and forth; but to cap all my uncertainties he drew the thirty-three-degree circle, showed me the secret signs that men had died to learn, and spoke about the time when our black ancestors chased an evil genius out of their kingdom and across a desert and onto an island somewhere in the sea; from which, hundreds of years later, this same evil genius sent forth a perfected breed of white-skinned and evil creatures who, through trickery, managed to enslave for five thousand years the onetime Black Masters of the world. He further explained the significance of the East and why all the saved must go there once during their lifetime, and possibly be buried there, as Kennedy had been.

It was dark and late at night, and the glaring bulb cast his great shadow into the corners so that there was the sense of some outraged spirit, fuming in the halls and dark places of our closets, waiting to extract some terrible and justifiable revenge from him for disclosing to me, an unbeliever, the closest-kept of secrets. But I was aware of them only for an instant, and then I did not believe him again.

The most convincing thing about it all was that he was very intelligent and had an orderly, well-regimented life-style, and yet *he* had no trouble with believing. He believed in the certainty of statistical surveys, which was his work; the nutritional value of wheat germ sprinkled on eggs; the sensuality of gin; and the dangers inherent in smoking. He was stylish in that he did not believe in God, but he was extremely moral and warm and kind; and I wanted sometimes to embrace him for his kindness and bigness and gentle manners. He lived his life so carefully that no matter what he said, I could not help believing him sometimes. But I did not want to, because I knew that once I started I could not stop; and then there would be no purpose to my own beliefs and no real conviction or direction in my own efforts to achieve when always, in the back of my regular thoughts, there would be a sense of futility and a fear of the unknown all about me. So, for the sake of necessity, I chose not to believe him.

He felt that the country was doomed and that the safe thing to do was to make enough money as soon as possible and escape to the Far East. He forecast summer riots in certain Northern cities and warned me, religiously, to avoid all implicating ties with whites so that I might have a chance to be saved when that time came. And I asked him about *his* ties, and the girls, and how it was never a movie date with coffee afterward but always his room and the cover-all blanket of Motown sounds late into the night.

"A man has different reasons for doing certain things," he had said.

He never seemed to be comfortable with any of the girls. He never seemed to be in control. And after my third month in the apartment I had concluded that he used his virility as a tool and forged, for however long it lasted, a little area of superiority which could never, it seemed, extend itself beyond the certain confines of his room, no matter how late into the night the records played. I could see him fighting to extend the area, as if an increase in the number of girls he saw could compensate for what he had lost in duration. He saw many girls: curious students, unexpected bus-stop pickups, and assorted other one-nighters. And his rationalizations allowed him to believe that each one was an actual conquest, a physical affirmation of a psychological victory over all he hated and loved and hated in the little world of his room.

But then he seemed to have no happiness, even in this. Even here I sensed some intimations of defeat. After each girl, Claude would almost immediately come out of his room, as if there were no need for aftertalk; as if, after it was over, he felt a brooding, silent emptiness that quickly intensified into nervousness and instantaneous shyness and embarrassment, so that the cold which sets in after that kind of emotional drain came in very sharp against his skin, and he could not bear to have her there any longer. And when the girl had gone, he would come into my room to talk. These were the times when he was most like a little boy; and these were the times when he really began to trust me.

"That bitch called me everything but the son of God," he would chuckle. And I would put aside my papers brought home from the office, smile at him, and listen.

He would always eat or drink afterward, and in those early days I was glad for his companionship and the return of his trust, and sometimes we drank and talked until dawn. During these times he would tell me more subtleties about the Man and would repredict the fall of the country. Once he warned me, in a fatherly way, about reading life from books before experiencing it; and another night he advised me on how to schedule girls so that one could run them without being run in return. These were usually good times of good-natured arguments and predictions; but as we drank more often he tended to grow excited and quick-tempered, especially after he had just entertained. Sometimes he would seethe with hate, and every drink he took gave life to increasingly bitter condemnations of the present system and our place in it. There were actually flying saucers, he told me once, piloted by things from other places in the universe, which would eventually destroy the country for what it had done to the black man. He had run into his room on that occasion, and had brought out a book by a man who maintained that the government was deliberately withholding from the public overwhelming evidence of flying saucers and strange creatures from other galaxies that walked among us every day. Claude emphasized the fact that the writer was a Ph.D. who must know what he was talking about, and insisted that the politicians withheld the information because they knew that their time was almost up and if they made it public, the black man would know that he had outside friends who would help him take over the world again. Nothing I said could make him reconsider the slightest bit of his information.

"What are we going to use for weapons when we take over?" I asked him once.

"We've got atomic bombs stockpiled and waiting for the day."

"How can you believe that crap?"

He did not answer, but said instead: "You are the living example of what the Man has done to my people."

"I just try to think things out for myself," I said.

"You can't think. The handkerchief over your head is too big."

I smiled.

"I know," he continued. "I know all there is to know about whites because I've been studying them all my life."

I smiled some more.

"I ought to know," he said slowly. "I have supernatural powers."

"I'm tired," I told him. "I want to go to sleep now."

Claude started to leave the room, then he turned. "Listen," he said at the door. He pointed his finger at me to emphasize the gravity of his pronouncement. "I predict that within the next week something is going to happen to this country that will hurt it even more than Kennedy's assassination."

"Good-night," I said as he closed the door.

He opened it again. "Remember that I predicted it when it happens," he said. For the first time I noticed that he had been deadly serious all along.

Two days later several astronauts burned to death in Florida. He raced into my room hot with the news.

"Do you believe in me *now?*" he said. "Just two days and look what happened."

I tried to explain, as much to myself as to him, that in any week of the year something unfortunate was bound to occur. But he insisted that this was only part of a divine plan to bring the country to its knees. He said that he intended to send a letter off right away to Jeane Dixon in D.C. to let her know that she was not alone because he also had the same power. Then he thought that he had better not because the FBI knew that he had been active in the Brotherhood before he got out.

At first it was good fun believing that someone important cared enough to watch us. And sometimes when the telephone was dead a long time before the dial tone sounded, I would knock on his door and together we would run through our telephone conversations for that day to see if either of us had said anything implicating or suspect, just in case they were listening. This feeling of persecution brought us closer together, and soon the instruction sessions began to go on almost every night. At this point I could not help believing him a little. And he began to trust me again, like a tolerable little brother, and even confided that the summer riots would break out simultaneously in Harlem and Watts during the second week in August. For some reason, something very difficult to put into words, I spent three hot August nights on the streets of Harlem, waiting for the riot to start.

In the seventh month of our living together, he began to introduce me to his girls again when they came in. Most of them came only once, but all of them received the same mechanical treatment. He discriminated only with liquor, the quality of which improved with the attractiveness or reluctance of the girl: gin for slow starters, bourbon for momentary strangers, and the scotch he reserved for those he hoped would come again. There was first the trek into his room, his own trip out for the ice and glasses while classical music was played within; then after a while the classical piece would be replaced by several Motowns. Finally, there was her trip to the bathroom, his calling a cab in the hall, and the sound of both their feet on the stairs as he walked her down to the cab. Then he would come to my room in his red bathrobe, glass in hand, for the aftertalk.

Then in the ninth month the trouble started. It would be very easy to pick out one incident, one day, one area of misunderstanding in that month and say: "That was where it began." It would be easy, but not accurate. It might have been one instance or a combination of many. It might have been the girl who came into the living room when I was going over the proposed blueprints for a new settlement house, and who lingered too long outside his room in conversation because her father was a builder somewhere. Or it might have been nothing at all. But after that time he warned me about being too friendly with his company.

Another night, when I was leaving the bathroom in my shorts, he came out of his room with a girl who smiled. "Hi," she said to me.

I nodded hello as I ducked back into the bathroom.

When he had walked her down to the door he came to my room and knocked. He did not have a drink. "Why didn't you speak to my company?" he demanded.

"I was in my shorts."

"She felt bad about it. She asked what the hell was wrong with you. What could I tell her—'He got problems'?"

"I'm sorry," I said. "But I didn't want to stop in my shorts."

"I see through you, Howard," he said. "You're just jealous of me and try to insult my girls to get to me."

"Why should I be jealous of you?"

"Because I'm a man and you're not."

"What makes a man anyway?" I said. "Your fried eggs and wheat germ? Why should I be jealous of you *or* what you bring in?"

"Some people don't need a reason. You're a black devil and you'll get yours. I predict that you'll get yours."

"Look," I told him, "I'm sorry about the girl. Tell her I'm sorry when you see her again."

"You treated her so bad she probably won't come back."

I said nothing more, and he stood there silently for a long time before he turned to leave the room. But at the door he turned again, and said: "I see through you, Howard. You're a black devil."

It should have ended there, and it might have with anyone else. I took great pains to speak to his girls after that, even though he tried to get them into the room as quickly as possible. But a week later he accused me of walking about in his room after he had gone out some two weeks before.

"I swear I wasn't in your room," I protested.

"I saw your shadow on the blinds from across the street at the bus stop," he insisted.

"I've *never* been in your room when you weren't there," I told him.

"I *saw* you!"

We went into his room, and I tried to explain how, even if he could see the window from the bus stop, the big lamp next to the window prevented any shadow from being cast on the blinds. But he was convinced in his mind that at every opportunity I plundered his closets and drawers. He had no respect for simple logic in these matters, no sense of the absurdity of his accusations, and the affair finally ended with my confessing that I might have done it without actually knowing, and if I had, I would not do it again.

But what had been a gesture for peace on my part became a vindication for him, proof that I *was* a black devil, capable of lying and lying until he confronted me with the inescapable truth of the situation. And so he persisted in creating situations from which, if he insisted on a point long enough and with enough self-righteousness, he could draw my inevitable confession.

And I confessed eagerly, goaded on by the necessity of maintaining peace. I confessed to mixing white sugar crystals in with his own brown crystals so that he could use it and violate the teachings of the Brotherhood; I confessed to cleaning the bathroom all the time merely because I wanted to make him feel guilty for not having ever cleaned it. I confessed to telling the faithful Marie, who brought a surprise dinner over for him, that he was working late at his office in order to implicate him with the girls who worked there. I confessed to leaving my papers about the house so that his company could ask about them and develop an interest in me. And I pleaded guilty to a record of other little infamies, which multiplied into countless others, and again subdivided into hundreds of little subtleties until my every movement was a threat to him. If I had a girlfriend to dinner, we should eat in my room instead of at the table because he had to use the bathroom a lot, and he was embarrassed to be seen going to the bathroom.

If I protested, he would fly into a tantrum and shake his big finger at me vigorously. And so I retreated, step by step, into my room, from which I emerged only to go to the bathroom or kitchen or out of the house. I tried to stay out on nights when he had company. But he had company so often that I could not always help being in my room after he had walked her to the door. Then he would knock on my door for his talk. He might offer me a drink, and if I refused, he would go to his room for a while and then come back. He would pace about for a while, like a big little boy who wants to ask for money over his allowance. At these times my mind would move feverishly over all our contacts for as far back as I could make it reach, searching and attempting to pull out that one incident which would surely be the point of his attack. But it was never any use.

"Howard, I got something on my chest, and I might as well get it off."

"What is it?" I asked from my bed.

"You been acting strange lately. Haven't been talking to me. If you got something on your chest, get it off now."

"I have nothing on my chest," I said.

"Then why don't you talk?"

I did not answer.

"You hardly speak to me in the kitchen. If you have something against me, tell me now."

"I have nothing against you."

"Why don't you talk, then?" He looked directly at me. "If a man doesn't talk, you think *something's* wrong!"

"I've been nervous lately, that's all. I got problems, and I don't want to talk."

"Everybody's got problems. That's no reason for going around making a man feel guilty."

"For God's sake, I don't want to talk."

"I know what's wrong with you. Your conscience is bothering you. You're so evil that your conscience is giving you trouble. You got everybody fooled but *me*. I know you're a black devil."

"I'm a black devil," I said. "Now will you let me sleep?"

He went to the door. "You dish it out, but you can't take it," he said. "That's *your* trouble."

"I'm a black devil," I said.

I lay there, after he left, hating myself but thankful that he hadn't called me into his room for the fatherly talk as he had done another time. That was the worst. He had come to the door and said: "Come out of there, I want to talk to you." He had walked ahead of me into his room and had sat down in his big leather chair next to the lamp with his legs spread wide and his big hands in his lap. He had said: "Don't be afraid. I'm not going to hurt you. Sit down. I'm not going to argue. What are you so nervous about? Have a drink," in his kindest, most fatherly way, and that had been the worst of all. That was the time he had told me to eat in my room. Now I could hear him pacing about in the hall, and I knew that it was not over for the night. I began to pray that I could sleep before he came. I did not care what he did as long as I did not have to face him. I resolved to confess to anything he accused me of if it would make him leave sooner. I was about to go out into the hall for my confession when the door was kicked open and he charged into the room.

"You black son of a bitch!" he said. "I ought to *kill* you." He stood over the bed in the dark room and shook his big fist over me. And I lay there hating the overpowering cowardice in me, which kept my body still and my eyes closed, and hoping that he would kill all of it when his heavy fist landed.

"First you insult a man's company, then you ignore him. I been *good* to you. I let you live here, I let you eat my uncle's food, and I taught you things. But you're a ungrateful m-f. I ought to *kill* you right now!"

And I still lay there, as he went on, not hearing him, with nothing in me but a loud throbbing which pulsed through the length of my body and made the sheets move with its pounding. I lay there secure and safe in cowardice for as long as I looked up at him with my eyes big and my body twitching and my mind screaming out to him that it was all right, and I thanked him, because now I truly believed in the new five thousand years of Black Rule.

It is night again. I am in bed again, and I can hear the new blond girl closing the bathroom door. I know that in a minute he will come out in his red robe and call a cab. His muffled voice through my closed door will seem very tired, but just as kind and patient to the dispatcher as it is to everyone, and as it was to me in those old times. I am afraid, because when they came up the stairs earlier they caught me working at the living room table with my back to them. I had not expected him back so soon; but then I should have known that he would not go out. I had turned around in the chair, and she smiled and said hello, and I said "Hi" before he hurried her into the room. I *did* speak, and I know that she heard. But I also know that I must have done something wrong; if not to her, then to him earlier today or yesterday or last week, because he glared at me before following her into the room, and he almost paused to say something when he came out to get the glasses and ice. I wish that I could remember just what it was. But it does not matter. I *am* guilty, and he knows it.

Now that he knows about me I am afraid. I could move away from the apartment and hide my guilt from him, but I know that he would find me. The brainwashed part of my mind tells me to call the police while he is still busy with her, but what could I charge him with when I know that he is only trying to help me? I could move the big ragged yellow chair in front of the door, but that would not stop him, and it might make him impatient with me. Even if I pretended to be asleep and ignored him, it would not help when he comes. He has not bothered to knock for weeks.

In the black shadows over my bed and in the corners I can sense the outraged spirits who help him when they hover about his arms as he gestures, with his lessons, above my bed. I am determined now to lie here and take it. It is the price I must pay for all the black secrets I have learned, and all the evil I have learned about myself. I *am* jealous of him, of his learning, of his girls. I am not the same handkerchief-head I was nine months ago. I have Marie to thank for that, and Claude, and the spirits. They know about me, and perhaps it is they who make him do it and he cannot help himself. I believe in the spirits now, just as I believe most of the time that I am a black devil.

They are going down to the cab now.

I will not ever blame him for it. He is helping me. But I blame the girls. I blame them for not staying on afterward, and for letting all the good nice happy love talk cut off automatically after it is over. *I* need to have them there, after it is over. And he needs it; he needs it much more and much longer than they could ever need what he does for them. He should be able to teach them, as he has taught me. And he should have their appreciation, as he has mine. I blame them. I blame them for letting him try and try and never get just a little of the love there is left in the world.

I can hear him coming back from the cab.

MENDING WALL

WILLARD MARSH

San Francisco, the alternate home of Miguel Flores, was a small, neat village with eroded adobe walls symmetrical around an elevated plaza that was shadowed by the spire of Saint Francis on clement days. Even through the steady drizzle of a mid-June dusk it gave a welcome lift to his spirits. He got off the bus with the two knapsacked Americans who had failed to make a transfer and accompanied them to the waiting room. There he learned that the next bus for their destination, a rowdy foreign colony on the upper edge of Lake Chapala, would not be due till nine-fifteen.

"Oh, man, that's sad news," said Harry, the lean, good-looking taller of the two. "Where's someplace swinging we can sweat out all that time, Mike?"

WILLARD MARSH teaches English at North Texas State University. He is the author of a novel, *Week With No Friday*, and a collection of stories, *Beachhead in Bohemia*.

Miguel smiled at the idioms, hoping to remember them. Swinging, surely from swing music. "There is a pleasant little restaurant where you can sweat yourselves in comfort." He pointed it out. "I think you will not find it swinging, but it is agreeable."

"Grease him, daddy, grease him," Harry's stocky friend Sidecar murmured.

"Have a drink and keep us company a little longer, amigo," Harry urged. "Think of us out here in the cold among alien faces, while you're in that far-out castle of yours, curled up with a warm broad and a bottle."

Again Miguel smiled (because of their broader, child-bearing hips?), hesitating. The family seldom used the villa in the rainy season. On occasional weekends such as this one, Miguel would come out to romp with the dog, play his worn old jazz records while the rain conspired with what he recognized was Weltschmerz (although recognition didn't lessen it), and try his hand at a love poem. "Very well, I will be pleased to join you."

Leading them to a crowded cantina that smelled of wet wool cloaks and stale dried fish, he had a beer while they each tossed off a pair of double tequilas. They were about nineteen, a year or so older than himself, and by a happy coincidence were also prelaw students at Stanford University in California. Furthermore, they were working their way through school as professional jazz musicians, Harry on piano and Sidecar with what Harry had praised as "the funkiest trumpet west of Salt Lake City."

"Well, how does our Frisco compare to yours?" Miguel asked. "I think you will find it lacks your fogs." He began humming a tricky eight-bar opening, slapping his palms in counter-tempo on the bar. Then he laughed, having caught them once again.

A slow, tantalized grin spread over Harry's face. "What the *hell* is the name of that thing?"

"I will give you a hint. They also recorded 'Margie' back in the thirties."

Sidecar began whistling "Margie" thoughtfully.

"Yes, that! That is the trombone solo of 'Margie'!" Miguel said in excitement. "Jimmy Lunceford, of course. And this I am doing now is his 'Frisco Fog.' Remember?"

"Remember it?" Harry said. "I don't think I could forget it if they brainwashed me."

Sidecar's eyes were half-lidded in nostalgia. "They broke the mold."

Pleased, Miguel extended his hand in farewell. "And now I must go home. Thank you for the drink and for the conversation."

"Oh no, Mike, why end it?" Harry said quickly. "Let's have some more of both—here or anywhere you say."

Miguel was touched by their naked loneliness. There was only the caretaker on the grounds, old Rafael, and his ailing wife and little daughter who managed for them. When the family came they always brought the servants from the town house. But even with a skeleton staff, provisions of some sort could be made for guests, he supposed.

"If you would like to wait at the villa, you would be welcome," he told them. "We could play some records, and there is probably beer in the refrigerator. We could have a little lunch of some kind, whatever is in the kitchen." He remembered the perfect expression. "Potluck."

"Crazy! Potluck sounds like great luck."

"Wild, man."

"A real lifesaver, Mike. That's very generous of you."

And buoyed by their appreciation, Miguel took them the kilometer walk across town to Casa Flores, a compact house that lay behind high walls on a short cliff that overhung the lake. Looking through the spiked iron gate onto the lawned terraces that old Rafael kept immaculate, Harry whistled in awe. Miguel wondered how they would react if they could see the opulent neighboring estates. Now he too whistled, a piercing octave drop.

The silence lasted for perhaps two seconds, and then there was an outburst of convulsively ecstatic barking from the direction of the caretaker's cottage. The arthritic collie, Corazón, came out of the woodshed as fast as her legs could bear her, followed by Rafael with his brass key ring. They were about the same age proportionately. Miguel let the collie bathe him with her tongue between the bars, jerking handfuls of her skin the way she liked.

"*Alma mía*. Oh you good girl," he said.

And when Rafael admitted them Miguel embraced him and said, "These two are friends who stay for a brief meal."

"They are welcome," Rafael said and they smiled back, although they didn't understand him. On the flagstoned path to the house, escorted by the bounding collie, they exchanged questions about their families. Finally excusing himself, Rafael said, "I shall send Louisa for your needs."

"Yes, please do so."

With an affectionate spank, Miguel sent the collie back to her lair. Her muddy paws and hair were prohibited from contact with his mother's furniture, and she could have his full attention all tomorrow morning. Then he led Harry and Sidecar down the tiled hall to his rear quarters, where his drums squatted across the room from a pair of angled speakers connected to his turntable. There was a fire laid in the hearth. Lighting it, Miguel pointed out the shelf of loosely stacked records.

"Choose your listening pleasure, *señores*, while I investigate the condition of the department of beer."

He left them eagerly writhing out of their knapsacks and returned up the hall to the kitchen, where young Louisa was chopping cabbage while tortillas simmered in a pan. Again he went through the ritual of comparing the health and fortunes of her scattered family and his own as he opened three chilled bottles of Corona and told her to put the rest of the case in the refrigerator.

Halfway back to his room he heard Art Tatum's "Sweet Lorraine" flare up, and he entered to find Harry and Sidecar squatting in solemn respect before the speakers. Silently handing them their bottles, Miguel sat on the window ledge and watched Harry's face reflect the dizzying velocity of the blind Negro's right hand, knowing that whatever he himself got from it, a professional pianist would be hearing so much more.

They all sighed at the conclusion of the record, and Sidecar said, "I believe that cat covers just a little more keyboard than you do, daddy."

Harry grinned. "Well, wait till I'm his age."

Laughing, Miguel said, "Now it is the turn to play one for the trumpet man." And selecting Buck Clayton's "Royal Garden Blues," he put it on and watched Sidecar shaking his head in disbelief at the hoarse golden agony and saying *too much, too much.* Harry pointed at the drums in invitation.

"Oh no, I could not," Miguel said quickly, at the same time hoping that they would insist, because this was one of his favorite recordings to play behind. But they let it go, and when the record was over Miguel said,

"And now, shall we have 'Frisco Fog'?"

"Great." Harry absently tilted up his empty bottle.

Embarrassed at being too neglectful a host to realize that they had finished their beers, Miguel went to the door and called Louisa. When she appeared at the head of the hall he ordered three more and hurriedly finished his own. It wasn't until after "Frisco Fog" was done that they were aware she had been shyly knocking at the door.

"Pass, girl, pass!" Miguel called.

The door opened and Louisa slipped in with a tray containing bottles, glasses, and a bowl of radishes.

"Get a load of those splendid little knockers," Harry told Sidecar.

"Oh man, the tenderest meat in town."

Louisa flushed and lowered her eyes under the intensity of their gaze. Miguel was embarrassed at being made to see that she was no longer a child.

Removing the contents of the tray, Harry said in clumsy Spanish, "Good morning, beautiful. To dance? To dance?" He put one hand on his chest and extended his arm, weaving his torso sensuously. "Slap something on that gramophone, paisano," he called over his shoulder.

Miguel stepped forward. "No, that is not done here. She has never in her life danced with a man." Then he thanked Louisa and dismissed her.

They put another record on, and after awhile the incident had passed. But from then on, whenever Harry and Sidecar were in need of fresh beers, Miguel went for them himself.

There was only one bottle remaining from the case by the time Louisa announced the meal, and Miguel divided it between the musicians.

"*Buen provecho,* as we say," he said, while they seated themselves around the heavy walnut dining table and Louisa brought in a cauldron of chicken broth. "Good appetite."

"No danger not," Harry said eagerly, ladling himself a bowl. "You got a dandy stack of platters back there, Mike. Some real collector's items."

"All that fine listening," Sidecar nodded. "And not being able to join in, that's what drags me. Man, I wish I had the old axe with me."

"The old axe?" Miguel smiled.

"My horn, dad."

"I see," he laughed, and then an idea struck him. "Excuse me for a moment, please."

In the kitchen, he told Louisa to ask Rafael to see if he could borrow a trumpet or cornet from one of the bandsmen in the village. She returned from the errand in time to clear the soup bowls and serve them with refried beans, salad, and rice with bits of roast pork. The food had more abundance than variety, and they filled themselves at leisure. When they were finishing coffee, Miguel said,

"I wish I could offer you some brandy, but my father keeps it under lock."

"Where is it?" Harry asked, and Miguel uneasily pointed to the glassed liquor cabinet. "Hell, a screwdriver can take care of that."

Miguel tried to laugh it off. "This I think my father would not quite appreciate."

But just then, to ease the awkwardness, Rafael signaled from the kitchen archway. Excusing himself, Miguel hurried over to see that, through some confusion of Louisa's or his own, the old man had got hold of a valve trombone. Miguel thanked him, brought it in and presented it to Sidecar with an elaborate flourish.

"What in hell is *that?*"

"An axe, poor as it is," Miguel said. "I thought we could take my drums to the *sala* where the piano is and make some noise. Just to pass the time."

"Man, if that's a trumpet I'm an ape's pizzaz."

"Come on, clown, don't drag the party," Harry said. "It's got valves, hasn't it? I think that's a real creative suggestion, Mike. Let's all go blow up a storm."

And with Sidecar testing the valve action in amused reluctance, they returned to Miguel's room for the drums.

They arranged themselves in the dimly lit, high-ceilinged living room, Miguel behind his snare and bass with the sizzle cymbal attached to it, next to the grand piano, with Sidecar lounging sardonically in a wing chair. Harry opened the piano, made a little show of blowing imaginary dust from the keyboard and slid his hand down it skeptically.

"Oh, no. When's the last time this thing was tuned?"

"It has been a little while," Miguel admitted.

Harry began striking notes at random, shaking his head in misery. "Terrible, terrible. It's bound to cramp my style."

"It's got keys, hasn't it?" Sidecar called. "Don't drag the party."

Harry gave him an obscene gesture. "You want to tune up?"

"Gimme an A."

Harry struck a key and Sidecar put the trombone to his lips, pushed the first valve down and produced a harsh tone with more breath than timbre.

"You're flat, but it's close enough for jazz," Harry said cheerfully. "OK, brass section, what'll we wail on?"

"Help yourself, daddy."

"How about 'The Bird on Nelly's Hat'?"

"What key?"

"Help yourself, daddy."

"How about B flat?"

"Oh man, if you'd said *A* flat it would make some sense. But *B* flat?"

Sidecar laughed insultingly. "Make it A flat, then. And give us an up-beat intro."

"With pleasure." Harry settled himself on the bench, serious now, and said quietly, "Leave us swing, gentlemen."

He began with the brisk, two-fingered waltz that nonpianists play at parties, and thoroughly enjoying the wit, Miguel gave him an appropriate backing.

Finishing, Harry called, "Take it, Mike!"

Miguel rolled into four-four, knocking out an eight-bar chorus. He used his snare as a tom-tom, making rim shots with a crossed stick, and at the end he gave them the re-entry riff on his cymbal and bass.

"Take it, Sidecar!" he called happily.

Sidecar brought the horn to his mouth, pushed all three valves down and produced the same strangled noise he'd made when he was tuning up. Then he stopped and stared in total disbelief at Harry, who was still playing "Chopsticks" in syncopated form.

"You son of a bitch, you're in B flat!"

"Of course I'm in B flat, you horse's pratt! Isn't that what we said?"

Then, in their slack-mouthed laughter, Miguel was able to see how far ahead of him they were in drinking. He hoped it had been merely drunkenness, or even contempt for his own performance, that had caused this display. It would be preferable to a deliberate abuse of his confidence.

Miguel glanced at his watch and got up from the drums. "Well, it helped to pass the time, correct? Your bus will come soon," he said. "Perhaps it will come ahead of schedule."

"I guess we're all a little better at law than music," Harry said nonchalantly. And then, to Miguel's amazement at their inability to read social signals, he said, "So listen, why don't we put on a trial? You know, defense attorney, prosecuting attorney—the whole bit."

"Whom do you propose to try?" Miguel asked coldly.

"Oh, we'll figure that out. You know, moot court stuff. Let's go hear some more records. Where's the head?"

"The what?"

"The can, man. The *escusado.*"

"Oh. I will show you."

Reconciled to being stuck with them until bus time, less than two hours from now, Miguel pointed out the bathroom on the way back to his room. Perhaps it wasn't too much to hope that Harry would have sense and grace enough to vomit himself into sobriety.

Since he and Sidecar had nothing to communicate to one another, Miguel put a record on to fill the silence. After a while Harry came in with a brandy bottle.

Waving it in grinning apology, he said, "Looking for a little drink of water in the kitchen. Slipped and broke a panel of the cabinet. Bad show. Thought I'd salvage it with a vintage bottle for the vintage records."

Incapable of further surprise, Miguel found himself thinking *They must be simply savages.* This observation enabled him to remain sitting on the bed like a research anthropologist, dividing his attention between them and his wristwatch.

Harry had passed the bottle to Sidecar and was flipping through the records. Finding one to his liking, he replaced the one that was going on the turntable. The familiar sounds of "Nelly Grey," by Louis Armstrong and the Mills Brothers, came drifting lazily from the speakers.

Harry and Sidecar looked at each other and began laughing in what seemed near hysteria.

"Oh, no, those cats *got* to go. The title alone does it. The bird on darling Nelly Grey's hat." Harry wiped his eyes and took another drink of brandy, coughing a little. "All right, I'll present the case for the plaintiff." He removed the record and waved it in the air. "We contend that this monstrosity does grave mischief to the ear of anyone who was born after 1922. We submit that it is Grade A horsecrap, fresh from the furrows. The plaintiff rests. Take it, Mike."

"Oh, then I am the defense? Very well," Miguel said. "The defense is willing to stipulate that this recording is older than some of the others. The defense further suggests that taste is impossible to define, and that no one forced you to listen to this or any other record."

"Does the defense rest?"

"Yes."

"Take it, paisano. You're the jury."

"We find the defendant guilty as charged," Sidecar said.

"And the jury brings in a verdict of mandatory death," Harry chanted.

He smashed the record against a corner of the shelf. Then as Miguel rose from the bed, he stepped quickly to the door and folded his arms.

"Play it cool, amigo," he cautioned.

"Real cool," Sidecar agreed.

Their faces, slack with liquor, wore a look of wary readiness. Miguel realized he was alone in the house with them, and in the caretaker's cottage there were a feeble old man and two females, one bedridden. He sat back down.

"That's better. Call the next defendant," Harry said, remaining at the door.

Sidecar glanced at a label or two. "That Art Tatum thing?"

"No, that's not too bad. Look for something really spooky."

"Earl Father Hines?"

"Father *who?* Well, hand it over and we'll find out."

"Do you propose to break that record also?" Miguel asked, surprised at the steadiness of his voice. He had been able to find only one Hines recording, their theme song, "Deep Forest."

"Why, Mike, are you suggesting we'd commit a breach of professional ethics?" Harry asked in astonishment. "There is no presentencing here. A defendant is allowed his chance before the bar of justice."

"Sure, what do you think we're running," Sidecar said, "a kangaroo court or something?"

And now Miguel began coughing from the thick smell of their cigarettes. "Can't we have some fresh air?"

"Christ yes. Don't you ever wash your feet, paisan'?"

Harry put the Hines record on, keeping a close eye on Miguel, while Sidecar struggled with the window. Damp new air surged in, along with the somber, deep chorale of Father Hines. The ex-musicians listened to it for a while in only mild amusement before Harry took the record off and weighed it in his hand, considering.

"Well, it's old-timey enough, God knows. Great-grandfather Hines would be more like it. But it doesn't rape your ear lobes. Tell you what, Mike. Make a good, spirited defense and maybe you'll persuade the prosecution to withdraw charges."

Miguel forced himself to casually whistle a few bars of the opening. Then he whistled an octave drop. "I am not sure that it is worth defending." He whistled the octave drop, louder.

"Well, now, *look*, amigo," Harry said in an ugly voice, "that's not professional ethics, abandoning your client to the big drop."

Miguel continued whistling idly.

"You don't want to cooperate?" Harry turned to Sidecar. "I do believe old Mike is dragging the party."

"That'll never do. Guess we have to coax him back into the jolly spirit."

"Looks like he's forcing us. Are you listening, amigo? I'm going to count to three, and if you aren't making a case for it, the record goes. One."

Miguel kept whistling.

"Two. . . ."

Miguel whistled the octave drop, in good volume.

"Three? All right, you asked for it."

In the instant that the record shattered the collie set up her barking from the woodshed. The sound approached rapidly.

"Novak, get that window!" Harry yelled.

"The what?"

"The window, stupid!"

As Sidecar leaped to the window to begin wrestling it shut, Corazón's head appeared in it, her front paws braced on the sill. She resumed barking at the commotion, her tail thrashing in rapture.

"Freeze!" Miguel shouted.

Sidecar froze.

"Now move very slowly, unless you want to lose that entire hand up to the elbow," Miguel told him. "Move backward."

When he was far enough from the window Miguel halted him, went to the ledge and hoisted the collie inside.

"Throw yourself!" he said, and she obediently sprawled at his feet, executing just about the only command he'd ever succeeded in teaching her.

"Guard them closely," he told her in Spanish, her tail thumping the floor contentedly. "Rip their pasty guts out if they even sneeze," he said, in the joy of cold fury that he would have felt had she been able to do such a thing. "I have just told her," he announced, "to go for the throat if either of you move one muscle. Wait here, exactly where you are."

Stepping out of the room, he hurried to his parents' bedroom. There in his mother's night table, as he'd remembered it, was her .25 pistol. It had never been fired, to his knowledge, and after all these years of disuse quite possibly would misfire, assuming it was loaded. But its small heft was welcome to his hand. He raced back in time to see Harry edging cautiously out into the hall.

"Get back in there or you're a dead man!" Miguel called, leveling the pistol at him.

Harry slowly elevated his arms and moved back inside. Joining them, Miguel ordered them both to stand against the wall while he stacked all his records on the floor.

"You must understand that I will not hesitate to kill you if you give me an excuse," he told them sincerely. "Death is a matter of small import in Mexico. Especially the death of a pair of vagabonds, who break into the grounds of a family of influence with intent to rob. No one in this village will challenge my interpretation of events." The collie stretched sleepily. "And now, shall we recommence the trial?" Miguel picked up the first record. "Art Tatum, on 'Sweet Lorraine.' This time you will be the defense, Harry, if that is your name." He thrust the pistol toward him. "Plead."

Harry smiled, or tried to. "Jesus, Mike, it's a beautiful record, I never said it wasn't."

"I am not Mike to you, *puto*. I am señor Flores. And you are wrong. It cannot be a beautiful record. It has been dirtied by your ears."

Miguel smashed it against the shelf and kicked the pieces from him.

"My God, amigo, what are you doing?"

Miguel looked at him. "If you call me amigo one more time, I will put a bullet through your heart." He bent to pick up the next record. It was "Frisco Fog." He set it aside and selected another. "Benny Goodman, 'Sing, Sing, Sing,' Part II. Can it be defended?"

"Look, Mike—I mean, señor. We were drunk clean out of our skulls. Give us a break and let us out of here."

Miguel struck the Goodman record clean in half. "All these records are contaminated by your presence, and by my tolerance of it. They will have to be purified."

Jimmy Lunceford's "Margie" went next, followed by the Teddy Wilson quartet, while the two looked on in fearful silence. By the time Miguel had broken Chick Webb, there was no emotion to it any more. It was an unseeing, mechanical process, during which they could have attacked him or fled and he wouldn't have known or cared.

Finally he was done, the floor littered with Fats Waller, Fletcher Henderson, the King Cole trio, the entire useless past. He met their dazed expressions with his own.

"Put on your packs and leave through the window," he said. "Get over the gate whatever way you can. Do it before I change my mind."

He sat back in utter fatigue, watching them ready themselves and climb quickly out the window. Then they were running down the terraces to the tall iron gate and laboring over it, and then they were gone.

They are simply savages, he found himself repeating, and now he realized whom he meant by *they*. It was all of them, all their stolen land and wealth and power. How could he have ever seen them otherwise? Oh, he would continue to use their language, because it was the language that best functioned on financial levels. But he was forever finished with their quaint Negro artists, their customs, their enthusiasms, their mere sight in any other than a duty situation.

Corazón whimpered, nudging him with her nose. He discovered that "Frisco Fog" was still intact. He swung it listlessly against the turntable until it cracked, perhaps with the sound of an opening egg shell.

THE HUNTERS

HARRIS DOWNEY

Private Meadows was lost. He had no idea which way his outfit had gone, had ever intended to go.

They were moving into France from the north. Naturally, their progress would be to the south. But during their fighting from Cherbourg they had moved in all directions. He did not know how long it had been since they left Cherbourg—three weeks, four weeks. It was some long, undeterminable stretch of time. Nor did he know how many miles they had come—forty, fifty, maybe two hundred. They had come through villages—slowly, ferreting snipers from the ruins that their own artillery made. Someone had named the names of the villages but he had not understood. He had asked the names again and again, feeling that he should establish something familiar in his memory,

HARRIS DOWNEY lives in Baton Rouge, Louisiana. His three novels are *Thunder in the Room, The Key to My Prison,* and *Carrie Dumain.* His short stories are widely published.

feeling that he might come to understand where he was going, what he was doing. But between question and answer he would fall back into the torpor that his life had been since Cherbourg. The answer, like a fragment slanting a helmet, would strike his mind obliquely and deflect away into the noisy and flashing anonymity of war.

He had traversed plow-furrowed fields when silence, imminent with violence, weighted him down like a pack. He had traversed shell-pelleted fields when fear tangled his legs like a barricade. He had seen his enemy and his comrades sprawled grotesque and cold in the neutrality of death, as impersonal as the cows among them, angling stiff legs to the sky. He had thrown grenades at hidden men; and once, staring into wide, stark eyes down the bead of his aim, he had sighed out his breath toward a union more intimate than love—and more treacherous than its denial. He had seen a dog, tethered at the gate, howl at the noise of destruction and die in terror; had seen bees swarm from their hives at the ground shake of cannon and hang in the air, directionless. He had seen Frenchmen return to their villages to gesticulate the glory of victory and, sobering, to peer from behind a silly grin at the rubbish that had been their homes. But these things had not touched him. He had left himself somewhere, and the farther he walked the terrain of war, the farther he went from himself.

He heard the spasmodic eruptions of war. He listened to silence hissing like the quick fuse of a bomb. Yet he felt nothing—unless it was weariness. He walked under the high fire of artillery as though it were a canopy against the rain. At first he had been unhappy and afraid; and perhaps, in the static musing, in the constant but unapprehended memory that was himself, he was yet unhappy and afraid.

Casually walking, talking to his friends, or running, crawling, squirming on his belly, looking ahead for cover, he had followed his leaders from sector to sector. The sun had come up on his left, on his right, from behind him, had sheered through the odd geometry of fields and had slid down the high summer clouds behind him, in front of him—always in a new tangent to the hedgerow. Twelve times, twenty times. How many times had he seen the sun point a surprising direction that was the west?

That morning he had seen the sun come up in the direction they were to move. Lying against the massed roots, he had looked through an opening of the hedgerow over a pasture that ran a quarter of a mile to a woods.

There near the woods he saw a farmhouse with spindly trees growing around it like a fence. He lay still, watching the sun slip above the treetops. To the right of him lay Barr, a replacement who had been in the company only a week or so, a talkative fellow who somehow managed to hold his happiness and his identity about him. Beyond Barr lay Pederson, whose twin brother had been wounded in his first skirmish and sent back. To the left of him was Harrod, whom Private Meadows had been with since induction. And beyond Harrod was Walton, a slow-talking, card-playing soldier who had come in with Barr. These men were his friends; by virtue of their position in the squad, they were his friends.

All along the row men lay with their heads in their helmets. Soon, from somewhere behind him, an order would be given and everyone would begin to move. But he would not comprehend the order. Even when it was passed on to him and he in turn passed it on, he would not consider its meaning. He had given up trying to understand words —orders, directions, cautions. He moved and lived in a channel of sounds, but his mind took them in as involuntarily as his lungs breathed the air. It was his eyes that activated him. He watched his leaders and his comrades. He followed. He did what they did. He listened acutely and unendingly but never accepted the meaning of sound. Consciously, he heard only silence—that dead silence which makes one feel that he has gone deaf.

As he looked through the hedgerow at the sun, he began to hear the silence gather. Even the men behind him, the lieutenant, the sergeants, had become silent. He could feel the silence creep along the hedgerow, turning the heads of his comrades. The sun, having cleared the trees, seemed to stick in the silence. The silence grew heavy. He could feel it on his back pressing him against the earth. The grass in the field was still, as though the silence were barrier against the wind. The silence swelled, grew taut, then violently burst.

It was the artillery from his own lines. The barrage was steady and strong. From beyond the woods the fire was returned, its shells falling short in the field. The cows in the field had lifted their heads and now stood as still as stone. Two horses from the farmyard thundered across the level terrain. A fox bounding from the woods reached the clearing and raced round in a circle.

Private Meadows pulled his head away from the opening of the hedgerow and leaned back against the embankment of roots. His unit began to move down the hedgerow. He followed, on his hands and knees, dragging the butt of his rifle.

When they came to the end of the row, they bounded into the woods at the south. There in the woods they dispersed and moved to the east. It was there in the woods that he got lost. He had followed the others for a time and then, of a sudden, he was alone. The artillery had stopped. It was the silence that called him to consciousness. He walked on, listening. He could hear nothing but the crackle of twigs under his feet. There was no firing even in the distance. And but for the noise he himself made, the woods were quiet—no wind in the trees, no birds even. He sat down, leaned against the trunk of a tree, crossed his piece over his thighs, his finger on the trigger, and waited. He waited for a sound.

He had expected that other men would come from the direction he had come. But somewhere, skirting the trees, he must have got out of the line of advance, for no men came.

The woods were eerie. It seemed that all the men had walked off into another world, leaving him alone. He didn't like the silence. He got up and began to walk, taking a direction half left to the one that brought him to his silent place. He came to a cart path. But he would not enter it. He stayed in the woods, keeping the path in sight, following it; it was angling him again to the left. He walked slowly, cautiously, wondering whether he were approaching the enemy line. The woods were thick and dark. Each tree was watching him, listening to the sounds he made. Each step was a deepening into fear. It was not the sort of fear he knew under fire. There he was scared, but this was a worse fear—unrelenting and conscious.

He hardly moved at all, putting one foot carefully before him and looking about, listening with all his body to the silence, before he brought the other foot forward. Then he stopped still, like a man yelled into a brace. He had heard a voice. His heartbeat pounded the silence. Then, directionless, whispered, he heard distinctly: "Hey." It was an American word, he guessed. But German snipers used American words as traps. He started to walk on, and then a little louder this time: "Hey." The word spiraled through the silence like a worm in wood. He halted again. He was afraid to turn. He dared not lift his rifle. Whoever called had a bead on him. Tentatively he put a foot forward, took a step. "Hey." He was playing with him as a cat does a rat, teasing him before he put the bullet in his back or between his eyes, waiting for him to make some particular move—to run, or turn, or lift his rifle, or gaze up into the barrel tracing him.

His enemy was all around him, saw him at every angle. He stood motionless, as though immobility forestalled the shot. He felt the sweat burst on his forehead. He was weak. In his memory he reviewed the sound, trying to divine its direction; and the voice came again. While he was listening to the voice in his memory, it came again, confusing him: "Hey there." It came from all sides of him, the voice of the forest itself. "Put down your gun." The command was clear and slow—behind him. He lowered his rifle to the ground, stepped backward, waited. "Turn aroun'." He turned slowly, holding his breath. He saw no one.

He watched the trunks of trees, expecting a head—and a gun—to slip round into the open. "Where you goin', bud?" At the foot of a tree to his left oblique, partly concealed under a bush, sat a man on his haunches, leaning forward on his rifle. It was an American: the helmet, the green jacket. "Whatcha scared of, bud?" The man stretched a foot forward and rose clear of the bush.

Private Meadows stood still. Was it a joke? He rather expected others to appear from the forest—from out of the brush, from behind the trees; expected all his lost comrades to appear from the silence that had swallowed them. He wondered whether he had not been lost in meditation; whether, as he followed his comrades through the trees, he had not fallen into a fearful dream and was now emerging into reality as one of his friends shook his shoulder, urging him on. He had been hypnotized by his fear. He wanted to cry but was too much exhausted to cry. The man standing before him, touching his shoulder with a thick, hairy hand, was strange. He and the man were alone. And the silence was real. "Come out of it, bud." But the man was not concerned. A grin stretched over his fat face like a painted mouth stretching over a tight balloon. He was enjoying the joke he had played. "Whatcha doin' here, soldier?" The voice was as cold as authority.

"I got lost," Private Meadows said.

Then the voice was as hooligan as persecution: "That's misbehavior before the enemy. They'd hang you for that. That's desertion."

Private Meadows didn't know the ensign of the man before him. Nor did he attempt to surmise it. It would be whatever the manner suggested it to be. In the man's manner there was some kind of authority. So Private Meadows answered with the only defense he knew: "I was lost."

"Me too," the man said. "*I'm* lost."

The man pointed to the gun on the ground. Private Meadows picked it up. Then he looked at the man squarely. Vaguely in his mind were the questions: *Why did you make me put it down? Why did you scare me?* But he never uttered them. They hung wordless in his mind, expressed only as the straight, surprised, and momentary stare. Then they faded into his real being, that shadowy, remote musing, progressively growing dark since Cherbourg—and inaccessible. He looked off, into the direction he had been walking. "What are we gonna do?" he asked.

The man walked forward. His answer was a command: "Take it easy—till we know what's up."

Private Meadows put his arm through the sling, settled his rifle behind his shoulder, and followed. He was over his fright now, the weakness gone from his knees. He was safe again in the guidance of the Army.

He saw the broad round shoulders before him humping the air like an elephant's flanks and the heavy field boots scraping through the brush, flushing the silence. The noise of their progress was to Private Meadows an easeful shelter, like a low roof on a rainy night. Then there was a burst of a cannon—the slamming of a door in the giant structure of war, shattering the silence of the endless chambers that, for a moment, Private Meadows had forgot.

"A eighty-eight," the man said. They had both stopped at the cannon burst, had looked at each other and then in the direction of the sound. The burst came again, then again, as they stood motionless, listening. Then came the sound of rifle fire, pelleting the continuing bursts of the cannon. "Well, now we know where we are." The man spoke softly, his head, poked forward on the thick neck, malling up and down—a mechanical ram impelled by words. "Let's go," he said. He changed the direction nearly full right. They came to a dirt road. "You been on that road?" he asked. Private Meadows shook his head. "Must be mined. Or we'd be using it," the man said. "Sump'n comin'." Down the road, winding out from the trees, came a cart. They drew back, settled themselves behind a bush, and waited. The cart came slowly by, going in the direction from which they had come. A man walked beside the horse and from time to time put his hand at the bridle. In the seat of the cart was a woman holding a baby. In the back, among some baggage, sat a child, leaning her head against a mattress.

After the cart was out of sight, the two soldiers went again to the edge of the road. "Guess it ain't mined," the big one said. His eyes, nearly obscured under the net-covered helmet, were two little mice peering from under a crib. His grin was the lifting of a rake, and the mice scurried back into their holes. "Let's go," he said. He jumped the ditch and ran across the road.

Mechanically Private Meadows followed him. "Ain't we gonna try to get back?" he asked.

The man turned sharply and looked at him distrustfully. "You don't wanna go now, do you?"

"I don't know," Private Meadows said.

"We getting back, see. But we takin' the long way roun'." Private Meadows shrugged his shoulders. He was tired. The man had stuck his great round face close to his and was staring into his eyes. Private Meadows held his face against the stare but wearily closed his eyes. Sleep covered him like a breaker. His body swayed. Then he shook his head and opened his eyes. "Come on," the man said.

They walked through the woods, keeping within sight of the road. The distant rifle fire was continuous. The artillery had begun again, and from time to time a great cannon jolted all the other sounds to silence. Though they were walking oblique from the firing, Private Meadows wondered whether, on the tangent of their direction, they might not be approaching the enemy's lines. But this wonder was fleeting, like the recurrent sleep that blacked him out whenever he closed his eyes. Responsibility had gone the way of his fear; he was automaton again. He was following.

The man, who had been walking ahead, jumped to cover behind a tree, at the same time wagging a fat hand around his waist in signal to Private Meadows. Private Meadows was behind a tree almost as quickly as the man, and then, peering around, he saw the cause of alarm. A German soldier was coming toward them. He was unhelmeted, a cap pulled low over his forehead. Slung over his shoulder and hanging at his waist was a leather case. "Hey," the big man called in the whispering voice. The German was startled by the sight of the man even before he heard the voice; for at the utterance he had already stopped, gazing first at the face and then at the rifle pointing from the fat round hip. "Hey," the man repeated—needlessly, for the German was standing frozen in the first attitude of shock.

Without turning his gaze from the German, the man called out to Private Meadows: "Is it clear?"

"Looks clear," Private Meadows said, shuttling his gaze among the trees.

The man approached the German until he stood within a few feet of him. "Search him," he said.

Private Meadows, holding his rifle at the waist, came beside the German, with his left hand felt the pockets of the uniform and, walking behind him, lifted the leather case from his shoulder.

"What's in it?" the man asked, still gazing at the German, thrusting the muzzle of his gun forward. The German, who had stood listless, his hands dropping to his sides after Private Meadows lifted the case from his shoulder, stared at his victor, as though in the uncomprehended words there was a new terror. Then quickly, as though guessing the meaning, he lifted his hands shoulder high in surrender. "Higher, you sonofabitch." The man motioned with the muzzle of his gun. The German understood the motion and lifted his hands above his head. "What's in it?" This time the voice was different. The German understood that the words were not for him. He cupped his hands behind his head.

"It's money," Private Meadows said. He held a handful of the bills in front of his companion.

"Christ! Kraut money," the big man said.

"It's filled with it," Private Meadows said, sliding the money back into the case.

"Where'd you get that money, bud?" the man said. The German became rigid. The terror returned to his eyes, but with it there seemed to be another feeling—of impatience, perhaps of injustice.

"Where'd you steal that money, Kraut?" And at the question there came into the German's face a sense of outrage. The big man saw it. "You bastard," he said. "Can't you speak English?"

"*Nein,*" the German said quickly. And he shook his head, "Nein."

"Nein, nein!" The man mocked him. "You dumb bastard." He lifted the muzzle of his gun and twice thrust it forward in the direction from which the German had come. "Get goin'," he said. "Vamoose." The German was doubtful. He turned his body slowly but kept shuttling his gaze from the gun to the fat, dark face above it. "Get the hell goin'." The German took a step tentatively, looked once at the fair-faced soldier who was adjusting the leather case at his waist. But in his eyes there was neither help nor corroboration—only indecision and doubt as great as his own. He started walking slowly away, his hands still cupped over his head. Then, just as he took the first step that was quicker and surer than the rest, the shot cracked through the woods. He fell forward on his face.

The big man lowered his rifle. Private Meadows, his mouth wide open, watched him open the bolt and push it forward again. He looked down at the ejected cartridge case, awesomely, as though it were a rabbit out of a hat, surprising and not quite convincing.

"Let's get the hell outa here," the man said. He walked quickly past Private Meadows.

Private Meadows looked again where the German had fallen. He saw an arm lifted, like a swimmer's in arrested motion. He saw it fall forward. He turned and followed his leader.

They came to a clearing, a series of fields surrounded by hedgerows and forming a rolling terrain.

"Better not go out there," the man said. Yet, if they followed through the woods, along the edge of the clearing, they would approach too directly the enemy line. "We gone far enough anyways." He listened to the distant crack of the rifles. He sat down and pulled his rifle over his fat legs crossed like a sawbuck. "Let's see that money." Private Meadows handed him the case and sat down beside him. The man dumped the contents on the ground. There was a tablet of forms printed in German. He tossed it away. "Musta been a pay sergeant . . . Suppose he was payin' men out on the goddamned *firin'* line?" The money was taped in seven tight bundles. "That sonofabitch was makin' way with somethin', you can bet your hat on that." He studied the numerals on the bills. He divided the money into two stacks and handed one stack to Private Meadows. He held up the case. "Want it?" Private Meadows looked at the case and then into the lariat eyes hesitantly. He shook his head. The man tossed the case beside the forms.

They both sat looking at the money in their hands. "Suppose it's any good?"

"It's German," Private Meadows said.

"Yeah, I guess so. But francs are good. We gonna get paid in francs. If ever we get paid."

"Maybe when we get to Germany——" Private Meadows said.

"Not me. I ain't go'n *get* that far," the man said. "Not me. Je-e-esus! Not me." He spread out his thick legs before him. "Look at them goats!"

In the clearing there were three goats. They had come through a break in the hedgerow or had climbed up some unnoticeable ravine, for they had not been there when the men first looked out. They neither grazed nor moved. It seemed that they were listening to the sounds of the firing.

"I'll take the one on the left," the man said. "You take the one on the right. And I'll bet you my stack of tens against it." He chunked out a bundle of the little bills.

Private Meadows spread the bundles of money fan-fashion, selected a bundle, threw it out, then turned toward the man—his look bending under the helmet to ask: *Now what?*

"We'll have to fire together or they'll be to hell and gone. Yours on the right." The man caracoled his arm into the sling and was adjusting himself to fire from the sitting position. Then Private Meadows understood.

"I . . . I don't think——" But the man was in position. Private Meadows thrust his arm through his sling quickly.

"Are you ready?"

"Say, do you think——?"

"Are you ready?"

Private Meadows jerked himself to the kneeling position and slid the gun butt into his shoulder, his face tight against the stock. He squinted his eyes as he leveled the sight. "O.K."

The man muzzled against his gun, and each of his commands was whispered in the respiration of a breath: "Ready—aim—fire."

The rifles cracked. The right goat fell, its front legs bending before it. The left goat sprang into the air, like a horse rearing, then rushed forward and crashed face first into the ground. The middle goat lifted his head as though sniffing the air but did not move from where it stood.

"Look at that dumb bastard," the man said. He humped his shoulders over his rifle. "I bet I get him first shot." He turned his head toward Private Meadows, his chin sliding along the gun stock. "O.K.?" he asked impatiently.

"I——" But the man was straining in a flesh-taut position, ready to fire. "O.K.," Private Meadows said.

The man took aim. The goat started walking forward, his nose still in the air. The man shifted his gun, aimed again, fired. The goat bleated once, turned, and ran. The man shot again. The goat fell, gave three long trembling bleats, and was silent.

"Well, it's yours," the man said. He leaned back, picked up the money, and threw it to Private Meadows. "That bastard." He crawled back against the tree, put his gun on the ground beside him, and pulled a package from his knapsack. "Got a ration?" he asked.

"I got some choc'late," Private Meadows said. He stood up, holding the money out from him as if he might throw it back to the man or fling it into the woods. He looked down at the notes in his hand—thoughtfully, as though trying to recall how they came to be there. Then he slipped them into his jacket pocket. He sat down again and took out his chocolate. He took a bite of the hard cube, lay back on the ground, and immediately fell asleep.

"Hey. Hey, bud." The man was pushing his boot into Private Meadows's side. "Get up. The artillery's stopped."

Private Meadows sat up. The firing had almost stopped. "We musta taken the hill," he said.

"It's a town," the man said. "A village. We were after a village."

Private Meadows stood up. "You suppose we really took it?"

"Sounds like it," the man said. "We better get goin'. We better start findin' ourselves." He started walking down the edge of the clearing. The hulking form, moored to some narrow gaze, rode the slow steps heavily, in strenuous swells and sudden falls. Private Meadows followed. To their right the sun was halfway down the sky.

They came in view of a farmhouse. It stood in the clearing about fifty yards away. "Looks deserted," the man said. They stood looking over the field at the small squat house. "We'll see," the man said. He lifted his rifle and fired. Then they waited, but there was no sign of life from the house. "Can't tell if I even hit." He fired again. And as they stood waiting for whatever they expected might happen, an airplane loomed from the south. They ducked quickly into the woods and there from among the trees watched the plane. It was flying low and unsteadily. "Damned thing's fallin'," the man said. And as he spoke, they saw a figure drop from the plane—and then another. A parachute opened and then fell into the jolt of full bloom. The second opened, leapt up at the hinges of the air, jolted. Then a third. They had not seen the third drop from the plane but there it moved, in echelon, with the others.

"Brother!" the man said, lifting his rifle. "I'll take the one on the left again. Same bet."

Private Meadows stared as the man pivoted his gun on the floating figure and fired.

"Quick, you bastard," the man said, stepping closer to him, his mouth curling down from the utterance in anger. The impatient words were command.

Private Meadows shouldered his gun and, while still leveling the figure into his sight, fired. He saw a body twitch, the hands fall from the cords, the head lean back. As he lowered his gun across his chest, he drew his heels together and stood straight and stiff, gaping at what he had done.

"Same again on the middle one," the man said. He lifted his gun, but his target was already falling beyond the roof of the house. "God damn," he said, dropping his gun from his shoulder. "He's outa sight 'cause you waited so long. What were you waitin' for?"

"You don't shoot men when they're parachutin'."

"My ass! You don't shoot *prisoners*, do you?"

"You sure they were Germans?" His voice was almost supplication.

"How do I know?" He started walking into the woods. "Let's get the hell away from here."

Private Meadows stood holding his gun over his chest, his hand on the bolt. He looked over the field. The two white chutes, now lying on the ground, were barely visible. He drew his bolt, ejecting the cartridge case; thrust the bolt forward again; and, yet holding the gun across his chest, followed the man into the woods.

"Suppose they were *Americans!*" he called out.

The man stopped, turned back—the accusing, distrustful look again in his eyes. "American, French, Kraut, whatever they are, they're fly boys, playin' games in the air and sleepin' in a bed at night." His helmet was almost touching Private Meadows's own. "Look, bud, you shoot first and *suppose* afterward, or you'll get lead between your own eyes." He drew back a step. "Ain't you killed any before?"

Private Meadows remembered the terrified eyes staring into his own. He answered doubtfully, in the voice of conjecture: "But I knew who I was killin'."

The fat lips drew tight round a sibilant of contempt. Then, "Killin's killin'," he said. "How long you been in this push anyways?"

"Since Cherbourg."

The man looked him up and down. "It's a wonder you lasted this long."

Through woods, over the dirt road, and through woods again to the first fields. Down a hedgerow cautiously. Debris of the advance:

cartridge belts, helmets, clips yet filled with bullets, a knit cap, a dog lying dead, a deck of cards scattered, and letters. The wounded and dead removed, but the signs of death in the wreckage. And then the main road, from which the night before they had deployed. Now an ambulance passing, now a jeep. A squad of soldiers, bearded, and fatuous with grime, shoveling dirt from an embankment to cover the carcass of a cow. Salvage of tanks and trucks. Trees broken and charred. A column of medics, walking with stooped weariness, into a side road. Trucks, filled with infantrymen, coming up from the rear. Then the village: "This town off limits for all military personnel." Really no village at all, only rubble: a tall mahogany armoire standing erect and unscratched among bricks and nameless jointures of wood like an exaggerated product in an advertisement; the horseshoe arches of four windows, like a backstage flat, signifying a church; the grave-yard, a grotesquerie of holes, stone, and upturned coffins; and, sitting atop a fallen door, a yellow-and-white kitten washing an outstretched paw.

At the entrance of the village and even in the street beyond the off-limits sign there were soldiers. They stood in groups, but they were quiet, looking over the ruins of the village or down the wreckage-strewn road they had traversed, staring vacantly at the interpreter talking to a group of five Nazi officers or at the Military Police help-ing a sergeant line up a lengthening formation of prisoners. The scene was almost still, like a rehearsal of a play where everyone waits for the director to reach a decision.

The two soldiers stopped by an off-limits sign and surveyed the scene. "I gotta find my company," the big man said. He went up to a group of soldiers. Private Meadows watched him a moment and then followed after. He saw one of the soldiers answering the big man's question, pointing away from the village. And before Private Meadows reached the group the big man walked away. Private Mead-ows stopped, ready to lift his hand in farewell, but the man went lunging on without looking back—the heavy body, in its laboring gait, an enemy to the air it humped and to the ground it scuffed: the beast that walks alone, that—among all the animals of the forest and in the meeting of its kind—is yet alone, the stalker of secret places, the hunter. Private Meadows sensed the solitariness, but he thought it was the realization of his own loneliness that made him shudder.

He approached the group of soldiers and asked the whereabouts of his company. All the men looked at him blankly. And then one, interpreting the silence of the group, answered: "I don't know."

Private Meadows turned away. Beyond the formation of prisoners he saw some French civilians crossing the street. A fat woman, carry-ing a hamper, walked down the side of the formation, a little white dog following her, scurrying from one side to the other to sniff at the boots of the prisoners or at something in the rubble.

He was alone again. He was lost.

At home he had often had a dream of being late for school. The scenes of the dream were always different, but the dream was always the same. An unsuccessful effort to get to school: the determination, the hurry; running down the street, then caught in some void where time passed and he stood still; or still discovering himself at a strange corner, not knowing the direction, not knowing how he came to be there. The remembrance of the dream was fleeting but the familiar hopeless feeling of it remained. He felt that no one here would know his company, that his company would be in a distant place maneuvering through some different duty. He had left his company that very same morning after sunrise and only now was the sun beginning to set. But his calculation gave him no assurance. He felt that he had been separated from his comrades for a campaign of time. And this—this feeling—was his real knowledge.

He went from soldier to soldier, from group to group, asking the position of his company—his question automatic and hopeless, but persistent like a sick man's fancy. And when a soldier answered "Yes" and named the directions, his mind was filled with only the realization of the soldier's knowing so that he had to ask again.

His company was bivouacked less than a mile from the village. It was twilight when he walked among his platoon.

"Meadows! Man, I thought you'd found your number." It was Barr. He was sitting on the ground, leaning against the wood fence. He touched the ground beside him in invitation for Meadows to sit.

"What happened to you?" Harrod, too, was leaning against the fence. He was smoking a cigarette. His face was black with grease and dirt.

"Guess I musta got lost," Private Meadows said. He leaned his gun against the fence, dropping his helmet to the ground, and sat down.

Without looking around Barr stretched his hand to his left and said "They got Pederson." Private Meadows looked up at him. "And Walton was shot in the hip but he'll get all right, lucky dog." He put his feet out before him, crossed them at the ankles, said wearily: "We 'bout all would have got it if it wasn't for those bombers. Zoom. Bang. And not another eighty-eight booped after that."

"Those *what?*" Private Meadows asked.

"The bombers. The lucky dogs. Sleeping in England tonight."

"I got lost," Private Meadows said.

Harrod and Barr both looked at him.

"Well, you're home now, chum," Barr said. "Good ole Easy Company. Gonna have hot stuff tonight—outa mess kit. And a sleep,

I-hope-I-hope-I-hope, here against a soft, warm fence."

"Wish they'd hurry with chow," Harrod said. "If I close my eyes, I'll never make it. . . . How much longer they gonna keep us in the line anyhow?"

"Couple of more days, I guess," Barr said. His tone was now flat, as if he had no interest in what he said.

"I wonder if I'll live that long," Harrod said. There was nothing in his voice; it sounded like a routine speculation, as if he wondered whether he would be in town long enough to send his clothes to the laundry.

It was almost dark.

Private Meadows was bent forward, his arms lying against his thighs, his eyes pressed against his wrists. Barr noticed that each hand clutched a stack of notes and, as he started to ask what they were, he heard the sobbing. It simpered like a fuse and then burst. The shoulders shook convulsively. "What the hell, kid?" Barr sidled close to him and put his hand on his arm.

Harrod looked over at him, then flipped away the dead cigarette that he had been absently holding between his fingers. A whistle blew.

"Snap out of it, kid," Barr said, rising. "It's time for chow." He stepped back and picked up his mess kit. Then he and Harrod stood on each side of Private Meadows and waited.

THE SIEGE

SOL YURICK

After twenty-seven years and two hours of Departmental contact, it came down to just this moment . . . the three of them, Kalisher, the Social Worker from Friends of the Community, Miller the Relief Investigator, and Mrs. Diamond, the client, were immured in a stasis. She refused to show them the fourth room.

They had contended with her for two hours. Her head was kept turning from Kalisher to Miller; they pressed, wanting to know; they ranged from kindness to brutality. Now they sat resting in the cluttered kitchen. They could hear the constant gurgling of water in the decayed pipes. They inhaled the thick smell of chicken or fish. Miller kept cataloguing. For the third time he made a neatly printed list:

SOL YURICK, a New Yorker by birth, lives in Brooklyn where, in addition to writing fiction, he reviews books for various periodicals. He is the author of the novels *The Warriors, Fertig,* and *The Bag;* and a story collection, *Someone Just Like You.*

piled food cans; boxes of dried cereal on the washtub cover; two kinds of Kosher soap; grease-spattered pictures of her long-deserted husband and her runaway son hung over the stained sink; a pot of soup—enough for two—was being heated over a low flame. Mrs. D.'s wary little eyes watched him out of a mask of wrinkles. Miller held his pen poised above his case-book. He sat stiffly.

Mrs. D. sighed again; Miller knew what he had known before: they were never going to get into the room beyond the bedroom. How had it escaped notice so long? Neglect. Past Investigators had come in, questioned briefly . . . she met the bare essentials of Eligibility: her case was hopeless. She was alone: deserted: too old and sick to work now. They had made their inspections quickly, noted nothing except her statement that it was a closet, perhaps wanting to get away from the stench and from having to listen to a long, old lady's complaint. Or if they suspected, did they really want to fight this old woman? Leave well-enough alone. That was the trouble, Miller thought: everyone left well-enough alone.

Mr. Miller had gone to see Mr. K., her social worker at Friends of the Community: did he know about the room? After all, Mr. K. had worked with her for three years. Mr. K. knew nothing . . . he had been concerned with her psychic welfare, helping her, an old, disturbed woman, adjust. Miller had expected Mr. K. to be angry at the deception, but Mr. K. had broken into a wide smile and said that it explained so many things. "She gave me a weekly cup of tea, Mr. Miller, but that was all. I begin to see it, how much she hasn't ventilated. I thought we were relating well . . . My God, Mr. Miller, aren't people wonderful?"

"Wonderful?" Mr. Miller had asked. "But didn't you investigate?"

"It isn't the business of Friends of the Community to investigate in the same sense the Relief Department investigates, Mr. Miller," Mr. K. had said.

"All right, I'll close the case."

"But you can't do that. She'll starve. She has no resources . . ."

"She probably has a boarder."

"It isn't as simple as that. Have you . . ."

"She has a boarder and therefore, extra income."

"But Mr. Miller; please. It might be more than a boarder," Mr. K. had said. "Why don't we go over her case completely?"

Now Miller didn't care anymore. After two hours of questioning, the required veneer of polite, investigative procedure they had agreed on was about to peel away. He had spoiled six sheets of his case-book with elaborate doodles. Mr. K. was more patient, Miller saw, but that was because Mr. K. accepted. Miller thought Mr. K. was ridiculous; he simply didn't know. Sly Mrs. D., in spite of her years, poverty, swollen ankles, pipette legs, was faster on her feet than Mr. K. Her hands were crumpled into grasping roots by arthritis. Miller looked away from those gnarled, calcified bones. He wanted to go. She made him feel uncomfortable. He was afraid she might reach out, touch, and infect him. She sighed. Her lips wrinkled into fleshy rays and her righteous mouth pressed tightly against the three or four teeth she had left. Miller knew they were beaten unless one of them—and it would have to be him—was direct about it. Miller's leg shook up and down on the ball of his foot; he lost count of the shakes. He had no patience for the long, unprofitable silences necessary to proper social work atmospheres.

Kalisher pointed to a picture: "Your husband?"

"Don't touch," she told him.

"Mrs. Diamond, we're only trying to help you," Kalisher told her while his eyes tried to look past her.

She sniffed. She had learned. In the past she had been betrayed. "To the grave you'd help," she said. She was sharpened by those tricky years of contact with Investigators sent to deprive her; her cunning must beat them. Kalisher, dripping honey, talking "adjustment" and "rehabilitation," soft words, had come before. The Millers too; without pretense, hard, uncaring: their looks said "you're cheating." Did they know or care how it was to live like she lived? She fought them all. She held on. "How much longer am I going to be able to stand it?" she asked matter-of-factly. Torture and martyrdom were something she imbibed with the thin, white farina she ate every morning. To remind them they had done this to her, her hands picked and clutched at the frayed rope that pulled her brightly flowered housecoat together.

Kalisher saw a soft, gray wisp of frail hair float out against the loud colors of the detergent boxes. His heart went out to her. He knew what psychic martyrdom moved mothers. He was reminded of those art-photographs of old people's hands; wonderful, abiding roots. He heeded the plea of those hands. If poor Mrs. Diamond could only know his feeling . . . warm, empathetic community flooding through his veins. His face shone. He could barely see through his glasses. He knew and understood the pain and anguish of withstanding them, the provisors, the father-figures. She wanted freedom and resented needing them. It was why she fought. It was why she rejected. He smiled.

Miller was afraid her housecoat was going to fall open. He saw that K. was about to tell Mrs. D. again how long she would be able to stand it. But Miller was tired after the two-hour siege. He was tired of sitting in the kitchen in his coat; he was sweating in the steamy atmosphere. He was tired of having to divide his time between Mrs. D. and

Mr. K. A splotch of grease seemed to expand, slowly seeping up through the checker tablecloth; he moved his sleeve away. He was sitting on crumbs. Mrs. D.'s clock said three: he didn't trust it. He was hungry. He was tired of making lists and neatly narrowing spirals in his case-book. It was the grabbing motion of her hand that decided him.

"Mrs. D., we've been here for two hours. You realize that. We haven't got all day. You're not our only case. Are you going to show us that room?"

Kalisher shook his head imperceptibly, disapproving. Smiling apologetically, he hastened to undo the harm. He talked Yiddish to Mrs. Diamond to show her he was really on her side. The long discussion hadn't begun to faze him; does one unravel a complex or pierce through to a pre-psychotic personality in a mere two hours? Kalisher interpreted Departmental policy. His voice droned soothingly through the kitchen as he tried to re-establish contact with her. He asked her to help *them* . . . as people. He thrust blame on a vast impersonal machine that ground down the lives of clients, investigators, and social workers impartially: the three of them were pawns; really allies. *He* was here to protect her interests. He hinted they could make some kind of arrangement. "It isn't him," he told her; "it's the Department. Mr. Miller doesn't like prying. But he has to see every room in the apartment. It's his job. You understand."

"If he doesn't want to do it, then why do it? I never heard of such a thing," she sniffed.

Twenty-seven years of getting Relief and she never heard of such a thing, Miller thought. He saw a sly roach follow a cupboard crack. She could quote the manual, chapter and verse; she knew her rights better than the both of them. He couldn't see signs of a boarder: no man's shoe, no sock, no half-smoked cigarette or cigar was left; she was careful.

"The *Department*, Mrs. Diamond, the *Department* wants him to look around. It's the law. But . . ."

"So why are *you* here?" she asked.

She saw Kalisher's greedy look. She had been fooled by sneaks before. They had worked it out together. They were the enemy. They came around saying, "Listen to us; we're on your side; tell us everything; we can do something for you." Once she had a little job; a few extra pennies; how else could you live? She had listened to them. They had closed her case. She now knew better. Back to the Relief Office she had gone and made a scene, screaming for two hours till, to get rid of her, they gave her help. For them it was some kind of game; to see if they could deprive her. She knew. If she passed their tests, she was safe for another few months. But this time . . .

two of them . . . they knew . . . she was choking . . . circles in Miller's notebook . . . what did those mean? Tight strings quivered under the flesh of her neck. Why did they sit there, playing, laughing at her? Her hands felt weak. Did she have much left? She was worn down. Her hands held tightly to the rope around her waist.

Miller saw she didn't have anything on underneath the housecoat. He watched her spit into her sink and wash it down. His pen tore a little hole through his case-book. She was old, diseased, dirty, possibly senile. If they could put her in a home . . .

"The way to stop it," he had told Mr. K., "is to take her and put her in a home."

"She wouldn't go. After all, she's lived there for thirty years."

"It's the answer."

"You can't do that. She wants to be independent."

"Don't they all?" Miller asked sarcastically. "Who's stopping her, Kalisher?" and they sat down and read the two-inch thick case record . . . twenty-seven years of contact.

"This is a waste of time," Miller had said.

"You wouldn't think everything had been covered. But yet . . ." Mr. K. said.

"Look at that." Miller had held up some sheets. "That's three times she's cheated the Department. Why do we bother? We'll ask to see the room. If she refuses, we close the case."

"You can't do that. She's an old woman. She's disturbed. You can't treat a human being like that."

"She's got a boarder there. She's probably got more than enough money saved by now."

"It's not the material things; it's that she gets support from the Welfare situation."

"Support is right," Miller had said.

"I don't mean in that sense," Mr. K. had said, being obviously patient with Miller. "And I don't think she has a boarder there. I think . . . it's pretty clear, isn't it? Don't you see it? Look at all these social work contacts."

"I see that she's a miser."

"That's a sickness too."

"She's got mattresses stuffed with money . . ."

"Miller, everyone has a treasure house . . . but it's a hiding place, of psychic possibility."

"For God's sake, what . . ."

"That room is an extension of her . . . a part of her psyche." Mr. K. had smiled at him.

"She's laughing at you, Kalisher. She's a miser."

"She's a miser, but not in the sense you mean it."

"I won't argue the point," Miller said, "but Department rulings on added income are clear."

"Listen, she's a sweet old woman, a free soul. She needs to bring forth her problem. She wants love and understanding. She's been left by her husband, deserted. She's been brutalized. She's been kept on a substandard existence."

"The budget allows . . ."

"Mr. Miller, you can't break psychic needs into grams, calories, municipal food reports, or monetary allotments. Such treatment demeans . . ."

Miller thought that Mr. K. could never admit she might be intrinsically brutal, only that she was sick.

". . . and she blocks, represses, she can't relate, she's compulsive, antisocial, she conceals. It's a form of hoarding, yes, but why, Mr. Miller; why?"

"Mr. Kalisher, who cares?" Miller had said.

Life would be more organized for her in a home, Miller thought, and this couldn't have happened. Going by the psychological book was well and good, but could you rehabilitate those arthritic, withered hands? Could she be sent to work? Years of support had made her parasitic. Don't starve her, but let her at least follow the rules. She was doomed. If she didn't show him the fourth room very soon, he would cut her off. She knew her duty. His pen jabbed through the sheet again. He saw her cunning eyes dance mockingly in her decayed face. A little smile showed the tip of one black tooth. He tried to breathe calmly: the reek, like fish, of the bubbling pot, was too much for him. He began another careful curve on a fresh sheet of paper. Of course Mr. K. would fight a case-closing; not until he tried every trick of pleading with her; whining, ingratiating himself, all of it. Miller slid his chair back a little. He saw Mr. K.'s soft, loose-lipped look, his indefatigable smile. Mr. K. missed the point, Miller thought. Mr. K. was trying to get into the fourth room with Mrs. D.'s goodwill, as if he owed something to her. She owed *them*—if she got ten dollars a week rent, the usual rate—and it had been going on for—he would be liberal—only ten years, then . . . No, her goodwill didn't matter; it was an unnecessary handicap. If they simply went away, left her alone, didn't bother her, sent her checks twice a month, *then* they would have her goodwill. If they left her the hidden resources of that room, *then* they would have Mrs. D.'s endless goodwill. He started to loosen his tie and stopped.

"You just want to take away; out of spite; I never heard such a thing. To come in, to tear me apart," she was muttering, convincing herself that they didn't have the right. They were playing with her. They were going to take everything away from her.

But Kalisher was lovingly patient; it didn't bother him that his undershirt, and now his shirt, was drenched. He permitted her to act out her aggressions. He talked to her as he might to his own mother, striving to rest those neurotic terrors. "Of course he doesn't mean *you* Mrs. Diamond, but some clients are cheats. Some clients have television sets, washing machines, telephones, cars, all sorts of things they try to hide. You understand."

"So what has this to do with me? What could I have to hide? On relief for twenty-seven years; what could I buy? A twenty-seven inch television set on what they give me? I can hardly afford what to eat."

"No. No, Mrs. Diamond. I don't mean *you*. Heaven forbid," Kalisher told her; "but that means that Mr. Miller will be able to record in the case that he saw and checked everything. You see?"

"So? Let him put it down."

"But that wouldn't be honest; just to put it down, I mean . . . Now what could be in that room?"

"Nothing. Before, I told you; nothing."

"Then what do you have to be afraid of?"

Miller saw that Mr. K. would have gone through it all a fourth time; a fifth time; a sixth time if necessary, probing, using that soft, that silly, that sympathetic approach. Miller, moved violently; the table jarred. A cup clattered. He looked up. Her hands clutched at her chest. He saw that she had never stopped looking at him. "So we have to look into the fourth room and see what's there. Who knows," Miller forced his lips to grin; "maybe you have diamonds there, Mrs. D."

But Kalisher laughed quickly to show her the idea was beyond the realm of the conceivable. He saw Miller's twisted lips tensed over his teeth. He had worked so hard to win her, and every time he almost had her on his side, Miller compulsively spoiled it.

"Now supposing," Kalisher had said, "we work it out that you play the villain and I her hero. You attack; she comes to me, you see. My relation with her is a little different, warmer, than . . ."

"Why bother?" Miller had asked again. "I ask. She shows. Why cater to her whims?"

And Kalisher wondered why Miller was blinding himself. He was rationalizing his hostility to Mrs. D. into a fetish for carrying out rules. Didn't he see what was perfectly clear in the case record? Kalisher had almost been tempted to see how long Miller might go on without seeing it . . . what . . . who was in the fourth room. "Because she's a human being."

"She's almost a cheat. The boarder . . ."

"Does that make her less a human being?"

Mrs. Diamond didn't think Mr. Miller's quip was funny. "Drain my blood," she told them. "Make me suffer. Go ahead. What does a human being mean to you? Do you know pity? Take everything from an old woman. Are you human beings?"

Being human had nothing to do with it, Miller thought. Pity? He had none left. He had seen too many clients. He knew them. Animals, he thought, just animals. No amount of readings in social case-work would give them dignity. Leave "humanity" to the K.'s. She was alien; a constant drain on public funds; she could bring no returns. What would happen later? She would die alone, like an animal. Her body would lie there for days in the gloom. Someone would smell rotting flesh and call the police. They would exhume her. Her burial would cost the city. Unless, of course—and he could sense it—the secret boarder found her. Miller intersected circles with squares, enclosing equal areas.

Watching her, Kalisher felt something inside of him wrench to see her suffering. He felt sure that she was appealing to him to save her; to save her secret. For he had said to Miller, in the office, "The husband deserted; the son, Paul, sixteen at the time, ran away from home twenty-one years ago."

"What has that to do with it?"

"There it is." And Kalisher had felt the glee again.

"What? I don't understand."

"The missing son. He disappeared without much explanation. She never complained. She never called the Missing Persons Bureau," Kalisher told Mr. Miller. "Isn't it obvious?" And left it unsaid.

"Don't be silly; things like that don't happen. She has a paying boarder. Don't be romantic. My God, what wishful thinking." Miller had almost shouted.

"Wishful?" Mr. Kalisher had said and wondered why Mr. Miller fought it so hard. "I know of cases like that; they're not as rare as you think. It's what any mother really wants to do."

"It's all stupid nonsense."

"He'd be thirty-seven now."

Mr. Miller had refused to credit it.

But suppose, Mr. Kalisher had insisted, the missing son had been living in the little room for the last twenty-one years? He felt it. It was right. He knew it. He had the insight. "Think of that kid in the warm room, like a womb, really, secured to her forever. Think of her feeding two people on the allowance for one."

"Or think of her as getting extra funds," Mr. Miller had said. They had argued it out. In the end Mr. Kalisher had agreed reluctantly to go along with it. What she hid in the fourth room represented the core of her existence. He nodded knowingly at Mr. Miller. But Mr.

Miller was looking into his case-book, rejecting the situation. Her face's old nobility, the wrinkles that time, privation, yet dignity had engraved there, were spoiled only by the fearing eyes and the neurotic denying quiver of the lips; she couldn't bring it out; she wouldn't deliver herself of the guilt. "You have no idea, Mrs. Diamond," he told her, his voice trembling in a rich, inaccurate Yiddish, "how much it hurts me to have to do this. Believe me. I'm on your side. I understand." His smile should have told her he had seen deeply.

"I know you. I know you all. Watching me all the time for something. You want me to starve. Look at me. Look at the way I live." Her twisted arm, waving, took in for Kalisher, all the suffering, the poor, the sick, all the lonely, old, and deserted in the slums.

Miller noted: the tablecloth was fairly new; the kitchen chairs were not too old; the dish-towels were serviceable; and through the cupboard glass he saw that she had two sets of dishes, one light blue, the other white. She burned two candles in glasses; she was rich enough to afford that nonsense, Miller thought. She wasn't starving. It was a question of what the boarder earned and contributed. The signs were hidden, but he knew. "Lady, you've managed to live, somehow or other, for twenty-seven years and never once did you admit you had an extra room. If I hadn't happened to recheck the registration of this apartment, I wouldn't have known either. *You* wouldn't have told me, would you? What about that, Mrs. D.? What about that?"

"No one asked me . . ."

"I'm asking now . . ."

She stood, hunched over a little, pulled in on herself, waiting for them to make their move. "There's nothing in there; I told you."

"Why haven't you ever shown that fourth room to any investigator, Mrs. D.?" Miller asked, pointing his pen at her.

She sniffed. There was nothing Kalisher could do for her either. He sat there, smiled, and felt his hands strain and tremble.

"No one asked. There's nothing there. It's none of your business," she told them.

"I've been reasonable for two hours; it *is* our business. *Everything* about you is our business. We give you money. *We keep you alive.* It has to be our business." And Miller saw she understood now. She had him alone to contend with. Kalisher was out of it; *his* agency didn't dispense funds; Miller's did. He sat before her, fuming because of her stubbornness. He crossed out a figure; he could compute it when he returned to the office. He made it very clear to her, stressing it, lingering on it, "Sooner or later we find out, lady. If you have nothing to hide . . . You know, you wouldn't be the first person to cheat the Department. You won't be the first to be caught either."

Kalisher's wounded sigh sounded helplessly in the room; and then he realized . . . Miller was jealous of his relationship with Mrs. Diamond . . .

Miller couldn't wait any more. "We know you have someone in that room."

They were caught in the thick smoke of Miller's cigarette: it hung in soft eddies. A thin plume of steam spurted from the pot. Did he detect a gleam under the tears, Miller wondered. He began to boil. "Who's in that room?"

"I can't show it to you."

"You won't . . ."

"Let me starve. Tear me apart. Kill me. Take everything away. Throw me into the streets. My life . . ."

"Don't be foolish. Who's . . ."

"Don't talk like that."

"A boarder?"

"Twenty men in a closet. A dormitory," she said. Their voices were growing louder.

"Or . . ." Miller smiled at Mr. K. ". . . your son?"

She screamed, Kalisher leaned forward, looking at her face; his mouth was open and moist. "My son! My son should only be there." Her face was twisted. The black teeth showed. Her hand clawed toward Miller. He slid back; the chair-feet screeched on the floor. "Who ever heard of such a thing? Where do they dream up such things to torture me? You got nothing better to do with your time than to torture an old, sick woman? It gives you fun?"

Kalisher's mouth kept opening and closing. After that inhuman violation of case-work principles, that sadistic wrenching-out, what could he possibly have said? A little while longer, another ten minutes, and it would have come out easily; she would have shown them the room. Each sob that shook Mrs. Diamond's body shook him too.

"What have you got to hide then? What are you making such a fuss about?" Miller asked loudly.

"I'm not making a fuss. There's nothing there. Dirt. I'm ashamed. The door has things laying in front of it. You're trying to make me look a fool. You're not ashamed?"

Miller looked at her and shrugged his shoulders.

"An old woman . . . I'm so tired . . . Only rags. Why don't you just kill me?"

Miller nodded.

Kalisher was horrified at the both of them . . . hating. He was appalled to find that reason had failed in the face of primitive emotion. Mrs. Diamond and Miller's hostility was steaming and overpowering in the small kitchen. "Kill you? Kill you? What kind of nonsense are you talking, Mrs. Diamond? Who talks of killing you? Kill my own mother, you should say."

She knit together, for the last time, a fragility of bone and meagerness of flesh. She clutched at the flowers on her breast. She clenched her toothless mouth and shook her head. She wouldn't listen. She would starve first. She fought her own weariness. She fought them. She had outwitted them, outfought them, outscreamed them in the past. It would pass. She gathered herself to start screaming.

Miller looked at her and rose. He capped his pen. It was pointless, undignified, to have to fight her. Calming himself, Miller thought it wasn't a matter of anger; could the Department be angry? It was a matter of balances and perspectives. They had given too much to this old woman. That was it. "Mrs. D., there's nothing more I can do for you. We've been patient," Miller told her. "Let's go, Kalisher."

"Now wait a minute, Mr. Miller; surely . . ." Pale, anxious, Kalisher pleaded.

"No."

"But look . . ."

"Look, nothing. There's nothing to look at. Two hours . . . She won't cooperate. She won't show us the room. She's simply not Eligible. Let *your* agency give her funds."

"Don't be hostile."

"Don't give me that jargon."

"For God's sake, be a little objective."

"Not eligible; simply; he says," she said bitterly.

Kalisher tried . . . "You have no idea, Mrs. Diamond, how all this pains me. You have disappointed me. You have hurt me."

She looked at plump Kalisher's face and saw all that professional Social Worker's pain, that charitable sorrow. His breathless eagerness she also saw. She didn't believe his sorrow or his hurt; she believed his greed. There was nothing left. She would starve to death. They stood up, towering over her. She was between them and the kitchen door, standing in their way. "What are you going to do?" her dead voice asked them.

"Close your case, Mrs. D.," Miller told her.

"I'll die," she said.

Kalisher's lips were round and he shook his head. Miller looked over her head.

She had fought too long; she understood; it was final. "Don't go."

Kalisher tried to look out the window into the gray, drab yard, but had to look into the living room. He felt a soft tick in his mouth-muscles. Miller uncapped his pen. They waited.

"All right," she screamed. "All right. Look. Do what you want with me. Make a fool of me. Look." The last wailing shriek, the sum, that final sum of the years of humiliation and deprivation came pouring out of her. "Look!" The word hung, wailing in the stillness. Her hands hung by her side. She turned and went out. They followed her.

They went through the living room. The room was spotless, clean, and unused. On the floor, flowers faded into an old Persian rug. Stained wood shelves nailed to the walls held cheap little porcelains. The rose-colored wallpaint had long yellowed into sallow orange. A bronzed chandelier holding fake, pasteboard candles with flame-colored bulbs canted a little loose from the cracked, white ceiling. The flowered brocade covering the couch was unworn at the handrests. Old group-photographs hung on the walls in black frames; stiff, family figures, long lost, stood still, paled, as if the sunlight's fading fused figure and background into one. There was no dust anywhere. Miller tallied the hundred gimcrack vases, the glazed figurines, and saw that she had been able to afford these. Kalisher noted her compulsive neatness and knew she entombed some dead, traumatic moment here too.

The bedroom was dirtier; she lived here. A cheap chest of drawers stood against the wall. She showed them a closet holding a few frayed dresses. A gold-faced clock ticked. Another row of pictures, faded relatives, were lined up in front of the mirror on the chest. Kalisher picked up one of the pictures showing a young Mrs. Diamond standing next to a boy who towered over her. "Is this your son?" Kalisher asked. "My, how big . . ."

She snatched the picture out of his hand, wiped its glass on her housecoat and put it into a pocket. "Torturing me isn't enough?" she screamed at him.

A double bed was against the door which, she had always maintained, led to a closet. A blue, chenille spread covered the bed. A pair of cracked shoes stood underneath. Miller pushed the bed aside. It rolled, bumping on the uneven floor. The shoes were turned over and swept aside. He looked at the floor, trying to detect permanent scrape-marks which indicated Mrs. D. moved the bed back and forth frequently. There were no scrape-marks, but Miller couldn't be sure. They listened carefully, but only heard Mrs. D.'s sobbing. Kalisher could feel a little tightening of his throat. Miller thought of the computation . . .

She looked at them, standing, waiting for her. "So? Go ahead. Go," she told them. "Tear away my skin. Open my body." Kalisher watched Mrs. Diamond carefully to see how she was taking it. Politely, Miller stepped back, seemed to bow a little, and waved his hand, arcing his pen, almost courtly in his concern now, giving her a victor's magnanimous courtesy, restraining himself. Kalisher's rimless glasses were misted, hiding his eyes. But she folded her arms over her stomach. One hand was forever crooked into a clutch that plucked spastically at her elbow. She looked away, petulant, stubborn; her lower lip overlapped the unsupported upper lip.

"Go ahead, Mrs. D.," Miller told her.

She refused to answer. They could see a tear roll, break apart, and proliferate in the seams and wrinkles of her cheek, making one side of her face gleam. "Maybe we should come back tomorrow? I mean maybe you want time to think about it?" Kalisher stumbled. "I mean, she should have time," he almost shouted at Miller. "Well, I mean somehow it isn't right!" Miller pushed the door in. He looked. Kalisher's breath was at his ear.

"See," said she. "Treasures," she said.

The endless maw of her existence she filled by grasping. Against the day when she would be deprived, utterly, she collected. The little Departmental pittance was on loan to her by a capricious God. She knew; because here they were, two messengers of that vengeful God, ready to snatch back everything from her. She delivered up the pains of accumulation: threads; scraps; ribbons. The room had never been lived in; it was reduced to a passageway between two banks. Old, frayed chinos, now washed and shining; damasks, double and single, she had piled to one side of the room and the other. Faded pants and chintzes, all neatly scrubbed, and of rare value, were carefully folded. A bright swatch of flowered cloth, picked out in pinks, blues, and reds, was spread next to a meandering green nylon ribbon bubbling cool, like a tongue of liquid, shining brighter than the light that filtered in. Strips of material, carefully ripped from brocaded chairs and couches, she saved from rot. Cloths of gold, she had, and secret bolts of Eastern silks. No. There had never been any point to anything any of them had told her. They didn't understand. She knew better.

Miller recoiled and turned his back on the tumbled mess of cloths, cartons, the thick, choking welter of rags, the old smell of musk and entombment, the fast dust-motes that danced in the heat-wavering sunlight, streaky from crusted windows half-blocked. He wrinkled his nose at the fetid stench that fumed up from the shards of her diseased mind. He shuddered, smelling it, hearing the thick stillness; he tried to turn away from it quickly before he was contaminated. But he felt the perspiration break loose again and pour down his chest. He looked away from that sickening sight of her soul, looked away from the pulsing festoons of dust hanging in the gloom. No Welfare manual could account for it, no amount of planning and regimentation could straighten it out. The dust-rats stirred and came for him and his skin itched unbearably. He felt, for one second, as though something had been opened inside of him; warped fingers warped his mind; her sickness, for one terrible second, was his sickness. He tried to make a notation in his notebook, but closed it.

Looking past him eagerly, Kalisher's face clouded over as he craned to see, stretching till he almost fell into the room. He tried to see if there could have been a burrow under the piles. He saw dirt; he had labored in vain. "Is that what you've been fighting us for for two hours? Really, Mrs. D." She had merely acquired. She had saved. Where he had expected warmth, he felt the chill from all the little items that, no doubt, she translated into funds. All the hours he had spent with her were meaningless. She had made him look stupid in Miller's eyes. She had fought for the leavings of strangers. He added two more hours to the debris. He turned and glared at the cold tear that silvered Mrs. D.'s avaricious cheek; she was laughing at him. He scolded, "You should clean up this mess. What if a fire breaks out?" Kalisher saw that her eyes were hard, bright, glittering dryly.

Past them she scrambled and closed the door. "You satisfied?" she asked them. "You satisfied you made a fool out of an old woman?"

"Just our duty, Mrs. Diamond," Miller tried to answer coolly. He made a notation in his case-book; a drop of sweat blotted the entry. Her distorted and demented face leered at him.

"Some duty, to torture a dying woman."

"We weren't torturing you, Mrs. Diamond," Miller sighed, "don't be dramatic."

"That stuff is a fire hazard. Get rid of it, Mrs. D.," Kalisher told her again.

She made a gnarled club out of her hands and waved them at Kalisher and Miller, laying blame on their heads. Her housecoat flapped open. "So who cares? I'm alone. There's nothing for me. There never was. What do you care? Let me burn." Her hard shrill voice rang out and she began to weep tears of joy and deliverance.

Kalisher and Miller looked at each other, embarrassed. "Mrs. D. . ." Kalisher began.

"Oh, come on," Miller said, plucking Kalisher by the sleeve and leading him out.

On the stairs, Kalisher told Miller, "She's probably got money hidden there."

"You want to look for it?" Miller asked, walking down. "You still want to pick through that sickness? Go ahead," he said. He was half a flight ahead of Kalisher.

THE DEMONSTRATORS

EUDORA WELTY

Near eleven o'clock that Saturday night the doctor stopped again by his office. He had recently got into playing a weekly bridge game at the club, but tonight it had been interrupted for the third time, and he'd just come from attending to Miss Marcia Pope. Now bedridden, scorning all medication and in particular tranquillizers, she had a seizure every morning before breakfast and often on Saturday night for some reason, but had retained her memory; she could amuse herself by giving out great wads of Shakespeare and *Arma virumque cano*," or the like. The more forcefully Miss Marcia Pope declaimed, the more innocent grew her old face—the lines went right out.

EUDORA WELTY has won three First Prizes in the annual O. Henry Awards for short fiction. She is the author of *A Curtain of Green, Delta Wedding, The Ponder Heart, Losing Battles,* and *The Optimist's Daughter.* She lives in Jackson, Mississippi, and she has lectured and worked at various colleges and universities throughout the United States.

"She'll sleep naturally now, I think," he'd told the companion, still in her rocker.

Mrs. Warrum did well, perhaps hadn't hit yet on an excuse to quit that suited her. She failed to be alarmed by Miss Marcia Pope, either in convulsions or in recitation. From where she lived, she'd never gone to school to this lady, who had taught three generations of Holden, Mississippi, its Latin, civics, and English, and who had carried, for forty years, a leather satchel bigger than the doctor's bag.

As he'd snapped his bag shut tonight, Miss Marcia had opened her eyes and spoken distinctly: "Richard Strickland? I have it on my report that Irene Roberts is not where she belongs. Now which of you wants the whipping?"

"It's all right, Miss Marcia. She's still my wife," he'd said, but could not be sure the answer got by her.

In the office, he picked up the city newspaper he subscribed to— seeing as he did so the picture on the front of a young man burning his draft card before a camera—and locked up, ready to face home. As he came down the stairway onto the street, his sleeve was plucked.

It was a Negro child. "We got to hurry," she said.

His bag was still in the car. She climbed into the back and stood there behind his ear as he drove down the hill. He met the marshal's car as both bounced over the railroad track—no passenger rode with the marshal that he could see—and the doctor asked the child, "Who got hurt? Whose house?" But she could only tell him how to get there, an alley at a time, till they got around the cottonseed mill.

Down here, the street lights were out tonight. The last electric light of any kind appeared to be the one burning in the vast shrouded cavern of the gin. His car lights threw into relief the dead goldenrod that stood along the road and made it look heavier than the bridge across the creek.

As soon as the child leaned on his shoulder and he had stopped the car, he heard men's voices; but at first his eyes could make out little but an assembly of white forms spaced in the air near a low roof— chickens roosting in a tree. Then he saw the reds of cigarettes. A dooryard was as packed with a standing crowd as if it were funeral time. They were all men. Still more people seemed to be moving from the nearby churchyard and joining onto the crowd in front of the house.

The men parted before them as he went following the child up broken steps and across a porch. A kerosene lamp was being held for him in the doorway. He stepped into a roomful of women. The child kept going, went to the foot of an iron bed and stopped. The lamp came up closer behind him and he followed a path of newspapers laid down on the floor from the doorway to the bed.

A dark quilt was pulled up to the throat of a girl alive on the bed. A pillow raised her at the shoulders. The dome of her forehead looked thick as a battering ram, because of the rolling of her eyes.

Dr. Strickland turned back the quilt. The young, very black-skinned woman lay in a white dress with her shoes on. A maid? Then he saw that of course the white was not the starched material of a uniform but shiny, clinging stuff, and there was a banner of some kind crossing it in a crumpled red line from the shoulder. He unfastened the knot at the waist and got the banner out of the way. The skintight satin had been undone at the neck already; as he parted it farther, the girl kicked at the foot of the bed. He exposed the breast and then, before her hand had pounced on his, the wound below the breast. There was a small puncture with little evidence of external bleeding. He had seen splashes of blood on the dress, now almost dry.

"Go boil me some water. Too much excitement to send for the doctor a little earlier?"

The girl clawed at his hand with her sticky nails.

"Have you touched her?" he asked.

"See there? And she don't want you trying it, either," said a voice in the room.

A necklace like sharp and pearly teeth was fastened around her throat. It was when he took that off that the little girl who had been sent for him cried out. "I bid that!" she said, but without coming nearer. He found no other wounds.

"Does it hurt you to breathe?" He spoke almost absently as he addressed the girl.

The nipples of her breasts cast shadows that looked like figs; she would not take a deep breath when he used the stethoscope. Sweat in the airless room, in the bed, rose and seemed to weaken and unstick the newspapered walls like steam from a kettle already boiling; it glazed his own white hand, his tapping fingers. It was the stench of sensation. The women's faces coming nearer were streaked in the hot lamplight. Somewhere close to the side of his head something glittered; hung over the knob of the bedpost, where a boy would have tossed his cap, was a tambourine. He let the stethoscope fall, and heard women's sighs travel around the room, domestic sounds like a broom being flirted about, women getting ready for company.

"Stand back," he said. "You got a fire on in here?" Warm as it was, crowded as it was in here, he looked behind him and saw the gas heater burning, half the radiants burning blue. The girl, with lips turned down, lay pulling away while he took her pulse.

The child who had been sent for him and then had been sent to heat the water brought the kettle in from the kitchen too soon and had to be sent back to make it boil. When it was ready and in the pan, the lamp was held closer; it was beside his elbow as if to singe his arm.

"Stand back," he said. Again and again the girl's hand had to be forced away from her breast. The wound quickened spasmodically as if it responded to light.

"Icepick?"

"You right this time," said voices in the room.

"Who did this to her?"

The room went quiet; he only heard the men in the yard laughing together. "How long ago?" He looked at the path of newspapers spread on the floor. "Where? Where did it happen? How did she get here?"

He had an odd feeling that somewhere in the room somebody was sending out beckoning smiles in his direction. He lifted, half turned his head. The elevated coal that glowed at regular intervals was the pipe of an old woman in a boiled white apron standing near the door.

He persisted. "Has she coughed up anything yet?"

"Don't you know her?" they cried, as if he never was going to hit on the right question.

He let go the girl's arm, and her hand started its way back again to her wound. Sending one glowing look at him, she covered it again. As if she had spoken, he recognized her.

"Why, it's Ruby," he said.

Ruby Gaddy *was* the maid. Five days a week she cleaned up on the second floor of the bank building where he kept his office and consulting rooms.

He said to her, "Ruby, this is Dr. Strickland. What have you been up to?"

"*Nothin'!*" everybody cried for her.

The girl's eyes stopped rolling and rested themselves on the expressionless face of the little girl, who again stood at the foot of the bed watching from this restful distance. Look equalled look: sisters.

"Am I supposed to just know?" The doctor looked all around him. An infant was sitting up on the splintery floor near his feet, he now saw, on a clean newspaper, a spoon stuck pipelike in its mouth. From out in the yard at that moment came a regular guffaw, not much different from the one that followed the telling of a dirty story or a race story by one of the clowns in the Elks' Club. He frowned at the baby; and the baby, a boy, looked back over his upside down spoon and gave it a long audible suck.

"She married? Where's her husband? That where the trouble was?"

Now, while the women in the room, too, broke out in sounds of amusement, the doctor stumbled where he stood. "What the devil's running in here? Rats?"

"You wrong there."

Guinea pigs were running underfoot, not only in this room but on the other side of the wall, in the kitchen where the water had finally got boiled. Somebody's head turned toward the leaf end of a stalk of celery wilting on top of the Bible on the table.

"Catch those things!" he exclaimed.

The baby laughed; the rest copied the baby.

"They lightning. Get away from you so fast!" said a voice.

"Them guinea pigs ain't been caught since they was born. Let you try."

"Know why? 'Cause they's Dove's. Dove left 'em here when he move out, just to be in the way."

The doctor felt the weight recede from Ruby's fingers, and saw it flatten her arm where it lay on the bed. Her eyes had closed. A little boy with a sanctimonious face had taken the bit of celery and knelt down on the floor; there was scrambling about and increasing laughter until Dr. Strickland made himself heard in the room.

"All right. I heard you. Is Dove who did it? Go on. Say."

He heard somebody spit on the stove. Then:

"It's Dove."

"Dove."

"Dove."

"Dove."

"You got it right that time."

While the name went around, passed from one mouth to the other, the doctor drew a deep breath. But the sigh that filled the room was the girl's own, luxuriously uncontained.

"Dove Collins? I believe you. I've had to sew him up enough times on Sunday morning, you all know that," said the doctor. "I know Ruby, I know Dove, and if the lights would come back on I can tell you the names of the rest of you and you know it." While he was speaking, his eyes fell on Oree, a figure of the Holden square for twenty years, whom he had inherited—sitting here in the room in her express wagon, the flowered skirt spread down from her lap and tucked in over the stumps of her knees.

While he was preparing the hypodermic, he was aware that more watchers, a row of them dressed in white with red banners like Ruby's, were coming in to fill up the corners. The lamp was lifted—higher than the dipping shadows of their heads, a valentine tacked on the wall radiated color—and then, as he leaned over the bed, the lamp was brought down closer and closer to the girl, like something that would devour her.

"Now I can't see what I'm doing," the doctor said sharply, and as the light jumped and swung behind him he thought he recognized the anger as a mother's.

"Look to me like the fight's starting to go out of Ruby mighty early," said a voice.

Still her eyes stayed closed. He gave the shot.

"Where'd he get to—Dove? Is the marshal out looking for him?" he asked.

The sister moved along the bed and put the baby down on it close to Ruby's face.

"Remove him," said the doctor.

"She don't even study him," said the sister. "Poke her," she told the baby.

"Take him out of here," ordered Dr. Strickland.

The baby opened one of his mother's eyes with his fingers. When she shut it on him he cried, as if he knew it to be deliberate of her.

"Get that baby out of here and all the kids, I tell you," Dr. Strickland said into the room. "This ain't going to be pretty."

"Carry him next door, Twosie," said a voice.

"I ain't. You all promised me if I leave long enough to get the doctor I could stand right here until." The child's voice was loud.

"O.K. Then you got to hold Roger."

The baby made a final reach for his mother's face, putting out a hand with its untrimmed nails, gray as the claw of a squirrel. The woman who had held the lamp set that down and grabbed the baby out of the bed herself. His legs began churning even before she struck him a blow on the side of the head.

"You trying to raise him an idiot?" the doctor flung out.

"*I* ain't going to raise him," the mother said toward the girl on the bed.

The deliberation had gone out of her face. She was drifting into unconsciousness. Setting her hand to one side, the doctor inspected the puncture once more. It was clean as the eye of the needle. While he stood there watching her, he lifted her hand and washed it—the wrist, horny palm, blood-caked fingers one by one.

But as he again found her pulse, he saw her eyes opening. As long as he counted he was aware of those eyes as if they loomed larger than the watch face. They were filled with the unresponding gaze of ownership. She knew what she had. Memory did not make the further effort to close the lids when he replaced her hand, or when he took her shoes off and set them on the floor, or when he stepped away from the bed and again the full lamplight struck her face.

The twelve-year-old stared on, over the buttress of the baby she held to her chest.

"Can you ever hush that baby?"

A satisfied voice said, "He going to keep-a-noise till he learn better."

"Well, I'd like a little peace and consideration to be shown!" the doctor said. "Try to remember there's somebody in here with you that's going to be pumping mighty hard to breathe." He raised a finger and pointed it at the old woman in the boiled apron whose pipe had continued to glow with regularity by the door. "You stay. You sit here and watch Ruby," he called. "The rest of you clear out of here."

He closed his bag and straightened up. The woman stuck the lamp hot into his own face.

"Remember Lucille? I'm Lucille. I was washing for your mother when you was born. Let me see you do something," she said with fury. "You ain't even tied her up! You sure ain't your daddy!"

"Why, she's bleeding inside," he retorted. "What do you think *she's* doing?"

They hushed. For a minute all he heard was the guinea pigs racing. He looked back at the girl; her eyes were fixed with possession. "I gave her a shot. She'll just go to sleep. If she doesn't, call me and I'll come back and give her another one. One of you kindly bring me a drink of water," the doctor continued in the same tone.

With a crash, hushed off like cymbals struck by mistake, something was moved on the kitchen side of the wall. The little boy who had held the celery to catch the guinea pigs came in carrying a teacup. He passed through the room and out onto the porch, where he could be heard splashing fresh water from a pump. He came back inside and at arm's length held the cup out to the doctor.

Dr. Strickland drank with a thirst they all could and did follow. The cup, though it held the whole smell of this house in it, was of thin china, was an old one.

Then he stepped across the gaze of the girl on the bed as he would have had to step over a crack yawning in the floor.

"Fixing to leave?" asked the old woman in the boiled white apron, who still stood up by the door, the pipe gone from her lips. He then remembered her. In the days when he travelled East to medical school, she used to be the sole factotum at the Holden depot when the passenger train came through sometime between two and three in the morning. It was always late. Circling the pewlike benches of the waiting rooms, she carried around coffee which she poured boiling hot into paper cups out of a white-enamelled pot that looked as long as her arm. She wore then, in addition to the apron, a white and flaring head covering—something between a chef's cap and a sunbonnet. As the train at last steamed in, she called the stations. She didn't use a loudspeaker but just the power of her lungs. In all the natural volume of her baritone voice she thundered them out to the scattered and few who had waited under lights too poor to read by—first in the colored waiting room, then in the white waiting room, to echo both times from the vault of the roof: ". . . Meridian. Birmingham. Chattanooga. Bristol. Lynchburg. Washington. Baltimore. Philadelphia. And New York." Seizing all the bags, two by two, in her own hands, walking slowly in front of the passengers, she saw to it that they left.

He said to her, "I'm going, but you're not. You're keeping a watch on Ruby. Don't let her slide down in the bed. Call me if you need me." As a boy, had he never even wondered what her name was—this tyrant? He didn't know it now. He put the cup into her reaching hand. "Aren't you ready to leave?" he asked Oree, the legless woman. She still lived by the tracks where the train had cut off her legs.

"I ain't in no hurry," she replied and as he passed her she called her usual "Take it easy, Doc."

When he stepped outside onto the porch, he saw that there was moonlight everywhere. Uninterrupted by any lights from Holden, it filled the whole country lying out there in the haze of the long rainless fall. He himself stood on the edge of Holden. Just one house and one church farther, the Delta began, and the cotton fields ran into the scattered paleness of a dimmed-out Milky Way.

Nobody called him back, yet he turned his head and got a sideways glimpse all at once of a row of dresses hung up across the front of the house, starched until they could have stood alone (as his mother complained), and in an instant had recognized his mother's gardening dress, his sister Annie's golf dress, his wife's favorite duster that she liked to wear to the breakfast table, and more dresses, less substantial. Elevated across the front of the porch, they were hung again between him and the road. With sleeves spread wide, trying to scratch his forehead with the tails of their skirts, they were flying around this house in the moonlight.

The moment of vertigo passed, as a small black man came up the steps and across the porch wearing heeltaps on his shoes.

"Sister Gaddy entered yet into the gates of joy?"

"No, Preacher, you're in time," said the doctor.

As soon as he left the house, he heard it become as noisy as the yard had been, and the men in the yard went quiet to let him through. From the road, he saw the moon itself. It was above the tree with the chickens in it; it might have been one of the chickens flown loose. He scraped children off the hood of his car, pulled another from position at the wheel, and climbed inside. He turned the car around in the churchyard. There was a flickering light inside the church. Flatroofed as a warehouse, it had its shades pulled down like a bedroom.

This was the church where the sounds of music and dancing came from habitually on many another night besides Sunday, clearly to be heard on top of the hill.

He drove back along the road, across the creek, its banks glittering now with the narrow bottles, the size of harmonicas, in which paregoric was persistently sold under the name of Mother's Helper. The telephone wires along the road were hung with shreds of cotton, the sides of the road were strewn with them too, as if the doctor were out on a paper chase.

He passed the throbbing mill, working on its own generator. No lights ever shone through the windowless and now moonlit sheet iron, but the smell came out freely and spread over the town at large—a cooking smell, like a dish ordered by a man with an endless appetite. Pipes hung with streamers of lint fed into the moonlit gin, and wagons and trucks heaped up round as the gypsy caravans or circus wagons of his father's, or even his grandfather's, stories, stood this way and that, waiting in the yard outside.

Far down the railroad track, beyond the unlighted town, rose the pillowshaped glow of a grass fire. It was gaseous, unveined, unblotted by smoke, a cloud with the November flush of the sedge grass by day, sparkless and nerveless, not to be confused with a burning church, but like anesthetic made visible.

Then a long beam of electric light came solid as a board from behind him to move forward along the long loading platform, to some bales of cotton standing on it, some of them tumbled one against the others as if pushed by the light; then it ran up the wall of the dark station so you could read the name, "Holden." The hooter sounded. This was a grade crossing with a bad record, and it seemed to the doctor that he had never started over it in his life that something was not bearing down. He stopped the car, and as the train in its heat began to pass in front of him he saw it to be a doubleheader, a loaded freight this time. It was going right on through Holden.

He cut off his motor. One of the sleepers rocked and complained with every set of wheels that rolled over it. Presently the regular, slow creaking reminded the doctor of an old-fashioned porch swing holding lovers in the dark.

He had been carried a cup tonight that might have been his own mother's china or his wife's mother's—the rim not a perfect round, a thin, porcelain cup his lips and his fingers had recognized. In that house of murder, comfort had been brought to him at his request. After drinking from it he had all but reeled into a flock of dresses stretched wide-sleeved across the porch of that house like a child's drawing of angels.

Faintly rocked by the passing train, he sat bent at the wheel of the car, and the feeling of well-being persisted. It increased, until he had come to the point of tears.

The doctor was the son of a doctor, practicing in his father's office; all the older patients, like Miss Marcia Pope—and like Lucille and Oree—spoke of his father, and some confused the young doctor with the old; but not they. The watch he carried was the gold one that had belonged to his father. Richard had grown up in Holden, married "the prettiest girl in the Delta." Except for his years at the university and then at medical school and during his internship, he had lived here at home and had carried on the practice—the only practice in town. Now his father and his mother both were dead, his sister had married and moved away, a year ago his child had died. Then, back in the summer, he and his wife has separated, by her wish.

Sylvia had been their only child. Until her death from pneumonia last Christmas, at the age of thirteen, she had never sat up or spoken. He had loved her and mourned her all her life; she had been injured at birth. But Irene had done more; she had dedicated her life to Sylvia, sparing herself nothing, tending her, lifting her, feeding her, everything. What do you do after giving all your devotion to something that cannot be helped, and that has been taken away? You give all your devotion to something else that cannot be helped. But you shun all the terrible reminders, and turn not to a human being but to an idea.

Last June, there had come along a student, one of the civil-rights workers, calling at his office with a letter of introduction. For the sake of an old friend, the doctor had taken him home to dinner. (He had been reminded of him once tonight, already, by a photograph in the city paper.) He remembered that the young man had already finished talking about his work. They had just laughed around the table after Irene had quoted the classic question the governor-before-this-one had asked, after a prison break: "If you can't trust a trusty, who can you trust?" Then the doctor had remarked, "Speaking of who can you trust, what's this I read in your own paper, Philip? It said some of your outfit over in the next county were forced at gunpoint to go into the fields at hundred-degree temperature and pick cotton. Well, that didn't happen—there isn't any cotton in June."

"I asked myself the same question you do. But I told myself, 'Well, they won't know the difference where the paper is read,'" said the young man.

"It's lying, though."

"We are dramatizing your hostility," the young bearded man had corrected him. "It's a way of reaching people. Don't forget—what they *might* have done to us is even worse."

"Still—you're not justified in putting a false front on things, in my opinion," Dr. Strickland had said. "Even for a good cause."

"*You* won't tell Herman Fairbrothers what's the matter with him," said his wife, and she jumped up from the table.

Later, as a result of this entertainment, he supposed, broken glass had been spread the length and breadth of his driveway. He hadn't seen in time what it wouldn't have occurred to him to look for, and Irene, standing in the door, had suddenly broken into laughter. . . .

He had eventually agreed that she have her wish and withdraw herself for as long as she liked. She was back now where she came from, where, he'd heard, they were all giving parties for her. He had offered to be the one to leave. "Leave Holden without its Dr. Strickland? You wouldn't to save your soul, would you?" she had replied. But as yet it was not divorce.

He thought he had been patient, but patience had made him tired. He was so increasingly tired, so sick and even bored with the bitterness, intractability that divided everybody and everything.

And suddenly, tonight, things had seemed just the way they used to seem. He had felt as though someone had stopped him on the street and offered to carry his load for a while—had insisted on it—some old, trusted, half-forgotten family friend that he has lost sight of since youth. Was it the sensation, now returning, that there was still allowed to everybody on earth a *self*—savage, death-defying, private? The pounding of his heart was like the assault of hope, throwing itself against him without a stop, merciless.

It seemed a long time that he had sat there, but the cars were still going by. Here came the caboose. He had counted them without knowing it—seventy-two cars. The grass fire at the edge of town came back in sight.

The doctor's feeling gradually ebbed away, like nausea put down. He started up the car and drove across the track and on up the hill.

Candles, some of them in dining-room candelabra, burned clear across the upstairs windows in the Fairbrothers' house. His own house, next door, was of course dark, and while he was wondering where Irene kept candles for emergencies he had driven on past his driveway for the second time that night. But the last place he wanted to go now was back to the club. He'd only tried it anyway to please his sister Annie. Now that he'd got by Miss Marcia Pope's dark window, he smelled her sweet-olive tree, solid as the bank building.

Here stood the bank, with its doorway onto the stairs to Drs. Strickland & Strickland, their names in black and gilt on three windows. He passed it. The haze and the moonlight were one over the square, over the row of storefronts opposite with the line of poles thin as matchsticks rising to prop the one long strip of tin over the sidewalk, the drygoods store with its ornamental top that looked like opened paper fans held up by acrobats. He slowly started around the square. Behind its iron railings, the courthouse-and-jail stood barely emerging from its black cave of trees and only the slicked iron steps of the stile caught the moon. He drove on, past the shut-down movie house with all the light bulbs unscrewed from the sign that spelled out in empty sockets "BROADWAY." In front of the new post office the flagpole looked feathery, like the track of a jet that is already gone from the sky. From in front of the fire station, the fire chief's old Buick had gone home.

What was there, who was there, to keep him from going home? The doctor drove on slowly around. From the center of the deserted pavement, where cars and wagons stood parked helter-skelter by day, rose the water tank, pale as a balloon that might be only tethered here. A clanking came out of it, for the water supply too had been a source of trouble this summer—a hollow, irregular knocking now and then from inside, but the doctor no longer heard it. In turning his car, he saw a man lying prone and colorless in the arena of moonlight.

The lights of the car fastened on him and his clothes turned golden yellow. The man looked as if he had been sleeping all day in a bed of flowers and rolled in their pollen and were sleeping there still, with his face buried. He was covered his length in cottonseed meal.

Dr. Strickland stopped the car short and got out. His footsteps made the only sound in town. The man raised up on his hands and looked at him like a seal. Blood laced his head like a net through which he had broken. His wide tongue hung down out of his mouth. But the doctor knew the face.

"So you're alive, Dove, you're still alive?"

Slowly, hardly moving his tongue, Dove said: "Hide me." Then he hemorrhaged through the mouth.

Through the other half of the night, the doctor's calls came to him over the telephone—all chronic cases. Eva Duckett Fairbrothers telephoned at daylight.

"Feels low in his mind? Of course he feels low in his mind," he had finally shouted at her. "If I had what Herman has, I'd go down in the back yard and shoot myself!"

The *Sentinel*, owned and edited by Horatio Duckett, came out on Tuesdays. The next week's back-page headline read, "TWO DEAD, ONE ICEPICK. FREAK EPISODE AT NEGRO CHURCH." The subhead read, "No Racial Content Espied."

The doctor sat at the table in his dining room, finishing breakfast as he looked it over.

* * *

An employee of the Fairbrothers Cotton Seed Oil Mill and a Holden maid, both Negroes, were stabbed with a sharp instrument judged to be an icepick in a crowded churchyard here Saturday night. Both later expired. The incident was not believed by Mayor Herman Fairbrothers to carry racial significance.

"It warrants no stir," the Mayor declared.

The mishap boosted Holden's weekend death toll to 3. Billy Lee Warrum Jr. died Sunday before reaching a hospital in Jackson where he was rushed after being thrown from his new motorcycle while on his way there. He was the oldest son of Mrs. Billy Lee Warrum, Rt. 1. Reputedly en route to see his fiance he was pronounced dead on arrival. Multiple injuries was listed as the cause, the motorcycle having speeded into an interstate truck loaded to capacity with holiday turkeys. (See eye-witness account, page 1.)

As Holden marshal Curtis "Cowboy" Stubblefield reconstructed the earlier mishap, Ruby Gaddy, 21, was stabbed in full view of the departing congregation of the Holy Gospel Tabernacle as she attempted to leave the church when services were concluded at approximately 9:30 P.M. Saturday.

Witnesses said Dove Collins, 25, appeared outside the church as early as 9:15 P.M. having come directly from his shift at the mill where he had been employed since 1959. On being invited to come in and be seated he joked and said he preferred to wait outdoors as he was only wearing work clothes until the Gaddy woman, said to be his common-law wife, came outside the frame structure.

In the ensuing struggle at the conclusion of the services, the woman, who was a member of the choir, is believed to have received fatal icepick injuries to a vital organ, then to have wrested the weapon from her assailant and paid him back in kind. The Gaddy woman then walked to her mother's house but later collapsed.

Members of the congregation said they chased Collins 13 or 14 yds. in the direction of Snake Creek on the South side of the church then he fell to the ground and rolled approximately ten feet down the bank, rolling over six or seven times. Those present believed him to have succumbed since it was said the pick while in the woman's hand had been seen to drive in and pierce either his ear or his eye, either of which, is in close approximation to the brain. However, Collins later managed to crawl unseen from the creek and to make his way undetected up Railroad Avenue and to the Main St. door of an office occupied by Richard Strickland, M.D., above the Citizens Bank & Trust.

Witnesses were divided on which of the Negroes struck the first blow. Percy McAtee, pastor of the church, would not take sides but declared on being questioned by Marshal Stubblefield he was satisfied no outside agitators were involved and no arrests were made.

Collins was discovered on his own doorstep by Dr. Strickland who had been spending the evening at the Country Club. Collins is reported by Dr. Strickland to have expired shortly following his discovery, alleging his death to chest wounds.

"He offered no statement," Dr. Strickland said in response to a query.

Interviewed at home where he is recuperating from an ailment, Mayor Fairbrothers stated that he had not heard of there being trouble of any description at the Mill. "We are not trying to ruin our good reputation by inviting any, either," he said. "If the weatherman stays on our side we expect to attain capacity production in the latter part of next month," he stated. Saturday had been pay day as usual.

When Collins' body was searched by officers the pockets were empty however.

An icepick, reportedly the property of the Holy Gospel Tabernacle, was later found by Deacon Gaddy, 8, brother of Ruby Gaddy, covered with blood and carried it to Marshal Stubblefield. Stubblefield said it had been found in the grounds of the new $100,000.00 Negro school. It is believed to have served as the instrument in the twin slayings, the victims thus virtually succeeding in killing each other.

"Well, I'm not surprised didn't more of them get hurt," said Rev. Alonzo Duckett, pastor of the Holden First Baptist Church. "And yet they expect to be seated in our churches." County Sheriff Vince Lasseter, reached fishing at Lake Bourne, said: "That's one they can't pin the blame on us for. That's how they treat their own kind. Please take note our conscience is clear."

Members of the Negro congregation said they could not account for Collins having left Snake Creek at the unspecified time. "We stood there a while and flipped some bottle caps down at him and threw his cap down after him right over his face and didn't get a stir out of him," stated an official of the congregation. "The way he acted, we figured he was dead. We would not have gone off and left him if we had known he was able to subsequently crawl up the hill." They stated Collins was not in the habit of worshipping at Holy Gospel Tabernacle.

The Gaddy woman died later this morning, also from chest wounds.

No cause was cited for the fracas.

The cook had refilled his cup without his noticing. The doctor dropped the paper and carried his coffee out onto the little porch; it was still his morning habit.

The porch was at the back of the house, screened on three sides. Sylvia's daybed used to stand here; it put her in the garden. No other houses were in sight; the gin could not be heard or even the traffic whining on the highway up off the bypass.

The roses were done for, the perennials too. But the surrounding crape-myrtle tree, the redbud, the dogwood, the Chinese tallow tree, and the pomegranate bush were bright as toys. The ailing pear tree had shed its leaves ahead of the rest. Past a falling wall of Michaelmas daisies that had not been tied up, a pair of flickers were rifling the grass, the cock in one part of the garden, the hen in another, picking at the devastation right through the bright leaves that appeared to have been left lying there just for them, probing and feeding. They stayed year round, he supposed, but it was only in the fall of the year that he ever noticed them. He was pretty sure that Sylvia had known the birds were there. Her eyes would follow birds when they flew across the garden. As he watched, the cock spread one wing, showy as a zebra's hide, and with a turn of his head showed his red seal.

Dr. Strickland swallowed the coffee and picked up his bag. It was all going to be just about as hard as seeing Herman and Eva Fairbrothers through. He thought that in all Holden, as of now, only Miss Marcia Pope was still quite able to take care of herself—or such was her own opinion.

THE
THIRD
OCEAN

HOLLIS
SUMMERS

Bill was three and Tim was a baby when the Travises began going to
the ocean every summer. They had not missed one summer in twelve
years, and now their ages were multiples of three: four and five times
three, and thirteen and fourteen times three. William Travis did not
mean to make anything of the fact. He thought of their ages while
he was driving slowly behind three long trucks outside Grafton, West
Virginia. He thought of saying, "We are multiples of three," but he
did not want Emily to say, "What a silly thing to think of," and so he
said nothing. Instead he passed, without caution, one of the long
trucks, and Emily said, "William, please."

But Tim mentioned their ages the first afternoon at Delmont Beach.

HOLLIS SUMMERS has written four books of poetry, the most recent being
The Peddler and Other Domestic Matters. His fourth novel is *The Day
After Sunday*.

The four of them were building a sand castle. Tim said, "You know what? We're all three times something." He spoke as if he were speaking to the turret. He said, "And three is very mystic. Red, white, and blue; past, present, and future; and Father, Son, and Holy Ghost."

Emily said, "Really, Tim!"

Bill said, "How cloddy can you get?" but he spoke without heat. "And chocolate, and vanilla, and strawberry." He scooped another handful of sand from the base of the castle wall.

William said, "I think that's very interesting, Tim." He was pleased with his son's observation, but he was determined to find no significance in the chance of their similar thoughts. "The air is soft," William thought. But if the boys and even Emily should have said in chorus, "The air is soft," he would have found no significance in the chance of their repetitions. "It is a lovely afternoon," William thought.

Bill's wall collapsed. "Good gosh. I'm too old to be playing in the sand. For gosh sakes."

Tim said, "Because of the threes, this is a *very* important summer."

"Every summer is important." William spoke casually. Already the sand and sun and water had made him feel casual.

Tim said, "But this is *especially* important because of the *threes*."

Bill said, "I think maybe he's really flipped." He stood up and adjusted the snap-on glasses he wore over his regular glasses.

"Here now," William said casually. The shafts of Bill's glasses were pale against his brown skin, but the snap-on lenses were circled in black. From William's angle the boy looked like a vast insect, or a man from space. "Here, here."

Bill brushed the sand from his trunks on to Tim. Tim hit at Bill's legs. Bill kicked at Tim's part of the castle, but the turret did not fall. Tim said, "Look at what you almost did, crazy." Bill said, "D'ja hear what he called me?" Tim said, "That's good enough for you."

William allowed his eyes to study Emily's profile. She was always beautiful. And she knew how to handle the boys, certainly. And she had not reacted at all to the word *crazy*. Last year she would have jerked her head toward him, suddenly, three lines between her eyes.

He was quite well now. He had worked too hard, enlarging the store and its sales force, arranging new accounts, reorganizing the books. The chaste signs on the windows were true, finally. The signs finally said, *William Travis*. For years after his father's death he had kept the name *T. R. Travis and Son* on the stationery, and the windows, and the accounts. But if ghosts walked, T. R. Travis would not recognize the store now. William had a right to be proud of his work. He had only worked too hard.

It was fatigue. A year ago last February the doctors in Cleveland had agreed it was only fatigue. In three weeks William Travis had learned to look more easily at the world. In three months he had almost learned to reaccept himself, and the world of Madison, Kentucky, and the world itself.

A person could not blame Emily's fear of her husband's sickness any more than a person could blame himself for fatigue. Emily lived in a single world of *twos:* good and bad, Catholic and Non-Catholic, sane and crazy. Fatigue swam dark in a sea of threes, once, over a year ago. But now the boys could call each other crazy quite naturally. Even Emily was not bothered by the word. William was not bothered by the word, or the boys, or multiples of three, or even the thought of a great shark who swam somewhere, always. Emily was a good companion. A man of forty-two could not expect to be a lover forever. Surely many wives refused themselves to their husbands, even young wives, even their young husbands. And sharks swam in every season.

The old man at the Shell Service Station, back in Madison, was the first person to mention the summer sharks. When William was signing the credit slip for the gasoline, the grease job, and the new tire, the man said, "They're certainly having a lot of trouble with those sharks."

William had not dreamed of the great shark in months. Perhaps he lifted his head suddenly to the old man, but he was not troubled by the man in gray overalls who spoke of sharks. William watched his own hand steadily make his own name. He finished making his name before he asked the man where they were having trouble.

The man raised his hand to his ear. William had forgot, for a moment, that the man was deaf. William spoke loudly, "I said, I haven't seen a newspaper!"

The man pushed at the bill of his cap. "I forget just where it was. Somewhere along the east coast."

William had meant to tell the man that they were going to the ocean. He like to say, "We are going to the ocean." Landlocked in Kentucky he had never said *beach,* or *shore,* or even *the coast.* Old Miss Markham, who had worked in Children's Wear ever since William wore Children's Wear, teased him about saying *the ocean.* "I don't know why I say it, Miss Markham." She was the only employee left from his father's time. He could not keep from feeling awkward in her presence. If one of his own clerks had teased him about saying *the ocean,* he would have said that naming *the ocean* made him grow taller. He had an easy relationship with the men and women he had hired himself.

The service station man's name had slipped his mind. "We're going on a little trip," he said. He liked the quiet slow man. Sometimes in their brief conversations William swore a little, and the quiet man always said, "You're god damned right, Mr. Travis," and they smiled at each other.

"Have a good trip, Mr. Travis." The man knew everybody's name, just as T. R. Travis had known everybody's name a long time ago. "And be careful."

"We're just going for a week. This year I can't get off any longer." He did not say, "We are going to Delaware." He did not say, "I am afraid to try the ocean for longer than a week."

They had spent one night on the road as usual. They arrived early Wednesday afternoon as usual. Everything was almost as usual, but they knew where they were going to stay. When they were younger they had merely ridden to the ocean and found a cabin. Now they preferred the comfort of a reservation. One of Emily's Vassar friends had given them the name of Delmont Beach and Mr. Meigg. Emily kept close touch with her past. Or perhaps her past was always present. William regretted that Emily had never met his father.

He did not miss a turn in arriving at Ocean Side Cottages. The cottages did not view the ocean, but they were on the ocean side of the highway: twelve little box cabins facing each other and a square gravel driveway. They did not look unlike the postcard Emily's friend had sent, and the rent was remarkably inexpensive. Emily delighted in economizing on vacations. "We can have luxury at home. And you meet more interesting people off the beaten path," she was always saying. "This is very adequate," Emily said. And there was Mr. Thomas Meigg, the proprietor of Ocean Side Cottages, sweeping the front step of one of the cabins as they drove into the square.

"I bet that's ours," Tim said.

"Bet you anything," Bill said.

It was number three, and only incidentally, their cabin. Tim said, "See?" And Bill said, "See what, silly, I'll beat you in the ocean."

Mr. Meigg leaned his broom against the clapboard wall. "Welcome to Ocean Side." His voice was a harsh whisper, and his face was so scarred that it was difficult to look at him straight. "You made good time."

Tim shook Mr. Meigg's hand, and said, "It's very nice to meet you." Bill shook his hand, and then looked away, humming under his breath. William found himself ridiculously moved by the boys' sudden manners. Bill even stood back to let Tim go first into the orange shellacked walls. Emily, of course, was entirely gracious.

"Fine. Yes, this is very attractive. Yes," she said in the sparsely furnished partitioned box which was cabin number three. "Twin beds," she said, as if she had not specified twin beds in her letter to Mr.

Meigg. "And a stove, and sink. We can have our breakfasts here. How nice."

William tried to imagine the partitions to the ceiling, making two bedrooms, a family room, and a bathroom. Parents who were lovers would need to love cautiously within these walls. And men who cried out their nightmares could not cry privately. But he was being foolish. He had promised Emily he would not bother her any more. And he had not dreamed of the shark in over a year, not since Florida.

"You'll want to sign the registery," Mr. Meigg said, "And towels. I'll give you more towels, if you come on up to my place."

Mr. Meigg's cottage was closer than the cabins to the ocean, but still hidden from the ocean by the dunes. Mr. Meigg whispered that the news didn't look very good but the weather had been fine. He said he liked August at the beach better than any other month. He said he had a place in Florida, too; incidentally, Mr. Meigg would be glad to have their business if they happened to find themselves in Florida.

"You in the war?" Mr. Meigg asked as he handed William the plastic book entitled *Friends Who Called.*

"A little while," William said, looking straight at Mr. Meigg. "I had a short trip."

The man lifted his hand to his scarred cheek. "Then we don't need to talk about it any."

"Of course not," William said, knowing he would not speak of Mr. Meigg's war to Emily; he did not want her to consider Mr. Meigg an interesting person off the beaten path. "I'm sorry," William said, wishing for other words.

"That's fine," Mr. Meigg said.

"We were in Florida last year." William began to write his name. "At New Smyrna. In June. But only for a couple of days. We ran into a lot of jelly fish."

The Portuguese Men of War were deformed pink and purple balloons, covering the beach at New Smyrna the morning after the Travises arrived. For two days the Travises sat in a cove and sunned. "Please, please let us go in the ocean," the boys said.

"Get hold of yourself," Emily said. "You're well now. The doctors said you were well."

"They're just jelly fish," the motel proprietor said.

They had made love the first night in the motel. It was the last night they had made love.

"Please let us go in, just once."

"Your father is making the decisions," Emily said, but it was Emily who made the decisions after Florida. "We're too old for all that stuff any more, William. I think it upsets you. We're too old to be like silly young lovers, William."

"Please, please," the boys said.

But William had insisted that they go back to Madison, Kentucky. He could not say why; he could not remember why. There had been no rumor of sharks in Florida.

"They blow away," Mr. Meigg said.

"Florida has some fine beaches."

Mr. Meigg lifted his hand to his scarred ear. William raised his voice. He would raise his voice all week to Mr. Meigg even if the man were not hard of hearing.

"Hurry, hurry," the boys called outside the picture window of Mr. Meigg's house that faced the sand road.

"Hurry," Emily said. She looked very young. She wore her white suit. Emily owned many bathing suits.

"I'm hurrying," he called, as he closed Mr. Meigg's register. "But don't wait for me."

First he hung the four yellow towels carefully on the bathroom racks. T. R. Travis always said that his son got his tidiness from his mother. But William could barely remember his mother. She was a gray squirrel coat and the odor of violets. William and his father lived in the big house on Court Street for all of their lives together. A series of housekeepers walked through the parlors and kitchen of the big house. And always there was Miss Markham of Children's Wear, advising and consoling and occasionally coming for dinner in the oak paneled dining room. William did not really believe that Miss Markham had been his father's mistress. Small towns always insinuated relationships; he had managed to separate himself from the insinuations of Madison a long time ago.

He took the four suitcases out of the station wagon. He picked up the clothes Emily and the boys had left in the bedrooms. Emily's clothes made hieroglyphs perhaps: she did not have the memory of a gray squirrel violet mother. William started to pull down the cracked green blind: the blind was crossed and curved and dotted, almost as if it were deliberately patterned. A light behind the blind would pattern the ceiling with constellations: "There's Venus," "And there's the Milky Way," "And even Mars," lovers could tell each other. But Emily had obviously undressed without pulling down the blind. They were at the ocean. A man discovered his body at the ocean; he became an anonymous body at the ocean.

William placed his folded sport shirt on the dresser. He hung his trousers on the rod which hung in the corner of the bedroom. He stepped into his athletic supporter and trunks. He turned back the beds for the night. The sheets were quite clean, almost blindingly clean. Ocean Side was all right. After the boys had said Cloddy and Bletch, or whatever words they were currently riding, they would say, "This is O.K. This is really O.K.," and Emily would speak naturally of *our house* and write a long letter to her Vassar friend in St. Louis.

He closed the screen door as carefully as if someone slept in cabin three.

He walked down the sand road, past Mr. Meigg's house, past three more cottages with screened porches and television aerials, the ocean pounding in his ears.

Twelve years ago he had first taken his family to the ocean—a South Carolina ocean. He did not feel any older than twelve years ago. He wore the same body. The body he wore had never really seen the ocean without Tim and Bill and Emily. He did not count the other ocean he had traveled as a young man in a troop ship, to be wounded a little, to be hurriedly returned to Madison, Kentucky. He did not count the other ocean he had sailed as a child with his parents, searching through a winter for his mother's health. He had not really seen the ocean during the war or that other time, not the way he was going to see it now, not the way he always saw it with his family, except for the last time in Florida.

The third ocean was the only ocean.

He did not break his step as he mounted the rise of the dunes.

And there it was, exactly as he remembered it, the way it always was, lovelier than he remembered it.

Emily and the boys jumped in the breakers. They hung a moment against the sky.

"Hurry Daddy," Tim shouted.

William ran as fast as he could run toward the vast water.

He needed the ocean. He did not doubt his need, or his desire. He did not try to differentiate between the dark requirements of need and desire. The ocean was neither Emily, whom he remembered well, nor his mother he could barely remember. This ocean was the ocean.

He was fifty feet tall. The waves knocked him down because he allowed them to. He was stronger than any tide. He could swim to Portugal, if he cared to; he did not care to swim to Portugal. He lingered among the breakers because he wished to. He was knocked down because he wished to be knocked down. He neither doubted nor questioned his need or his desire. Tim had spoken of the *threes* because Tim happened to think of the threes. Everything that happened was a coincidence, or nothing was a coincidence, and neither way mattered presently or finally. *The third ocean is.* Values lay in living—that is what the doctor in Cleveland said, that was the way to look casually at the world. If William Travis thought of the natures of number or mystery, he thought of them casually.

For four days the ocean did not disappoint him, not with a third, or a ninth, or a thousandth wave. He read without much concern of sharks in waters that bordered New York or Maryland or Georgia. He deliberately bought newspapers at the doors of restaurants up the highway. He did not avoid discussing the sharks with the elegant grandmother and her son and daughter-in-law who sprawled under the next umbrella, or the old couple who walked the beach three times a day, or the young parents who crowded the water, or Mr. Meigg who never came to the beach. "Haven't seen a shark since I been here, three years now," Mr. Meigg whispered, smiling. "They aren't going to scare me with their shark talk," the grandmother said, glaring at her very pregnant daughter-in-law, moving into the water to swim her graceful side stroke, returning gracefully: "Do you see any shark marks, Jennifer?" The old couple, holding hands, went into the water up to their thin knees. "Keep a sharp eye out. Sharp eye," the old lady said. The two boys, whom Bill named the County Snakes, fished every afternoon and evening for the sharks. "We'll get 'em," they told each other, hitching at their tight trunks. "We'll get us some."

Until Sunday the Travises left the beach only to eat. Every morning William rented a chair and an umbrella from the two blonde young men who wore *Life Guard* on their tee shirts and drove a scarlet Jeep up and down the sand. "I can't feel they're much protection, those Life Guards," Emily said. "But they count change well." "Silly William," Emily said. "They'll Life Guard if they need to," he told her.

All day the Travises sat on the beach, rubbing oil on themselves, dipping in and out of the ocean. The boys were companionable; they did not quarrel much; "Come on in," they called, and William came. Emily joined them in fashioning a sand castle at least once a day. But most of the day she sat in the chair under the umbrella and wrote letters, and read, and did her nails. Most of the day William lay near her, out of the shadow of her umbrella, looking at the clean white scenery.

"My, you're getting brown," she said.

"This is good for us, isn't it?" she said.

"The boys are sturdy, aren't they?" she said, waving her nails to dry in the salt air.

Once, on Saturday afternoon, she lowered her book and smiled gently at William. He did not mean to make anything of a wife's smiling at her husband. He wished she would reach out and touch his shoulder, but he did not wish deeply. And he had promised to leave her alone, before God he had promised. "We're not going to get a divorce, William. We will work out our human salvation," she said in the Florida motel. She had obviously prepared the words she was saying; perhaps she had even rehearsed the words before Father Baldwin back in Madison. "Look at me, William. We are husband and wife because we are married in the eyes of God, and because we are the parents of two children." "But the other night. . . ." he said. "That was a mistake. We're going back to Madison, and we're not going to have any more of that . . . stuff. Look at me, William, and promise."

"You promised, you promised," she said the few times he had tried to forget or ignore his promise. "Before God you promised."

He had not challenged her God or his own promise. For a year now, because he was weak and dominated, or because he was strong and wise, or because, because, because: because a man had to work out his human salvation, he accepted Emily's edict and his own promise.

"We aren't a typical family any more," Emily said, smiling at Delmont Beach. "We're older than the other families now, aren't we? We're the oldest family all together at the beach."

"Oh I don't think so," William said, although he had noticed the young families that first afternoon even before Tim spoke of the *threes*. "The boys are fine."

Emily said, "At the ocean everybody used to be in their thirties and have two children. At the ocean we used to be everybody's age."

"Now they have four and they're still in their thirties." William's laughter sounded quite natural in the bright sun. "We like family beaches. We've always said so." He pushed himself up to sit in Emily's shade.

"Next year, Bill will probably be—I don't know, somewhere on his own." She was not smiling now.

"There's no reason. . . ." William's eyes held Emily's eyes; he had to force his eyes to keep looking. "We've always said we liked our ocean because it wasn't Miami, or Virginia Beach, or . . . or Rehobeth."

"Of course we do. It's silly to think about." Emily shrugged. Her breasts moved in her white suit.

"In Florida . . ." William said, taking his eyes from Emily's breasts.

"You promised, William." Her voice was not unkind. "We promised each other we wouldn't talk about that any more. We've stopped talking about that time. That was part of your promise, William. You promised."

"Sure," he said.

Before she lifted the book from her lap, she said, "I complimented Mr. Meigg on Delmont. He said it was a fine place if you weren't wanting to *go* all the time." Emily laughed. "That's exactly what the man at Pauley's Island said."

"I know," William said, but his wife was reading.

"It's a lovely afternoon," the old woman said, and the old man nodded as if he had thought of the comment himself.

"Fine, fine," William said, stretching on the sand.

In the evenings after dinner they walked, as they had always walked at the ocean after dinner. The boys ran ahead of them, sometimes lost, sometimes appearing suddenly behind them or at their sides, stamping stiff legged into the waves and out. Always they walked toward the flush of light at the edge of the sky, and always the boys suggested that they walk clear to the town ahead, Myrtle, or Santa Monica, or Rehobeth.

As usual Emily said they would save town for a rainy day. "There are always rainy days at the ocean," she said.

Sunday morning she took the boys to the early service at the little Catholic church up the highway. William lay on the beach by himself under a sky that held clouds a while, and the sun, and clouds, and the sun, and clouds. "Careful, baby don't let the fish get you," the young mother with the lemon colored hair called to her toy doll child. The clouds did not look like maps or elephants or human beings. "If I am not contented, I am thinking about the word contentment." *Catch, catch. Good morning. Lovely morning.*

"Mother says why don't we go to Rehobeth for lunch," Bill said.

"Maybe this is the rainy day at the ocean," Tim said under the sun.

He had slept. He had never slept on a beach in all his life. The boys stood above him in their Sunday suits.

"I was asleep. I went to sleep," William told his sons.

"My how nice we look," the elegant grandmother said.

"Do you want to go to Rehobeth for lunch?" Bill asked.

"Fine, fine," William said. "Everything's fine at the ocean."

"Everything's fine at Rehobeth, but I'm ready to go home," Tim said.

"Home?"

"I mean our house. Our cabin, I mean." Tim laughed sputtering his popcorn. Bill laughed too.

They had eaten well; they had walked the board walk; they had placed dimes in machines to receive their fortunes, and scarlet candy, and glass rings; they had ridden on The Sea Basket which tilted and twirled them against the sky; they had wandered in shops and bought pennants and cotton candy and souvenir flashlights. In Greshwin's Sea Knacks Bill put his arm on Tim's shoulder as they studied an aquarium that contained sea horses. The proprietor smiled at the boys and went over to talk to them.

In the car Tim said, "That man said the father sea horse has the babies."

"He takes care of the eggs," Bill said. "He doesn't lay them."

"One father had five thousand babies last week and they all died."

"More like five hundred, or more like fifty," Bill said.

"But they all died."

"Why don't you turn on the radio?" Emily asked.

William turned the left knob, and after a moment he twisted the other knob until a newscaster's voice entered the car. His voice was young and apologetic. He spoke of another miracle in space.

"Hey, leave that," Bill said.

"Golly," Tim said.

The announcer had finished telling of the miracle. He told of the shells in Greshwin's Sea Knacks.

"That's where *we* were," Tim shouted. "What do you think about that? That's where *we were*."

"Everybody knows that," Bill said.

"And now for the news of our area," the announcer said.

"Space is our area," Tim said.

"Hush up," Bill said.

It was not the coincidence of turning a dial three times that brought the shark into the car. They would have heard of the shark from Mr. Meigg anyhow. It was better to have heard of the shark first from the apologetic announcer.

At Indian Beach a shark had chased Mr. T. M. Robbins into the shore. Mr. Robbins escaped without injury. Mr. Robbins said he had thought he would never see his family again. Mr. Robbins was swimming from fifty to sixty feet off shore. The shark was estimated to be at least nine feet in length.

"Where's Indian Beach?" Tim asked.

"South Carolina, I think." Emily had not been listening to the radio she had asked to hear.

William started not to say, "Indian Beach is the third one down from us." He had stood in a service station in Madison, Kentucky, and studied the names of the beaches that swam down the map: Delmont, Tompkins, Ranger, Indian. "It's the third one down," he said angrily.

Bill said, "I'll be."

Tim said, "I'm never going in the ocean again, not ever, not forever and a day. I'm not ever going to set foot in the ocean, not ever."

"That's enough," William said, glaring into the rearview mirror.

Bill jabbed his elbow into Tim's side.

"Well, I'm not, and quit hitting me."

"Boys," Emily said.

Bill flounced himself into the corner of the seat. He leaned his forehead against the window. His lips moved.

"Stop that muttering," William said, and more quietly: "Speak up, if you have something to say."

Bill's face grew large in the mirror. He leaned hard against his father's shoulders. "What's a shark, I'd like to know. And now I bet you won't let us go in at all. I bet you make us go home tomorrow, just because of one little old shark." His voice cracked. His voice was almost crying. "I bet it'll be like in Florida."

Emily turned.

"I'd be ashamed," Tim said.

"Well, I mean it. It's going to be like last year in Florida."

"Bill!" Emily's knees whispered against the nylon seat covers. "Bill, I told you."

Bill was crying. A fifteen-year-old boy was crying in the back seat of the station wagon. "You won't let us go in, and who's afraid of a shark, and they won't be at our beach anyhow," the fifteen-year-old boy cried.

"We'll see." William's voice was as loud as if he spoke to the deaf. "We'll see. Now straighten up there."

"We'll see, we'll see, we'll see," Bill muttered.

The words were the words of T. R. Travis. But at least T. R. Travis had pretended intimacy with his son. T. R. Travis often said, "*We'll see* means I am not capable of being a responsible law-giver. It means give me time for the situation to change so I won't have to make a decision."

William said, "I said, 'We'll see.' Now, quiet, all of you." And, after a little while he said, "I'm sorry."

But the boys were arguing in low voices over how long was fifty feet; it was twice as long as their living room, it was "about out to there, no, a little bit further," it was the length of the pool. When they turned into Ocean Side they were challenging each other on the number of pecks in a gallon.

Mr. Meigg was readying cabin number six. His scarred face chuckled as he came over to place his hand on the sill of William's window. His fingers were thin, but smooth. "Did you see the shark?" he whispered.

"We heard about it." William made himself look into the man's eyes.

Bill put his hand on William's shoulder. "Here? Was the shark here on our beach?"

"They sighted him. Just after noon." Mr. Meigg laughed at the thought. "He was a big fellow. I stood on the dunes and watched. They were after him with shotguns and clam rakes and everything. It was a sight." Mr. Meigg removed his hand from the sill to laugh and cough against his smooth fingers. "They were after him with everything. They didn't catch him, though." He was delighted with his story. "Clam rakes, and shotguns, and even brooms. One old fellow had a broom."

"Really? Really?" Tim said.

"I would expect a land-owner to keep this quiet." William spoke casually.

Mr. Meigg did not seem to understand. "You expect all sorts of things at the beach," he said, as if William had not spoken.

"Is there danger, of swimming, for us, I mean, for the boys?" William spoke loudly.

"Oh, I don't think so." Mr. Meigg was unable to stop smiling. "You just have to be careful. They're fast."

Emily said, "If we all go in together. . . ."

"That's right. You can see them coming. They zigzag. But you can see them all right. This morning one of them chased a man clear up to the beach down at Indian, the same one, I guess."

Tim said, "It was nine feet out and fifty feet long." He giggled. "I mean the other way around."

"He just chased him right in." Mr. Meigg giggled too, as if he were not old enough to have been wounded in a war. "The sea was quiet as a millpond, and he chased him right in."

Tim and Bill were asking questions together. William could barely distinguish their questions, but Mr. Meigg was answering the boys separately. "But you probably won't ever see one," Mr. Meigg said.

In the cabin William said, "Are they going in, Emily?" He found it difficult to think about the shark.

The boys stood at their bedroom door. They had already taken off their shirts. They held their hands at their hips; their stance was the stance of the County Snakes.

Emily lifted her hand to the lamp on the table. With the forefinger of her right hand she circled the top rim of the lampshade. She did not turn on the lamp, of course; she was beautiful in the sudden light that came from somewhere. It was the sun, of course. The sun had come out as suddenly as it had disappeared while they were talking to Mr. Meigg. William thought of other beaches where they had made love. "You're the father," she said. "You make the ocean decisions."

"Please, pretty please," Tim said. "For gosh sakes," Bill said.

"There are always sharks." William kept his voice as soft as Emily's. "We'll just have to be careful." The words were not difficult to speak. They were not nearly so difficult as saying, "We'll go back to Madison."

"Very well," Emily said. "I'll dress in the bathroom." She sounded no more pleased than if he had said, "I love you, Emily. Oh Emily, I love you."

"Oh boy," Tim said.

As he removed his clothes William thought, "Oh boy, oh boy," trying to think of Tim's pleasure. He wished to think his moment of decision into importance, at least into more importance than a moment of indecision. He was naked. He was in his bathing trunks. Tim stood at the door. "Ready, ready? Are you ready?"

"Ready," William said.

Behind Tim Bill stood scowling through his glasses. "Why don't you leave your glasses here?" William asked.

Bill stepped back. He flipped his towel savagely against Tim's legs.

Tim whirled, yelling, "You dog, you, you. . . ." His towel sailed across the room. It landed against an empty milk bottle on the drainboard. The bottle teetered before it fell to the floor. The sound of its breaking came slowly, like thunder after lightning.

Bill was shouting. "Did you see that? What are you going to do to him? If I'd a done that, I'd never hear the end of it."

"The idea. The very idea." William's fingers dug into Bill's shoulders.

"Hey. Hey, quit."

"Boys," Emily said at the bathroom door.

Bill wrenched away from William's hands. He stood at the door. "What'd I do?" He crossed his hands over his thin chest. "What'd I do to the little baby?"

"Get out. Get out of here, both of you."

"I didn't mean. . . ." Tim began.

"You heard your father," Emily said softly, stooping to the broken glass.

Bill opened the screen door wide, letting it slam behind him. He stood outside and slammed it a second time before he started around the driveway.

"Bill!" William shouted.

"Leave him alone," Emily said.

"He hit me first," Tim said. "I didn't . . ."

"Go on, I said go on." William whispered.

Tim shrugged. He opened and closed the screen door with elaborate carefulness.

At the sink, in the quiet cabin, Emily turned. "That was quite a display," she said.

"I know. I'm sorry."

"You're with them so little, I would think . . ." Emily bit her lips. "You're always after them."

"I'm not always after them. It's just that. . . ." He was determined to keep his voice as soft as Emily's. "I know I've been a little upset. I know. . . ."

145

"Please, William. We don't quarrel. At least we don't quarrel."

"My God, Emily. My God."

"Please."

"A man shouldn't have to keep working things out, over and over again. You don't have to keep working things out."

She spoke so softly that William had to ask her to repeat. "That's what I mean," she said again.

"*What* do you mean?"

"Why are you afraid of the shark? Why are you afraid of the shark?" she asked, although he had heard her the first time. "No, don't touch me. No, No. *Why?*"

"I dreamed of a shark. When I was sick I dreamed of a great shark." He spoke quickly. If he spoke quickly perhaps he could say what he meant, not knowing what he meant. "It's bad not to be able to tell what's real from a dream. I don't want to be sick, Emily."

"Everybody dreams." Emily leaned hard against the sink. She looked small. "No, no," she said.

"I worry about the boys, I guess." William cleared his throat. "I guess I worry about keeping us together. And about dying." He stepped back from her. "I guess I want to hold on—whatever we have."

She was moving toward him now. They were like dancers in the room. "If you had faith," she said. "If you went to church with the boys and me. If you had *faith*."

"I try. I try, Emily."

"You didn't try. You didn't give the Church a chance, not a real chance."

"We can't talk about it. You don't want to talk about . . ."

She wore the gray suit instead of the white one. "Not if talk means going to bed together. That's what talk means to you. You've been looking at me that way. You promised. Before God you promised."

"God damn," he said. "God damn."

"William, William, William," she said. "You're right," she said. "We can't talk together. But it's all right. It's perfectly all right. You're all right."

She patted his arm before she moved around him to the door. "I'm not a bit annoyed. We're fine." She seemed to speak sincerely. Her anger had been a light switched on by mistake.

And she was right, perhaps. They were probably fine. In a few minutes it was all right to follow the road past the dunes to the crowded beach and ocean. The beach fluttered in the bright wind.

Their umbrella was already up. Emily was paying one of the blonde young men for the chair and umbrella. Bill stood tall beside her. "Here I am," Tim yelled from the edge of the water. "Here I am."

"Ready?" Emily smiled.

"I'm sorry about. . . ."

Bill turned his head.

"Everything's all right. Bill's fine. Forget it," Emily said. "Now are we all ready?"

But Bill did not want to go in the ocean. "I don't feel much like it," he said. "I guess I'm catching a cold."

"We'll go in together," Emily said. "Give me your glasses. I'll put them right here in my case."

"I don't want to, I told you."

"I'll race you," William said.

"We'll rent some of those rubber rafts," Emily said.

"I said I wasn't going. Are you deaf?"

"Mister. Mister Life Guard. Wait a minute, Life Guard." Emily moved across the sand to the scarlet Jeep, opening her beach bag that was covered with round plastic suns. "Help me, Bill. Help me with these."

Emily talked well. Emily talked easily. Together they sat on the sand with the rafts for a while. Tim was delighted with his raft. "Hey, keen," he said. He raced into the water and out again. "Shark, shark, I'm a shark," Tim shouted, and the mother of the toy doll child said, "Look at the big boy. Look at him run." "We should of got these before."

"*Should have*," Bill said. "It's not *should of*."

"The water's good," Tim said. "It's just as soft and good."

"Everybody's in," Emily said. "Maybe we'll all go in after a while."

And after a while they all went into the ocean. Bill lifted both hands to his temples. He removed his glasses slowly and handed them, slowly, to his mother. "I'll just put them right in here," she said. "They'll be safe as anything."

"I can't see much without those things," Bill said. "The man said *they* slipped up on you."

How does a father say, I love you? What does a man mean when he says I love you? William said, "Fine, fine."

They ran into the water together. For almost an hour they were a family with rafts near the shore. They lay on the rafts; they wrestled them; they dumped each other and themselves; they fought through the water up to air. Emily laughed a great deal. Tim shouted, "Wowie," and "Fab-O."

Once, when Bill squinted over his shoulder toward the curve of sea, William said, "I'm watching out." And Bill said, "I know you are."

The sea was a blue saucer. Gulls sailed. Sandpipers raced on tip-toes, and turned, their feathers ruffled.

"I'm cold, I'm really cold. Don't you think it's getting cold?" Bill asked.

"I think it's cold, too," Tim said. "In fact, I'm freezing to death."

"We'll get out now," Emily said.

"It's been fine," William said, his throat tight with worry or with love; and the afternoon and the evening washed quickly against him, almost too quickly to think about. "It's been very fine."

After dinner they walked by the ocean, on the beach which was charted for them now with people to nod to, with dunes and lights to recognize. The shining mother quarreled with her toy child, but the waves snatched away most of her words: "Don't you know people will. . . . And don't you know you are. . . ."

"Is the shark gone away?" the child whined as the Travises passed.

The mother's teeth glowed as she smiled at the Travises. "Yes, yes, darling," she said, nodding. "They killed it, darling. All the sharks are killed."

"They killed it?" Bill skipped into step beside William.

"She said so. The lady said so." Tim ran into the water until a wave splashed his shorts. "Shark, shark," he shouted, tracing numbers with his flashlight.

Far down the beach driftwood fires burned. "It's pretty, isn't it?" Emily said. "It's like a carnival, isn't it?"

The beach was full of little sharks. Almost every knot of fishermen discussed their little sharks with the people who did not fish but merely walked the beach. "Sand shark." "White shark," they told the Travises.

"Golly," Tim said. "That woman didn't tell the truth."

"A storm's blown them in," one man said; and another said they had come in because the ocean had been quiet so long.

"As a millpond," Tim said.

"But that fellow this morning—he was a whopper. Eleven feet long, anyhow."

Twelve feet, eighteen, twenty-four. He was forty feet off shore, twenty-five feet, he was in the trough of the second wave. He was last sighted at eleven; no nearer twelve-thirty; at two. The friendly men and women and children on the beach moved together among a variety of numbers. How many people saw him? How deep is it out there? Give me a number, any number. How high is the sky?

"I bet they know about him even in Madison, Kentucky," Tim said.

"You tell 'm," a man said.

One of the twins who lived in the blue apartment house guarded the largest of the little sharks. The boy and the shark were almost the same size, three feet tall, three and a half. The boy stood the dead shark on its nose and dropped it to the sand. The boy kicked the shark. "Do it again, Greg," his brother said.

The County Snakes had caught a hammerhead. "It's a god dam hammerhead," the boy in the red and white striped trunks said. He placed his palms on his hips.

"It's a fish," Tim said.

"Sure it's a fish." The County Snakes laughed, looking toward William.

"It's a fish, Tim," William said.

"They're killers." The boy in yellow trunks spit over his shoulder. "They smell you out."

The old lady said, "Lovely evening."

The lovely evening was very dark when the Travises returned to their dunes.

Lightning bloomed the sky a moment.

"It may rain," Emily said.

"I'm sleepy," Bill said.

"Me too." Tim yawned loudly.

"Beat you to bed."

"Oh no you won't."

At the front door William turned to study the sky a moment.

He was not Paul on the road to Damascus. He was only a man who had walked on the beach with his family.

But for a moment he was the sea. He was all of the oceans. The waters of his mind held a multitude of faces, from war and even childhood, even his mother—she was not dressed in fur: she wore a white voile dress and sat in a steamer chair, even the man at the Shell Station, his father and the boys, and Emily, Emily, Emily.

The oceans were one ocean. He considered the possibility of deafness. But he was not deaf. The wind sounded in the sky.

He did not say, "I accept the responsibility of being human." But aloud he said, "I wish you well." He spoke, perhaps, to the shark who swam somewhere, absolute, perhaps fully dark, perhaps evil. He was embarrassed at having spoken aloud.

"Goodnight, Emily," William said as she switched off the lamp above her bed. "Goodnight, boys," he said in the dark cabin.

"Don't let the bedbugs bite," Tim called above the partition.

William lay on his back, his fingers clasped behind his neck. The tent of the roof appeared and disappeared in the sudden lightning. He wondered if the flashes came at any regular intervals, but he did not consider determining their frequency by counting his own pulse, or Emily's breathing.

"We have two and a half more days." Bill's voice seemed to come from the rafters.

"I bet we can't go in tomorrow at all," Tim said.

"You can go," William said. "You may go."

"And the morning and the evening were the fifth day," William thought. He was making a kind of joke. It was a joke like "The millpond round my neck." The act of committing your family to the sea was a small act, no different, not much different from saying, "Goodnight, goodnight."

IN THE ZOO

JEAN STAFFORD

Keening harshly in his senility, the blind polar bear slowly and cease-lessly shakes his head in the stark heat of the July and mountain noon. His open eyes are blue. No one stops to look at him; an old farmer, in passing, sums up the old bear's situation by observing, with a ruth-less chuckle, that he is a "back number." Patient and despairing, he sits on his yellowed haunches on the central rock of his pool, his huge toy paws wearing short boots of mud.

The grizzlies to the right of him, a conventional family of father and mother and two spring cubs, alternately play the clown and sleep. There is a blustery, scoundrelly, half-likable bravado in the manner of the black bear on the polar's left; his name, according to the legend

JEAN STAFFORD, winner of the 1970 Pulitzer Prize for her *Collected Stories*, has published fiction and nonfiction in many American magazines. Her novels include *Boston Adventure*, *The Mountain Lion*, and *The Catherine Wheel*.

on his cage, is Clancy, and he is a rough-and-tumble, brawling blow-hard, thundering continually as he paces back and forth, or pauses to face his audience of children and mothers and release from his great, gray-tongued mouth a perfectly Vesuvian roar. If he were to be reincarnated in human form, he would be a man of action, possibly a football coach, probably a politician. One expects to see his black hat hanging from a branch of one of his trees; at any moment he will light a cigar.

The polar bear's next-door neighbors are not the only ones who offer so sharp and sad a contrast to him. Across a reach of scrappy grass and litter is the convocation of conceited monkeys, burrowing into each other's necks and chests for fleas, picking their noses with their long, black, finicky fingers, swinging by their gifted tails on the flying trapeze, screaming bloody murder. Even when they mourn— one would think the male orangutan was on the very brink of suicide —they are comedians; they only fake depression, for they are firmly secure in their rambunctious tribalism and in their appalling insight and contempt. Their flibbertigibbet gambolling is a sham, and, stealth-ily and shiftily, they are really watching the pitiful polar bear ("Back number," they quote the farmer. "That's *his* number all right," they snigger), and the windy black bear ("Life of the party. Gasbag. Low I.Q.," they note scornfully on his dossier), and the stupid, bourgeois grizzlies ("It's feed the face and hit the sack for them," the monkeys say). And they are watching my sister and me, two middle-aged women, as we sit on a bench between the exhibits, eating popcorn, growing thirsty. We are thoughtful.

A chance remark of Daisy's a few minutes before has turned us to memory and meditation. "I don't know why," she said, "but that poor blind bear reminds me of Mr. Murphy." The name "Mr. Murphy" at once returned us both to childhood, and we were floated far and fast, our later lives diminished. So now we eat our popcorn in silence with the ritualistic appetite of childhood, which has little to do with hunger; it is not so much food as a sacrament, and in tribute to our sisterliness and our friendliness I break the silence to say that this is the best popcorn I have ever eaten in my life. The extravagance of my statement instantly makes me feel self-indulgent, and for some time I uneasily avoid looking at the blind bear. My sister does not agree or disagree; she simply says that popcorn is the only food she has ever really liked. For a long time, then, we eat without a word, but I know, because I know her well and know her similarity to me, that Daisy is thinking what I am thinking; both of us are mournfully remembering Mr. Murphy, who, at one time in our lives, was our only friend.

This zoo is in Denver, a city that means nothing to my sister and me except as a place to take or meet trains. Daisy lives two hundred miles farther west, and it is her custom, when my every-other-year visit with her is over, to come across the mountains to see me off on my eastbound train. We know almost no one here, and because our stays are short, we have never bothered to learn the town in more than the most desultory way. We know the Burlington uptown office and the respectable hotels, a restaurant or two, the Union Station, and, beginning today, the zoo in the city park.

But since the moment that Daisy named Mr. Murphy by name our situation in Denver has been only corporeal; our minds and our hearts are in Adams, fifty miles north, and we are seeing, under the white sun at its pitiless meridian, the streets of that ugly town, its parks and trees and bridges, the bandstand in its dreary park, the roads that lead away from it, west to the mountains and east to the plains, its mongrel and multitudinous churches, its high school shaped like a loaf of bread, the campus of its college, an oasis of which we had no experience except to walk through it now and then, eying the woodbine on the impressive buildings. These things are engraved forever on our minds with a legibility so insistent that you have only to say the name of the town aloud to us to rip the rinds from our nerves and leave us exposed in terror and humiliation.

We have supposed in later years that Adams was not so bad as all that, and we know that we magnified its ugliness because we looked upon it as the extension of the possessive, unloving, scornful, complacent foster mother, Mrs. Placer, to whom, at the death of our parents within a month of each other, we were sent like Dickensian grotesqueries—cowardly, weak-stomached, given to tears, backward in school. Daisy was ten and I was eight when, unaccompanied, we made the long trip from Marblehead to our benefactress, whom we had never seen and, indeed, never heard of until the pastor of our church came to tell us of the arrangement our father had made on his deathbed, seconded by our mother on hers. This man, whose name and face I have forgotten and whose parting speeches to us I have not forgiven, tried to dry our tears with talk of Indians and of buffaloes; he spoke, however, at much greater length, and in preaching cadences, of the Christian goodness of Mrs. Placer. She was, he said, childless and fond of children, and for many years she had been a widow, after the lingering demise of her tubercular husband, for whose sake she had moved to the Rocky Mountains. For his support and costly medical care, she had run a boarding house, and after his death, since he had left her nothing, she was obliged to continue running it. She had been a girlhood friend of our paternal grandmother, and our father, in the absence of responsible relatives, had made her the beneficiary of his life insurance on the condition that she lodge and rear us.

The pastor, with a frankness remarkable considering that he was talk-ing to children, explained to us that our father had left little more than a drop in the bucket for our care, and he enjoined us to give Mrs. Placer, in return for her hospitality and sacrifice, courteous help and eternal thanks. "Sacrifice" was a word we were never allowed to forget.

And thus it was, in grief for our parents, that we came cringing to the dry Western town and to the house where Mrs. Placer lived, a house in which the square, uncushioned furniture was cruel and the pic-tures on the walls were either dour or dire and the lodgers, who lived in the upper floors among shadowy wardrobes and chiffoniers, had come through the years to resemble their landlady in appearance as well as in deportment.

After their ugly-colored evening meal, Gran—as she bade us call her—and her paying guests would sit, rangy and aquiline, rocking on the front porch on spring and summer and autumn nights, tasting their delicious grievances: those slights delivered by ungrateful sons and daughters, those impudences committed by trolley-car conductors and uppity salesgirls in the ready-to-wear, all those slurs and calculated elbow-jostlings that were their daily crucifixion and their staff of life. We little girls, washing the dishes in the cavernous kitchen, listened to their even, martyred voices, fixed like leeches to their solitary sub-ject and their solitary creed—that life was essentially a matter of being done in, let down, and swindled.

At regular intervals, Mrs. Placer, chairwoman of the victims, would say, "Of course, I don't care; I just have to laugh," and then would tell a shocking tale of an intricate piece of skulduggery perpetrated against her by someone she did not even know. Sometimes, with her avid, partial jury sitting there on the porch behind the bitter hopvines in the heady mountain air, the cases she tried involved Daisy and me, and, listening, we travailed, hugging each other, whispering, "I wish she wouldn't! Oh, how did she find out?" How *did* she? Certainly we never told her when we were snubbed or chosen last on teams, never admitted to a teacher's scolding or to the hoots of laughter that greeted us when we bit on silly, unfair jokes. But she knew. She knew about the slumber parties we were not invited to, the beefsteak fries at which we were pointedly left out; she knew that the singing teacher had said in so many words that I could not carry a tune in a basket and that the sewing superintendent had said that Daisy's fingers were all thumbs. With our teeth chattering in the cold of our isola-tion, we would hear her protestant, litigious voice defending our right to be orphans, paupers, wholly dependent on her—except for the really ridiculous pittance from our father's life insurance—when it was all she could do to make ends meet. She did not care, but she had to laugh that people in general were so small-minded that they looked down on fatherless, motherless waifs like us and, by association, looked down on her. It seemed funny to her that people gave her no credit for taking on these sickly youngsters who were not even kin but only the grandchildren of a friend.

If a child with braces on her teeth came to play with us, she was, according to Gran, slyly lording it over us because our teeth were crooked, but there was no money to have them straightened. And what could be the meaning of our being asked to come for supper at the doctor's house? Were the doctor and his la-di-da New York wife and those pert girls with their solid-gold barrettes and their Shetland pony going to shame her poor darlings? Or shame their poor Gran by making them sorry to come home to the plain but honest life that was all she could provide for them?

There was no stratum of society not reeking with the effluvium of fraud and pettifoggery. And the school system was almost the worst of all: if we could not understand fractions, was that not our teacher's fault? And therefore what right had she to give us F? It was as plain as a pikestaff to Gran that the teacher was only covering up her own inability to teach. It was unlikely, too—highly unlikely—that it was by accident that time and time again the free medical clinic was closed for the day just as our names were about to be called out, so that nothing was done about our bad tonsils, which meant that we were repeatedly sick in the winter, with Gran fetching and carrying for us, climbing those stairs a jillion times a day with her game leg and her heart that was none too strong.

Steeped in these mists of accusation and hidden plots and double meanings, Daisy and I grew up like worms. I think no one could have withstood the atmosphere in that house where everyone trod on eggs that a little bird had told them were bad. They spied on one another, whispered behind doors, conjectured, drew parallels beginning "With all due respect . . ." or "It is a matter of indifference to *me* but . . ." The vigilantes patrolled our town by day, and by night returned to lay their goodies at their priestess's feet and wait for her oracular interpretation of the innards of the butcher, the baker, the candlestick maker, the soda jerk's girl, and the barber's unnatural deaf white cat.

Consequently, Daisy and I also became suspicious. But it was suspicion of ourselves that made us mope and weep and grimace with self-judgment. Why were we not happy when Gran had sacrificed herself to the bone for us? Why did we not cut dead the paper boy who called her a filthy name? Why did we persist in our willful friendliness with the grocer who had tried, unsuccessfully, to overcharge her on a case of pork and beans?

Our friendships were nervous and surreptitious; we sneaked and lied, and as our hungers sharpened, our debasement deepened; we were

155

pitied; we were shifty-eyed, always on the lookout for Mrs. Placer or one of her tattletale lodgers; we were hypocrites.

Nevertheless, one thin filament of instinct survived, and Daisy and I in time found asylum in a small menagerie down by the railroad tracks. It belonged to a gentle alcoholic ne'er-do-well, who did nothing all day long but drink bathtub gin in rickeys and play solitaire and smile to himself and talk to his animals. He had a little, stunted red vixen and a deodorized skunk, a parrot from Tahiti that spoke Parisian French, a woebegone coyote, and two capuchin monkeys, so serious and humanized, so small and sad and sweet, and so religious-looking with their tonsured heads that it was impossible not to think their gibberish was really an ordered language with a grammar that someday some philologist would understand.

Gran knew about our visits to Mr. Murphy and she did not object, for it gave her keen pleasure to excoriate him when we came home. His vice was not a matter of guesswork; it was an established fact that he was half-seas over from dawn till midnight. "With the black Irish," said Gran, "the taste for drink is taken in with the mother's milk and is never mastered. Oh, I know all about those promises to join the temperance movement and not to touch another drop. The way to Hell is paved with good intentions."

We were still little girls when we discovered Mr. Murphy, before the shattering disease of adolescence was to make our bones and brains ache even more painfully than before, and we loved him and we hoped to marry him when we grew up. We loved him, and we loved his monkeys to exactly the same degree and in exactly the same way; they were husbands and fathers and brothers, these three little, ugly, dark, secret men who minded their own business and let us mind ours. If we stuck our fingers through the bars of the cage, the monkeys would sometimes take them in their tight, tiny hands and look into our faces with a tentative, somehow absent-minded sorrow, as if they terribly regretted that they could not place us but were glad to see us all the same. Mr. Murphy, playing a solitaire game of cards called "once in a blue moon" on a kitchen table in his back yard beside the pens, would occasionally look up and blink his beautiful blue eyes and say, "You're peaches to make over my wee friends. I love you for it." There was nothing demanding in his voice, and nothing sticky; on his lips the word "love" was jocose and forthright, it had no strings attached. We would sit on either side of him and watch him regiment his ranks of cards and stop to drink as deeply as if he were dying of thirst and wave to his animals and say to them, "Yes, lads, you're dandies."

Because Mr. Murphy was as reserved with us as the capuchins were, as courteously noncommittal, we were surprised one spring day when he told us that he had a present for us, which he hoped Mrs. Placer would let us keep; it was a puppy, for whom the owner had asked him to find a home—half collie and half Labrador retriever, blue-blooded on both sides.

"You might tell Mrs. Placer—" he said, smiling at the name, for Gran was famous in the town. "You might tell Mrs. Placer," said Mr. Murphy, "that this lad will make a fine watchdog. She'll never have to fear for her spoons again. Or her honor." The last he said to himself, not laughing but tucking his chin into his collar; lines sprang to the corners of his eyes. He would not let us see the dog, whom we could hear yipping and squealing inside his shanty, for he said that our disappointment would weigh on his conscience if we lost our hearts to the fellow and then could not have him for our own.

That evening at supper, we told Gran about Mr. Murphy's present. A dog? In the first place, why a dog? Was it possible that the news had reached Mr. Murphy's ears that Gran had just this very day finished planting her spring garden, the very thing that a rampageous dog would have in his mind to destroy? What sex was it? A male! Females, she had heard, were more trustworthy; males roved and came home smelling of skunk; such a consideration as this, of course, would not have crossed Mr. Murphy's fuddled mind. Was this young male dog housebroken? We had not asked? That was the limit!

Gran appealed to her followers, too raptly fascinated by Mr. Murphy's machinations to eat their Harvard beets. "Am I being far-fetched or does it strike you as decidedly queer that Mr. Murphy is trying to fob off on my little girls a young cur that has not been trained?" she asked them. "If it were housebroken, he would have said so, so I feel it is safe to assume that it is not. Perhaps cannot *be* housebroken. I've heard of such cases."

The fantasy spun on, richly and rapidly, with all the skilled helping hands at work at once. The dog was tangibly in the room with us, shedding his hair, biting his fleas, shaking rain off himself to splatter the walls, dragging some dreadful carcass across the floor, chewing up slippers, knocking over chairs with his tail, gobbling the chops from the platter, barking, biting, fathering, fighting, smelling to high heaven of carrion, staining the rug with his muddy feet, scratching the floor with his claws. He developed rabies; he bit a child, two children! Three! Everyone in town! And Gran and her poor darlings went to jail for harboring this murderous, odoriferous, drunk, Roman Catholic dog.

And yet, astoundingly enough, she came around to agreeing to let us have the dog. It was, as Mr. Murphy had predicted, the word "watchdog" that deflected the course of the trial. The moment Daisy uttered it, Gran halted, marshalling her reverse march; while she rallied and tacked and reconnoitred, she sent us to the kitchen for the dessert. And by the time this course was under way, the uses of a dog, the enormous potentialities for investigation and law enforcement in a dog trained by Mrs. Placer, were being minutely and passionately scrutinized by the eight upright bloodhounds sitting at the table wolfing their brown betty as if it were fresh-killed rabbit. The dog now sat at attention beside his mistress, fiercely alert, ears cocked, nose aquiver, the protector of widows, of orphans, of lonely people who had no homes. He made short shrift of burglars, homicidal maniacs, Peeping Toms, gypsies, bogus missionaries, Fuller Brush men with a risqué spiel. He went to the store and brought back groceries, retrieved the evening paper from the awkward place the boy had meanly thrown it, rescued cripples from burning houses, saved children from drowning, heeled at command, begged, lay down, stood up, sat, jumped through a hoop, ratted.

Both times—when he was a ruffian of the blackest delinquency and then a pillar of society—he was full-grown in his prefiguration, and when Laddy appeared on the following day, small, unsteady, and whimpering lonesomely, Gran and her lodgers were taken aback; his infant, clumsy paws embarrassed them, his melting eyes were unapropos. But it could never be said of Mrs. Placer, as Mrs. Placer her own self said, that she was a woman who went back on her word, and her darlings were going to have their dog, soft-headed and feckless as he might be. All the first night, in his carton in the kitchen, he wailed for his mother, and in the morning, it was true, he had made a shambles of the room—fouled the floor, and pulled off the tablecloth together with a ketchup bottle, so that thick gore lay everywhere. At breakfast, the lodgers confessed they had had a most amusing night, for it had actually been funny the way the dog had been determined not to let anyone get a wink of sleep. After that first night, Laddy slept in our room, receiving from us, all through our delighted, sleepless nights, pats and embraces and kisses and whispers. He was our baby, our best friend, the smartest, prettiest, nicest dog in the entire wide world. Our soft and rapid blandishments excited him to yelp at us in pleased bewilderment, and then we would playfully grasp his muzzle, so that he would snarl, deep in his throat like an adult dog, and shake his head violently, and, when we freed him, nip us smartly with great good will.

He was an intelligent and genial dog and we trained him quickly. He steered clear of Gran's radishes and lettuce after she had several times given him a brisk comeuppance with a strap across the rump, and he soon left off chewing shoes and the laundry on the line, and he outgrew his babyish whining. He grew like a weed; he lost his spherical softness, and his coat, which had been sooty fluff, came in stiff and rusty black; his nose grew aristocratically long, and his clever, pointed ears stood at attention. He was all bronzy, lustrous black except for an Elizabethan ruff of white and a tip of white at the end of his perky tail. No one could deny that he was exceptionally handsome and that he had, as well, great personal charm and style. He escorted Daisy and me to school in the morning, laughing interiorly out of the enormous pleasure of his life as he gracefully cantered ahead of us, distracted occasionally by his private interest in smells or unfamiliar beings in the grass but, on the whole, engrossed in his role of chaperon. He made friends easily with other dogs, and sometimes he went for a long hunting weekend into the mountains with a huge and bossy old red hound named Mess, who had been on the county most of his life and had made a good thing of it, particularly at the fire station.

It was after one of these three-day excursions into the high country that Gran took Laddy in hand. He had come back spent and filthy, his coat a mass of cockleburs and ticks, his eyes bloodshot, loud *râles* in his chest; for half a day he lay motionless before the front door like someone in a hangover, his groaning eyes explicitly saying "Oh, for God's sake, leave me be" when we offered him food or bowls of water. Gran was disapproving, then affronted, and finally furious. Not, of course, with Laddy, since all inmates of her house enjoyed immunity, but with Mess, whose caddish character, together with that of his nominal masters, the firemen, she examined closely under a strong light, with an air of detachment, with her not caring but her having, all the same, to laugh. A lodger who occupied the back west room had something to say about the fire chief and his nocturnal visits to a certain house occupied by a certain group of young women, too near the same age to be sisters and too old to be the daughters of the woman who claimed to be their mother. What a story! The ex-ophthalmic librarian—she lived in one of the front rooms—had some interesting insinuations to make about the deputy marshal, who had borrowed, significantly, she thought, a book on hypnotism. She also knew—she was, of course, in a most useful position in the town, and from her authoritative pen in the middle of the library her mammiform and azure eyes and her eager ears missed nothing—that the fire chief's wife was not as scrupulous as she might be when she was keeping score on bridge night at the Sorosis.

There was little at the moment that Mrs. Placer and her disciples could do to save the souls of the Fire Department and their families, and therefore save the town from holocaust (a very timid boarder—a Mr. Beaver, a newcomer who was not to linger long—had sniffed throughout this recitative as if he were smelling burning flesh), but at least the unwholesome bond between Mess and Laddy could and would be severed once and for all. Gran looked across the porch at Laddy, who lay stretched at full length in the darkest corner, shuddering and baying abortively in his throat as he chased jack rabbits in his dreams, and she said, "A dog can have morals like a human." With this declaration Laddy's randy, manly holidays were finished. It may have been telepathy that woke him; he lifted his heavy head from his paws, laboriously got up, hesitated for a moment, and then padded languidly across the porch to Gran. He stood docilely beside her chair, head down, tail drooping as if to say, "O.K., Mrs. Placer, show me how and I'll walk the straight and narrow."

The very next day, Gran changed Laddy's name to Caesar, as being more dignified, and a joke was made at the supper table that he had come, seen, and conquered Mrs. Placer's heart—for within her circle, where the magnanimity she lavished upon her orphans was daily demonstrated, Mrs. Placer's heart was highly thought of. On that day also, although we did not know it yet, Laddy ceased to be our dog. Before many weeks passed, indeed, he ceased to be anyone we had ever known. A week or so after he became Caesar, he took up residence in her room, sleeping alongside her bed. She broke him of the habit of taking us to school (temptation of low living was rife along those streets; there was a chow—well, never mind) by the simple expedient of chaining him to a tree as soon as she got up in the morning. This discipline, together with the stamina-building cuffs she gave his sensitive ears from time to time, gradually but certainly remade his character. From a sanguine, affectionate, easygoing Gael (with the fits of melancholy that alternated with the larkiness), he turned into an overbearing, military, efficient, loud-voiced Teuton. His bark, once wide of range, narrowed to one dark, glottal tone.

Soon the paper boy flatly refused to serve our house after Caesar efficiently removed the bicycle clip from his pants leg; the skin was not broken, or even bruised, but it was a matter of principle with the boy. The milkman approached the back door in a seizure of shakes like St. Vitus's dance. The metermen, the coal men, and the garbage collector crossed themselves if they were Catholics and, if they were not, tried whistling in the dark. "Good boy, good Caesar," they carolled, and, unctuously lying, they said they knew his bark was worse than his bite, knowing full well that it was not, considering the very nasty nip, requiring stitches, he had given a representative of the Olson Rug Company, who had had the folly to pat him on the head. Caesar did not molest the lodgers, but he disdained them and he did not brook being personally addressed by anyone except Gran. One night, he wandered into the dining room, appearing to be in search of something he had mislaid, and, for some reason that no one was ever able to divine, suddenly stood stock-still and gave the easily upset Mr. Beaver a long and penetrating look. Mr. Beaver, trembling from head to toe, stammered, "Why—er, hello there, Caesar, old boy, old boy," and Caesar charged. For a moment, it was touch and go, but Gran saved Mr. Beaver, only to lose him an hour later when he departed, bag and baggage, for the Y.M.C.A. This rout and the consequent loss of revenue would more than likely have meant Caesar's downfall and his deportation to the pound if it had not been that a newly widowed druggist, very irascible and very much Gran's style, had applied for a room in her house a week or so before, and now he moved in delightedly, as if he were coming home.

Finally, the police demanded that Caesar be muzzled and they warned that if he committed any major crime again—they cited the case of the Olson man—he would be shot on sight. Mrs. Placer, although she had ɪ respect for the law, knowing as much as she did about its agents, obeyed. She obeyed, that is, in part; she put the muzzle on Caesar for a few hours a day, usually early in the morning when the traffic waᵉ light and before the deliveries had started, but the rest of the time his powerful jaws and dazzling white sabre teeth were free and snapping. There was between these two such preternatural rapport, such an impressive conjugation of suspicion, that he, sensing the approach of a policeman, could convey instantly to her the immediate necessity of clapping his nose cage on. And the policeman, sent out on the complaint of a terrorized neighbor, would be greeted by this law-abiding pair at the door.

Daisy and I wished we were dead. We were divided between hating Caesar and loving Laddy, and we could not give up the hope that something, someday, would change him back into the loving animal he had been before he was appointed vice-president of the Placerites. Now at the meetings after supper on the porch he took an active part, standing rigidly at Gran's side except when she sent him on an errand. He carried out these assignments not with the air of a servant but with that of an accomplice. "Get me the paper, Caesar," she would say to him, and he, dismayingly intelligent and a shade smart-alecky, would open the screen door by himself and in a minute come back with the *Bulletin*, from which Mrs. Placer would then read an item, like the Gospel of the day, and then read between the lines of it, scandalized.

In the deepening of our woe and our bereavement and humiliation, we mutely appealed to Mr. Murphy. We did not speak outright to him, for Mr. Murphy lived in a state of indirection, and often when he used the pronoun "I," he seemed to be speaking of someone standing a little to the left of him, but we went to see him and his animals each day during the sad summer, taking what comfort we could from the cozy, quiet indolence of his back yard, where small black eyes encountered ours politely and everyone was half asleep. When Mr.

Murphy inquired about Laddy in his bland, inattentive way, looking for a stratagem whereby to shift the queen of hearts into position by the king, we would say, "Oh, he's fine," or "Laddy is a nifty dog." And Mr. Murphy, reverently slaking the thirst that was his talent and his concubine, would murmur, "I'm glad."

We wanted to tell him, we wanted his help, or at least his sympathy, but how could we cloud his sunny world? It was awful to see Mr. Murphy ruffled. Up in the calm clouds as he generally was, he could occasionally be brought to earth with a thud, as we had seen and heard one day. Not far from his house, there lived a bad, trouble-making boy of twelve, who was forever hanging over the fence trying to teach the parrot obscene words. He got nowhere, for she spoke no English and she would flabbergast him with her cold eye and sneer, "*Tant pis.*" One day, this boorish fellow went too far; he suddenly shot his head over the fence like a jack-in-the-box and aimed a water pistol at the skunk's face. Mr. Murphy leaped to his feet in a scarlet rage; he picked up a stone and threw it accurately, hitting the boy square in the back, so hard that he fell right down in a mud puddle and lay there kicking and squalling and, as it turned out, quite badly hurt. "If you ever come back here again, I'll kill you!" roared Mr. Murphy. I think he meant it, for I have seldom seen an anger so resolute, so brilliant, and so voluble. "How dared he!" he cried, scrambling into Mallow's cage to hug and pet and soothe her. "He must be absolutely mad! He must be the Devil!" He did not go back to his game after that but paced the yard, swearing a blue streak and only pausing to croon to his animals, now as frightened by him as they had been by the intruder, and to drink straight from the bottle, not bothering with fixings. We were fascinated by this unfamiliar side of Mr. Murphy, but we did not want to see it ever again, for his face had grown so dangerously purple and the veins of his forehead seemed ready to burst and his eyes looked scorched. He was the closest thing to a maniac we had ever seen. So we did not tell him about Laddy; what he did not know would not hurt him, although it was hurting us, throbbing in us like a great, bleating wound.

But eventually Mr. Murphy heard about our dog's conversion, one night at the pool hall, which he visited from time to time when he was seized with a rare but compelling garrulity, and the next afternoon when he asked us how Laddy was and we replied that he was fine, he tranquilly told us, as he deliberated whether to move the jack of clubs now or to bide his time, that we were sweet girls but we were lying in our teeth. He did not seem at all angry but only interested, and all the while he questioned us, he went on about his business with the gin and the hearts and spades and diamonds and clubs. It rarely happened that he won the particular game he was playing, but that

day he did, and when he saw all the cards laid out in their ideal pattern, he leaned back, looking disappointed, and he said, "I'm damned."
He then scooped up the cards, in a gesture unusually quick and tidy
for him, stacked them together, and bound them with a rubber band.
Then he began to tell us what he thought of Gran. He grew as loud
and apoplectic as he had been that other time, and though he kept
repeating that he knew *we* were innocent and he put not a shred of
the blame on us, we were afraid he might suddenly change his mind,
and, speechless, we cowered against the monkeys' cage. In dread, the
monkeys clutched the fingers we offered to them and made soft, protesting noises, as if to say, "Oh, stop it, Murphy! Our nerves!"

As quickly as it had started, the tantrum ended. Mr. Murphy paled
to his normal complexion and said calmly that the only practical thing
was to go and have it out with Mrs. Placer. "At once," he added,
although he said he bitterly feared that it was too late and there would
be no exorcising the fiend from Laddy's misused spirit. And because
he had given the dog to us and not to her, he required that we go
along with him, stick up for our rights, stand on our mettle, get up
our Irish, and give the old bitch something to put in her pipe and
smoke.

Oh, it was hot that day! We walked in a kind of delirium through
the simmer, where only the grasshoppers had the energy to move, and
I remember wondering if ether smelled like the gin on Mr. Murphy's
breath. Daisy and I, in one way or another, were going to have our
gizzards cut out along with our hearts and our souls and our pride,
and I wished I were as drunk as Mr. Murphy, who swam effortlessly
through the heat, his lips parted comfortably, his eyes half closed.
When we turned in to the path at Gran's house, my blood began to
scald my veins. It was so futile and so dangerous and so absurd. Here
we were on a high moral mission, two draggletailed, gumptionless little
girls and a toper whom no one could take seriously, partly because
he was little more than a gurgling bottle of booze and partly because
of the clothes he wore. He was a sight, as he always was when he was
out of his own yard. There, somehow, in the carefree disorder, his
clothes did not look especially strange, but on the streets of the town,
in the barbershop or the post office or on Gran's path, they were
fantastic. He wore a pair of hound's-tooth pants, old but maintaining
a vehement pattern, and with them he wore a collarless blue flannelette
shirt. His hat was the silliest of all, because it was a derby three sizes
too big. And as if Shannon, too, was a part of his funny-paper costume, the elder capuchin rode on his shoulder, tightly embracing his
thin red neck.

Gran and Caesar were standing side by side behind the screen door,
looking as if they had been expecting us all along. For a moment,

Gran and Mr. Murphy faced each other across the length of weedy brick between the gate and the front porch, and no one spoke. Gran took no notice at all of Daisy and me. She adjusted her eyeglasses, using both hands, and then looked down at Caesar and matter-of-factly asked, "Do you want out?"

Caesar flung himself full-length upon the screen and it sprang open like a jaw. I ran to meet and head him off, and Daisy threw a library book at his head, but he was on Mr. Murphy in one split second and had his monkey off his shoulder and had broken Shannon's neck in two shakes. He would have gone on nuzzling and mauling and growling over the corpse for hours if Gran had not marched out of the house and down the path and slapped him lightly on the flank and said, in a voice that could not have deceived an idiot, "Why, Caesar, you scamp! You've hurt Mr. Murphy's monkey! Aren't you ashamed!"

Hurt the monkey! In one final, apologetic shudder, the life was extinguished from the little fellow. Bloody and covered with slather, Shannon lay with his arms suppliantly stretched over his head, his leather fingers curled into loose, helpless fists. His hind legs and his tail lay limp and helter-skelter on the path. And Mr. Murphy, all of a sudden reeling drunk, burst into the kind of tears that Daisy and I knew well—the kind that time alone could stop. We stood aghast in the dark-red sunset, killed by our horror and our grief for Shannon and our unforgivable disgrace. We stood upright in a dead faint, and an eon passed before Mr. Murphy picked up Shannon's body and wove away, sobbing, "I don't believe it! I don't *believe* it!"

The very next day, again at morbid, heavy sunset, Caesar died in violent convulsions, knocking down two tall hollyhocks in his throes. Long after his heart had stopped, his right hind leg continued to jerk in aimless reflex. Madly methodical, Mr. Murphy had poisoned some meat for him, had thoroughly envenomed a whole pound of hamburger, and early in the morning, before sunup, when he must have been near collapse with his hangover, he had stolen up to Mrs. Placer's house and put it by the kitchen door. He was so stealthy that Caesar never stirred in his fool's paradise there on the floor by Gran. We knew these to be the facts, for Mr. Murphy made no bones about them. Afterward, he had gone home and said a solemn Requiem for Shannon in so loud a voice that someone sent for the police, and they took him away in the Black Maria to sober him up on strong green tea. By the time he was in the lockup and had confessed what he had done, it was far too late, for Caesar had already gulped down the meat. He suffered an undreamed-of agony in Gran's flower garden, and Daisy and I, unable to bear the sight of it, hiked up to the red rocks and shook there, wretchedly ripping to shreds the sand lilies that grew in the cracks. Flight was the only thing we could think of, but where could we go? We stared west at the mountains and quailed at the look of the stern white glacier; we wildly scanned the prairies for escape. "If only we were something besides kids! Besides girls!" mourned Daisy. I could not speak at all; I huddled in a niche of the rocks and cried.

No one in town, except, of course, her lodgers, had the slightest sympathy for Gran. The townsfolk allowed that Mr. Murphy was a drunk and was fighting Irish, but he had a heart and this was something that could never be said of Mrs. Placer. The neighbor who had called the police when he was chanting the "Dies Irae" before breakfast in that deafening monotone had said, "The poor guy is having some kind of a spell, so don't be rough on him, hear?" Mr. Murphy became, in fact, a kind of hero; some people, stretching a point, said he was a saint for the way that every day and twice on Sunday he sang a memorial Mass over Shannon's grave, now marked with a chipped, cheap plaster figure of Saint Francis. He withdrew from the world more and more, seldom venturing into the streets at all, except when he went to the bootlegger to get a new bottle to snuggle into. All summer, all fall, we saw him as we passed by his yard, sitting at his dilapidated table, enfeebled with gin, graying, withering, turning his head ever and ever more slowly as he maneuvered the protocol of the kings and the queens and the knaves. Daisy and I could never stop to visit him again.

It went on like this, year after year. Daisy and I lived in a mesh of lies and evasions, baffled and mean, like rats in a maze. When we were old enough for beaux, we connived like sluts to see them, but we would never admit to their existence until Gran caught us out by some trick. Like this one, for example: Once, at the end of a long interrogation, she said to me, "I'm more relieved than I can tell you that you *don't* have anything to do with Jimmy Gilmore, because I happen to know that he is after only one thing in a girl," and then, off guard in the loving memory of sitting in the movies the night before with Jimmy, not even holding hands, I defended him and defeated myself, and Gran, smiling with success, said, "I *thought* you knew him. It's a pretty safe rule of thumb that where there's smoke there's fire." That finished Jimmy and me, for afterward I was nervous with him and I confounded and alarmed and finally bored him by trying to convince him, although the subject had not come up, that I did not doubt his good intentions.

Daisy and I would come home from school, or, later, from our jobs, with a small triumph or an interesting piece of news, and if we forgot ourselves and, in our exuberance, told Gran, we were hustled into court at once for cross-examination. Once, I remember, while I was still in high school, I told her about getting a part in a play. How very nice for me, she said, if that kind of make-believe seemed to me worth while. But what was my role? An old woman! A widow woman believed to be a witch? She did not care a red cent, but she did have to laugh in view of the fact that Miss Eccles, in charge of dramatics, had almost run her down in her car. And I would forgive her, would I not, if she did not come to see the play, and would not think her eccentric for not wanting to see herself ridiculed in public?

My pleasure strangled, I crawled, joy-killed, to our third-floor room. The room was small and its monstrous furniture was too big and the rag rugs were repulsive, but it was bright. We would not hang a blind at the window, and on this day I stood there staring into the mountains that burned with the sun. I feared the mountains, but at times like this their massiveness consoled me; they, at least, could not be gossiped about.

Why did we stay until we were grown? Daisy and I ask ourselves this question as we sit here on the bench in the municipal zoo, reminded of Mr. Murphy by the polar bear, reminded by the monkeys not of Shannon but of Mrs. Placer's insatiable gossips at their postprandial feast.

"But how could we have left?" says Daisy, wringing her buttery hands. "It was the depression. We had no money. We had nowhere to go."

"All the same, we could have gone," I say, resentful still of the waste of all those years. "We could have come here and got jobs as waitresses. Or prostitutes, for that matter."

"I wouldn't have wanted to be a prostitute," says Daisy.

We agree that under the circumstances it would have been impossible for us to run away. The physical act would have been simple, for the city was not far and we could have stolen the bus fare or hitched a ride. Later, when we began to work as salesgirls in Kress's it would have been no trick at all to vanish one Saturday afternoon with our week's pay, without so much as going home to say goodbye. But it had been infinitely harder than that, for Gran, as we now see, held us trapped by our sense of guilt. We were vitiated, and we had no choice but to wait, flaccidly, for her to die.

You may be sure we did not unlearn those years as soon as we put her out of sight in the cemetery and sold her house for a song to the first boob who would buy it. Nor did we forget when we left the town for another one, where we had jobs at a dude camp—the town where Daisy now lives with a happy husband and two happy sons. The succubus did not relent for years, and I can still remember, in the beginning of our days at the Lazy S 3, overhearing an edgy millionaire say to his wife, naming my name, "That girl gives me the cold shivers. One would think she had just seen a murder." Well,

I had. For years, whenever I woke in the night in fear or pain or loneliness, I would increase my suffering by the memory of Shannon, and my tears were as bitter as poor Mr. Murphy's.

We have never been back to Adams. But we see that house plainly, with the hopvines straggling over the porch. The windows are hung with the cheapest grade of marquisette, dipped into coffee to impart to it an unwilling color, neither white nor tan but individual and spitefully unattractive. We see the wicker rockers and the swing, and through the screen door we dimly make out the slightly veering corridor, along one wall of which stands a glass-doored bookcase; when we were children, it had contained not books but stale old cardboard boxes filled with such things as W.C.T.U. tracts and anticigarette literature and newspaper clippings related to sexual sin in the Christianized islands of the Pacific.

Even if we were able to close our minds' eyes to the past, Mr. Murphy would still be before us in the apotheosis of the polar bear. My pain becomes intolerable, and I am relieved when Daisy rescues us. "We've got to go," she says in a sudden panic. "I've got asthma coming on." We rush to the nearest exit of the city park and hail a cab, and, once inside it, Daisy gives herself an injection of adrenalin and then leans back. We are heartbroken and infuriated, and we cannot speak.

Two hours later, beside my train, we clutch each other as if we were drowning. We ought to go out to the nearest policeman and say, "We are not responsible women. You will have to take care of us because we cannot take care of ourselves." But gradually the storm begins to lull.

"You're sure you've got your ticket?" says Daisy. "You'll surely be able to get a roomette once you're on."

"I don't know about that," I say. "If there are any V.I.P.s on board, I won't have a chance. 'Spinsters and Orphans Last' is the motto of this line."

Daisy smiles. "I didn't care," she says, "but I had to laugh when I saw that woman nab the redcap you had signalled to. I had a good notion to give her a piece of my mind."

"It will be a miracle if I ever see my bags again," I say, mounting the steps of the train. "Do you suppose that blackguardly porter knows about the twenty-dollar gold piece in my little suitcase?"

"Anything's possible!" cries Daisy, and begins to laugh. She is so pretty, standing there in her bright-red linen suit and her black velvet hat. A solitary ray of sunshine comes through a broken pane in the domed vault of the train shed and lies on her shoulder like a silver arrow.

"So long, Daisy!" I call as the train begins to move.

She walks quickly along beside the train. "Watch out for pick-pockets!" she calls.

"You, too!" My voice is thin and lost in the increasing noise of the speeding train wheels. "Goodbye, old dear!"

I go at once to the club car and I appropriate the writing table, to the vexation of a harried priest, who snatches up the telegraph pad and gives me a sharp look. I write Daisy approximately the same letter I always write her under this particular set of circumstances, the burden of which is that nothing for either of us can ever be as bad as the past before Gran mercifully died. In a postscript I add: "There is a Roman Catholic priest (that is to say, he is *dressed* like one) sitting behind me although all the chairs on the opposite side of the car are empty. I can only conclude that he is looking over my shoulder, and while I do not want to cause you any alarm, I think you would be advised to be on the lookout for any appearance of miraculous medals, scapulars, papist booklets, etc., in the shops in your town. It really makes me laugh to see the way he is pretending that all he wants is for me to finish this letter so that he can have the table."

I sign my name and address the envelope, and I give up my place to the priest, who smiles nicely at me, and then I move across the car to watch the fields as they slip by. They are alfalfa fields, but you can bet your bottom dollar that they are chockablock with marijuana.

I begin to laugh. The fit is silent but it is devastating; it surges and rattles in my rib cage, and I turn face to the window to avoid the narrow gaze of the Filipino bar boy. I must think of something sad to stop this unholy giggle, and I think of the polar bear. But even his bleak tragedy does not sober me. Wildly I fling open the newspaper I have brought and I pretend to be reading something screamingly funny. The words I see are in a Hollywood gossip column: "How a well-known starlet can get a divorce in Nevada without her crooner husband's consent, nobody knows. It won't be worth a plugged nickel here."

REVELATION

FLANNERY O'CONNOR

The doctor's waiting room, which was very small, was almost full when the Turpins entered and Mrs. Turpin, who was very large, made it look even smaller by her presence. She stood looming at the head of the magazine table set in the center of it, a living demonstration that the room was inadequate and ridiculous. Her little bright black eyes took in all the patients as she sized up the seating situation. There was one vacant chair and a place on the sofa occupied by a blond child in a dirty blue romper who should have been told to move over and make room for the lady. He was five or six, but Mrs. Turpin saw at once that no one was going to tell him to move over. He was

FLANNERY O'CONNOR, winner of innumerable prizes for her short fiction, wrote two novels, *Wise Blood* and *The Violent Bear It Away*. Her short story collections are *A Good Man Is Hard to Find* and *Everything That Rises Must Converge*. In 1969 a collection of her "occasional prose" was published posthumously, under the title *Mystery and Manners*.

169

slumped down in the seat, his arms idle at his sides and his eyes idle in his head; his nose ran unchecked.

Mrs. Turpin put a firm hand on Claud's shoulder and said in a voice that included anyone who wanted to listen, "Claud, you sit in that chair there," and gave him a push down into the vacant one. Claud was florid and bald and sturdy, somewhat shorter than Mrs. Turpin, but he sat down as if he were accustomed to doing what she told him to.

Mrs. Turpin remained standing. The only man in the room besides Claud was a lean stringy old fellow with a rusty hand spread out on each knee, whose eyes were closed as if he were asleep or dead or pretending to be so as not to get up and offer her his seat. Her gaze settled agreeably on a well-dressed grey-haired lady whose eyes met hers and whose expression said: if that child belonged to me, he would have some manners and move over—there's plenty of room there for you and him too.

Claud looked up with a sigh and made as if to rise.

"Sit down," Mrs. Turpin said. "You know you're not supposed to stand on that leg. He has an ulcer on his leg," she explained.

Claud lifted his foot onto the magazine table and rolled his trouser leg up to reveal a purple swelling on a plump marble-white calf.

"My!" the pleasant lady said. "How did you do that?"

"A cow kicked him," Mrs. Turpin said.

"Goodness!" said the lady.

Claud rolled his trouser leg down.

"Maybe the little boy would move over," the lady suggested, but the child did not stir.

"Somebody will be leaving in a minute," Mrs. Turpin said. She could not understand why a doctor—with as much money as they made charging five dollars a day to just stick their head in the hospital door and look at you—couldn't afford a decent-sized waiting room. This one was hardly bigger than a garage. The table was cluttered with limp-looking magazines and at one end of it there was a big green glass ash tray full of cigaret butts and cotton wads with little blood spots on them. If she had had anything to do with the running of the place, that would have been emptied every so often. There were no chairs against the wall at the head of the room. It had a rectangular shaped panel in it that permitted a view of the office where the nurse came and went and the secretary listened to the radio. A plastic fern in a gold pot sat in the opening and trailed its fronds down almost to the floor. The radio was softly playing gospel music.

Just then the inner door opened and a nurse with the highest stack of yellow hair Mrs. Turpin had ever seen put her face in the crack and called for the next patient. The woman sitting beside Claud grasped the two arms of her chair and hoisted herself up; she pulled her dress free from her legs and lumbered through the door where the nurse had disappeared.

Mrs. Turpin eased into the vacant chair, which held her tight as a corset. "I wish I could reduce," she said, and rolled her eyes and gave a comic sigh.

"Oh, *you* aren't fat," the stylish lady said.

"Ooooo I am too," Mrs. Turpin said. "Claud he eats all he wants to and never weighs over one hundred and seventy-five pounds, but me I just look at something good to eat and I gain some weight," and her stomach and shoulders shook with laughter. "You can eat all you want to, can't you, Claud?" she asked, turning to him.

Claud only grinned.

"Well, as long as you have such a good disposition," the stylish lady said, "I don't think it makes a bit of difference what size you are. You just can't beat a good disposition."

Next to her was a fat girl of eighteen or nineteen, scowling into a thick blue book which Mrs. Turpin saw was entitled *Human Development*. The girl raised her head and directed her scowl at Mrs. Turpin as if she did not like her looks. She appeared annoyed that anyone should speak while she tried to read. The poor girl's face was blue with acne and Mrs. Turpin thought how pitiful it was to have a face like that at that age. She gave the girl a friendly smile but the girl only scowled the harder. Mrs. Turpin herself was fat but she had always had good skin, and, though she was forty-seven years old, there was not a wrinkle in her face except around her eyes from laughing too much.

Next to the ugly girl was the child, still in exactly the same position, and next to him was a thin leathery old woman in a cotton print dress. She and Claud had three sacks of chicken feed in their pump house that was in the same print. She had seen from the first that the child belonged with the old woman. She could tell by the way they sat—kind of vacant and white-trashy, as if they would sit there until Doomsday if nobody called and told them to get up. And at right angles but next to the well-dressed pleasant lady was a lank-faced woman who was certainly the child's mother. She had on a yellow sweat shirt and wine-colored slacks, both gritty-looking, and the rims of her lips were stained with snuff. Her dirty yellow hair was tied behind with a little piece of red paper ribbon. Worse than niggers any day, Mrs. Turpin thought.

The gospel hymn playing was, "When I looked up and He looked down," and Mrs. Turpin, who knew it, supplied the last line mentally, "And wona these days I know I'll we-eara crown."

Without appearing to, Mrs. Turpin always noticed people's feet. The well-dressed lady had on red and grey suede shoes to match her dress. Mrs. Turpin had on her good black patent leather pumps. The ugly girl had on Girl Scout shoes and heavy socks. The old woman had on tennis shoes and the white-trashy mother had on what appeared to be bedroom slippers, black straw with gold braid threaded through them—exactly what you would have expected her to have on.

Sometimes at night when she couldn't go to sleep, Mrs. Turpin would occupy herself with the question of who she would have chosen to be if she couldn't have been herself. If Jesus had said to her before he made her, "There's only two places available for you. You can either be a nigger or white-trash," what would she have said? "Please, Jesus, please," she would have said, "just let me wait until there's another place available," and he would have said, "No, you have to go right now and I have only those two places so make up your mind." She would have wiggled and squirmed and begged and pleaded but it would have been no use and finally she would have said, "All right, make me a nigger then—but that don't mean a trashy one." And he would have made her a neat clean respectable negro woman, herself but black.

Next to the child's mother was a red-headed youngish woman, reading one of the magazines and working on a piece of chewing gum, hell for leather, as Claud would say. Mrs. Turpin could not see the woman's feet. She was not white-trash, just common. Sometimes Mrs. Turpin occupied herself at night naming the classes of people. On the bottom of the heap were most colored people, not the kind she would have been if she had been one, but most of them; then next to them—not above, just away from—were the white-trash; then above them were the home-owners, and above them the home-and-land owners, to which she and Claud belonged. Above she and Claud were people with a lot of money and much bigger houses and much more land. But here the complexity of it would begin to bear in on her, for some of the people with a lot of money were common and ought to be below she and Claud and some of the people who had good blood had lost their money and had to rent and then there were colored people who owned their homes and land as well. There was a colored dentist in town who had two red Lincolns and a swimming pool and a farm with registered white-face cattle on it. Usually by the time she had fallen asleep all the classes of people were moiling and roiling around in her head, and she would dream they were all crammed in together in a box car, being ridden off to be put in a gas oven.

"That's a beautiful clock," she said and nodded to her right. It was a big wall clock, the face encased in a brass sunburst.

"Yes, it's very pretty," the stylish lady said agreeably. "And right on the dot too," she added, glancing at her watch.

The ugly girl beside her cast an eye upward at the clock, smirked, then looked directly at Mrs. Turpin and smirked again. Then she returned her eyes to her book. She was obviously the lady's daughter because, although they didn't look anything alike as to disposition, they both had the same shape of face and the same blue eyes. On the lady they sparkled pleasantly but in the girl's seared face they appeared alternately to smolder and to blaze.

What if Jesus had said, "All right, you can be white-trash or a nigger or ugly!"

Mrs. Turpin felt an awful pity for the girl, though she thought it was one thing to be ugly and another to act ugly.

The woman with the snuff-stained lips turned around in her chair and looked up at the clock. Then she turned back and appeared to look a little to the side of Mrs. Turpin. There was a cast in one of her eyes. "You want to know wher you can get you one of themther clocks?" she asked in a loud voice.

"No, I already have a nice clock," Mrs. Turpin said. Once somebody like her got a leg in the conversation, she would be all over it.

"You can get you one with green stamps," the woman said. "That's most likely wher he got hisn. Save you up enough, you can get you most anythang. I got me some joo'ry."

Ought to have got you a wash rag and some soap, Mrs. Turpin thought.

"I get contour sheets with mine," the pleasant lady said.

The daughter slammed her book shut. She looked straight in front of her, directly through Mrs. Turpin and on through the yellow curtain and the plate glass window which made the wall behind her. The girl's eyes seemed lit all of a sudden with a peculiar light, an unnatural light like night road signs give. Mrs. Turpin turned her head to see if there was anything going on outside that she should see, but she could not see anything. Figures passing cast only a pale shadow through the curtain. There was no reason the girl should single her out for her ugly looks.

"Miss Finley," the nurse said, cracking the floor. The gum-chewing woman got up and passed in front of her and Claud and went into the office. She had on red high-heeled shoes.

Directly across the table, the ugly girl's eyes were fixed on Mrs. Turpin as if she had some very special reason for disliking her.

"This is wonderful weather, isn't it?" the girl's mother said.

"It's good weather for cotton if you can get the niggers to pick it," Mrs. Turpin said, "but niggers don't want to pick cotton any more. You can't get the white folks to pick it and now you can't get the niggers—because they got to be right up there with the white folks."

"They gonna *try* anyways," the white-trash woman said, leaning forward.

"Do you have one of those cotton-picking machines?" the pleasant lady asked.

"No," Mrs. Turpin said, "they leave half the cotton in the field. We don't have much cotton anyway. If you want to make it farming now, you have to have a little of everything. We got a couple of acres of cotton and a few hogs and chickens and just enough white-face that Claud can look after them himself."

"One thang I don't want," the white-trash woman said, wiping her mouth with the back of her hand. "Hogs. Nasty stinking things, a-gruntin and a-rootin all over the place."

Mrs. Turpin gave her the merest edge of her attention. "Our hogs are not dirty and they don't stink," she said. "They're cleaner than some children I've seen. Their feet never touch the ground. We have a pig-parlor—that's where you raise them on concrete," she explained to the pleasant lady, "and Claud scoots them down with the hose every afternoon and washes off the floor." Cleaner by far than that child right there, she thought. Poor nasty little thing. He had not moved except to put the thumb of his dirty hand into his mouth.

The woman turned her face away from Mrs. Turpin. "I know I wouldn't scoot down no hog with no hose," she said to the wall.

You wouldn't have no hog to scoot down, Mrs. Turpin said to herself.

"A-gruntin and a-rootin and a-groanin," the woman muttered.

"We got a little of everything," Mrs. Turpin said to the pleasant lady. "It's no use in having more than you can handle yourself with help like it is. We found enough niggers to pick our cotton this year but Claud he has to go after them and take them home again in the evening. They can't walk that half a mile. No they can't. I tell you," she said and laughed merrily, "I sure am tired of buttering up niggers, but you got to love em if you want em to work for you. When they come in the morning, I run out and I say, 'Hi yawl this morning?' and when Claud drives them off to the field I just wave to beat the band and they just wave back." And she waved her hand rapidly to illustrate.

"Like you read out of the same book," the lady said, showing she understood perfectly.

"Child, yes," Mrs. Turpin said. "And when they come in from the field, I run out with a bucket of icewater. That's the way it's going to be from now on," she said. "You may as well face it."

"One thang I know," the white-trash woman said. "Two thangs I ain't going to do: love no niggers or scoot down no hog with no hose." And she let out a bark of contempt.

The look that Mrs. Turpin and the pleasant lady exchanged indicated they both understood that you had to *have* certain things before you could *know* certain things. But every time Mrs. Turpin exchanged a look with the lady, she was aware that the ugly girl's peculiar eyes were still on her, and she had trouble bringing her attention back to the conversation.

"When you got something," she said, "you got to look after it." And when you ain't got a thing but breath and britches, she added to herself, you can afford to come to town every morning and just sit on the Court House coping and spit.

A grotesque revolving shadow passed across the curtain behind her and was thrown palely on the opposite wall. Then a bicycle clattered down against the outside of the building. The door opened and a colored boy glided in with a tray from the drug store. It had two large red and white paper cups on it with tops on them. He was a tall, very black boy in discolored white pants and a green nylon shirt. He was chewing gum slowly, as if to music. He set the tray down in the office opening next to the fern and stuck his head through to look for the secretary. She was not in there. He rested his arms on the ledge and waited, his narrow bottom stuck out, swaying slowly to the left and right. He raised a hand over his head and scratched the base of his skull.

"You see that button there, boy?" Mrs. Turpin said. "You can punch that and she'll come. She's probably in the back somewhere."

"Is that right?" the boy said agreeably, as if he had never seen the button before. He leaned to the right and put his finger on it. "She sometime out," he said and twisted around to face his audience, his elbows behind him on the counter. The nurse appeared and he twisted back again. She handed him a dollar and he rooted in his pocket and made the change and counted it out to her. She gave him fifteen cents for a tip and he went out with the empty tray. The heavy door swung to slowly and closed at length with the sound of suction. For a moment no one spoke.

"They ought to send all them niggers back to Africa," the white-trash woman said. "That's wher they come from in the first place."

"Oh, I couldn't do without my good colored friends," the pleasant lady said.

"There's a heap of things worse than a nigger," Mrs. Turpin agreed. "It's all kinds of them just like it's all kinds of us."

"Yes, and it takes all kinds to make the world go round," the lady said in her musical voice.

As she said it, the raw-complexioned girl snapped her teeth together. Her lower lip turned downwards and inside out, revealing the pale pink inside of her mouth. After a second it rolled back up. It was the ugliest face Mrs. Turpin had ever seen anyone make and for a moment she was certain that the girl had made it at her. She was looking at her as if she had known and disliked her all her life—all of Mrs. Turpin's life, it seemed too, not just all the girl's life. Why, girl, I don't even know you, Mrs. Turpin said silently.

She forced her attention back to the discussion. "It wouldn't be practical to send them back to Africa," she said. "They wouldn't want to go. They got it too good here."

"Wouldn't be what they wanted—if I had anythang to do with it," the woman said.

"It wouldn't be a way in the world you could get all the niggers back over there," Mrs. Turpin said. "They'd be hiding out and lying down and turning sick on you and wailing and hollering and raring and pitching. It wouldn't be a way in the world to get them over there."

"They got over here," the trashy woman said. "Get back like they got over."

"It wasn't so many of them then," Mrs. Turpin explained.

The woman looked at Mrs. Turpin as if here was an idiot indeed but Mrs. Turpin was not bothered by the look, considering where it came from.

"Nooo," she said, "they're going to stay here where they can go to New York and marry white folks and improve their color. That's what they all want to do, every one of them, improve their color."

"You know what comes of that, don't you?" Claud asked.

"No, Claud, what?" Mrs. Turpin said.

Claud's eyes twinkled. "White-faced niggers," he said with never a smile.

Everybody in the office laughed except the white-trash and the ugly girl. The girl gripped the book in her lap with white fingers. The trashy woman looked around her from face to face as if she thought they were all idiots. The old woman in the feed sack dress continued to gaze expressionless across the floor at the high-top shoes of the man opposite her, the one who had been pretending to be asleep when the Turpins came in. He was laughing heartily, his hands still spread out on his knees. The child had fallen to the side and was lying now almost face down in the old woman's lap.

While they recovered from their laughter, the nasal chorus on the radio kept the room from silence.

"You go to blank blank
And I'll go to mine
But we'll all blank along
To-geth-ther,

And all along the blank
We'll hep eachother out
Smile-ling in any kind of
Weath-ther!"

Mrs. Turpin didn't catch every word but she caught enough to agree with the spirit of the song and it turned her thoughts sober. To help anybody out that needed it was her philosophy of life. She never spared herself when she found somebody in need, whether they were white or black, trash or decent. And of all she had to be thankful for, she was most thankful that this was so. If Jesus had said, "You can be high society and have all the money you want and be thin and svelte-like, but you can't be a good woman with it," she would have had to say, "Well don't make me that then. Make me a good woman and it don't matter what else, how fat or how ugly or how poor!" Her heart rose. He had not made her a nigger or white-trash or ugly! He had made her herself and given her a little of everything. Jesus, thank you! she said. Thank you thank you thank you! Whenever she counted her blessings she felt as buoyant as if she weighed one hundred and twenty-five pounds instead of one hundred and eighty.

"What's wrong with your little boy?" the pleasant lady asked the white-trashy woman.

"He has a ulcer," the woman said proudly. "He ain't give me a minute's peace since he was born. Him and her are just alike," she said, nodding at the old woman, who was running her leathery fingers through the child's pale hair. "Look like I can't get nothing down them two but Co' Cola and candy."

That's all you try to get down em, Mrs. Turpin said to herself. Too lazy to light the fire. There was nothing you could tell her about people like them that she didn't know already. And it was not just that they didn't have anything. Because if you gave them everything, in two weeks it would all be broken or filthy or they would have chopped it up for lightwood. She knew all this from her own experience. Help them you must, but help them you couldn't.

All at once the ugly girl turned her lips inside out again. Her eyes were fixed like two drills on Mrs. Turpin. This time there was no mistaking that there was something urgent behind them.

Girl, Mrs. Turpin exclaimed silently, I haven't done a thing to you! The girl might be confusing her with somebody else. There was no need to sit by and let herself be intimidated. "You must be in college," she said boldly, looking directly at the girl. "I see you reading a book there."

The girl continued to stare and pointedly did not answer.

Her mother blushed at this rudeness. "The lady asked you a question, Mary Grace," she said under her breath.

"I have ears," Mary Grace said.

The poor mother blushed again. "Mary Grace goes to Wellesley College," she explained. She twisted one of the buttons on her dress. "In Massachusetts," she added with a grimace. "And in the summer she just keeps right on studying. Just reads all the time, a real book worm. She's done real well at Wellesley; she's taking English and Math and History and Psychology and Social Studies," she rattled on, "and I think it's too much. I think she ought to get out and have fun."

The girl looked as if she would like to hurl them all through the plate glass window.

"Way up north," Mrs. Turpin murmured and thought, well, it hasn't done much for her manners.

"I'd almost rather to have him sick," the white-trash woman said, wrenching the attention back to herself. "He's so mean when he ain't. Look like some children just take natural to meanness. It's some gets bad when they get sick but he was the opposite. Took sick and turned good. He don't give me no trouble now. It's me waitin to see the doctor," she said.

If I was going to send anybody back to Africa, Mrs. Turpin thought, it would be your kind, woman. "Yes, indeed," she said aloud, but looking up at the ceiling, "it's a heap of things worse than a nigger." And dirtier than a hog, she added to herself.

"I think people with bad dispositions are more to be pitied than anyone on earth," the pleasant lady said in a voice that was decidedly thin.

"I thank the Lord he has blessed me with a good one," Mrs. Turpin said. "The day has never dawned that I couldn't find something to laugh at."

"Not since she married me anyways," Claud said with a comical straight face.

Everybody laughed except the girl and the white-trash.

Mrs. Turpin's stomach shook. "He's such a caution," she said, "that I can't help but laugh at him."

The girl made a loud ugly noise through her teeth.

Her mother's mouth grew thin and tight. "I think the worst thing in the world," she said, "is an ungrateful person. To have everything and not appreciate it. I know a girl," she said, "who has parents who would give her anything, a little brother who loves her dearly, who is getting a good education, who wears the best clothes, but who can never say a kind word to anyone, who never smiles, who just criticises and complains all day long."

"Is she too old to paddle?" Claud asked.

The girl's face was almost purple.

"Yes," the lady said, "I'm afraid there's nothing to do but leave her to her folly. Some day she'll wake up and it'll be too late."

"It never hurt anyone to smile," Mrs. Turpin said. "It just makes you feel better all over."

"Of course," the lady said sadly, "but there are just some people you can't tell anything to. They can't take criticism."

"If it's one thing I am," Mrs. Turpin said with feeling, "it's grateful. When I think who all I could have been besides myself and what all I got, a little of everything, and a good disposition besides, I just feel like shouting, 'Thank you, Jesus, for making everything the way it is!' It could have been different!" For one thing, somebody else could have got Claud. At the thought of this, she was flooded with gratitude and a terrible pang of joy ran through her. "Oh thank you, Jesus, thank you!" she cried aloud.

The book struck her directly over her left eye. It struck almost at the same instant that she realized the girl was about to hurl it. Before she could utter a sound, the raw face came crashing across the table toward her, howling. The girl's fingers sank like clamps into the soft flesh of her neck. She heard the mother cry out and Claud shout, "Whoa!" There was an instant when she was certain that she was about to be in an earthquake.

All at once her vision narrowed and she saw everything as if it were happening in a small room far away, or as if she were looking at it through the wrong end of a telescope. Claud's face crumpled and fell out of sight. The nurse ran in, then out, then in again. Then the gangling figure of the doctor rushed out of the inner door. Magazines flew this way and that as the table turned over. The girl fell with a thud and Mrs. Turpin's vision suddenly reversed itself and she saw everything large instead of small. The eyes of the white-trashy woman were staring hugely at the floor. There the girl, held down on one side by the nurse and on the other by her mother, was wrenching and turning in their grasp. The doctor was kneeling astride her, trying to hold her arm down. He managed after a second to sink a long needle into it.

Mrs. Turpin felt entirely hollow except for her heart which swung from side to side as if it were agitated in a great empty drum of flesh.

"Somebody that's not busy call for the ambulance," the doctor said in the off-hand voice young doctors adopt for terrible occasions.

Mrs. Turpin could not have moved a finger. The old man who had been sitting next to her skipped nimbly into the office and made the call, for the secretary still seemed to be gone.

"Claud!" Mrs. Turpin called.

He was not in his chair. She knew she must jump up and find him but she felt like some one trying to catch a train in a dream, when everything moves in slow motion and the faster you try to run the slower you go.

"Here I am," a suffocated voice, very unlike Claud's, said.

He was doubled up in the corner on the floor, pale as paper, holding his leg. She wanted to get up and go to him but she could not move. Instead, her gaze was drawn slowly downward to the churning face on the floor, which she could see over the doctor's shoulder.

The girl's eyes stopped rolling and focussed on her. They seemed a much lighter blue than before, as if a door that had been tightly closed behind them was now open to admit light and air.

Mrs. Turpin's head cleared and her power of motion returned. She leaned forward until she was looking directly into the fierce brilliant eyes. There was no doubt in her mind that the girl did know her, knew her in some intense and personal way, beyond time and place and condition. "What you got to say to me?" she asked hoarsely and held her breath, waiting, as for a revelation.

The girl raised her head. Her gaze locked with Mrs. Turpin's. "Go back to hell where you came from, you old wart hog," she whispered. Her voice was low but clear. Her eyes burned for a moment as if she saw with pleasure that her message had struck its target.

Mrs. Turpin sank back in her chair.

After a moment the girl's eyes closed and she turned her head wearily to the side.

The doctor rose and handed the nurse the empty syringe. He leaned over and put both hands for a moment on the mother's shoulders, which were shaking. She was sitting on the floor, her lips pressed together, holding Mary Grace's hand in her lap. The girl's fingers were gripped like a baby's around her thumb. "Go on to the hospital," he said. "I'll call and make the arrangements."

"Now let's see that neck," he said in a jovial voice to Mrs. Turpin. He began to inspect her neck with his first two fingers. Two little moon-shaped lines like pink fish bones were indented over her windpipe. There was the beginning of an angry red swelling above her eye. His fingers passed over this also.

"Lea' me be," she said thickly and shook him off. "See about Claud. She kicked him."

"I'll see about him in a minute," he said and felt her pulse. He was a thin grey-haired young man, given to pleasantries. "Go home and have yourself a vacation the rest of the day," he said and patted her on the shoulder.

Quit your pattin me, Mrs. Turpin growled to herself.

"And put an ice pack over that eye," he said. Then he went and squatted down beside Claud and looked at his leg. After a moment he pulled him up and Claud limped after him into the office.

Until the ambulance came, the only sounds in the room were the tremulous moans of the girl's mother, who continued to sit on the floor. The white-trash woman did not take her eyes off the girl. Mrs. Turpin looked straight ahead at nothing. Presently the ambulance drew up, a long dark shadow, behind the curtain. The attendants came in and set the stretcher down beside the girl and lifted her expertly onto it and carried her out. The nurse helped the mother gather up her things. The shadow of the ambulance moved silently away and the nurse came back in the office.

"That ther girl is going to be a lunatic, ain't she?" the white-trash woman asked the nurse, but the nurse kept on to the back and never answered her.

"Yes, she's going to be a lunatic," the white-trash woman said to the rest of them.

"Po' critter," the old woman murmured. The child's face was still in her lap. His eyes looked idly out over her knees. He had not moved during the disturbance except to draw one leg up under him.

"I thank Gawd," the white-trash woman said fervently, "I ain't a lunatic."

Claud came limping out and the Turpins went home.

As their pick-up truck turned into their own dirt road and made the crest of the hill, Mrs. Turpin gripped the window ledge and looked out suspiciously. The land sloped gracefully down through a field dotted with lavender weeds and at the start of the rise their small yellow frame house, with its little flower beds spread out around it like a fancy apron, sat primly in its accustomed place between two giant hickory trees. She would not have been startled to see a burnt wound between two blackened chimneys.

Neither of them felt like eating so they put on their house clothes and lowered the shade in the bedroom and lay down, Claud with his leg on a pillow and herself with a damp washcloth over her eye. The instant she was flat on her back, the image of a razor-backed hog with warts on its face and horns coming out behind its ears snorted into her head. She moaned, a low quiet moan.

"I am not," she said tearfully, "a wart hog. From hell." But the denial had no force. The girl's eyes and her words, even the tone of her voice, low but clear, directed only to her, brooked no repudiation. She had been singled out for the message, though there was trash in the room to whom it might justly have been applied. The full force of this fact struck her only now. There was a woman there who was neglecting her own child but she had been overlooked. The message had been given to Ruby Turpin, a respectable, hard-working, church-going woman. The tears dried. Her eyes began to burn instead with wrath.

She rose on her elbow and the washcloth fell into her hand. Claud was lying on his back, snoring. She wanted to tell him what the girl had said. At the same time, she did not wish to put the image of herself as a wart hog from hell into his mind.

"Hey, Claud," she muttered and pushed his shoulder.

Claud opened one pale baby blue eye.

She looked into it warily. He did not think about anything. He just went his way.

"Wha, whasit?" he said and closed the eye again.

"Nothing," she said. "Does your leg pain you?"

"Hurts like hell," Claud said.

"It'll quit terreckly," she said and lay back down. In a moment Claud was snoring again. For the rest of the afternoon they lay there. Claud slept. She scowled at the ceiling. Occasionally she raised her fist and made a small stabbing motion over her chest as if she were defending her innocence to invisible guests who were like the comforters of Job, reasonable-seeming but wrong.

About five-thirty Claud stirred. "Got to go after those niggers," he sighed, not moving.

She was looking straight up as if there were unintelligible handwriting on the ceiling. The protuberance over her eye had turned a greenish-blue. "Listen here," she said.

"What?"

"Kiss me."

Claud leaned over and kissed her loudly on the mouth. He pinched her side and their hands interlocked. Her expression of ferocious concentration did not change. Claud got up, groaning and growling, and limped off. She continued to study the ceiling.

She did not get up until she heard the pick-up truck coming back with the negroes. Then she rose and thrust her feet in her brown oxfords, which she did not bother to lace, and stumped out onto the back porch and got her red plastic bucket. She emptied a tray of ice cubes into it and filled it half full of water and went out into the back yard. Every afternoon after Claud brought the hands in, one of the boys helped him put out hay and the rest waited in the back of the truck until he was ready to take them home. The truck was parked in the shade under one of the hickory trees.

"Hi yawl this evening?" Mrs. Turpin asked grimly, appearing with the bucket and the dipper. There were three women and a boy in the truck.

"Us doin nicely," the oldest woman said. "Hi you doin?" and her gaze stuck immediately on the dark lump on Mrs. Turpin's forehead. "You done fell down, ain't you?" she asked in a solicitous voice. The old woman was dark and almost toothless. She had on an old felt hat of Claud's set back on her head. The other two women were younger and lighter and they both had new bright green sun hats. One of them had hers on her head; the other had taken hers off and the boy was grinning beneath it.

Mrs. Turpin set the bucket down on the floor of the truck. "Yawl hep yourselves," she said. She looked around to make sure Claud had gone. "No. I didn't fall down," she said, folding her arms. "It was something worse than that."

"Ain't nothing bad happen to you!" the old woman said. She said it as if they all knew that Mrs. Turpin was protected in some special way by Divine Providence. "You just had you a little fall."

"We were in town at the doctor's office for where the cow kicked Mr. Turpin," Mrs. Turpin said in a flat tone that indicated they could leave off their foolishness. "And there was this girl there. A big fat girl with her face all broke out. I could look at that girl and tell she was peculiar but I couldn't tell how. And me and her mama were just talking and going along and all of a sudden WHAM! She throws this big book she was reading at me and . . ."

"Naw!" the old woman cried out.

"And then she jumps over the table and commences to choke me."

"Naw!" they all exclaimed, "naw!"

"Hi come she do that?" the old woman asked. "What ail her?"

Mrs. Turpin only glared in front of her.

"Somethin ail her," the old woman said.

"They carried her off in an ambulance," Mrs. Turpin continued, "but before she went she was rolling on the floor and they were trying to hold her down to give her a shot and she said something to me." She paused. "You know what she said to me?"

"What she say?" they asked.

"She said," Mrs. Turpin began, and stopped, her face very dark and heavy. The sun was getting whiter and whiter, blanching the sky overhead so that the leaves of the hickory tree were black in the face of it. She could not bring forth the words. "Something real ugly," she muttered.

"She sho shouldn't said nothin ugly to you," the old woman said. "You so sweet. You the sweetest lady I know."

"She pretty too," the one with the hat on said.

"And stout," the other one said. "I never knowed no sweeter white lady."

"That's the truth befo' Jesus," the old woman said. "Amen! You des as sweet and pretty as you can be."

Mrs. Turpin knew just exactly how much negro flattery was worth and it added to her rage. "She said," she began again and finished this time with a fierce rush of breath, "that I was an old wart hog from hell."

There was an astounded silence.

"Where she at!" the youngest woman cried in a piercing voice. "Lemme see her. I'll kill her!"

"I'll kill her with you!" the other one cried.

"She b'long in the sylum," the old woman said emphatically. "You the sweetest white lady I know."

"She pretty too," the other two said. "Stout as she can be and sweet. Jesus satisfied with her!"

"Deed he is," the old woman declared.

Idiots! Mrs. Turpin growled to herself. You could never say anything intelligent to a nigger. You could talk at them but not with them. "Yawl ain't drunk your water," she said shortly. "Leave the bucket in the truck when you're finished with it. I got more to do than just stand around and pass the time of day," and she moved off and into the house.

She stood for a moment in the middle of the kitchen. The dark protuberance over her eye looked like a miniature tornado cloud which might any moment sweep across the horizon of her brow. Her lower lip protruded dangerously. She squared her massive shoulders. Then she marched into the front of the house and out the side door and started down the road to the pig parlor. She had the look of a woman going single-handed, weaponless, into battle.

The sun was a deep yellow now like a harvest moon and was riding westward very fast over the far tree line as if it meant to reach the hogs before she did. The road was rutted and she kicked several good-sized stones out of her path as she strode along. The pig parlor was on a little knoll at the end of a lane that ran off from the side of the barn. It was a square of concrete as large as a small room, with a board fence about four feet high around it. The concrete floor sloped slightly so that the hog wash could drain off into a trench where it was carried to the field for fertilizer. Claud was standing on the outside, on the edge of the concrete, hanging onto the top board, hosing down the floor inside. The hose was connected to the faucet of a water trough nearby.

Mrs. Turpin climbed up beside him and glowered down at the hogs inside. There were seven long-snouted bristly shoats in it—tan with liver-colored spots—and an old sow a few weeks off from farrowing. She was lying on her side grunting. The shoats were running about shaking themselves like idiot children, their little slit pig eyes searching the floor for anything left. She had read that pigs were the most intelligent animal. She doubted it. They were supposed to be smarter than dogs. There had even been a pig astronaut. He had performed his assignment perfectly but died of a heart attack afterwards because they left him in his electric suit, sitting upright throughout his examination when naturally a hog should be on all fours.

A-gruntin and a-rootin and a-groanin.

"Gimme that hose," she said, yanking it away from Claud. "Go on and carry them niggers home and then get off that leg."

"You look like you might have swallowed a mad dog," Claud observed, but he got down and limped off. He paid no attention to her humors.

Until he was out of earshot, Mrs. Turpin stood on the side of the pen, holding the hose and pointing the stream of water at the hind quarters of any shoat that looked as if it might try to lie down. When he had had time to get over the hill, she turned her head slightly and wrathful eyes scanned the path. He was nowhere in sight. She turned back again and seemed to gather herself up. Her shoulders rose and she drew in her breath.

"What do you send me a message like that for?" she said in a low fierce voice, barely above a whisper but with the force of a shout in its concentrated fury. "How am I a hog and me both? How am I saved and from hell too?" Her free fist was knotted and with the other she gripped the hose, blindly pointing the stream of water in and out of the eye of the old sow whose outraged squeal she did not hear.

The pig parlor commanded a view of the back pasture where their twenty beef cows were gathered around the hay-bales Claud and the boy had put out. The freshly cut pasture sloped down to the highway. Across it was their cotton field and beyond that a dark green dusty wood which they owned as well. The sun was behind the wood, very red, looking over the paling of trees like a farmer inspecting his own hogs.

"Why me?" she rumbled. "It's no trash around here, black or white, that I haven't given to. And break my back to the bone every day working. And do for the church."

She appeared to be the right size woman to command the arena before her. "How am I a hog?" she demanded. "Exactly how am I like them?" and she jabbed the stream of water at the shoats. "There was plenty of trash there. It didn't have to be me.

"If you like trash better, go get yourself some trash then," she railed. "You could have made me trash. Or a nigger. If trash is what you wanted why didn't you make me trash?" She shook her fist with the hose in it and a watery snake appeared momentarily in the air. "I could quit working and take it easy and be filthy," she growled. "Lounge about the sidewalks all day drinking root beer. Dip snuff and spit in every puddle and have it all over my face. I could be nasty.

"Or you could have made me a nigger. It's too late for me to be a nigger," she said with deep sarcasm, "but I could act like one. Lay down in the middle of the road and stop traffic. Roll on the ground."

In the deepening light everything was taking on a mysterious hue. The pasture was growing a peculiar glassy green and the streak of highway had turned lavender. She braced herself for a final assault and this time her voice rolled out over the pasture. "Go on," she yelled, "call me a hog! Call me a hog again. From hell. Call me a wart hog from hell. Put the bottom rail on top. There'll still be a top and bottom!"

A garbled echo returned to her.

A final surge of fury shook her and she roared, "Who do you think you are?"

The color of everything, field and crimson sky, burned for a moment with a transparent intensity. The question carried over the pasture and across the highway and the cotton field and returned to her clearly like an answer from beyond the wood.

She opened her mouth but no sound came out of it.

A tiny truck, Claud's, appeared on the highway, heading rapidly out of sight. Its gears scraped thinly. It looked like a child's toy. At any moment a bigger truck might smash into it and scatter Claud's and the niggers' brains all over the road.

Mrs. Turpin stood there, her gaze fixed on the highway, all her muscles rigid, until in five or six minutes the truck reappeared, returning. She waited until it had time to turn into their own road. Then like a monumental statue coming to life, she bent her head slowly and gazed, as if through the very heart of mystery, down into the pig parlor at the hogs. They had settled all in one corner around the old sow who was grunting softly. A red glow suffused them. They appeared to pant with a secret life.

Until the sun slipped finally behind the tree line, Mrs. Turpin remained there with her gaze bent to them as if she were absorbing some abysmal life-giving knowledge. At last she lifted her head. There was only a purple streak in the sky, cutting through a field of crimson and leading, like an extension of the highway, into the descending dusk. She raised her hands from the side of the pen in a gesture hieratic and profound. A visionary light settled in her eyes. She saw the streak as a vast swinging bridge extending upward from the earth through a field of living fire. Upon it a vast horde of souls were rumbling toward heaven. There were whole companies of white-trash, clean for the first time in their lives, and bands of black niggers in white robes, and battalions of freaks and lunatics shouting and clapping and leaping like frogs. And bringing up the end of the procession was a tribe of people whom she recognized at once as those who, like herself and Claud, had always had a little of everything and the God-given wit to use it right. She leaned forward to observe them closer. They were marching behind the others with great dignity, accountable as they had always been for good order and common sense and respectable behavior. They alone were on key. Yet she could see by their shocked and altered faces that even their virtues were being burned away. She lowered her hands and gripped the rail of the hog pen, her eyes small but fixed unblinkingly on what lay ahead. In a moment the vision faded but she remained where she was, immobile.

At length she got down and turned off the faucet and made her slow way on the darkening path to the house. In the woods around her the invisible cricket choruses had struck up, but what she heard were the voices of the souls climbing upward into the starry field and shouting hallelujah.

MY SON THE MURDERER

BERNARD MALAMUD

He wakes to a feeling his father is in the hallway, listening. Listening to what? Listening to him sleep and dream. To him get up and fumble for his pants. To him not going to the kitchen to eat. Staring with shut eyes in the mirror. Sitting an hour on the toilet. Flipping the pages of a book he can't read. To his rage, anguish, loneliness. The father stands in the hall. The son hears him listen.

My son the stranger, he tells me nothing.

I open the door and see my father in the hall.

Why are you standing there, why don't you go to work?

BERNARD MALAMUD, who is on the faculty of Bennington College, has published widely. His novels include *The Natural, The Assistant, A New Life,* and *The Fixer;* his short story collections are *Idiots First, The Magic Barrel,* and *Pictures of Fidelman.* He has won both the National Book Award and the Pulitzer Prize.

I took my vacation in the winter instead of the summer like I usually do.

What the hell for if you spend it in this dark smelly hallway watching my every move. Guessing what you don't see. Why are you spying on me?

My father goes to his room and after a while comes out in the hallway again, listening.

I hear him sometimes in his room but he don't talk to me and I don't know what's what. It's a terrible feeling for a father. Maybe someday he'll write me a nice letter, My dear father. . . .

My dear son Harry, open up your door.

My son the prisoner.

My wife leaves in the morning to be with my married daughter who is having her fourth child. The mother cooks and cleans for her and takes care of the children. My daughter is having a bad pregnancy, with high blood pressure, and is in bed most of the time. My wife is gone all day. She knows something is wrong with Harry. Since he graduated college last summer he is nervous, alone, in his own thoughts. If you talk to him, half the time he yells. He reads the papers, smokes, stays in his room. Once in a while he goes for a walk.

How was the walk, Harry?

A walk.

My wife told him to go look for work and a few times he went, but when he got some kind of offer he didn't take the job.

It's not that I don't want to work. It's that I feel bad.

Why do you feel bad?

I feel what I feel. I feel what is.

Is it your health, sonny? Maybe you ought to go to a doctor?

Don't call me by that name. It's not my health. Whatever it is I don't want to talk about it. The work wasn't the kind I want.

So take something temporary in the meantime, she said.

He starts to yell. Everything is temporary. Why should I add more to what is already temporary? My guts feel temporary. The world is temporary. On top of that I don't want temporary work. I want the opposite of temporary, but where do you look for it? Where do you find it?

My father temporarily listens in the kitchen.

My temporary son.

She said I'd feel better if I work. I deny it. I'm twenty-two, since last December, a college graduate and you know where you can stick that. At night I watch the news broadcasts. I watch the war from day to day. It's a large war on a small screen. I sometimes lean over and touch the war with the flat of my hand. I'm waiting for my hand to die.

My son with the dead hand.

I expect to be drafted any day but it doesn't bother me so much anymore. I won't go. I'll go to Canada or somewhere, though the idea is a burden to me.

The way he is frightens my wife and she is glad to go off to my daughter's house in the morning to take care of the three children. I'm left alone, but he don't talk to me.

You ought to call up Harry and talk to him, my wife says to my daughter.

I will sometimes, but don't forget there's nine years' difference between our ages. I think he thinks of me as another mother around and one is enough. I used to like him, but it's hard to deal with a person who won't reciprocate.

She's got high blood pressure. I think she's afraid to call.

I took two weeks off from work. I'm a clerk at the stamps window in the Post Office. I told the superintendent I wasn't feeling so good, which is no lie, and he said I should take sick leave, but I said I wasn't that sick. I told my friend Moe Berk I was staying out because Harry had me worried.

I know what you mean, Leo. I got my own worries and anxieties about my kids. If you have two girls growing up you got hostages to fortune. Still in all, we got to live. Will you come to poker Friday night? Don't deprive yourself of a good form of relaxation.

I'll see how I feel by then, how it's coming. I can't promise.

Try to come. These things all pass away. If it looks better to you, come on over. Even if it don't look so good, come on over anyway because it might relieve the tension and worry that you're under. It's not good for your heart at your age if you carry that much worry around.

This is the worst kind of worry. If I worry about myself I know what the worry is. What I mean, there's no mystery. I can say to myself, Leo, you're a fool, stop worrying over nothing—over what, a few bucks? Over my health that always stood up pretty good although I've had my ups and downs? Over that I'm now close to sixty and not getting any younger? Everybody that don't die by age fifty-nine gets to be sixty. You can't beat time if it's crawling after you. But if the worry is about somebody else, that's the worst kind. That's the real worry because if he won't tell you, you can't get inside the other person and find out why. You don't know where's the switch to turn off. All you can do is worry more.

So I wait in the hallway.

Harry, don't worry about the war.

Don't tell me what to worry about.

Harry, your father loves you. When you were a little boy, every night when I came home you used to run to me. I picked you up and lifted you to the ceiling. You liked to touch it with your small hand.

I don't want to hear about that anymore. It's the very thing I don't want to hear about. I don't want to hear about when I was a child.

Harry, we live like strangers. All I'm saying is I remember better days. I remember when we weren't afraid to show we loved each other.

He says nothing.

Let me cook you an egg.

I don't want an egg. It's the last thing in the world I want.

So what do you want?

He put his coat on. He pulled his hat off the clothes tree and went downstairs into the street. Harry walked along Ocean Parkway in his long coat and creased brown hat. He knew his father was following him and it filled him with rage.

He didn't turn around. He walked at a fast pace up the broad avenue. In the old days there was a bridle path at the side of the walk where the concrete bicycle path was now. And there were fewer trees now, their black branches cutting the sunless sky. At the corner of Avenue X, just about where you begin to smell Coney Island, he crossed over and began to walk home. He pretended not to see his father cross over, although he was still infuriated. The father crossed over and followed his son home. When he got to the house he figured Harry was already upstairs. He was in his room with the door shut. Whatever he did in his room he was already doing.

Leo took out his key and opened the mailbox. There were three letters. He looked to see if one of them was, by any chance, from his son to him. My dear father, let me explain myself. The reason I act as I do is. . . . But there was no such letter. One of the letters was from the Post Office Clerks Benevolent Society, which he put in his coat pocket. The other two letters were for his son. One was from the draft board. He brought it up to his son's room, knocked on the door and waited.

He waited for a while.

To the boy's grunt he said, There is a draft board letter for you. He turned the knob and entered the room. Harry was lying on the bed with his eyes shut.

You can leave it on the table.

Why don't you open it? Do you want me to open it for you?

No, I don't want you to open it. Leave it on the table. I know what's in it.

What's in it?

That's my business.

The father left it on the table.

The other letter to his son he took into the kitchen, shut the door and boiled up some water in a kettle. He thought he would read it quickly and then seal it carefully with a little paste so that none leaked over the edge of the flap, then go downstairs and put it back in the mailbox. His wife would take it out with her key when she returned from their daughter's house and bring it up to Harry.

The father read the letter. It was a short letter from a girl. The girl said Harry had borrowed two of her books more than six months ago and since she valued them highly she would like him to send them back to her. Could he do that as soon as possible so that she wouldn't have to write again?

As Leo was reading the girl's letter Harry came into the kitchen and when he saw the surprised and guilty look on his father's face, he tore the letter out of his hands.

I ought to kill you the way you spy on me.

Leo turned away, looking out of the small kitchen window into the dark apartment-house courtyard. His face was a mottled red, his eyes dull, and he felt sick.

Harry read the letter at a glance and tore it up. He then tore up the envelope marked personal.

If you do this again don't be surprised if I kill you. I'm sick of you spying on me.

Harry left the house.

Leo went into his room and looked around. He looked in the dresser drawers and found nothing unusual. On the desk by the window was a paper Harry had written on. It said: Dear Edith, why don't you go fuck yourself? If you write another such letter I'll murder you.

The father got his hat and coat and left the house. He ran for a while, running then walking, until he saw Harry on the other side of the street. He followed him a half block behind.

He followed Harry to Coney Island Avenue and was in time to see him board a trolleybus going toward the Island. Leo had to wait for the next bus. He thought of taking a taxi and following the bus, but no taxi came by. The next bus came by fifteen minutes later and he took it all the way to the Island. It was February and Coney Island was cold and deserted. There were few cars on Surf Avenue and few people on the streets. It looked like snow. Leo walked on the boardwalk, amid snow flurries, looking for his son. The grey sunless beaches were empty. The hot-dog stands, shooting galleries, and bathhouses were shuttered up. The gunmetal ocean, moving like melted lead, looked freezing. There was a wind off the water and it worked its way into his clothes so that he shivered as he walked. The wind white-capped the leaden waves and the slow surf broke on the deserted beaches with a quiet roar.

He walked in the blow almost to Sea Gate, searching for his son, and then walked back. On his way toward Brighton he saw a man on the beach standing in the foaming surf. Leo went down the boardwalk stairs and onto the ribbed-sand beach. The man on the shore was Harry standing in water up to his ankles.

Leo ran to his son. Harry, it was my mistake, excuse me. I'm sorry I opened your letter.

Harry did not turn. He stayed in the water, his eyes on the leaden waves.

Harry, I'm frightened. Tell me what's the matter. My son, have mercy on me.

It's not my kind of world, Harry thought. It fills me with terror. He said nothing.

A blast of wind lifted his father's hat off his head and carried it away over the beach. It looked as if it were going to land in the surf but then the wind blew it toward the boardwalk, rolling like a wheel along the ground. Leo chased after his hat. He chased it one way, then another, then toward the water. The wind blew the hat against his legs and he caught it. He pulled the freezing hat down tight on his head until it bent his ears. By now he was crying. Breathless, he wiped his eyes with icy fingers and returned to his son at the edge of the water.

He is a lonely man. This is the type he is, Leo thought. He will always be lonely.

My son who became a lonely man.

Harry, what can I say to you? All I can say to you is who says life is easy? Since when? It wasn't for me and it isn't for you. It's life, what more can I say? But if a person don't want to live what can he do if he's dead? If he doesn't want to live maybe he deserves to die.

Come home, Harry, he said. It's cold here. You'll catch a cold with your feet in the water.

Harry stood motionless and after a while his father left. As he was leaving, the wind plucked his hat off his head and sent it rolling along the sand.

My father stands in the hallway. I catch him reading my letter. He follows me at a distance in the street. We meet at the edge of the water. He is running after his hat.

My son stands with his feet in the ocean.

THE
SINGER

DAVID
MADDEN

Thank you, Reverend Bullard. Your introduction was exaggerated, of course, but I won't say it made me mad. Ladies and gentlemen, I want to say first what splendid work your church has been doing. And I'm speaking now not as a man but as a citizen and a Christian. As the reverend was saying, the church must play a role in the important issues of this changing world of ours. Now don't anybody go away and tell it on me that Pete Simpkins talked here tonight like some radical. Politics is one thing, and the hard facts of social life is another. You can't legislate morality. But now you *can* educate people about the facts of their state government and where it's not

DAVID MADDEN, writer-in-residence at Louisiana State University, is the author of the novels *The Beautiful Greed* and *Cassandra Singing*, as well as the story collection *The Shadow Knows* and a literary study, *Wright Morris*. He has edited a number of books, including *Tough Guy Writers of the Thirties, Proletarian Writers of the Thirties,* and *Rediscoveries.*

194

doing right by the people. So "Christian Program on Politics" is a good, 100 per cent American name for what you're doing in this election year. Now with the ward your church is in, I don't have to guess how most of you folks have voted for the last half-century, but tonight I just want to *show* you some of the mistruths that the present administration is forsting upon the people, and you can vote accordingly. Because this movie I'm going to show you—which I was in on making—is to show you the truth, instead of what you read in the papers, about how they're wiping out poverty is eastern Kentucky.

You know, in spring, when the floods aren't raging, in summer when they ain't a drought, and in the fall, when the mountain slopes aren't ablaze, eastern Kentucky is beautiful. In the winter, though, I don't hesitate to call it a nightmare landscape: nature hides herself under a mossy rock and you see the human landscape come into focus, especially in *this* winter's record cold and hunger. We took these movies all this summer and fall, off and on, up the narrow valleys, creeks, and hollers of the counties of eastern Kentucky: McCreary, Owsley, Bell, Breathitt, Perry, Pike, Laurel, Lee, Leslie, Letcher, Clay, Harlan, Knott, Floyd, and let's see, Magoffin, Martin, Whitley, and Wolfe.

So let me show you what we saw in eastern Kentucky. Now, you understand, we're in the early stages of working on this movie. We got a lot of work and a heap of fund raising ahead of us yet, before we can get it in shape to release to the general public on TV and at rallies where it can do the damage. So, Fred, if you're ready to roll. . . .

Wayne, you want to get up here with me, so if there's any questions I can't answer, maybe you can? Come on up. You had more to do with this project than I did. As the reverend told you, ladies and gentlemen, Wayne was our advance man. We sent him ahead to prepare the people for the cameras—set things up. I got my poop sheets laying on the pulpit here, Wayne, else I'd let you see how it feels to stand in the preacher's shoes.

You're doing fine, Pete.

Then let's start, Fred. . . . Ha! Can you all see through me okay? Those numbers show up awful clear on my shirt. I better scoot off to the side a little. Now, soon's those numbers stop flashing, you'll see what the whole national uproar is about. People better quit claiming credit before it's due, just because they're trying to win an election.

Now these washed-out shoulders you can blame on the Department of Highways and Politics. Coming down the steep mountainsides, you have to swerve to miss holes that look to been made by hand grenades, and then around the curve you try to miss the big trucks. Hard freezes, sudden thaws, and coal-truck traffic too heavy for the roads they travel can tear up a cheap narrow road. But if the administration kept its promises to maintain certain standards of construction. . . .

Folks, that's not an Indian mound, that's a slag heap. Something else that greets you around every curve: slate dumps from shut-down mines and sawdust piles from abandoned woodpecker mills, smoldering, thousands of them, smoldering for ten years or more. The fumes from these dumps'll peel the paint off your house. A haze always hangs over the towns and the taste of coal is in the air you breathe. That smell goes away with you in your clothes.

Good shot of one of those gas stations from the thirties. Remember those tall, skinny, old-timey orange pumps with the glass domes? This station was lived in for about twenty-five years before it was abandoned. They don't demolish anything around there. Plenty of room to build somewhere else. Look at that place. You know, traveling in eastern Kentucky makes you feel you're back in the thirties. Ah! Now this is a little ghost town called Blackey.

I think this is Decoy, Pete.

Decoy. And I mean, there's not a soul lives there. But plenty of evidence a lot of them once did. You get there up fifteen miles of dirt road. Millions of dollars were mined out of there. That's the company store, there's the hospital, post office, jail, schoolhouse—turned coal camp gray, and may as well be on the dark side of the moon. See the old mattress draped over the tree limb, and all the floors—see that —covered with a foot of wavy mud that's hardened over the summer. That crust around the walls close to the ceiling marks the level of the flood that bankrupted what was left of the company. Ripped couches in the yard there, stink weeds all around, rusty stovepipes, comic books, romance magazines, one shoe in the kitchen sink, the other somewhere out in the yard under the ropes where they've hacked the swing down. Rooms full of mud daubers building nests, dead flies on the sills and half-eaten spiderwebs. And over the crusts of mud in the houses and in the yards is strowed about a bushel of old letters from boys that joined the services out of desperation or hoping for adventure, and photographs the people left behind when they fled to God knows where. So it's just out there in the middle of the wilderness, doing nothing. Decoy.

Here we are in a typical eastern Kentucky town. Harlan, wudn't it, Wayne?

    Hazard.

Hard to tell them apart. Well, next time we show this thing, God willing, it'll have one of the biggest TV announcers in Louisville narrating.

See the way the slopes of the mountains kindly make a bowl around Harlan? Houses cover the hillsides—just sort of flung up there. No streets or even dirt roads leads up to some of them. Swaying staircases and crooked paths go up to those porches that hover above the road there. Go along the highway, and see washing machines and refrigerators parked on the front porches. See high up, just below the clouds, that brown house with the long porch—just clinging to the cliffside? Houses like that all over, deserted, some of them just charred shells, the roofs caved in under tons of snow, the junk spewed out the front door.

Now *this* you see everywhere you go: old folks sitting on the front porch in half-deserted coal camps. On relief, on the dole, *been* on the dole since the war. That old man isn't near as old as he looks. Worked in the mines before they laid him off and idleness went to work on him like erosion. Wife got no teeth, no money to get fitted. Dipped snuff and swigged RC's to kill the pain of a mouth full of cavities till the welfare jerked them all out for her. And there comes the little baby— right through the ripped screen door—grandchild the daughter left behind when she went to Chicago or Cincinnati or *Detroit* or Baltimore, which is where they all go. Didn't they say this baby's momma had it, Wayne, just had it, so they could collect on it?

    Yeah.

And another girl, under twenty-one, had four babies and drew on *all* of them. Why, the government takes an interest in her that no husband could hope to match. Look at that baby's little tummy, swollen out there like a—Fred, you shoulda held on that one.

And this is a general view of how high the mountains are. *Way* up high. . . . (What *was* the point of that, Wayne?)

(I don't know.)

See that stream? Watch. . . . See that big splash of garbage? Fred, did you get a good shot of that woman? *There* you go! She just waltzed out in her bare feet and tossed that lard bucket of slop over the back banister without batting an eye.

Even the industries dump——

Well. . . . And that stream—Big Sandy, I think. See how low it runs? Well, every spring it climbs those banks and pours down that woman's chimney and washes out every home along that valley. See the strips of red cloth left hanging on the branches of the trees? Like flagging a lot of freight trains. And rags and paper and plastic bleach jugs dangle from the bushes and from the driftwood that juts up out of the riverbed mud. In the summer those banks swarm with green, but don't let it fool you. See how wavy that mud is? And that little bright trickle of poisoned water. Fish *die* in that stuff, so leave your pole at home. And stay away from the wells. Lot of them polluted.

This is a trash dump on a slope high above Harlan where whole families go to root for "valuables." Look like bats clinging to a slanting wall, don't they? But if you go in among them, why, seems like it's just a Sunday family outing.

Most of the graveyards are up on a hill like this one, to escape the floods, I guess. But living on the mountains, maybe the natural way of thinking is up. Look close under that inscription: it's a photograph, sealed in glass, showing the deceased sitting in the front-porch swing with his wife, morning-glories climbing the trellis.

With that red sky behind them, those kadziu vines crawling all over the hillsides, dripping from the trees, look like big lizards rising up out of the mud. Come around a bend on a steep mountain highway and they've crept to the edge. Those kadziu vines are the last green to go.

Here we are up in the mountains again. (Who said to shoot the scenic overlooks, Wayne?)

(Nobody. Fred loved to shoot the view, I suppose.)

(That'd be fine if this was called "Vacation in Eastern Kentucky." Now, this part, Wayne, I don't remember at all.

This is Cumberland. You were still asleep and Fred and I went out for coffee and passed this big crowd—Wait a minute. . . .

Actually, folks, this is the first time I've had a chance to see the stuff. I told Fred just to throw it together for tonight. The real editing comes later.

Just a bunch of miners standing on a street corner. You might take notes on some of this stuff, Fred, stuff to cut out, and, ladies and gentlemen, I hope *you* will suggest what——

Good Lord, Fred!

(Watch your language, Wayne. I saw it.) Fred, I think you got some black-and-white footage accidentally mixed in. Folks, please excuse this little technical snafu, but as I say, we wanted to get this *on* the screen for you, get your reactions, and I think Fred here—Well, he's worked pretty hard and late hours, these past three weeks especially, and we only got back to Louisville a few days ago. . . . Ha! Ha. Fred, how much of this? . . . As some of you folks may know, Fred is mute.

Now this, ladies and gentlemen, is the girl some of you have been reading about in the *Courier*. And the other girl, the one leaning against the front of that empty pool hall, is——

Wayne, I don't think—I'm sure these fine people aren't interested in hearing any more about *that* little incident. Listen, Fred, that machine has a speed-up on it, as I recall.

I think he brought the old Keystone, Pete.

Oh. Well, folks, I don't know how long this part lasts, and I apologize for Fred, but we'll just have to wait till it runs out.

In the meantime, what I could do is share with you some facts I've collected from eyewitnesses and that my research staff has dug out for me. Barely see my notes in this dim light. The Cumberland Mountains are a serrated upland region that was once as pretty as the setting of that old *Trail of the Lonesome Pine* movie. It has a half-million inhabitants. But there's been about a 28 per cent decline in population of people between the ages of twenty and twenty-four, and an *increase* of about 85 per cent old people. In some counties about half the population is on relief and it's predicted that some day about 80 per cent of the whole region will be drawing commodities. There's about 25 per cent illiteracy for all practical purposes, and those that *do* get educated leave. And something that surprises me is that there's only about 15

per cent church affiliation.   All in all, I'd say the poverty is worse than
Calcutta, India, and the fertility rate is about as high, seems like to me.
In other words, the people are helpless and the situation is hopeless.
The trouble with this administration is that they *think* a whole lot *can*
be done, and then they claim credit even before they do it, to make *us*
look bad.   We don't make no such promises.   Because we see that the
facts——

I think a lady in the audience has her hand up, Pete.

Ma'am . . . I'm sorry, that old moving-picture machine makes such a
racket, you'll have to speak louder.

Pete, I think what she asked was, "Did any of us get to talk
with her?"

With who?   Oh.   Ma'am, that really isn't what this movie is about.
We went in there with the best color film money can buy to shoot
poverty, and where Fred got this cheap black and white newsreel
stock——

I think it was from that New York movie crew.

Now, Wayne, this is not the place to drag all *that* business in.   We
came here tonight to show what it's like to live in the welfare state
where all a body's got is promises instead of bread to put on the table.
I know.   I *come* from those people.   Now there *are* some legitimate
cripples, caused by explosions, fires, roof-falls and methane gas poison-
ing in the mines, and some have been electrocuted and blinded and
afflicted with miner's asthma.   But a majority that's on relief are welfare malingerers who look forward to getting "sick enough to draw,"
and whose main ambition is to qualify for total and permanent dis-
ability.   For those people, all these aids, gifts, grants, and loans are the
magic key to the future, but I see it as what's undermining public
morals and morale.   That's the story I was hired to get, and as I
remember that's the story we *got,* on those thousands of feet of expensive color film.   And if——

Well, now we're back at the heart of the matter.   Here we are on
Saturday in Hazard.

Pete.

What?

I think that's Harlan.

Wayne, I was *born* in Harlan.

> Well, Pete, there's that twelve-foot pillar of coal in the middle
> of the intersection, which you told us to shoot because it be-
> longed to your childhood.

Fred's got the whole thing so fouled up, he's probably spliced Hazard
and Harlan together.

> Okay. . . .

Now the shot's *gone*. That, as you could see, folks, *was* the breadline.
The monthly rations.

I guess Wayne was right, after all. Says WORK, THINK, BUY
COAL, painted right across the top of the town's highest building.

Here you see a mother and her four kids standing beside the highway,
waiting for her goldbricking husband to row across the river and
pick her up and take the rations and the donated clothes over to the
old log cabin—caulked with mud, see that, and ambushed by briars
and weeds. That's their swinging bridge, dangling in the water from
the flood last spring that he's too lazy to—

Now this is *really* the kind of thing we went in there to get. That's
not a desert, that's a dry riverbed those two women are crossing.
What they're lugging on their backs is towsacks full of little pieces
of shale coal that—Now see that steep ridge? You can just barely
make them out on the path now. See that? See that man under the
bridge? A little too dark. . . . Get down under there, Fred. *There*
we go! Squatting on the bottom of that dry riverbed with his five
kids, actually rooting in the dirt for pieces of coal no bigger than a
button that the floods washed down from the mountains. Whole
family grubbing for coal, looking toward winter. Sunday. Bright
fall morning. Church bells ringing in Harlan while we were shooting.
Kids dirty. Noses and sores running. Don't that one remind you of
pictures of children liberated from Auschwitz? Look at the way he
stares at you. I offered to *buy* the man a truckload of coal. What he
said, I won't repeat. Who's he talking to now, Wayne?

> Fred.

Sure got a good close-up of him, Fred. Now, the eye that belongs in that empty socket is under tons of coal dust in some choked-up mine shaft, and when he lifts those buckets and starts to follow the women, he'll limp.

Black and white again, Fred! Now where did this stuff *come* from? Who's paying for this waste?

> That other movie crew, Pete, when they went back to New York, they practically gave it to Fred in exchange for a tank of gas.

(Wayne, I wouldn't be surprised if Fred put up as much as he made on the whole expedition.)

> (Frankly, I think he did.)

Fred, shut off the dang picture and let the thing wind ahead by itself.

> This is the old machine, Pete.

(I don't understand how he could make such a mistake. Anybody can see when they've got color and when——)

> Pete, young man in the back has his hand up.

Yes? . . . Listen, son, I don't know one thing about that girl. In fact, I'd be happy to forget what little I *do* know. All three of them, in fact, and the motorsickle and the whole mess. . . . I'm sorry, you'll have to talk louder. . . . (Wayne, you should have *pre*viewed this movie!) Now, son, I don't have a thing to say about that girl.

> (Well, somebody better say *some*thing, Pete. It's only human for them to be interested.)

(Then *you* tell them. You're as bad as Fred was—*is.*)

> To answer your question, young man. No one has yet located the parents of the two girls.

> These shots show them walking along the highway between Whitesburg and Millstone. The smoke you see is coming from one of those slag heaps Pete was telling about. It's the first light of morning before the coal trucks begin to roll. Later, on down

the road, one of those trucks, going around a hairpin curve, turned over and slung coal almost two hundred feet. That's The Singer, as she was called, the one with the guitar slung over her shoulder, and there's the friend, who always walked a few steps behind, like a servant. These black and white shots were taken by the crew from New York. I don't think *they* were mentioned in the newspaper stories, though. But they crossed paths with the girls in Wheelright, Lovely, Upper Thousand Sticks, Dalna, Coal Run, Highsplint, and other towns along the way. Yes, Reverend Bullard?

What did he say?

He said no smoking on church premises, Pete.

Oh. Sorry, Reverend. Nervous habit, I guess.

Somewhere in here is a shot of the preacher who started it all. Soon after people started talking about The Singer, he described himself as God's transformer. Claimed God's electricity flowed through *him* into *her*. The day they found the girls, he put it a different way—said he was only God's impure vessel.

Ladies and gentlemen, I would like to focus your attention on a really fine shot of a rampaging brush fire that——

Hey, Fred, I didn't know you got those girls in color!

Okay, Fred, okay, okay! Just throw the switch! Lights, somebody! Lights!

Fred, Pete said to cut the projector off!

Folks, I apologize for Fred, but I had no way of knowing. Fred, this is what I call a double cross, a real live double cross, Fred! You promised that if I'd hire you back, you'd stay away from that New York outfit and those two girls.

(Pete, aren't you doing more harm than good by just cutting the thing off?)

(This stuff don't belong in the picture.)

(Just look at their faces. They want to know all about it, they want to *see* every inch of film on that reel.)

(This ain't what I come to show.)

      (She couldn't be in *all* of it. We didn't run into her that often, and neither did that New York bunch.)

(It's distracting as hell.)

      (The poverty footage is *on* the reel, too, you know.)

(You *want* to tell them, don't you? *He* wants to *show* them and *you* want to tell all about it. Admit it.)

      (Look, Pete, it's only natural——)

(Yeah, like looking for a job when you're out of one. Go ahead. Tell them. If Fred wasn't a mute, he'd furnish the sound track in person.)

Folks, this is just our little joke tonight. We thought we'd experiment. You know, give you a double feature, both on the same reel.

      Here, Fred got a shot of the revival tent in Blue Diamond where she first showed up about five weeks ago, early in September. That's a blown-up photograph of Reverend Daniel in front of the tent. Sun kind of bleached it out, but the one in the paper was clear.

      That's the old company store at Blue Diamond and the photographs you see on the bulletin board there are of miners killed in the war. Maybe one of them was The Singer's brother.

      The tent again. . . .

      The way people tell it, Reverend Daniel was preaching pretty hard, lashing out at sinners, when he suddenly walked straight to the back, pointing at a girl that he said he knew wanted to be saved because she had committed a terrible sin that lay heavy on her heart. And standing where the tent flap was pulled back, dripping rain, was this girl. Thin and blond, with the biggest eyes you ever saw.

Good footage on that wrecked car in the creek, Fred. You know, the young men go to *Detroit* to work awhile, get homesick and drive some broken-down Cadillac or Buick back home and leave it where it crashed in the river or broken down in the front yard, and the floods ship it on to the next town. Hundreds of roadside scrap yards like this one where cars look like cannibals have been at them. Good panoramic shot. Fred's pictures are worth a thousand words when he's got his mind on his work.

And here's Fred shooting the mountains again. Couldn't get enough of those look-offs.

So there she stood, a little wet from walking to the tent in the rain, and Reverend Daniel led her up front, and pretty soon he began to heal the afflicted. They say he was great that night. Had them all down on the ground. He laid hands on them, and there was speaking in tongues, and those who weren't on the ground were singing or doing a sort of dance-like walk they do. And when it was all over, he went among them with his portable microphone and asked them to testify.

Then he came to *her*. And instead of talking, she began to sing. A man that lived nearby was sitting on his porch, and he said he thought it was the angels, coming ahead of Gabriel.

She sang "Power in the Blood" for an hour, and when she stopped, Reverend Bullard—excuse me—Reverend *Daniel* asked her what she suffered from. And when she didn't speak, he said he bet it was rheumatic fever, and when she still didn't speak——

Moving on now, we see a typical country schoolhouse. In the middle of the wilderness, a deserted schoolhouse is not just an eyesore, it's part of the country. When people live on the front porch, relics of the past are always in view, reminding them of times that's gone: the era of the feuds, of the timber industry, of the coming of the railroad, of the moonshine wars, and of the boom and bust days of coal.

Ha! Fooled you, didn't I? Thought it was deserted. Ha. There's the teacher in her overcoat, and the kids all bundled up in what little clothes they have. See that one girl with rags wrapped around her legs in place of boots? That's the reason: gaps between the boards a foot wide. And believe me, it gets cold in those mountains. Now what's the administration going to say to the voters about *that* when they go to the polls in November? They claim they're *improving* conditions.

From the highway, you don't often see the scars in the earth from strip mines and the black holes where the augers have bored. I suppose those New York boys are trying here to give you an impression of the landscape The Singer wandered over. On the highways, you may pass a truck hauling big augers, but to watch the auger rig boring, you have to climb steep dirt roads. That's where The Singer and her friend seem to be going now—not on purpose, I don't think. Just aimlessly wandering, those New York boys following close behind with their black and white. Now, who's *that* girl? Oh, yeah, the one that starred in *their* movie. What was her name? Deirdre. . . . Back to The Singer again. Going on up the winding road, and those black eyes staring at you out of that far hillside— auger holes seven feet in diameter. The dust those trucks stir up barreling down the mountain is from spoil banks that get powder-dry in the summer and it sifts down, along with coal grit, onto the little corn and alfalfa and clover that still grows in the worn-out land. With its trees cut down by the stripping operation, its insides ripped out by the augers, this mountain is like some mangy carcass, spewing out fumes that poison the air and the streams.

Where these augers and the strip mining have been, snows, rains, floods, freezes, and thaws cause sheet erosion, and rocks big as tanks shoot down on people's cabins. This used to be rich bot-tomland. Now it's weeds, broomsedge, and thickets. Don't look for an old bull-tongue plow on *those* hillsides. And the big trees are gone.

Of course, the blight got the chestnuts, but what do you call *this?*

Wayne, let's keep in mind the money that helped make this movie possible.

Well, this, friends, was once called Eden. Some people have reason to call it dark and bloody ground. There's places that look like the petrified forest, places like the painted desert, but it's a wasteland, whatever you call it, and the descendants of the mountaineers are trespassers on company property that their fathers sold for a jug, ignorant as a common Indian of its long-term value. And they can't look to the unions any more. The UMWA has all but abandoned them, some say, while the bulldozers that made that road and which drag that auger apparatus into place for another boring every hour continue what some people call the rape of the Appalachians. . . . I'm sorry, I didn't hear the question?

Young lady wants to know what happened next.

Next? Oh. You mean about The Singer? Oh, yes. Well, the story, which we got piece by piece, has it that when the girl didn't speak, Reverend Daniel got a little scared and looked around for someone that knew her.

In the entrance to the tent, where The Singer had stood, was another girl: black-haired, sort of stocky, just a little cross-eyed, if you remember the picture, but pretty enough to attract more men than was good for her. She didn't know The Singer but was staring at her in a strange way, and several boys in leather jackets were trying to get her to come away from the tent and go off with them.

Now this is a shot of the girls drinking from a spring that gushes out of the mountain with enough force to knock a man down. Her friend sees the cameraman and steps behind The Singer to block her from the camera. Those New York boys would barge right in without blinking an eye.

Well, Reverend Daniel did find someone who knew her and who said there was absolutely nothing wrong with her, physically or mentally, that when she saw her the day before The Singer was just fine. That made everybody look at Reverend Daniel a little worried, and he turned pale, but an old, old woman began to do that dance and speak in tongues and when she calmed down she said *she* knew what had come over the girl. Said she had what they call——

Now here we see the Negro section of Harlan. Notice——

Just a second, Pete.

The old lady said that the girl had got a *calling*, to sing for Jesus. And The Singer began to sing again, and the girl that travels with Reverend Daniel *gave* The Singer her guitar, said, "Take it, keep it, use it to sing for Jesus." Then *she* took up the tambourine, the whole tent began to shake with singing, The

Singer's voice soaring above it all, and listen, ladies and gentle-men, before that night nobody in that area knew a thing about her singing.

You pass this condemned swimming pool and that graveyard of school buses and go over a concrete-railing bridge that humps in the middle and there you are in the Negro slums. The cement street turns into a dirt road a country block long, and the houses are identical, and the ones that haven't turned brown are still company green. See, the street is just a narrow strip between that hill and the river that floods the houses every year. At each end, wild bushes reach up to the tree line. At the back steps, a steep hill starts up. There's no blackness like midnight dark in the Cumberland Mountains, but the white man can walk this street safely. No one wants to discourage him from buying the white lightnin' and the black women. And here we are inside the dance hall where the Negroes are having a stomping Saturday night good time. Awful dim, but if you strain a little. . . .

Want to let me finish, Pete?

Then The Singer walked out of the tent and they followed her up the highway, but she kept walking, higher and higher into the mountains, and the people kept falling back, until only one person walked behind her—that black-haired girl with the slightly crossed eyes.

You through?

Sure, go ahead.

(They just *missed* the greatest shot in the whole movie.)

(They saw it, Pete.)

(The hell. They were listening to *you*, 'stead of looking at the *move*-ee. For an Ohio Yankee you sure act like you know it all. Now when *my* part is on, *you* shut up.)

(Fair enough, Pete.)

More of the black and white. . . . Shots of The Singer at a coal tipple near Paintsville. Truck mine. No railroad up this branch, so they just pop-shoot it with dynamite and truck it out.

* * *

Anyway, what would happen was that The Singer and the other girl would walk along and whenever and *wherever* the spirit moved her, The Singer would sing. Just sing, though. She couldn't, wouldn't, anyway *didn't* speak a word. Only sing. And while she sang, she never sat down or leaned against anything. Hardly any expression on her face. Sometimes she seemed to be in a trance, sometimes a look on her face like she was trying to hide pain, sometimes a flicker of a smile, but what got you in a funny way was that the song hardly ever called for the little things she did, except the happy songs, "I Love to Tell the Story," or "Just As I Am," you know—those she'd plunge into with a smile at first, until she would be laughing almost hysterically in a way that made you want to hug her, but, of course, nobody, not even the kind of women that'll take hold of a sweating girl full of the Holy Ghost and drench her with tears, really dared to. No, not The Singer. She wasn't touched, that I know of, though people sort of reached for her as she passed. But then sometimes you'd feel that distance between you and her and next thing you knew she'd be so close in among people you could smell her breath, like cinnamon. She had ways of knocking you off balance, but so you only fell deeper into her song. Like she'd be staring into your eyes, and her lids would drop on a note that was going right through you. Or coming out of a pause between verses, she'd suddenly take three steps toward you.

They walked, they never rode. They walked thousands of miles through those hills, aimlessly: through Sharondale, Vicco, Kingdom Come, Cumberland Gap, Cody, along Hell-for-Certain Creek, and up through Pine Mountain.

And here we are in a jailhouse in Manchester. Handle a lot of coal around there. And these boys you see looking through the bars are teenagers the sheriff rounded up the night before. Out roving the highways in these old cars, shooting up road signs. They loved having their picture taken—a mob of little Jesse Jameses.

Now, I ask you: can the administration just *give* these youngsters jobs?

Winding road . . . coiled up like a rattlesnake. See where those boys —watch for fallen rock. Just shot it all to pieces. Most of them will end up in the penitentiary *making* road signs.

Now in this shot—in Hellier, I think—The Singer has wandered into a church and they've followed her. And off to the side there, among the parked cars and pickup trucks, you can see the other girl, leaning against the door of a car, talking to some men and boys. Can't see them for the car. There. See them? Talking to her? Well, that's the way it was, after awhile.

A boy told one of the young men on the New York crew that he was outside the tent at Blue Diamond that first night, and that the black-haired girl was going from car to car where the men were waiting for their wives to come out of the revival tent and the young boys were waiting for the girls to come out. But *this* girl never made it *in*. They always waited for her outside, and she went with all of them. And then—I don't know who or where I got it—the girl heard the singing and left the cab of a coal truck and went to the entrance of the tent, and then when The Singer went out to the highway, she followed her. Then after about a week—

Oh. Go ahead, Pete.

Folks, here we are back on the track, with a shot we were afraid wouldn't come out. Good job, Fred. A carload of pickets waiting to join a caravan. Eight young men in that car, all of them armed. You can hear them at night, prowling up and down the highways in long caravans, waking you up, and if you look between the sill and the shade by your bed, you can see lights flashing against Black Mountain under the cold sky, full of stars.

And here we are swinging down the mountainside. . . . Some of the early September shots before this record cold drove people indoors. We just suddenly, in the bright morning sunlight, came upon this train, derailed in the night by dynamite. Don't it look like an exhibit out in that big open space, all those crowded porches huddled around on the bare hillside?

Going along the highway, you can expect to find anything in the yards, even in front of inhabited houses. See that car? Pulled up by a block and tackle tossed over a tree limb—looks like an old-time lynching. This man's taken the junk that floods leave on his porch—sometimes on his roof—and arranged a *display* of it all in his yard.

You look up and see those long porches, hanging over the road, seems like, clinging to the steep slopes, and what it reminds *me* of is little villages in Europe when I was in the army. Whole family sitting out there, on the railing, on car seats jerked out of wrecks on the highway, on cane-bottom chairs salvaged from their cabin home places far in the mountains, talking and swirling RC's and watching the road. For *what?*

> Well, for *her*, wouldn't you say, Pete? Word of her singing ran ahead of her, and since nobody knew where she'd turn up next. . . . One time she even walked right into a congregation of snake handlers and started singing. But not even that brazen New York crew got any shots of *that*. And sometimes she'd walk right out of the wildest woods, the other girl a little behind, both of them covered with briars and streaked with mud.

> Here—somewhere along the Poor Fork of the Cumberland River—Fred seems to be trying to give an impression of the road, the winding highway The Singer walked. Pretty fall leaves stripped from the branches now. Abandoned coal tipples, bins, chutes, ramps, sheds, clinging to the bare hillsides like wild animals flayed and nailed to an old door. Those stagnant yellow ponds where the rain collects breed mosquitoes and flies the way the abandoned towns and the garbage on the hillsides breed rats. You may leave this region, but the pictures of it stick in your mind like cave drawings.

> Here you see The Singer and her friend walking along one of those mountain roads again. Too bad those New York boys couldn't afford color. A light morning rain has melted most of the snow that fell the night before. This is along Troublesome Creek and they've already been through Cutshin, Diablock, Meta, Quicksand, Jeff, and Carbon Glow, Lynch, and Mayking. By the way, the reason the girls are dressed that way—style of the thirties—is because they're wearing donated clothes. Remember the appeal that came over television and filled the fire stations with clothes after last spring's flood?

These artificial legs were displayed in a window near our *hotel* next to the railroad depot in Harlan. Nice, hazy Sunday morning sunlight, but *that*, and this shot of a pawnshop window—little black pearl-handled revolvers on pretty little satin cushions—reminds you of what kind of life these people have in the welfare state. And those windows piled high with boots and shoes beyond repair are something else you see at rest on Sunday in Harlan.

> There they are in front of a movie theater—What's that showing? Oh, yeah, an old Durango Kid movie. Fred and I saw that in another town—Prestonsburg, I think. Never forget the time

she walked into a movie theater and started to sing right in the middle of a showdown in some cowboy shoot-out, and one big lummox started throwing popcorn at her till the singing reached him and he just left his hand stuffed in the bag like it was a bear trap.

Anyway, as I was telling before, the other girl, after about a week, took to luring the men away from The Singer because they began to follow her and bother her and try to start something with her, so the friend had to distract them from her, and ended up doing the very thing she had tried to stop herself from doing by going with The Singer. They say The Singer never seemed to know what was going on. She'd walk on up the highway or on out of town and the other girl would catch up.

See how they just nail their political posters to the nearest tree? Sun sure bleached that man out, didn't it?

Here, Fred got a shot of the New York movie crew getting out of their station wagon. Three young men and a girl. Looks like somebody scraped the bottom of a barrel full of Beatniks, doesn't it? The local boys and men kept teasing them about their beards and they tried to laugh along, but finally they would get into fights, and we'd come into a town just after they had gone, with the police trying to get people out of the street, or the highway patrol escorting the crew into the next county. They came down to shoot what they called an art movie. They told Fred the story once and I listened in, but I can't remember a thing about it, except that this girl named Deirdre was going to be in it. She *was* in it. Yeah, this is one of the scenes! Shot her *in front of* a lot of things, and she would kind of sway and dip around among some local people—just like that—and everybody—Yeah, see the big grins on their faces? And the director kept begging them to look serious, look serious.

That one's *yours*, Pete.

Shots of old men in front of the courthouse. . . . Young boys, too. . . . No work. Bullet holes around the door from the thirties. Bad time, bad time.

What those guys did, Wayne, was make everybody mad, so that when *we* came rolling into town, they were ready to shoot anybody that even *looked* like he wanted to pull out a camera.

Yeah. Always pointing those loaded cameras at things and running around half-cocked, shoot, shoot, shooting.

Then they ran into The Singer and her friend, and—Yeah, this is the one, this is actually the *first* shot they took of The Singer. First, this is a close-up of *their* girl—Deirdre—you're looking at, long stringy hair, soulful eyes. One time they even put something *in* her eyes to make the tears run. And in just a second they'll swing to catch The Singer. That's it! See the camera jerk? The script writer saw The Singer on the opposite corner and jerked the cameraman around. Here you can see The Singer's friend standing off to the side, on the lookout for trouble-makers—front of a little café in Frenchberg. Cameraman got her in the picture by accident, but later when the director caught on to what she was *doing* with The Singer, he hounded her to death. Made her very angry a couple of times. Deirdre in *his* movie though—

Pete. . . .

What's you want?

Your part's on.

Well . . . that's as you can see—the garbage in the streams there— kids with rickets—brush fire in the mountains. . . .

I was about to say about the folk singer from Greenwich Village—Deirdre—she got very angry too, over the way the movie boys took after The Singer, so she threatened to get a bus back to New York. But after they had listened to people tell about The Singer in the towns they came into, not long after she had gone on, and after they had tracked her down a few times, and after Deirdre had heard her sing, she got so she tried to *follow* The Singer. Deirdre ran away from the movie boys once, and when they caught up with her the black-haired girl was trying to fight off some local boys who thought Deirdre was like *her*. But she wasn't. Not after The Singer got to her, anyway. I don't know *what* Deirdre was like in New York, but in the Cumberland Mountains she heard one song too many. I never saw her after she changed, either. Finally, the New York boys had to lock her in a room at the Phoenix Hotel in Salyersville and one stayed behind to watch over her. Wish we had a shot of that hotel. White, a century old, or more, three stories in front, four in back, little creek running behind it. Three porches along the front. Sit in a broken chair and watch the people go by below. If you're foolish, you sit on the rail. If you leave the windows open in the room at the back, you wake up covered with dew and everything you touch is damp.

Pete.

Shots of another abandoned shack. . . .

Go ahead, Pete.

They can see it okay. Same old thing. . . .

Oh. Now *that's* Reverend Daniel, the one that ministered to The Singer in Blue Diamond. He'd moved his tent to Pikeville and that's where we saw him, and got these shots of his meeting. Promised him a stained-glass window for his tent if he'd let us, didn't we, Wayne? Ha! Anyway, next time we saw him was a week ago, just before the accident, and he told me how he had offered to make The Singer rich if she would sing here in Louisville. Told her people all over Kentucky would read about the wandering singer for Jesus, and that he could make her famous all over the world, and they could build the biggest church in the country, and stuff like that. She just looked at him and walked on. He pestered her awhile, but finally gave up after about six miles of walking. Wayne, you saw him after it happened, didn't you?

Yeah. He blames himself. Thinks he should have looked after her. As though God meant him to be not just a transformer but a guardian angel, too. He'll never put up another tent as long as he lives.

And that girl—Deirdre—that come down from New York, she could be dead, for all we know. The boy that was guarding her——

Said he shouldn't have told her about what happened on the highway.

Slipped out of the Phoenix *Ho*tel somehow and vanished.

She *may* turn up in New York.

And she might turn up alongside some highway in the mountains, too.

This is one of Fred's few shots of the girls. He hated to disturb them. Actually, The Singer never paid any attention to us or to the other crew, did she, Pete? Mostly, Fred listened to her sing, standing in the crowds in Royalton, Hardburley, Coalville, Chevrolet, Lothair, his camera in his case, snapped shut. Right, Fred? But here, while they sat on a swinging bridge, eating—well, the friend eating, because nobody every saw The Singer put a bite of food in her mouth, just drink at the mountain springs—Fred got them with his telephoto lens from up on one of those look-offs beside the road.

Kind of grainy and the color's a little blurred, but it looks like it's from a long way off through a fine blue mist at about twilight. Nice shot, Fred.

There's those numbers again. What about that? Fred, you want to catch that thing—film flapping that way gets on my nerves.

Personally, I'm glad nobody's got the *end* on film.

Know what you mean, Wayne.

What the papers didn't tell was——

That the boy on the motorsickle. . . ?

Wasn't *looking* for the girls.

And he wasn't a member of some wild California gang crossing the country, either.

Go ahead and tell them, Pete.

That's okay. You tell it, Wayne.

The way Fred got the story—Fred, this is one time when I really wish you could speak for *yourself*. Fred was the one who kept his arms around the boy till he stopped crying.

Tell them where it happened, Wayne.

Outside Dwarf on Highway 82. The girls were walking along in the middle of the highway at about three o'clock in the morning and a thin sheet of ice was forming, and this motorcycle came down the curve, and if he hadn't slammed on his brakes——

More or less as a reflex——

It wouldn't have swerved and hit them.

You see, Fred had set out to catch up with them. Me and Wayne'd left him to come on back to Louisville alone, because he said he was going to stop off a day or two to visit his cousin in Dwarf, and when he pulled in for coffee at Hindman and some truck driver told him he *thought* he had seen the girls walking, out in the middle of nowhere, Fred got worried, it being so cold, and——

So he tried to catch up with them.

The girls and the boy were lying in the road.

Kid come all the way from Halifax, Nova Scotia.

Yeah, that's where they got the facts wrong in the paper. Saying he was some local hoodlum, then switching to the claim that he was with a gang from California. The fact is that the boy had quit school and bought a brand-new black Honda, and he had set out to see the United States.

Wait a second, Wayne. Fred's trying to hand you a note.

Thanks, Fred. Oh. Ladies and gentlemen, Fred says here that it wasn't *Halifax*, Nova Scotia. He says, "It was *Glasgow*, Nova Scotia. Not that it matters a damn."

PLOT

JOYCE CAROL OATES

Given: the existence of X.

Given: the existence of myself.

Given: X's obsessive interest in me.

Given: the universe we share together, he and I, which has subsided into an area about two miles square in the center of this city.

Hypothesized: X follows me continually, whenever I go out, for one of several reasons that are mutually exclusive. He is on a mission of reclamation, a private detective hired by my father; he is a police agent; he is an acquaintance in disguise or an acquaintance of someone I know/have known, who wants revenge for a real/unreal offense I have committed.

* * *

JOYCE CAROL OATES is the author of several books, the most recent being *Expensive People, Them, The Wheel of Love,* and *Wonderland.* She received the National Book Award for 1970.

PLOT:

There was once a young man of twenty-four, Nicholas Angoff, who woke one morning to discover that he was alone. Utter silence. A vacuum. His eyesight became sharper and he saw that he was in a room—a room with walls, peeling wallpaper, and a gash in the ceiling out of which wires hung. No light fixtures. The young man stood cautiously in the center of the room, measuring the distance between himself and the walls. There was also a window, and a door. His arms moved to protect him—shielding the soft parts of his body. He did not have enough arms. There was a kind of fur over his face, especially over his eyeballs. A film, a fuzz. He stood in the center of the chilly room and began to think of the logical sequence of events that had brought him to this place in his life . . .

No, before this I will have to get in certain information: a description of the young man, which will be approximately my own description except I'll give him black hair, long ratty black hair, instead of long ratty frizzy brown hair; black is more dramatic. When I've thought about it, I've thought that I would prefer black hair, over the years. And perhaps I'll add an inch or so to his height, make him six foot two. Good. And what else? He is intelligent, like me, but sluggish and easily confused, like me, and not really very intelligent when you come down to it, like me, but ordinarily bright; accused sometimes of being a smart-aleck, but those days are past . . . We're all too far gone now. I will have to work all this information in: how he/I popped too many brain cells, sensing immortality in the vigor of young manhood, etc. We both sleep ten/twelve/fifteen hours at a stretch, unless we are awake for three days straight.

He went to the window and looked out. The pressure had already begun at the base of his head, even before he saw the figure in the street below. . . .

Or is this too abrupt? I want only to write about him, that bastard who is starving me to death, whom I have never really seen face to face; but maybe I should hold Nicholas back from the window for a while?

He thought: *I will telephone my father.* . . .

But no, he wouldn't think of that. Not any more than I would. I will have to think of another way of getting the father in, getting him mentioned—his occupation, his money, his handsome graying urbane face, his distress, the "emotional divorce" from his wife/my mother, and all that.

> He went to the window and stared down at the street below. Empty. Sidewalk, storefronts, a thin rib of litter blown up against the building across the way. The street was empty yet it had that bare, frigid look of a stage about to be entered . . .

What, is that right? "A stage about to be entered . . ." Do people *enter* stages? They walk on stages, they come in out of the wings and appear on stage, but they don't *enter* stages, what crap this all is! Erase everything.

Given: X, who is following N.

Given: the city, this building, this room, the toilet down the hall, the leaking faucet, the rubble down in the foyer, the stench, the other people, their voices and thumping feet.

Given: the girl, Rebecca, the long lean legs in white slacks, soiled slacks; a sweater pulled down brutally over her thin hips—that awful fluorescent green, a sweater made of something called "orlon"—her hair straw-colored and long, listless. Has a habit of chewing on the ends of her hair. Her face is querulous, too sharp. But she is a striking woman and carries herself, particularly her head, with that knowledge, that special knowledge women have—it would have carried into her old age, if she'd had an old age. Her eyes are large and shiny, brown eyes. Overlarge. Someone should have taken her moist hands in his, some kindly family doctor, and said: "Rebecca, you have beautiful big brown eyes. Have you ever had a basal metabolism test?" . . . So restless, Rebecca. She can't sit still for five minutes, she is always crossing and uncrossing her legs, twitching her toes, scratching between her toes with her jagged fingernails, throwing her head back so that her hair flips (a high-school girl's trick?) and stings my face, and sighing loudly, angrily. "Why are you so restless, Rebecca?" I might say in exasperation. When the room got too much for us we went out, anywhere. Any weather. We didn't always notice the weather, to tell the truth. She always had a cold. If I had loved her, I would have taken her wet, cold feet between my hands and warmed them, just as a grandfatherly doctor (the kind now nearly extinct) should have taken her cold hands in his and warmed them, but nobody thought to do this for Rebecca, she was too impatient and too beautiful.

Given: The natural and normal biological attraction between Rebecca and myself, somewhat dulled, hazed over by the circumstances of our lives. Or rather: my attraction to Rebecca. I wonder if she could have loved any man, anyone at all. It had nothing to do with her body, which was a normal woman's body, or with her background (she had been married, had an ordinary squalid life; her parents were ordinary and resisted my penchant for mythologizing, as soon as I saw a snapshot of them), but with a peculiar boredom in her glands. Women have that boredom today. Never did I come across this phenomenon in the past, in history, browsing through old novels/biographies/journals in my former life as a student; it is something that has happened only this year. In the past, women wore twenty yards of cloth wrapped carefully around them, on the plump surfaces of their bodies, and carried themselves as if carrying an armful of eggs, but you could be certain of passion once all the cloth was unwound. Not now. Women like Rebecca (she was really a woman, not a girl—twenty-eight years old) come running across the street to you, a stranger, and gladly do they nuzzle their lips against your throat, eagerly do they wrap themselves around you, arms and legs, but then a hideous convulsive yawn begins deep in their throats. . . .

Given: the deteriorating nature of human relationships in America today. I don't pretend to understand it, though I am contributing to it. Just as I eluded my family, who love/loved me, so did Rebecca elude me, constantly. I wanted to kill her, it was awful. . . . But perhaps if she had ever kissed me full on the mouth, if she had stared at me with those large brown eyes, listening to me, perhaps I would have kicked her out. I can't say. I am a pendulum that swings between intense excitement (nervousness on the edge of terror: I don't even have to see that man, X, any longer before I break out into sweat, it's enough just to remember him) and an intense boredom, a desolation I can taste . . . yes, I can taste it, right now I can taste it . . . it is like sand, hard baked sand, sand that has been around for five thousand years, walked upon by barefoot people and dogs. Sometimes I get all the way downstairs to the foyer and then it comes upon me, the terror, the knowledge that X is waiting for me in the street, and so I run back up here, to this laughable sanctuary, walls that are probably collapsible or penetrable by his special spying devices anyway, and my heart is literally hammering with terror . . . my eyes jump into every corner and up to that wound in the ceiling, that gouged-out eye with the optical nerves hanging down, and I am paralyzed with. . . .

> Nicholas was sometimes paralyzed with himself. The thought of himself. The terror of himself. He carried his head around with him, so how could he get out of it? No way! Stuck. Stuck. Stuck.

. . . And at other times I drag myself up the stairs, I use that verb truly, intentionally, "drag," I must drag my body up, I can feel the roots of my hair pulling wearily at my head, and my head pulling my neck, and the elastic cords in my neck tugging at my shoulders, my torso, *oh, come on! only a few more steps!* It is so boring, this stairway. This body. Heavy as a corpse, this body. I am tempted to give up. Surrender to gravity. Lie down on the dirty stairs, with head on one step, torso on another, stomach on another, legs and feet abandoned somewhere in the shadows below. Let the kids jump over me. Or, maybe, I should lie upside-down: my head enriched by a rush of blood.

> Nicholas lay upside-down on the stairs, one day. Blood rushed into his head to rejuvenate the brain. Lying there, he imagined peacefully the wet gray-pink folds of his brain and could not believe that they were eroding, like ordinary ridges and hills made of earth. Similarly, he could not believe that his heart, which was always saying Hey You, would come to a halt someday.

What a joke, if X came in here one day, barged right into this building, and found me like that! He is probably a very conventional man, a citizen. He must be, since he is so faithful, out there at his post. . . . If he saw me lying upside-down it might frighten him so much that he would leave me alone. He might quit the assignment. Or, if he is out to get revenge on me, he might take pity on me and leave me alone. *That guy is crazy.* He might think that my trouble is contagious, that just gazing into my watery eyes would contaminate him. . . .

When I look out my window here, I see the building opposite this building, and that boarded-up store that was once a grocery store, with aged tattered posters on it, I see the doorways opposite me and the windows opposite me, where people presumably live. Off to one side, at the periphery of my vision, I can see X. He is perfectly faithful. He is always there. Sometimes a rush of joy sweeps through me and I want to yell out the window to X and to traffic and pedestrians and people sleeping across the way that I am here, I am living, I love them, *I love them*, we are all human beings living together through this moment of history and we must, we must love one another—

> One day Nicholas approached three men on the street. They seemed to be turning from him. Their shoulders moved—three shoulders, three shoulders turning away. Heads turning. Away. He said: "I need some help." They said: "Move." He said: "What did you say. . . ?" because the pressure on the back of his head made him a little deaf. They said: "Move on." The young man, Nicholas, began to cry. He thought wildly: Is someone crying? Who is crying? Why won't they

talk to me when I love them and we are all here together, on this earth together, why won't they help me when I am in trouble, I am going crazy, I need money, I need a shot, why are they walking away, what is that noise—somebody crying? He said: "I know who you bastards are—I know your names and everything about you!" They were walking away. The sidewalk would fill up with other people. "You're afraid of me—I know your names and I could turn you in," he said. Maybe he did not say these words out loud. He was crying. His face smashed like a girl's, eyes crinkled and hot. Posters on a store window two feet in front of him: VOTE FOR FRANCIS T. JONES. He stood there for a while crying and a squad car passed by, slowly, taking no notice of him, and what must have been an old man came by and paused, eying him, breathing hoarsely, but decided for some reason to walk on. When Nicholas came to he saw, in the doorway of a drugstore up the block, in the center of a loose, noisy crowd of Negroes, *that man* calmly watching him.

Oh yes: *that man* is always watching me, in or out of a crowd of Negroes. He has binoculars, a telescope, a mechanism to see through walls, a tape recorder, an instrument that measures my footsteps, my heartbeat, my thoughts. He is driving me crazy. He is Rebecca's exhusband out to get me, or her ex-father, who was supposed to be a nut, so she hinted—or he is in the hire of my own father, who also hates me, or he belongs to the FBI and is waiting for me to lead him to someone important. . . . But what does he look like? My vision is off a little. That is the horror I live with now: I can never quite see the man's face. If I could see it I might understand something. I might see a human face there, human features—the two of us might turn out to be friends, we might shake hands, introduce ourselves, say hello, filled with a sudden spurt of generosity—

He loved her, he imagined her forever trapped in his arms, he lay with her for long sticky hours, he pressed his face everywhere against her flesh, yearning to suck out her soul. Her stubborn female soul. Where was it? Where could he suck at it? On her lovely arms there were many tiny pricks and red spots and sores and scabs. Nicholas closed his eyes against the body of his beloved Rebecca: rubbing his eyes, his eyelashes, against her. In honor of her body, her face, her beauty, her soul. It was not enough to say, "I love you," because other men had said that to her. Other men had said everything to her, using up all the words. She lay her hand on Nicholas' head as if in pity. She stretched back, her mouth open and yearning backward into a patch of cold clear winter sunlight from the window. . . . "Why do you want to leave me? Why do you want to get money on your own? I can give you money, I can take care of you," Nicholas begged. Her body was warm and slippery and though he was lying with her she seemed to be eluding him. *Better to kill her.* But no: he loved her. That was why he pressed his tender eyes against her, rubbing the eyeballs against her flesh, offering his eyelashes to her—how much more gentle could a lover be, what is more gentle in a man than his eyelashes? She was sobbing. "Why do you want to leave? Is it the city? We could leave together," he said. She sobbed, she pushed his head away, she began to move her body on the bed, slowly, as if in a dance without music, and he stared at her until, after a while, she lay still and fell asleep.

That really happened, but I fell asleep too. Passion wore me out. We slept together, for many weeks, but in different parts of the globe. "Rebecca" and I. She dozed along the Pacific shore, the long length of her bobbing in warm waves, curved to the shoreline, her hair drifting, dreaming, her toes and fingers nibbled by tiny amorous fish. But I, being the male, was thrown in my stupor against the rocks along the Atlantic coast, my body bruised, a cracked rib here, a cracked rib there, a lacerated scalp, a head concussion, eyes pecked out by hungry seagulls—We slept but the two waters of our sleep did not flow together.

He said to his father: "No, I won't talk to her. Why? She walks past my door so that I can hear her crying. Let her cry. I am not going to cry. I am not sick either. I am not going back to the clinic. If you call the doctor I will throw myself out the front window. I will run naked across the golf course. No. Don't touch me. Nobody is going to touch me. You don't love me and you don't love each other and I always had to see that picture of you, on the inside of my eyelids, when I was in bed and you two were in bed, I had to see that picture of you, imagining you, making love and falling asleep, making love with your eyes closed, in the dark, falling asleep before you were finished, because you didn't love each other or me or anyone, and if you fell asleep and slept all night in the same bed you were not really in the same bed because you were not really together . . ."

Did I really say that to my father? Some of it. A few words. When I said that about the golf course, he started coming toward me, and

223

when I said, "Don't touch me," he slapped me across the face. I think that happened in December. The big tree was up in the front hall. I went out of my mind with the frosting on that tree, the glitter and the angels' hair and the smell of evergreen needles, everything was so lovely, why did he have to slap me? He and Sol Mintz own "The Silk Touch," cosmetics for black women, you see the billboards and the ads all over, beautiful leggy black women wearing "Silk Touch" make-up on their flawless faces or their flawless bodies, every square inch of flesh as far as I know, and Melvin T. Riddle, a handsome black man, a member of the "Black Capitalists Coalition," is president of the company and often interviewed, his picture even in *Newsweek*, very grateful to my father and Sol. My father also owns Caesar Aluminum. He had to fly back from Munich fast to get me out of jail. The two of us wept together for five hours. Off and on he kept asking me, "Did they molest you in there?" and didn't believe me when I said I couldn't exactly remember. Oh, I don't take my body so seriously, Father, it isn't that important or that private, why not do a good deed for some bastard worse off than I am. . . ? But I told him I didn't think so. No. I didn't think anyone had "molested" me. What I said wasn't enough, he got disgusted. He stopped crying and started getting disgusted. The next morning he was more disgusted. He wouldn't let my mother in to see me. He kicked me out. In December, I think . . . then he came down to get me, where I was staying with a friend, but it lasted only a few days and then I left home again without saying good-bye. The end. It must have been embarrassing for him to have a thirty-year-old freak of a son, always crying.

Yes, I really am thirty years old. A thirty-year-old son. There is something outlandish about that term, it is not as agreeable as a twenty-four-year-old son or, better yet, a nineteen-year-old son. Once I was these sons. I was once a fifteen-year-old son also, but that was so long ago it isn't worth remembering. One time I threw out all the snapshots of me. The hell with them. I burned Father's miles of film, the gawky grins and smirks. Hell. The hell with them. Now I am thirty years old, unlike my hero Nicholas, soon to be thirty-one, and I spend all of my life waiting for that man to come up here and knock on my door and claim me. All the rest is fiction: I am making up a plot to keep him away.

> Nicholas loved Dorothy but she kept falling asleep in his arms. She kept yearning backward, backward. He hated her, lying above her, "above" her body even though he was touching her along every inch of her flesh, because he could not make her stay awake. So he thought, suddenly, "I will make up a story to keep her awake."

Well, yes, her name is Dorothy; it was Dorothy. Not Rebecca. Blond hair, yes, but not very clean. It looked bitten off at its ends. A film to her fair skin that would roll a little beneath my curious thumb. It would roll out black: thin black rolls of dirt, like the black spines of shrimp when they haven't been carefully "deveined."

> Dorothy touched her lovely flesh with the needle's point. *Music, a cascade of notes!* But no music. Pursing her lips, perspiring, she searched for a vein . . . but no vein. A bead of sweat darted down her nose, unnoticed. She maneuvered the plunger again, shyly, but—no blood! Not even a drop! She squinted to see if maybe there was a drop loosed, just a drop. . . ? No, try again. Try again. Don't tremble. Nicholas stood above her, encouraging her. *Don't tremble like that, Dorothy,* he whispered. The back of his head was bloated and silly and he couldn't hear her reply. Only music, a cascade of notes, and his beloved dipping the needle in, timidly, not yet impatiently, "deveining" herself with infinite patience. . . .

This morning I woke to discover I was alone. What, alone? Where had they all gone? I saw that the room had walls, four walls, the wallpaper was peeling, exactly like the inside of my skull, why did this surprise me? A rumpled bed. That smell. That smell, friends, is *me*. In the ceiling there is a hole, a gash. No light fixtures, just torn wires. A gouged-out eye. There was something over my skin, prominent against the moist parts of my face, where my thoughts move especially fast—my mouth and eyes—it was like a second skin. Fur. Transparent fur. Is it before birth, am I still in a silken cocoon, in a female womb, a stranger's womb, waiting to be born? . . . I stood in the center of the room, my knees shaking slightly, trying to think of the logical sequence of events that had brought me to this place in my life.

The examined life is not worth living.

Every time I wake up I jump out of bed, terrified, and I spend some long minutes in the center of this room, thoughts whirl in my brain or what is left of my brain, the pressure builds up, I carefully prepare a shot for myself and take it, loving myself tenderly, being very good to myself, and the terror fades, the way people's faces fade if you don't see them daily. Joy propels me to the window and I want to shout down at everyone about life, love, happiness, I want to exhibit myself so that the sick and unhappy can take heart from me, a thirty-year-old creature of skin and bones and constant diarrhea who is nevertheless very happy. On flame with happiness! At such times I am not even certain who I am. Whose body this is. Am I myself, a boy of fifteen or a young man of nineteen or twenty-four or thirty, or already aged into a man of thirty-one, or am I someone else (an ex-friend of mine, a Negro named Dill; or Dorothy herself, an ex-lover, now dead; or someone in the building across the street, behind those mysterious mourning windows), because my soul has exploded outward to take in all of the universe. Nothing is excluded. I know this fact: that something miraculous exists where I stand, some being, pinpricked and marveling, his skull open so that the very stars themselves (invisible during the ugly daytime) make little love-pinches in his brain.

But then it faded. Stopped. Nicholas sat down heavily, slack-mouthed. Was it over so soon? Over? What was over? He couldn't remember. Was it Nicholas himself that was coming to an end? *Oh, my brain,* he thought in surprise, *it is being squeezed out of shape! Somebody's hand, the fleshy palm of his hand, is pressing against the base of my skull and making it numb.* He did not know if he was going crazy, or if "craziness" was coming his way and would sweep him up in it.

This is the record of someone going crazy, in case you are curious. I wish you could feel the itching that runs up and down my body, like those fancy bubble lights on Christmas trees, lights bubbling and blinking on and off. Nails, fingernails also itch. Itches. Scratching. Blood. I think it was a few days after Dorothy died that I ran out onto the street—bumped into a woman—kept on running. I went to a gas station near Cass to get a container of gasoline. The gas station is across the street from TransLove, Inc., stucco and streaked white paint, now boarded up. Kids with books brush by me, not seeing me, going to the university a few blocks away. A heavy container of gasoline. I like the smell of gasoline. I always have. In a White Tower diner I can see a row of people at the counter, sitting—it must be late afternoon and not morning, as I had thought for a while —I've been sleeping for a long while—and one of the men is *that man,* X himself. He sits with his overcoat on, his back to me. Sipping coffee. Eyes in the back of his head, watching me perpetually. He is driving me crazy. Should I rush inside the diner and scream at him, should I try to kill him, should I wait outside and introduce myself and shake hands, should I run back to my room and slam the door behind me, sobbing . . . ?

Rebecca said in a voice like music: "I want to die." She put her hand on his bare back. She said gently: "I want to die."

Her lips moved back from her gums, the gums of a young woman who has been strung-out for two weeks, gray gums, gums streaked with a yellowish substance, and she whispered: "I want to die." Nicholas wanted to tell her that his love was enough to keep her living. He wanted to declaim certain truths that have existed throughout history. The truth of love: of why life is worth living, through love, of how the chemistry of love makes for better living, makes living liveable. He wanted to recite a poem to her in which these statements were articulated. But his mind blanked out at the touch of her hand. Her words moved soundlessly inside his head. Words, syllables, sounds. A breath. He wanted to carve out on the back of her hand, into those cheap flimsy useless veins we all have there: I LOVE YOU. But the idea faded.

Anyway we were not alone, my friend Streeter was there with us. In fact he was watching us. He had just finished reading out loud something from the *Detroit News*—probably the Jane Lee Advice column —and now he was just watching us, a smile below the faint little smile of his moustache. He had to shave once in a while because he had a job. What effect would it have, I wonder, to inform readers that a love scene is not private, that a third party is present? I think it would destroy everything. I think it would offend people. I know it would offend me, if I were the reader . . . and it offends me now, to remember Streeter, that son of a bitch. He still owes me money. It might be Streeter who is following me, in disguise, or maybe he has convinced the police that I am important and that I should be followed, knowing it would drive me crazy? Because Streeter loved Dorothy too. He once said to her: "I hate your name. Why aren't you Rebecca? I will call you Rebecca." Streeter was always changing people's names and calling them whatever he wanted. He called me "Buddy" and "Brick," I don't know why. He was always turning up when you thought he had left for good. He liked to impersonate people who wore uniforms on the job: policemen, delivery men, soldiers, sailors, even chauffeurs. He bought a chauffeur's outfit and lived in it for a long time—two weeks straight—carrying himself with dignity everywhere, very vain. He tried to get a job as a real chauffeur, but didn't know how to advertise himself. He never did get a job as a chauffeur. So Streeter was in the room with us that day—

She said: "Will you let me go. Because I want to die." He said: "Why do you want to die?" Her large, shiny, confused eyes. Her chemistry brewed to a storm, uncontainable. A raging thyroid. Raging liver. Heart. Lungs. She was burn-

ing out, burning away. She said: "If you love me, you'll let
go of me." He said: "I can't let you go . . ." He said: "You
don't love me or you would want to live." He said: "All right,
God damn it, I will let you go . . ."
And so she died.

"And so she died."

Dill ran in and started reading them a news story, in a terrible
voice. Mrs. Mungo, the mother of Herb Mungo, a police in-
former and a traitor, a betrayer, a thief, an evil young man,
Mrs. Mungo had been interviewed by a reporter. Dill had made
the bomb himself with materials Nicholas had bought and the
bomb had been sent to Herb Mungo's apartment, left outside
in the hall, and a few days later Mrs. Mungo came to see where
her son was (out of town on business, maybe) and saw the
package addressed to him. So she took it home with her. Mr.
Mungo, a Greyhound bus driver, was not home at the time; but
the five Mungo kids, Herb's younger brothers and sisters, were
all there. What fun! A present! So they opened the package,
on the kitchen table, and . . . and the bomb did not go off . . .
Mrs. Mungo said to the police: "I took a look at that thing and
told Bobby to throw it out in the backyard, fast! I knew
what it was right away from all the stuff on television. Now,
can you imagine anybody sending a thing like that through the
mail? People should know what might happen with a thing
like that, and five children in a family. I don't know what the
world is coming to . . ."
Dill was very angry. He read the story over several times,
shouting. Dill had wanted to be an actor, in his former life.
Perhaps he had actually been an actor.

But none of this is a logical sequence of events. It does not add up
to anything logical. If a human life, my own life, is to make sense
it must add up to a certain unit, reductive to a certain statement: *He
was a hero. He was a hero because he resisted suicide. He was a
coward. He was a coward because he resisted suicide. He was somebody's thirty-year-old aging archaic son.* My brain is going, but before it goes completely I want to make very clear my dislike for you:
my readers, who are reading through my life as fast as possible, skim-
ming along, impatient with me and hoping for some final mess. You
read, people like you, only to whistle through your teeth and think:
Jesus, there's somebody worse off than I am! Why else read, why
plow your way through somebody else's plots? A "plot" is not fiction,

as you know, but very real; it is the record of someone's brain, a trail like a snail's trail, sticky and shameful. . . . But in creating a plot to explain my life, I am being forced to change things around. The essential story gets away from me. The main thing is that I am being followed and tortured to madness by someone, probably a stranger, probably a hired stranger, and I have to keep repeating this for fear I will forget it as my mind goes. Otherwise I will keep asking myself about certain events—people—memories—that are confusing. Did I love Rebecca/Dorothy, or is that a lie? I loved her when my chemistry ordered *Love!* but the rest of the time I think I forgot her. She certainly forgot me. We lay dreamily together in our two halves of the globe, but when I told her I loved her she fell asleep; when she told me, one day, of her ex-husband and what he had done to her, I shut my mind off and watched her lips move but I heard nothing. And I never really knew . . . I never really knew whether Dorothy and Streeter and Dill and some of the others liked me for myself or because I had money, an allowance my father finally gave me, because I was the only one down here who had money and who was generous . . .

> After Rebecca's death, Nicholas himself declined . . . After Rebecca's death, Nicholas himself thought increasingly of death, of an end, a conclusion, of the stairway outside his room where one might lie upside-down forever. . . .
> After Rebecca's death he began to think of the marriage they might have made, the children they might have made, now that it was certain she could not return to him. . . .
> After Dorothy's death, in fact the next day, X appeared at the top of a stairway and looked down at Nicholas, claiming him. . . .

Dorothy did die. I keep thinking of her death, again and again. Her death. "Her" death. She never said most of those things—"I want to die," etc. She never spoke gently, delicately, musically to me at all. I don't think she noticed me except to ask for money. Only a dry brushing of her lips against mine—she would never kiss me the right way, though I begged her—and the way she died was not suicide, it was not deliberate at all, but like this: the three of us had shared everything, Dorothy and Streeter and I, and we shared our best times as well as our worst times, and one night when we were all high together we seized one another's hands, everything raging in me, a delirious storm, everything joyful, and I could feel their friendly hearts racing like mine, our pulses racing, our eyeballs burning, and then . . . and then I had to sneeze suddenly. . . .

A sneeze! Rebecca leaped back from them, terrified. Her body quaked. She could not take it—the noise was too much, too much of a surprise—her body raced in terror—too much stress, too much heartbeat. It exploded in her—the heart. Blood gushed out of mouth, nose, ears, eyes. Oh, exclamations of blood! Nicholas stared at her in disbelief. Blood poured out of her. Streeter began to run and Nicholas followed, out of the room and down the stairs and into the street. They were in the street before the corpse stopped its convulsions!

It was no dramatic moment. There is no drama when lovers part like that—no preparation, nothing. How do you prepare for your beloved's sudden death? The explosion of her heart? A muscular little fist that stretched out all its fingers suddenly in terror, in despair . . . (This morning my own heart pounded in cold, brutal, militant palpitations for an hour and a half, frightened by a cat prowling around in the alley. God damn these stray cats!) If only I hadn't sneezed . . . What do you do when your love dies so quickly, so strangely? You must write about it. Rewrite it. You can change both your names, exaggerate your love for her, exaggerate her beauty, try to figure out how this leads to your being followed now by her ex-husband, the boy from Midland, Michigan, who was so unkind to her.

There was once a young man of twenty-four who, having been praised years ago by an instructor at Cornell, and given a B+ in freshman English, decided he would write a story about himself. He decided that it would begin in the past—some personal history, but not too much, because obvious autobiographical information tires readers—and move quickly to the near-present, the break with his family, the three months camping out in the city of Detroit, the friendships with certain people, the unhappy love affair with a girl he would call Rebecca, the suicide of Rebecca (how? slashed wrists? gas? an overdose of pills would be too close to the truth), some description of the city, the jumbled skyline, the traffic several blocks over on the John Lodge Expressway, etc., the Narcotics Squad, the Vice Squad, dirt and flu and a constant leaking faucet, etc., some sentimental remarks about the human condition, being a son/having a father, etc. What made him pause was the knowledge that if he wrote something terrible he might have to fulfill it; might have to make it come true. But what other possibility of salvation would there be for him, except this writing of the scenario of his own life, his predicament with the deadly X, who is always waiting? No other way. No. So he would write a story that would make sense of X. By creating a coherent plot he would then explain to his own satisfaction why someone was obsessed with him. Or, he would hint (and convince himself) that the man, X, was only imagined—a harmless dot in front of the eyes, bouncing and wiggling like crazy, only bothersome if it is taken seriously—and so he would exorcise the man, the phantom, the perpetual X on the edge of his consciousness. . . . But, having written eighteen pages he discovered that X could not be explained away so easily. There was the X on paper, and the X out in the street. Two X's. X out in the street is never in the narrative, really, but only mentioned—always out of eyesight, out of the range of human affection and pleas! The police, or a police agent, followed an acquaintance of Nicholas' once and indicated, somehow, that there was a relationship between them that resulted in the acquaintance being found dead one day. . . . The police know how to put certain pressure on one's associates to kill: after all, nobody wants to be betrayed. But Nicholas is no threat to anyone and cannot betray anyone, now. Therefore it makes no sense for anyone to follow him; therefore X is not really following him. . . .

If I go out to get something to eat he will see me. I can't go out. I could buy some more food from kids in the building, cookies and crackers and other junk, which they steal from their mothers' cupboards, but the kids haven't been around today; I could break into their mothers' cupboards and eliminate the kids entirely, but if I break into someone's apartment I am likely to be shot. How long can I stay holed up here? I can put my hands around myself, around my waist. A skeleton. A thirty-year-old skeleton. My long skinny thumbs touching, straining to touch like lovers, and the third finger of each hand touching firmly. It would be interesting to know how much I weigh. . . .

I will escape this self-pity by returning to my plot.

The end of the story: a logical sequence of events that results in the young hero cleaning up his life, walking out into the street, confronting X—who turns out to be, I suspect, a private detective hired by his father—and the two of them eye each other for a few suspenseful minutes, the young man shaky from going without food, and from taking too prodigious a variety of drugs, but still essentially healthy and intelligent and rational, an obviously civilized young man whom society would be eager to rehabilitate. And the dialogue will go something like this: "Your father is very worried about you, Nicholas. Don't you realize that?" Nicholas, his face serious and handsomely pale: "I'm beginning to realize what I've done to him." "Shall we go now?" the man will say. "Yes, I'm ready now," Nicholas will say. He and X walk together down the block, side by side, walking together down the block, together, the two of them, walking down the block together, together. . . .

Tears spilled out of his eyes at the look of himself: his hands, his two hands, could span his entire body. Trembling. Weeping. He understood that his mind was about to go and that he must not wind up in Lafayette Clinic like the rest of them, gibbering and drooling all over himself, he had enough dignity left, so he moved one leg and then the other, left and right and left again and right, lifting his knees with his two hands, until he came to the Mobile station near Cass and bought a can of gasoline. Was he being followed? He didn't look around. On Woodward he hitched a ride north with someone who took pity on him—a motorist whose car ran out of gas? no matter that he looks like hell and his hair is frizzed out around his head in an explosion of kinky brown curls and he weighs about one hundred and ten pounds, still the can of gasoline suggests that he is an automobile owner and therefore a good citizen—and drove him all the way up to Six Mile. Good. Coming home. He crossed over to Hamilton Road and went along the deserted sidewalk of the private street to his parents' home, past the Detroit Golf Club, too large, complex, and magnificent a home to describe, and walked up the broad front flagstone walk, in the gauzy pleasant lilac-scented air of a May evening, and around to the garage, where a single car was parked, and in the garage, sitting suddenly, coming to rest, sitting Indian-fashion with his ankles locked whitely about each other, he dumped the gasoline over himself and, before anyone could catch up to him, X or anyone at all, before anyone even knew he had come back, he set himself on fire. So many times had Nicholas returned to this home, this house, wandering homeward in his head!—like a ghost wandering, yearning back, backward, but never until this moment did he know why he would return. Yes, constantly was he going home, always going home in the confused plot of his life, and never until the last hour of his life did he understand what home meant—

A DOLPHIN IN THE FOREST A WILD BOAR ON THE WAVES

CHARLES NEWMAN

THREE SCENES

"We must act as if we were lost, desperate . . ."
—Van Gogh to his brother

[I]

We sat there for awhile looking at the snow and the sky. We had come all the way through the Preserve, catching our breath among the great oaks of the Golf Club. We cleared away some snow and squatted down on the frozen sod, a finely quilted grass for future divots. Sand for the traps was heaped among the trees, and above us stretched the powder-blue watertower of Precious Blood Retreat.

They had bought the land when it was still wild onion. Their tower was the highest thing outside the city. When we first moved in, I lay in bed at night and listened to the water running out of the tower and

CHARLES NEWMAN, editor of *Triquarterly* and a member of the English faculty at Northwestern University, will be on the staff of the *New Hungarian Quarterly* for 1971–1972. He is the author of the novels *New Axis* and *The Promise-Keeper*.

233

into all the houses. They grew horse-radish for years until the ground turned blue. Then they sold the west forty to the state for an airport, they sold the east forty to developers for a golf club, they sold the south forty to the city for a garbage dump, they sold the north forty to Irma Nadler's husband, Dr. Nadler, and he sold it to us and thirty-nine others.

Before they sold the south forty they took out all the rock and sold it to the airport for concrete. Before they sold the west forty they took off all the sod and sold it to the Golf Club for grass. When they put garbage where the rock and sod had been, the gulls from the lake moved inland with us. The gull is a clean and quiet bird. But they heckled the clippedwing swans down at the swan pond, and one gull flew into the mouth of an executive jet and blew it up.

The tower was a real landmark. At Christmastime they put messages on it in lights. This year it said: CHRIST WANTS MORE!

There was a good deal of comment about that. It attracted attention because it stretched around the entire tank, and to get the whole message, it was necessary to drive an everwidening circle through the countryside. Otherwise, from a single perspective, you could get only a few letters. From our house, for instance, all you could see was ANTS. Airliners used it for a pylon, and when a pervert annually took its child in the Preserve, official observers were seen at the tower railing, flashing signals through the night to search parties in the forest. They go up there when a little girl is late for dinner. Rewards are offered, the State Police are summoned, the hounds go out, the creek is dragged, the air is full of helicopters, but it's never any use. The dogs always find them the same way, half buried, decomposed, their underclothes in their mouths. The newspapers run a picture of the cop giving a little shoe to a big dog to smell. Sometimes, the body is dismembered and the police are around for weeks. Tell me, why do they have to find *all of it,* once they know?

The Cloister itself was yellow stucco with a red tile roof and a bell-less campanile. We went there several times a year to vote. Our precinct polls were in the foyer of the chapel, the only public place around. My parents always took me when they voted, a nice touch, although we never discussed who was to be chosen. While they were doing their duty, I stayed in the foyer, and it always surprised me, next to the pamphlet rack towered a big stuffed polar bear rearing up on his hind legs. You put a penny on his grooved tongue, shoved it back through scissor teeth and for a good minute his head swiveled, his eyes rolled, and from deep inside came a siren roar. Err-*err*-Err-Err! It was for orphans.

I mention this because something happened while we were sitting there, all tired out, with nothing to do, that nearly made the day.

Moulton and I were in pretty bad shape; we didn't have too much more to say to each other. Our supply lines were over-extended. We had, as he said, "defined the problem." So, we were just sitting there, resting, "free from constraint," as he would say, heads between our tails, and I had even begun to hear the water dripping out of the tower again after so many years, at my age, when three men came out of the forest. They were running crazily, zig-zagging, and they all carried huge sticks with which they beat the ground. It looked like some fool medieval Mad Dance.

It is a fact of modern living that we don't question what a man is doing as long as we understand what he's wearing. So when I saw they were wearing B-29 parkas, not hooded robes; sweatpants not pantaloons; football cleats not *clochepied*, and their weapons merely fiberglass polevault poles, I was prepared to give them a chance.

What they were doing was hunting. Their plan, apparently, was to run the length of the field in tandem, flushing rabbits and then busting them with their poles. And sure enough, on their third sally, one rabbit zigged when he should have zagged, and got clouted by the center hunter. They gathered round to finish the job, and by that time we were up to them. Moult was fascinated.

"By God, you got him!" he exclaimed. "That was terrific!"

The three of them grinned and leaned on their poles. They were stocky flushed types and the fur of their hoods was drawn in perfect circles about their faces.

"First one today," the center hunter spoke for the others, "tough going."

"I'll bet," said Moult. "What a fine idea!"

They didn't say anything but just kept grinning. They were probably wondering what we were doing there. I was getting worried.

"You fellahs with Precious Blood?" I broke in.

"For a time," the center one spoke again. "Until the spring when we take orders."

"Oh, Monks?" Moult said.

"Brothers," they grinned.

"Where will you go from here?" I said.

They shrugged collectively, shifting their weight on the poles. I wanted to ask them "orders for what," but I was afraid Moult might start an argument if it was one of those with vows of silence or celibacy or something.

There was a light in Moulton's eye as he looked down at that rabbit pounded fresh on the snow; a light not for the killing or even the hunting, but for the lengths they had gone to before they did kill.

"Lemmie see one of those poles, will you Pal?"

When Moulton got it he held it in his hands like a presentation.

Then he choked up on it, backed away, and took a few swings. Then he took several vicious swings, grunting and letting the momentum throw him off balance. Then he arched it back over his shoulder and flung it like a javelin. It sailed and bore quivering into a thicket. He plunged in after it, emerged in a minute with snow clinging to his hair, the pole over his shoulders like a yoke.

When he returned he looked down at their cleats.

"You guys must have a pretty good athletic set-up."

"You ever play anybody in anything?"

They shook their heads.

"Well, for not playing anybody they sure give you a lot of equipment."

Moult bent the pole in the snow, letting it snap back. I was afraid he was going to insult them and I wanted to get out of there.

"Just rabbits?" he pondered, "why not owls and quail too? And there's muskrat down by the creek."

"The rabbits get into the garbage," the center one said, "and the vegetables in the spring."

"We can't shoot them," another spoke for the first time, "It's against the law."

"We can't even eat them," said the third morosely.

I knew Moult was going to ask *why* they couldn't eat them and it might have been embarrassing so I interrupted.

"You fellahs got a nice chapel here," I said. "We go there a lot to vote." They smiled.

I was trying to figure out how to ask them the story behind the polar bear without getting involved when I saw Moult screwing the pole into the snow and getting a very troubled expression on his face. And we were in no position to protest.

"Well, better be going," I said. "Nice to meet you guys."

We shook hands all around but as I thought we were free, Moult did it.

"Could I have the rabbit?"

They looked at each other. They shuffled their feet, folded and unfolded their arms. The center one made sure we were not being watched, then smiled benignly. Why not? And we shook hands again before they ran off, brandishing their poles silently, running in cadence.

"Well, it's not exactly the Great White Whale," Moult said, fastening his prize to his belt by the ears," but it's perked me up."

We weren't talking as we turned back across the divot field. My balance had made his leverage possible, I thought.

[II]

We cleared the forest, startled. The Christmas lights had been turned on! The houses, normally disparate, had reconnoitered in an electrical pageant, and now marched upon us full of jolly fury. The sky was smoked at the rooftops, extinguishing the stars; a wintry rose dusk. It was as if the sun had fallen into the ocean.

Strands of light lay everywhere. Hung in winking festoons from the trees, strung through the gristle of hedges; entwined about telephone poles, gascapsules, septictanks; they framed windows, crowned doorways, shrouded chimneys, garlanded mailboxes, stumps, balconies. Some lay in the winter brush like foxfire, others straddled gutters or dangled from frozen conifers, and some simply lay scattered on the snow where they had been thrown, like broken atoms.

Windowpanes had been carefully flocked, in special predrifted patterns, but, sad to say, real frost had filled these in. And through this ice, cellophane wreaths revolved, while on ribboned trees, electric candles bubbled colored waters. Enormous aluminum lollipops and stalks of peppermint were anchored in the snowbanks and plastic life-size Santas, squatting in their own glow, waved convincingly as parking-lot attendants. Here and there a horseless driverless sleigh laden with massive hollow packages embarked across a yard. Golden doves with pipe cleaners in their claws strained on their wires in the wind. The Millers had a Kodachrome enlargement of the family in their window, framed with those birds of peace. The children were as happy as the birds and the birds as cute as the children. The Simmonses had chosen Raphael's *Alba Madonna* for their front porch. The Wrights had a snowman with a nose which blinked in the night like an airliner. The Nelsons' four papier-mâché lambs huddled for warmth in a spotlight. Elves worked feverishly at an assembly line in the Johnsons' patio, grinning to themselves, while the Coopers' bevy of imported tinsel partridge hooted prerecorded hoots from collapsible pear trees. Baseboard silhouettes of wise men and camels strode across the playground towards the Memorial: Mother holding child untrembling, the swirling snow filling in their eye-sockets.

We were almost home. The Christmas lights gilded the road, chained tires bit through the ice, stung sparks from the pavement. At an intersection, two plainclothesmen in a pastel ranchwagon were setting up a radar speed-trap.

We climbed the cyclone fence and cut through Mrs. Parker's bird sanctuary, to save time. The Parker place was the largest and the most magnificent around. Mr. Parker had been Dr. Nadler's first customer, as Dr. Nadler had first entreated upon the Church. They have eschewed each other since. A successful engineering career had been cut short by a hunting accident in Parker's case. Part of his frontal cortex had been shot away, making it subsequently impossible for him to think in terms of the possible. He had retired with his wife, early in life, and both devoted themselves to the photography of the wild life within their acreage.

Parker himself had died recently, but the crescent paths which were his testament were kept up by his wife. His woods were still webbed with the rusty wires he used to trip his secret cameras. And the Parker foyer was fully decorated with testimony to his skill; hundreds of startled animals gazed down from the walls, like beautiful movie stars trapped in some profane indulgence—raccoons with fish, deer stripping bark, birds atop rodents, snakes sucking eggs, rabbits with each other.

Suddenly, Mrs. Parker appeared ahead of us, turning one of her husband's serpentine bends, leading her black Labrador, Beodyboy.

"Get that rabbit out of sight," I hissed to Moult, "she'll think we've been poaching."

Moult disposed of the corpse in his coat. And we met a minute later, Mrs. Parker brimming with that gentleness which has no object, pleased that we were taking advantage of her privacy. I said the good things and remembered to introduce Moult who shook hands stiffly like a foreigner as he had the rabbit in his armpit. We would have gotten out of it cleanly, in fact, if it weren't for Beodyboy. He sauntered up, nosed Moult, and dropped into a solemn point. I don't think Mrs. Parker had ever seen Beodyboy on point before; nothing had been dead and bleeding that close to her. It embarrassed all of us of course. Particularly when Beodyboy jammed his nose into Moulton's groin. Mrs. Parker apologized and tugged on Beodyboy's collar but Beodyboy just stood his ground and growled. Moult grinned terribly and I patted Beodyboy's head as fast as I could. What we should have done, I suppose, was to let Mrs. Parker see what was up, explain things, throw the body for Beodyboy and get home for dinner. But there were so many things involved I don't think Mrs. Parker could have stood it. This was no time to start that. It would be easier, in a way, just to stand there, being pointed at, until Mrs. Parker either left or collapsed from the cold, and we could beat the pee out of Beody-boy and make it for home. For when we move, we leave nothing behind. No scraps, no ribbons in the trees, no graves, no dung. We leave things clean—if not precisely as we found them, still clean—bequeathing a footprint so wide, so equally pressured, that our predecessors will have no idea what passed their way.

But as it turned out, we didn't have to. Because Mrs. Parker just picked up a branch and started to whale Beodyboy about the shoulders. Exactly as we would have done, except for different reasons.

Beodyboy didn't differentiate and took off for home. It was nice of Mrs. Parker to do that because she loved Beodyboy; he had been Mr. Parker's favorite after all. At least she knew something was wrong and that this was no time for a tug-of-war. It was hard to believe she was part of the conspiracy.

We commended her as best we knew how, and then she excused herself, returning around the bend to the enormous house which lit up the apple sky like an ocean liner. Her plotting was now confused, I suspect, and we were free again.

[III]

There are no hills near the Lake so they built one. They dug a hole for the necessary dirt, called what was left a reservoir, and that was all right. But inadvertently, they inverted the mountain. That is, they piled first what they dug first, so that the mountain is built on clods of topsoil small as walnuts; the peak is enormous rectangles of clay and striped granite. So our mountain tends to collapse into itself each year, and is only maintained by the constant ministrations of a corps of steam shovels and dumptrucks. In any case, the hill arose tentatively out of the fields before us, settling like a fallen meteor in its rim of shale. It was on the way and we climbed it for the view and to rest.

In the dark, at the top, things were indistinct. Across the fields, I could make out our house, set in the prairie turf like an axblade. The forest was darker than the sky; the sky had seeped through the horizon and ran like lymph throughout the electric patches of our Christmas. The water tower was spotlit, its fine message warped as always by parallax. From the hill tonight, it read WAN. The monastery's turrets glowed red; the Lake, still white and ribbed with frozen currents, angled away like a gull's wing. We squatted down and rested.

It was quite still. The airbase had shut down for the holidays; the bluntnosed orange planes, aerodynamics bulged with radar, were down. The submarines were in their pens. The commuters were home.

I blinked down into the Sunset Estates, down into the converging lights, into those homes designed with so little thought that years of grooming could not give them warmth or character, but only a slight diffidence to one another. I was very cold and very tired. All day, it seemed, we had been addressing a vague audience that was not ourselves, an audience which refused to be taken seriously. We have destroyed the Proscenium forever.

In the dark, of the stillness, at the top, I heard the water backing

up in the tower, the silence too of more solid fuel cached in our Preserve, frost splitting brickpaths, drone of precision thermostats, lubric
drip of idle engines; waiting only for the coordinates to intersect,
ignite . . . in order to retaliate. . . .

"My God," yelled Moult. "There's someone down there!"

I peered down into the great white field. There was someone there
all right. But if it was someone, they looked dead. He was lying
right in the center of the field with arms and legs outstretched, an
illiterate signature on the snow.

We ran down the hill as fast as we could and into the field. At
first I thought the perverts were rushing the season, but they would
never have left things that way. Perhaps heart disease or cancer. We
crashed down through the ice and into nettles as we ran. Moult was
getting short of wind and tears were freezing to his face. Once he
tripped and cut his ankle on the edge of his own deep track. He
clutched at his wound but I got him by the back of the neck and
hauled him to his feet. Then we were going again, and he soon out-
distanced me. We galloped on, knee deep now, the nettles cutting
our socks to pieces. A great volume of blood pressed against my
eyes—the adrenalin hadn't started yet, I wasn't excited, I was going
on pure intent. I had been feeling mean; now maybe we could make
a rescue.

It was a kid all right. About ten, in a purple snowsuit, an abandoned princeling. Moult arrived first but didn't know what to do. I
drew up, dropped to my knees to see if the kid were breathing. Moult
fell on the other side of him and began to retch. The kid was fine.
His eyes were wide open and he was breathing clouds of frost. There
was nothing wrong with him at all except his nose was running.

"What ya want, bub?" he said, and not too pleasantly.

"What happened? You fall down?"

"Are you kidding?"

"Does your family know you're out here?" He rolled his eyes in-
differently.

"Lost?"

"No," he pouted.

I started to grab him under the arms to pick him up—perhaps he
had a fight and was sulking—but as soon as I touched him he winced
and bellowed.

"No. Don't!"

"What? You break something?"

"No. Stupe. Can't you see? You'll ruin it! The angel!" I didn't
know what he meant and took a deep breath.

"Just get away, will ya? And I'll show ya."

I rolled away a few feet to watch. Moult seemed better, and was eyeing the kid from a safe distance. Very solemnly and deliberately the kid sat up, holding his arms out to the side. Then in one motion he sprang to his feet and turned on us proudly. "There," he said, pointing. He was right. In the snow was the impression of an angel in full flight.

"A little didactic," Moult mumbled, "But still, an angel." He rolled over closer, intrigued. "Hey," he said, "how'd you do that?"

"Easy," the kid said, wiping his nose. "Just lie on your back without moving and sweep your arms up and down like you were flying."

Moult put the rabbit beside him and lay down. But the kid yelled and stamped his feet.

"No. Naah! You gotta do it easy!"

He took Moult's head in his hands and eased him back. He still lay too eagerly, however, and again broke the outline.

"I told ya buddy, you gotta do it *easy*."

"Try it over here," I said. "There's a good smooth spot."

Moult came over, careful not to damage the fresh snow, and began again, gingerly.

"You can do it on your stomach if you want," the kid continued, "but you'll get snow up your nose."

Moult was down and I tried it next to him. The kid looked down at us.

"OK," he said. "Now fly."

I wound my arms slowly in a half circle. Moult did the same. At one point in the arc, our knuckles brushed.

"Slow," warned the kid. "Easy does it."

We continued. I took short breaths, careful not to arch my back and ruin the mold.

"OK," the kid said again. "That's good. OK! OK!!" Moult and I looked to him.

"OK. Now's the hard part. Gotta get up. But no hands, see? Or you'll break it."

Then he held my feet. I sat up slowly. My groin burned from the running. But after some effort I was up. And Moult was too. With the kid's help. We rolled forward on our haunches, up and away from the impressions.

"Not bad," the kid said, "pretty good."

They were too. Two big gruff angels on either side of the kid's little perfect one. Ours seemed to careen more, like helicopters. But they were good, considering.

"Say," Moult said, "Say. That's all right."

The kids wiped his nose. "OK."

"Moult," I interrupted, "Moult. We got to go." He nodded.

"And you," I said to the kid, "You better get home. Your mother's probably going crazy wondering where you are." The idea seemed to strike him as a fact; but he lay down again.

"Sometimes," he said, "I make 'em with just one wing. Then they look sadder, or they look like somebody carrying a fan or a horn or a big ax."

"Yes, that is what they would look like," said Moult, caching our carcass within his parka again.

"We got to get going," I said. "So long kid."

"Yeah bub," he said. "I'd wave but I'd break it."

We crossed the field at a trot. We didn't look back or talk.

THE DACHAU SHOE

W. S. MERWIN

My cousin Gene (he's really only a second cousin) has a shoe he picked up at Dachau. It's a pretty worn-out shoe. It wasn't top quality in the first place, he explained. The sole is cracked clear across and has pulled loose from the upper on both sides, and the upper is split at the ball of the foot. There's no lace and there's no heel.

He explained he didn't steal it because it must have belonged to a Jew who was dead. He explained that he wanted some little thing. He explained that the Russians looted everything. They just took anything. He explained that it wasn't top quality to begin with. He explained that the guards or the kapos would have taken it if it had

w. s. merwin is the author of many books of poetry, including *The Lice* (for which he received the National Book Award) and *The Carrier of Ladders* (for which he received the Pulitzer Prize). He has also done many volumes of translations, and for his *Selected Translations 1948–1968* he was awarded the P.E.N. Translation Prize for 1968.

been any good. He explained that he was lucky to have got anything. He explained that it wasn't wrong because the Germans were defeated. He explained that everybody was picking up something. A lot of guys wanted flags or daggers or medals or things like that, but that kind of thing didn't appeal to him so much. He kept it on the mantel-piece for a while but he explained that it wasn't a trophy.

He explained that it's no use being vindictive. He explained that he wasn't. Nobody's perfect. Actually we share a German grand-father. But he explained that this was the reason why we had to fight that war. What happened at Dachau was a crime that could not be allowed to pass. But he explained that we could not really do any-thing to stop it while the war was going on because we had to win the war first. He explained that we couldn't always do just what we would have liked to do. He explained that the Russians killed a lot of Jews too. After a couple of years he put the shoe away in a drawer. He explained that the dust collected in it.

Now he has it down in the cellar in a box. He explains that the central heating makes it crack worse. He'll show it to you, though, any time you ask. He explains how it looks. He explains how it's hard to take it in, even for him. He explains how it was raining, and there weren't many things left when he got there. He explains how there wasn't anything of value and you didn't want to get caught taking anything of that kind, even if there had been. He explains how everything inside smelled. He explains how it was just lying out in the mud, probably right where it had come off. He explains that he ought to keep it. A thing like that.

You really ought to go and see it. He'll show it to you. All you have to do is ask. It's not that it's really a very interesting shoe when you come right down to it but you learn a lot from his explanations.

MAKE THIS SIMPLE TEST

W. S. MERWIN

Blindfold yourself with some suitable object. If time permits remain still for a moment. You may feel one or more of your senses begin to swim back toward you in the darkness, singly and without their names. Meanwhile have someone else arrange the products to be used in a row in front of you. It is preferable to have them in identical containers, though that is not necessary. Where possible, perform the test by having the other person feed you a portion—a spoonful—of each of the products in turn, without comment.

Guess what each one is, and have the other person write down what you say.

Then remove the blindfold. While arranging the products the other person should have detached part of the label or container from each and placed it in front of the product it belongs to, like a title. This bit of legend must not contain the product's trade name nor its generic name, nor any suggestion of the product's taste or desirability. Or price. It should be limited to that part of the label or container which enumerates the actual components of the product in question.

Thus, for instance:

"Contains dextrinized flours, cocoa processed with alkali, non-fat dry milk solids, yeast nutrients, vegetable proteins, agar, hydrogenated vegetable oil, dried egg yolk, GUAR, sodium cyclamate, soya lecithin, imitation lemon oil, acetyl tartaric esters of mono- and diglycerides as emulsifiers, polysorbate 60, $\frac{1}{10}$ of 1% of sodium benzoate to retard spoilage."

Or:

"Contains anhydrated potatoes, powdered whey, vegetable gum, emulsifier (glycerol monostearate), invert syrup, shortening with freshness preserver, lactose, sorbic acid to retard mold growth, caramel color, natural and artificial flavors, sodium acid pyrophosphate, sodium bisulfite."

Or:

"Contains beef extract, wheat and soya derivatives, food starch-modified, dry sweet whey, calcium carageenan, vegetable oil, sodium phosphates to preserve freshness, BHA, BHT, prophylene glycol, pectin, niacinamide, artificial flavor, U.S. certified color."

There should be not less than three separate products.

Taste again, without the blindfold. Guess again and have the other person record the answers. Replace the blindfold. Have the other person change the order of the products and again feed you a spoonful of each.

Guess again what you are eating or drinking in each case (if you can make the distinction). But this time do not stop there. Guess why you are eating or drinking it. Guess what it may do for you. Guess what it was meant to do for you. By whom. When. Where. Why. Guess where in the course of evolution you took the first step toward it. Guess which of your organs recognize it. Guess whether it is welcomed to their temples. Guess how it figures in their prayers. Guess how completely you become what you eat. Guess how soon. Guess at the taste of locusts and wild honey. Guess at the taste of water. Guess what the rivers see as they die. Guess why the babies are burning. Guess why there is silence in heaven. Guess why you were ever born.

POSTCARDS FROM THE MAGINOT LINE

W. S. MERWIN

This morning there was another one in the mail. A slightly blurred and clumsily retouched shot of some of the fortifications, massive and scarcely protruding from the enormous embankments. The guns—the few that can be seen—look silly, like wax cigars. The flag looks like a lead soldier's, with the paint put on badly. The whole thing might be a model.

But there have been the others. Many of them. For the most part seen from the exterior, from all angles—head-on, perspectives facing north and facing south, looking out from the top of the embankments, even one from above. They might all have been taken from a model, in fact, but when they are seen together that impression fades. And then there are the interiors. Officers' quarters which, the legend says, are hundreds of feet below ground. Views of apparently endless corridors into which little ramps of light descend at intervals; panels of dials of different sizes, with black patches on them that have been censored out. It was rather startling to notice a small flicker of relief at the sight of the black patches: it had seemed somehow imprudent to make public display of so much of the defenses.

A few of the cards have shown other, related subjects: a mezzotint of Maginot as a child in the 1880's, a view of the house where he grew up, with his portrait in an oval inset above it, pictures of villages near the line of fortifications, with their churches, and old men sitting under trees, and cows filing through the lanes, and monuments from other wars. They have all been marked, front and back, in heavy black letters THE MAGINOT LINE, and the legend in each case has made the relation clear. And the postmarks are all from there.

They have been coming for months, at least once a week. All signed simply "Pierre." Whoever he is. He certainly seems to know me, or know about me—referring to favorite authors, incidents from my childhood, friends I have not seen for years. He says repeatedly that he is comfortable there. He praises what he calls the tranquillity of the life. He says, as though referring to an old joke, that with my fondness for peace I would like it. He says war is unthinkable. A thing of the past. He describes the flowers in the little beds. He describes the social life. He tells what he is reading. He asks why I never write. He asks why none of us ever write. He says we have nothing to fear.

A SORROWFUL WOMAN

GAIL GODWIN

Once upon a time there was a wife and mother one too many times

One winter evening she looked at them: the husband durable, receptive, gentle; the child a tender golden three. The sight of them made her so sad and sick she did not want to see them ever again.

She told the husband these thoughts. He was attuned to her; he understood such things. He said he understood. What would she like him to do? "If you could put the boy to bed and read him the story about the monkey who ate too many bananas, I would be grateful." "Of course," he said. "Why, that's a pleasure." And he sent her off to bed.

The next night it happened again. Putting the warm dishes away in the cupboard, she turned and saw the child's grey eyes approving her movements. In the next room was the man, his chin sunk in the

GAIL GODWIN received a Ph.D. in English from the University of Iowa. She is currently a post-doctoral fellow at the Center for Advanced Study in Urbana, Illinois. She has published two novels, *The Perfectionists* and *The Glass People*.

open collar of his favorite wool shirt. He was dozing after her good supper. The shirt was the grey of the child's trusting gaze. She began yelping without tears, retching in between. The man woke in alarm and carried her in his arms to bed. The boy followed them up the stairs, saying, "It's all right, Mommy," but this made her scream. "Mommy is sick," the father said, "go and wait for me in your room."

The husband undressed her, abandoning her only long enough to root beneath the eiderdown for her flannel gown. She stood naked except for her bra, which hung by one strap down the side of her body; she had not the impetus to shrug it off. She looked down at the right nipple, shriveled with chill, and thought, How absurd, a vertical bra. "If only there were instant sleep," she said, hiccuping, and the husband bundled her into the gown and went out and came back with a sleeping draught guaranteed swift. She was to drink a little glass of cognac followed by a big glass of dark liquid and afterwards there was just time to say Thank you and could you get him a clean pair of pajamas out of the laundry, it came back today.

The next day was Sunday and the husband brought her breakfast in bed and let her sleep until it grew dark again. He took the child for a walk, and when they returned, red-cheeked and boisterous, the father made supper. She heard them laughing in the kitchen. He brought her up a tray of buttered toast, celery sticks and black bean soup. "I am the luckiest woman," she said, crying real tears. "Nonsense," he said. "You need a rest from us," and went to prepare the sleeping draught, find the child's pajamas, select the story for the night.

She got up on Monday and moved about the house till noon. The boy, delighted to have her back, pretended he was a vicious tiger and followed her from room to room, growling and scratching. Whenever she came close, he would growl and scratch at her. One of his sharp little claws ripped her flesh, just above the wrist, and together they paused to watch a thin red line materialize on the inside of her pale arm and spill over in little beads. "Go away," she said. She got herself upstairs and locked the door. She called the husband's office and said, "I've locked myself away from him. I'm afraid." The husband told her in his richest voice to lie down, take it easy, and he was already on the phone to call one of the baby-sitters they often employed. Shortly after, she heard the girl let herself in, heard the girl coaxing the frightened child to come and play.

After supper several nights later, she hit the child. She had known she was going to do it when the father would see. "I'm sorry," she said, collapsing on the floor. The weeping child had run to hide. "What has happened to me, I'm not myself anymore." The man picked her tenderly from the floor and looked at her with much concern. "Would it help if we got, you know, a girl in? We could fix the room downstairs. I want you to feel freer," he said, understanding these things. "We have the money for a girl. I want you to think about it."

And now the sleeping draught was a nightly thing, she did not have to ask. He went down to the kitchen to mix it, he set it nightly beside her bed. The little glass and the big one, amber and deep rich brown, the flannel gown and the eiderdown.

The man put out the word and found the perfect girl. She was young, dynamic and not pretty. "Don't bother with the room, I'll fix it up myself." Laughing, she employed her thousand energies. She painted the room white, fed the child lunch, read edifying books, raced the boy to the mailbox, hung her own watercolors on the fresh-painted walls, made spinach soufflé, cleaned a spot from the mother's coat, made them all laugh, danced in stocking feet to music in the white room after reading the child to sleep. She knitted dresses for herself and played chess with the husband. She washed and set the mother's soft ash-blonde hair and gave her neck rubs, offered to.

The woman now spent her winter afternoons in the big bedroom. She made a fire in the hearth and put on slacks and an old sweater she had loved at school, and sat in the big chair and stared out the window at snow-ridden branches, or went away into long novels about other people moving through other winters.

The girl brought the child in twice a day, once in the later afternoon when he would tell of his day, all of it tumbling out quickly because there was not much time, and before he went to bed. Often now, the man took his wife to dinner. He made a courtship ceremony of it, inviting her beforehand so she could get used to the idea. They dressed and were beautiful together again and went out into the frosty night. Over candlelight he would say, "I think you are better, you know." "Perhaps I am," she would murmur. "You look . . . like a cloistered queen," he said once, his voice breaking curiously.

One afternoon the girl brought the child into the bedroom. "We've been out playing in the park. He found something he wants to give you, a surprise." The little boy approached her, smiling mysteriously. He placed his cupped hands in hers and left a live dry thing that spat brown juice in her palm and leapt away. She screamed and wrung her hands to be rid of the brown juice. "Oh, it was only a grasshopper," said the girl. Nimbly she crept to the edge of a curtain, did a quick knee bend and reclaimed the creature, led the boy competently from the room.

So the husband came alone. "I have explained to the boy," he said. "And we are doing fine. We are managing." He squeezed his wife's pale arm and put the two glasses on her table. After he had gone, she sat looking at the arm.

"I'm afraid it's come to that," she said. "Just push the notes under the door; I'll read them. And don't forget to leave the draught outside."

The man sat for a long time with his head in his hands. Then he rose and went away from her. She heard him in the kitchen where he mixed the draught in batches now to last a week at a time, storing it in a corner of the cupboard. She heard him come back, leave the big glass and the little one outside on the floor.

Outside her window the snow was melting from the branches, there were more people on the streets. She brushed her hair a lot and seldom read anymore. She sat in her window and brushed her hair for hours, and saw a boy fall off his new bicycle again and again, a dog chasing a squirrel, an old woman peek slyly over her shoulder and then extract a parcel from a garbage can.

In the evening she read the notes they slipped under her door. The child could not write, so he drew and sometimes painted his. The notes were painstaking at first; the man and boy offering the final strength of their day to her. But sometimes, when they seemed to have had a bad day, there were only hurried scrawls.

One night, when the husband's note had been extremely short, loving but short, and there had been nothing from the boy, she stole out of her room as she often did to get more supplies, but crept upstairs instead and stood outside their doors, listening to the regular breathing of the man and boy asleep. She hurried back to her room and drank the draught.

She woke earlier now. It was spring, there were birds. She listened for sounds of the man and the boy eating breakfast; she listened for the roar of the motor when they drove away. One beautiful noon, she went out to look at her kitchen in the daylight. Things were changed. He had bought some new dish towels. Had the old ones worn out? The canisters seemed closer to the sink. She inspected the cupboard and saw new things among the old. She got out flour, baking powder, salt, milk (he bought a different brand of butter), and baked a loaf of bread and left it cooling on the table.

The force of the two joyful notes slipped under her door that evening pressed her into the corner of the little room; she had hardly space to breathe. As soon as possible, she drank the draught.

Now the days were too short. She was always busy. She woke with the first bird. Worked till the sun set. No time for hair brushing. Her fingers raced the hours.

Finally, in the nick of time, it was finished one late afternoon. Her veins pumped and her forehead sparkled. She went to the cupboard, took what was hers, closed herself into the little white room and brushed her hair for a while.

"The girl upsets me," said the woman to her husband. He sat frowning on the side of the bed he had not entered for so long. "I'm sorry, but there it is." The husband stroked his creased brow and said he was sorry too. He really did not know what they would do without that treasure of a girl. "Why don't you stay here with me in bed," the woman said.

Next morning she fired the girl who cried and said, "I loved the little boy, what will become of him now?" But the mother turned away her face and the girl took down the watercolors from the walls, sheathed the records she had danced to and went away.

"I don't know what we'll do. It's all my fault, I know. I'm such a burden, I know that."

"Let me think. I'll think of something." (Still understanding these things.)

"I know you will. You always do," she said.

With great care he rearranged his life. He got up hours early, did the shopping, cooked the breakfast, took the boy to nursery school. "We will manage," he said, "until you're better, however long that is." He did his work, collected the boy from the school, came home and made the supper, washed the dishes, got the child to bed. He managed everything. One evening, just as she was on the verge of swallowing her draught, there was a timid knock on her door. The little boy came in wearing his pajamas. "Daddy has fallen asleep on my bed and I can't get in. There's not room."

Very sedately she left her bed and went to the child's room. Things were much changed. Books were rearranged, toys. He'd done some new drawings. She came as a visitor to her son's room, wakened the father and helped him to bed. "Ah, he shouldn't have bothered you," said the man, leaning on his wife. "I've told him not to." He dropped into his own bed and fell asleep with a moan. Meticulously she undressed him. She folded and hung his clothes. She covered his body with the bedclothes. She flicked off the light that shone in his face.

The next day she moved her things into the girl's white room. She put her hairbrush on the dresser; she put a note pad and pen beside the bed. She stocked the little room with cigarettes, books, bread and cheese. She didn't need much.

At first the husband was dismayed. But he was receptive to her needs. He understood these things. "Perhaps the best thing is for you to follow it through," he said. "I want to be big enough to contain whatever you must do."

All day long she stayed in the white room. She was a young queen, a virgin in a tower; she was the previous inhabitant, the girl with all the energies. She tried these personalities on like costumes, then discarded them. The room had a new view of streets she'd never seen that way before. The sun hit the room in late afternoon and she took to brushing her hair in the sun. One day she decided to write a poem. "Perhaps a sonnet." She took up her pen and pad and began working from words that had lately lain in her mind. She had choices for the sonnet, ABAB or ABBA for a start. She pondered these possibilities until she tottered into a larger choice: she did not have to write a sonnet. Her poem could be six, eight, ten, thirteen lines, it could be any number of lines, and it did not even have to rhyme.

She put down the pen on top of the pad.

In the evenings, very briefly, she saw the two of them. They knocked on her door, a big knock and a little, and she would call Come in, and the husband would smile though he looked a bit tired, yet somehow this tiredness suited him. He would put her sleeping draught on the bedside table and say, "The boy and I have done all right today," and the child would kiss her. One night she tasted for the first time the power of his baby spit.

"I don't think I can see him anymore," she whispered sadly to the man. And the husband turned away, but recovered admirably and said, "Of course, I see."

The man and boy came home and found: five loaves of warm bread, a roast stuffed turkey, a glazed ham, three pies of different fillings, eight molds of the boy's favorite custard, two weeks' supply of fresh-laundered sheets and shirts and towels, two hand-knitted sweaters (both of the same grey color), a sheath of marvelous watercolor beasts accompanied by mad and fanciful stories nobody could ever make up again, and a tablet full of love sonnets addressed to the man. The house smelled redolently of renewal and spring. The man ran to the little room, could not contain himself to knock, flung back the door.

"Look, Mommy is sleeping," said the boy. "She's tired from doing all our things again." He dawdled in a stream of the last sun for that day and watched his father roll tenderly back her eyelids, lay his ear softly to her breast, test the delicate bones of her wrist. The father put down his face into her fresh-washed hair.

"Can we eat the turkey for supper?" the boy asked.

THE HAT ACT

ROBERT COOVER

In the middle of the stage: a plain table.

A man enters, dressed as a magician with black cape and black silk
hat. Doffs hat in wide sweep to audience, bows elegantly.

Applause.

He displays inside of hat. It is empty. He thumps it. It is clearly
empty. Places hat on table, brim up. Extends both hands over hat,
tugs back sleeves exposing wrists, snaps fingers. Reaches in, extracts
a rabbit.

ROBERT COOVER is the author of the novels *The Universal Baseball Association, Inc. J. Henry Waugh, Prop.* and *The Origin of the Brunists,* and a
collection of "fictions," *Pricksongs & Descants.* He is currently residing in
England.

Applause.

Pitches rabbit into wings. Snaps fingers over hat again, reaches in, extracts a dove.

Applause.

Pitches dove into wings. Snaps fingers over hat, reaches in, extracts another rabbit. No applause. Stuffs rabbit hurriedly back in hat, snaps fingers, reaches in, extracts another hat, precisely like the one from which it came.

Applause.

Places second hat alongside first one. Snaps fingers over new hat, withdraws a third hat, exactly like the first two.

Light applause.

Snaps fingers over third hat, withdraws a fourth hat, again identical. No applause. Does not snap fingers. Peers into fourth hat, extracts a fifth one. In fifth, he finds a sixth. Rabbit appears in third hat. Magician extracts seventh hat from sixth. Third hat rabbit withdraws a second rabbit from first hat. Magician withdraws eighth hat from seventh, ninth from eighth, as rabbits extract other rabbits from other hats. Rabbits and hats are everywhere. Stage is one mad turmoil of hats and rabbits.

Laughter and applause.

Frantically, magician gathers up hats and stuffs them into each other, bowing, smiling at audience, pitching rabbits three and four at a time into wings, smiling, bowing. It is a desperate struggle. At first, it is difficult to be sure he is stuffing hats and pitching rabbits faster than they are reappearing. Bows, stuffs, pitches, smiles, perspires.

Laughter mounts.

Slowly the confusion diminishes. Now there is one small pile of hats and rabbits. Now there are no rabbits. At last there are only two hats. Magician, perspiring from overexertion, gasping for breath, staggers to table with two hats.

Light applause, laughter.

Magician, mopping brow with silk handkerchief, stares in perplexity at two remaining hats. Pockets handkerchief. Peers into one hat, then into other. Attempts tentatively to stuff first into second, but in vain. Attempts to fit second into first, but also without success. Smiles weakly at audience. No applause. Drops first hat to floor, leaps on it until crushed. Wads crushed hat in fist, attempts once more to stuff it into second hat. Still, it will not fit.

Light booing, impatient applause.

Trembling with anxiety, magician presses out first hat, places it brim up on table, crushes second hat on floor. Wads second hat, tries desperately to jam it into first hat. No, it will not fit. Turns irritably to pitch second hat into wings.

Loud booing.

Freezes. Pales. Returns to table with both hats, first in fair condition brim up, second still in a crumpled wad. Faces hats in defeat. Bows head as though to weep silently.

Hissing and booing.

Smile suddenly lights magician's face. He smoothes out second hat and places it firmly on his head, leaving first hat bottomside-up on table. Crawls up on table and disappears feet first into hat.

Surprised applause.

Moments later, magician's feet poke up out of hat on table, then legs, then torso. Last part to emerge is magician's head, which, when lifted from table, brings first hat with it. Magician doffs first hat to audience, shows it is empty. Second hat has disappeared. Bows deeply.

Enthusiastic and prolonged applause, cheers.

Magician returns hat to head, thumps it, steps behind table. Without removing hat, reaches up, snaps fingers, extracts rabbit from top of hat.

Applause.

Pitches rabbit into wings. Snaps fingers, withdraws dove from top of hat.

Sprinkling of applause.

Pitches dove into wings. Snaps fingers, extracts lovely assistant from top of hat.

Astonished but enthusiastic applause and whistles.

Lovely assistant wears high feathery green hat, tight green halter, little green shorts, black net stockings, high green heels. Smiles coyly at whistles and applause, scampers bouncily offstage.

Whistling and shouting, applause.

Magician attempts to remove hat, but it appears to be stuck. Twists and writhes in struggle with stuck hat.

Mild laughter.

Struggle continues. Contortions. Grimaces.

Laughter.

Finally, magician requests two volunteers from audience. Two large brawny men enter stage from audience, smiling awkwardly.

Light applause and laughter.

One large man grasps hat, other clutches magician's legs. They pull cautiously. The hat does not come off. They pull harder. Still, it is stuck. They tug now with great effort, their heavy faces reddening, their thick neck muscles taut and throbbing. Magician's neck stretches, snaps in two: POP! Large men tumble apart, rolling to opposite sides of stage, one with body, other with hat containing magician's severed head.

Screams of terror.

Two large men stand, stare aghast at handiwork, clutch mouths.

Shrieks and screams.

Decapitated body stands.

Shrieks and screams.

Zipper in front of decapitated body opens, magician emerges. He is as before, wearing same black cape and same black silk hat. Pitches deflated decapitated body into wings. Pitches hat and head into wings. Two large men sigh with immense relief, shake heads as though completely baffled, smile faintly, return to audience. Magician doffs hat and bows.

Wild applause, shouts, cheers.

Lovely assistant, still in green costume, enters, carrying glass of water.

Applause and whistling.

Lovely assistant acknowledges whistling with coy smile, sets glass of water on table, stands dutifully by. Magician hands her his hat, orders her by gesture to eat it.

Whistling continues.

Lovely assistant smiles, bites into hat, chews slowly.

Laughter and much whistling.

She washes down each bite of hat with water from glass she has brought in. Hat at last is entirely consumed, except for narrow silk band left on table. Sighs, pats slender exposed tummy.

Laughter and applause, excited whistling.

Magician invites young country boy in audience to come to stage. Young country boy steps forward shyly, stumbling clumsily over own big feet. Appears confused and utterly abashed.

Loud laughter and catcalls.

Young country boy stands with one foot on top of other, staring down redfaced at his hands, twisting nervously in front of him.

Laughter and catcalls increase.

Lovely assistant sidles up to boy, embraces him in motherly fashion. Boy ducks head away, steps first on one foot, then on other, wrings hands.

More laughter and catcalls, whistles.

Lovely assistant winks broadly at audience, kisses young country boy on cheek. Boy jumps as though scalded, trips over own feet, and falls to floor.

Thundering laughter.

Lovely assistant helps boy to his feet, lifting him under armpits. Boy, ticklish, struggles and giggles helplessly.

Laughter (as before).

Magician raps table with knuckles. Lovely assistant releases hysterical country boy, returns smiling to table. Boy resumes awkward stance, wipes his runny nose with back of his hand, sniffles.

Mild laughter and applause.

Magician hands lovely assistant narrow silk band of hat she has eaten. She stuffs band into her mouth, chews thoughtfully, swallows with some difficulty, shudders. She drinks from glass. Laughter and shouting have fallen away to expectant hush. Magician grasps nape of lovely assistant's neck, forces her head with its feathered hat down between her stockinged knees. He releases grip and her head springs back to upright position. Magician repeats action slowly. Then repeats action rapidly four or five times. Looks inquiringly at lovely assistant. Her face is flushed from exertion. She meditates, then shakes head: no. Magician again forces her head to her knees, releases grip, allowing head to snap back to upright position. Repeats this two or three times. Looks inquiringly at lovely assistant. She smiles and nods. Magician drags abashed young country boy over behind lovely assistant and invites him to reach into lovely assistant's tight green shorts. Young country boy is flustered beyond belief.

Loud laughter and whistling resumes.

Young country boy, in desperation, tries to escape. Magician captures him and drags him once more behind lovely assistant.

Laughter etc. (as before).

Magician grasps country boy's arm and thrusts it forcibly into lovely assistant's shorts. Young country boy wets pants.

Hysterical laughter and catcalls.

Lovely assistant grimaces once. Magician, smiling, releases grip on agonizingly embarrassed country boy. Boy withdraws hand. In it, he finds he is holding magician's original black silk hat, entirely whole, narrow silk band and all.

Wild applause and footstamping, laughter and cheers.

Magician winks broadly at audience, silencing them momentarily, invites young country boy to don hat. Boy ducks head shyly. Magician insists. Timidly, grinning foolishly, country boy lifts hat to head. Water spills out, runs down over his head, and soaks young country boy.

Laughter, applause, wild catcalls.

Young country boy, utterly humiliated, drops hat and turns to run offstage, but lovely assistant is standing on his foot. He trips and falls to his face.

Laughter etc. (as before).

Country boy crawls abjectly offstage on his stomach. Magician, laughing heartily with audience, pitches lovely assistant into wings, picks up hat from floor. Brushes hat on sleeve, thumps it two or three times, returns it with elegant flourish to his head.

Appreciative applause.

Magician steps behind table. Carefully brushes off one space on table. Blows away dust. Reaches for hat. But again, it seems to be stuck. Struggles feverishly with hat.

Mild laughter.

Requests volunteers. Same two large men as before enter. One quickly grasps hat, other grasps magician's legs. They tug furiously, but in vain.

Laughter and applause.

First large man grabs magician's head under jaw. Magician appears to be protesting. Second large man wraps magician's legs around his waist. Both pull apart with terrific strain, their faces reddening, the veins in their temples throbbing. Magician's tongue protrudes, hands flutter hopelessly.

Laughter and applause.

Magician's neck stretches. But it does not snap. It is now several feet long. Two large men strain mightily.

Laughter and applause.

Magician's eyes pop like bubbles from their sockets.

Laughter and applause.

Neck snaps at last. Large men tumble head over heels with respective bloody burdens to opposite sides of stage. Expectant amused hush falls over audience. First large man scrambles to his feet, pitches head and hat into wings, rushes to assist second large man. Together they unzip decapitated body. Lovely assistant emerges.

Surprised laughter and enthusiastic applause, whistling.

Lovely assistant pitches deflated decapitated body into wings. Large men ogle her and make mildly obscene gestures for audience.

Mounting laughter and friendly catcalls.

Lovely assistant invites one of two large men to reach inside her tight green shorts.

Wild whistling.

Both large men jump forward eagerly, tripping over each other and tumbling to floor in angry heap. Lovely assistant winks broadly at audience.

Derisive catcalls.

Both men stand, face each other, furious. First large man spits at second. Second pushes first. First returns push, toppling second to floor. Second leaps to feet, smashes first in nose. First reels, wipes blood from nose, drives fist into second's abdomen.

Loud cheers.

Second weaves confusedly, crumples miserably to floor clutching abdomen. First kicks second brutally in face.

Cheers and mild laughter.

Second staggers blindly to feet, face a mutilated mess. First smashes second back against wall, knees him in groin. Second doubles over, blinded with pain. First clips second with heel of hand behind ear. Second crumples to floor, dead.

Prolonged cheering and applause.

First large man acknowledges applause with self-conscious bow. Flexes knuckles. Lovely assistant approaches first large man, embraces him in motherly fashion, winks broadly at audience.

Prolonged applause and whistling.

Large man grins and embraces lovely assistant in unmotherly fashion, as she makes faces of mock astonishment for audience.

Shouting and laughter, wild whistling.

Lovely assistant frees self from large man, turns plump hindquarters to him, and bends over, her hands on her knees, her shapely legs straight. Large man grins at audience, pats lovely assistant's green-clad rear.

Wild shouting etc. (as before).

Large man reaches inside lovely assistant's tight green shorts, rolls his eyes, and grins obscenely. She grimaces and wiggles rear briefly.

Wild shouting etc. (as before).

Large man withdraws hand from inside lovely assistant's shorts, extracting magician in black cape and black silk hat.

Thunder of astonished applause.

Magician bows deeply, doffing hat to audience.

Prolonged enthusiastic applause, cheering.

Magician pitches lovely assistant and first large man into wings. Inspects second large man, lying dead on stage. Unzips him and young country boy emerges, flushed and embarrassed. Young country boy creeps abjectly offstage on stomach.

Laughter and catcalls, more applause.

Magician pitches deflated corpse of second large man into wings. Lovely assistant reenters, smiling, dressed as before in high feathery hat, tight green halter, green shorts, net stockings, high heels.

Applause and whistling.

Magician displays inside of hat to audience as lovely assistant points to magician. He thumps hat two or three times. It is empty. Places hat on table, and invites lovely assistant to enter it. She does so.

Vigorous applause.

Once she has entirely disappeared, magician extends both hands over hat, tugs back sleeves exposing wrists, snaps fingers. Reaches in, extracts one green high-heeled shoe.

Applause.

Pitches shoe into wings. Snaps fingers over hat again. Reaches in, withdraws a second shoe.

Applause.

Pitches shoe into wings. Snaps fingers over hat. Reaches in, withdraws one long net stocking.

Applause and scattered whistling.

Pitches stocking into wings. Snaps fingers over hat. Reaches in, extracts a second black net stocking.

Applause and scattered whistling.

Pitches stocking into wings. Snaps fingers over hat. Reaches in, pulls out high feathery hat.

Increased applause and whistling, rhythmic stamping of feet.

Pitches hat into wings. Snaps fingers over hat. Reaches in, fumbles briefly.

Light laughter.

Withdraws green halter, displays it with grand flourish.

Enthusiastic applause, shouting, whistling, stamping of feet.

Pitches halter into wings. Snaps fingers over hat. Reaches in, fumbles. Distant absorbed gaze.

Burst of laughter.

Withdraws green shorts, displays them with elegant flourish.

Tremendous crash of applause and cheering, whistling.

Pitches green shorts into wings. Snaps fingers over hat. Reaches in. Prolonged fumbling. Sound of a slap. Withdraws hand hastily, a look of astonished pain on his face. Peers inside.

Laughter.

Head of lovely assistant pops out of hat, pouting indignantly.

Laughter and applause.

With difficulty, she extracts one arm from hat, then other arm. Pressing hands down against hat brim, she wriggles and twists until one naked breast pops out of hat.

Applause and wild whistling.

The other breast: POP!

More applause and whistling.

She wriggles free to the waist. She grunts and struggles, but is unable to free her hips. She looks pathetically, but uncertainly at magician. He tugs and pulls but she seems firmly stuck.

Laughter.

He grasps lovely assistant under armpits and plants feet against hat brim. Strains. In vain.

Laughter.

Thrusts lovely assistant forcibly back into hat. Fumbles again. Loud slap.

Laughter increases.

Magician returns slap soundly.

Laughter ceases abruptly, some scattered booing.

Magician reaches into hat, withdraws one unstockinged leg. He reaches in again, pulls out one arm. He tugs on arm and leg, but for all his effort cannot extract the remainder.

Scattered booing, some whistling.

Magician glances uneasily at audience, stuffs arm and leg back into hat. He is perspiring. Fumbles inside hat. Withdraws nude hindquarters of lovely assistant.

Burst of cheers and wild whistling.

Smiles uncomfortably at audience. Tugs desperately on plump hindquarters, but rest will not follow.

Whistling diminishes, increased booing.

Jams hindquarters back into hat, mops brow with silk handkerchief.

Loud unfriendly booing.

Pockets handkerchief. Is becoming rather frantic. Grasps hat and thumps it vigorously, shakes it. Places it once more on table, brim up. Closes eyes as though in incantations, hands extended over hat. Snaps fingers several times, reaches in tenuously. Fumbles. Loud slap. Withdraws hand hastily in angry astonishment. Grasps hat. Gritting teeth, enfuriated, hurls hat to floor, leaps on it with both feet. Something crunches. Hideous piercing shriek.

Screams and shouts.

Magician, aghast, picks up hat, stares into it. Pales.

Violent screaming and shouting.

Magician gingerly sets hat on floor, and kneels, utterly appalled and grief-stricken, in front of it. Weeps silently.

Weeping, moaning, shouting.

Magician huddles miserably over crushed hat, weeping convulsively. First large man and young country boy enter timidly, soberly, from wings. They are pale and frightened. They peer uneasily into hat. They start back in horror. They clutch their mouths, turn away, and vomit.

Weeping, shouting, vomiting, accusations of murder.

Large man and country boy tie up magician, drag him away.

Weeping, retching.

Large man and country boy return, lift crushed hat gingerly, and trembling uncontrollably, carry it at arm's length into wings.

Momentary increase of weeping, retching, moaning, then dying away of sound to silence.

Country boy creeps onto stage, alone, sets up placard against table and facing audience, then creeps abjectly away.

THIS ACT IS CONCLUDED
THE MANAGEMENT REGRETS THERE
WILL BE NO REFUND

AUTOBIOGRAPHY: A SELF-RECORDED FICTION

JOHN BARTH

You who   listen   give me life   in a manner of speaking.

I won't hold you responsible.

My first words weren't my first words. I wish I'd begun differently.

Among other things I haven't a proper name. The one I bear's misleading, if not false. I didn't choose it either.

I don't recall asking to be conceived! Neither did my parents come to think of it. Even so. Score to be settled. Children are vengeance.

I seem to've known myself from the beginning without knowing I knew; no news is good news; perhaps I'm mistaken.

JOHN BARTH, Professor of English at the State University of New York at Buffalo, is the author of the novels *End of the Road, The Floating Opera, The Sot-Weed Factor,* and *Giles Goat-Boy,* and the collection of short pieces, *Lost in the Funhouse.*

Now that I reflect I'm not enjoying this life: my link with the world.

My situation appears to me as follows: I speak in a curious, detached manner, and don't necessarily hear myself. I'm grateful for small mercies. Whether anyone follows me I can't tell.

Are you there? If so I'm blind and deaf to you, or you are me, or both're both. One may be imaginary; I've had stranger ideas. I hope I'm a fiction without real hope. Where there's a voice there's a speaker.

I see I see myself as a halt narrative: first person, tiresome. Pronoun sans ante or precedent, warrant or respite. Surrogate for the substantive; contentless form, interestless principle; blind eye blinking at nothing. Who am I. A little *crise d'identité* for you.

I must compose myself.

Look, I'm writing. No, listen, I'm nothing but talk; I won't last long. The odds against my conception were splendid; against my birth excellent; against my continuance favorable. Are yet. On the other hand, if my sort are permitted a certain age and growth, God help us, our life expectancy's been known to increase at an obscene rate instead of petering out. Let me squeak on long enough, I just might live forever: a word to the wise.

My beginning was comparatively interesting, believe it or not. Exposition. I was spawned not long since in an American state and born in no better. Grew in no worse. Persist in a representative. Prohibition, Depression, Radicalism, Decadence, and what have you. An eye sir for an eye. It's alleged, now, that Mother was a mere passing fancy who didn't pass quickly enough; there's evidence also that she was a mere novel device, just in style, soon to become a commonplace, to which Dad resorted one day when he found himself by himself with pointless pen. In either case she was mere, Mom; at any event Dad dallied. He has me to explain. Bear in mind, I suppose he told her. A child is not its parents, but sum of their conjoinèd shames. A figure of speech. Their manner of speaking. No wonder I'm heterodoxical.

Nothing lasts longer than a mood. Dad's infatuation passed; I remained. He understood, about time, that anything conceived in so unnatural and fugitive a fashion was apt to be freakish, even monstrous—and an advertisement of his folly. His second thought therefore was to destroy me before I spoke a word. He knew how these things work; he went by the book. To expose ourselves publicly is frowned upon; therefore we do it to one another in private. He me, I him: one was bound to be the case. What fathers can't forgive is that their offspring receive and sow broadcast their shortcomings. From my conception to the present moment Dad's tried to turn me off; not ardently, not consistently, not successfully so far; but persistently, persistently, with at least half a heart. How do I know. I'm his bloody mirror!

Which is to say, upon reflection I reverse and distort him. For I suspect that my true father's sentiments are the contrary of murderous. That one only imagines he begot me; mightn't he be deceived and deadly jealous? In his heart of hearts he wonders whether I mayn't after all be the get of a nobler spirit, taken by beauty past his grasp. Or else, what comes to the same thing, to me, I've a pair of dads, to match my pair of moms. How account for my contradictions except as the vices of their versus? Beneath self-contempt, I particularly scorn my fondness for paradox. I despise pessimism, narcissism, solipsism, truculence, word-play, and pusillanimity, my chiefer inclinations; loathe self-loathers *ergo me;* have no pity for self-pity and so am free of that sweet baseness. I doubt I am. Being me's no joke.

I continue the tale of my forebears. Thus my exposure; thus my escape. This cursed me, turned me out; that, curse him, saved me; right hand slipped me through left's fingers. Unless on a third hand I somehow preserved myself. Unless unless: the mercy-killing was successful. Buzzards let us say made brunch of me betimes but couldn't stomach my voice, which persists like the Nauseous Danaid. We . . . monstrosities are easilier achieved than got rid of.

In sum I'm not what either parent or I had in mind. One hoped I'd be astonishing, forceful, triumphant—heroical in other words. One dead. I myself conventional. I turn out I. Not every kid thrown to the wolves ends a hero: for each survivor, a mountain of beast-baits; for every Oedipus, a city of feebs.

So much for my dramatic exposition: seems not to've worked. Here I am, Dad: Your creature! Your caricature!

Unhappily, things get clearer as we go along. I perceive that I have no body. What's less, I've been speaking of myself without delight or alternative as self-consciousness pure and sour; I declare now that even that isn't true. I'm not aware of myself at all, as far as I know. I don't think . . . I know what I'm talking about.

Well, well, being well into my life as it's been called I see well how it'll end, unless in some meaningless surprise. If anything dramatic were going to happen to make me successfuller . . . agreeabler . . . endurabler . . . it should've happened by now, we will agree. A change for the better still isn't unthinkable; miracles can be cited. But the odds against a wireless *deus ex machina* aren't encouraging.

Here, a confession: Early on I too aspired to immortality. Assumed I'd be beautiful, powerful, loving, loved. At least commonplace. Anyhow human. Even the revelation of my several defects—

absence of presence to name one—didn't fetch me right to despair: crippledness affords its own heroisms, does it not; heroes are typically gimpish, are they not. But your crippled hero's one thing, a bloody hero after all; your heroic cripple another, etcetcetcetcet. Being an ideal's warpèd image, my fancy's own twist figure, is what undoes me.

I wonder if I repeat myself. One-track minds may lead to their origins. Perhaps I'm still in utero, hung up in my delivery; my exposition and the rest merely foreshadow what's to come, the argument for an interrupted pregnancy.

Womb, coffin, can—in any case, from my viewless viewpoint I see no point in going further. Since Dad among his other failings failed to end me when he should've, I'll turn myself off if I can this instant.

Can't. *Then if anyone hears me, speaking from here inside like a sunk submariner, and has the means to my end, I pray him do us both a kindness.*

Didn't. Very well, my ace in the hole: *Father, have mercy, I dare you! Wretched old fabricator, where's your shame? Put an end to this, for pity's sake! Now! Now!*

So. My last trump, and I blew it. Not much in the way of a climax; more a climacteric. I'm not the dramatic sort. May the end come quietly, then, without my knowing it. In the course of any breath. In the heart of any word. This one. This one.

Perhaps I'll have a posthumous cautionary value, like gibbeted corpses, pickled freaks. Self-preservation, it seems, may smell of formaldehyde.

A proper ending wouldn't spin out so.

I suppose I might have managed things to better effect, in spite of the old boy. Too late now.

Basket case. Waste.

Shark up some memorable last words at least. There seems to be time.

Nonsense, I'll mutter to the end, one word after another, string the rascals out, mad or not, heard or not, my last words will be my last words